We That Are Left

Also by Juliet Greenwood and available from Honno

Eden's Garden

We That Are Left

by

Juliet Greenwood

HONNO MODERN FICTION

First published by Honno

'Ailsa Craig', Heol y Cawl, Dinas Powys, Wales, CF64 4AH

1 2 3 4 5 6 7 8 9 10

print ISBN: 978-1-906784-99-7
ebook ISBN: 978-1-909983-05-2

Published with the financial support of the Welsh Books Council.

The author wishes to acknowledge the award of a Writer's Bursary from
Literature Wales for the purpose of completing this novel.

Cover images: John Hague and Michael Wadlow

Cover design: Simon Hicks

Printed by Gomer Press

For my family

'They shall not grow old as we that are left grow old...'
For the Fallen *Laurence Binyon*

My subject is War, and the pity of War.
Wilfred Owen

Prologue

1925

The door had not changed. Weathered and cracked, hidden by
ivy tumbling over the high, stone walls, it was scarcely visible
from the cliff path. I glanced back towards the sea. A first touch
of autumn had settled over Cornwall, bringing stillness and a
soft, hazy sunshine. Far below, in the curve of the bay, Port Helen
basked, fishing boats swaying gently in the harbour. Just beyond
the walls, cliff steps still led down to the sheltered beach and
rocky cove, its waters deep green and clear as glass.

I should not have come. I paused, hand resting on the latch,
as memories crowded in like ghosts. My home, which I had
thought I would never see again. And here I was, creeping back
in through the secret ways like a thief.

The door creaked on its hinges, brushing aside a clump of
nettles, opening up into a wilderness of tall grasses and teasels,
interspersed with saplings. On either side, fruit bushes and
brambles led to pear and apple trees, windfalls rotting at their feet.
Peach trees lined the far wall, fruit already withering on the branch.
Several panes of the once pristine greenhouses were broken,
allowing vines to escape, prisoners reaching towards the light.

Above the greenhouses rose the familiar tiled roofs, the towers
and turrets and gothic arched windows. The stone had turned
pale honey in the afternoon sun, but the windows glinted, grimy
and dark, letting in no light. I shivered.

A whisper stirred amongst the grasses, echoes of laughter, of
children racing around the central pond and out along the paths
between the vegetable beds. Of voices murmuring in the cool of
evening, when the day's work was done.

I had been a child here. Kept safe behind Hiram's walls or

swimming in the smooth circle of sea in Hiram Cove. I thought my children would grow up here, and that I would never leave.

But that was a long time ago. Before I understood the terrible things that human beings can do to each other.

Footsteps crunched on the gravel leading to the front of the house. I could put this off no longer. I had come to put things right.

Slowly, I made my way between the tangled roses and sprawl of rosemary and lavender, between the bright butterflies and the bees and the hover of small flies. Back to Hiram Hall.

Part One

Chapter One

AUGUST 1ST, 1914

It was the day of raspberries and champagne, the day the world changed.

We had another long, hot summer that year and the fruit in the kitchen garden had ripened early. By the first of August, Cook had already made jams and preserves for the winter and delicious ice cream with the last of the ice. So that day, Hugo's birthday, the only fresh raspberries were the small wild ones along the edges of the flat meadow above the house. When Cook muttered she had no girl spare to collect them, I jumped at the chance to leave supervising the flowers and the meticulous laying of the table in the capable hands of Mrs Pelham, the Housekeeper, and escape with my cousin Alice out onto the cliffs.

It was Alice who first heard the staccato of an engine high above. 'Look!' She pointed to a bi-plane coming over the sea. 'Lucky pilot.' She sighed. 'Can you imagine the freedom? He must be able to see to France from there.'

I paused, hands filled with raspberries. 'How does it stay up?'

'I couldn't even begin to guess. But they say people are already attempting to fly around the world. Can you imagine? The whole world.'

The hum of the engine grew louder every minute.

'I wonder where it's going.'

'London, maybe. The aristocracy are said to see them as toys to show off to each other. Even more than automobiles. It must be *so* thrilling.'

'And terrifying.' I shuddered. Hugo had acquired first a stately Rover, then a large and gleaming Rolls Royce Silver Ghost, both of which he drove often. Despite my husband's frequent assurances that he would never go near the Silver Ghost's potential top speed of twenty-four miles an hour while I was with him, I still found it unnerving being hurtled through the countryside in such a cumbersome machine.

The bi-plane was now almost directly above our heads, soaring against the clear blue sky. It was a miracle. A new world, about which I knew nothing.

And then, as we watched, the engine stuttered. It coughed and spluttered, then started up again. I began to breathe.

Too soon. This time the engine cut out completely. The wings angled, this way and that, as if attempting to find a level, as it drifted crazily out of the sky towards us.

Alice grasped my shoulders, pulling me beneath the nearest tree. 'It's going to crash!'

It was coming down fast. All we could do was watch. The engine coughed, again and again, like a creature gasping for air. At the last minute it came back to life. The bi-plane rose, soaring above the house and gardens and back out over the sea.

'That was terrifying!' My cousin's cheeks were flushed. She sounded more exhilarated than alarmed. 'Look, he's coming round again.'

The bi-plane had banked and was making a more controlled descent to the meadow. 'There must be some fault. He's going to land.'

We watched as the craft came in low, bouncing over the rough grass before swerving around and staggering to a stop.

'Oh my goodness!' Alice grabbed my hand, pulling me hurtling down the bank. 'Come on, Elin. He might be injured. We might have to pull him free before flames engulf everything.'

By the time we reached the crash, half a dozen servants were rushing from the Hall. Despite Alice's fears, the pilot swung down from the cockpit and jumped to the floor. He seemed unconcerned about any danger, too busy inspecting the undercarriage for damage.

'Are you hurt?' demanded Alice, breathlessly.

'Not in the least.'

Alice and I stared at each other.

The pilot pulled off goggles and a fur cap, revealing curling fair hair and a deeply tanned face. 'Although I'm not sure this thing is going to get any further without help. I might have to impose on you and beg a bed for the night,' she added with a grin.

'Of course,' I said. *A woman who flew over the sea, all on her own.* The wild child in me – the one that had once regularly escaped my governess' lessons on decorum for the rows of beans and the tangle of grape vines, drunk on the vivid scent of blackberries and the green sweetness of peapods, the one I tried so hard to put behind me now – was bewitched. 'You must be our guest. I'll ask Cook to add an extra place for dinner.'

My husband, who hated any change to his plans, would be cross. I took another glance at the pilot. She was young, only a few years older than me, twenty-five at the most, and possessed a self-assurance and a striking beauty I could only dream of. Perhaps Hugo would not be so cross.

'Thank you. I'm afraid the best I can offer you in return is good French brandy. If the bottle is still intact.' She climbed up and half disappeared into the cockpit, emerging with a brandy bottle and a wicker basket. 'Here,' she said, dropping the basket at my feet. 'French cheese and a loaf. All the way from Paris this morning.'

'Paris?' She must be joking.

She handed down the brandy and reached back inside. 'Aha. I knew I had some wine left somewhere.' She brought out a bottle and dusted it down on her flying jacket. 'No point in leaving it in here. It was a dreadful nuisance rolling around at my feet.

Nowhere to put bottles, you see. That's something I must work out for next time.'

She jumped down once more. 'Margaret Northholme,' she announced, holding out her hand.

I shook it a little tentatively. 'Elin Helstone. And this is my cousin, Alice Griffiths.'

'*Lady* Margaret Northholme?' I'd never heard such hero worship in my cousin's voice.

Lady Margaret grinned, slightly mischievous, slightly peeved. 'You read the papers, then.'

'Oh yes.' Alice turned to me. 'Lady Margaret is famed for her exploits. She bet recently that she could fly the Channel.'

Lady Margaret laughed. 'I not only flew the Channel, but on to Paris and back again.' She looked a little rueful. 'I was intending to make it to London tonight, but my navigation must be a little out. There is supposed to be a reception party waiting for me somewhere, so I could refuel. I must have mistaken the coastline. Plan was to follow the cliffs and glide my way. I should have had enough fuel with the help of the updrafts to get to Portsmouth. I don't suppose you have a telephone?'

'There's one in the house,' I said. 'And you'll be more than welcome to stay the night, if your machine can't be fixed before morning. We always have a guest room made up.'

'Thank you. I'll telephone my cousin Owen, and he can tell the others there's been a change of plan.' She strung a small canvas knapsack over her back and picked up the wicker basket. 'I won't suggest they all come haring down here this evening. Besides, I'm tired. I could hardly keep my eyes open with nothing but sea beneath me. And that engine needs a good checking over. Sounded a bit more than just a lack of fuel.' She smiled. 'I've no real desire to spend a night in a field between here and Richmond Hill, surrounded by cows. So thank you, Mrs Helstone, I shall impose on you. I've won my bet: tomorrow will be soon enough to return home.' She came to a halt, biting her lip. 'I mean, you don't mind, do you? Owen is right, I'm terribly rude and I only ever think of my own convenience.'

'Not at all,' I replied, smiling at this childlike openness beneath her veneer of sophistication.

Lady Margaret beamed. 'Oh, I'm so glad.' She eyed me with a slightly unnerving frankness. 'Most people are terribly shocked when they first meet me, but you weren't. I'm glad I landed here. I can see we are going to be the most tremendous friends.' Her eyes were twinkling once more. 'And I expect I shall drag you into all sorts of trouble. I can't help myself.'

I found myself smiling.

I led the way along the cliffs, with Alice and Lady Margaret deep in conversation behind me.

'No trouble is there, Mrs Helstone?' remarked the Head Gardener, as he shooed his unwilling flock back within the high walls of the kitchen garden. His glance towards Lady Margaret was severe.

'Not at all, Mr Wiltshire,' I replied, as if I hadn't noticed. 'Lady Margaret is quite unhurt. She will be staying with us until her friends can come to fetch her.'

'Very well, Mrs Helstone.' Mr Wiltshire had begun his apprenticeship at Hiram when Prince Albert was still alive. He was slightly mollified by Lady Margaret's title. I heard Alice stifle a giggle.

We hurried our guest between the apple trees and the row of peach fans on the sunniest wall, dodging wheelbarrows and the curious grins of the new lads from Port Helen being trained up to Mr Wiltshire's exacting standards.

As we shot through the archway to the front, several automobiles were already parked on the gravel and yet more making their way up the drive. Mr Ford of Applebourne, a large manor house just outside Plymouth, emerged from the latest model Silver Ghost, a vehicle of such splendour it quite eclipsed even Hugo's pride and joy. Mr Ford handed down his daughter Cicely, a pale, excruciatingly shy girl of fifteen, while instructing his driver to find a convenient place to park. The driver would then join the others heading for the servants' dining room.

Mr Ford came to a halt mid-sentence, jaw dropping in disbelief at a young woman in men's trousers, without even a coat to shield her modesty, striding towards them.

'We must hurry, Cicely, my dear, we can't have you catching cold,' he announced, ushering his daughter, who had turned quite pink, towards the safety of the front door.

'They never mind dancing girls,' announced Lady Margaret to the world in general. 'But a hint that a lady's legs might be created for her own convenience rather than their amusement, and off they go in a fit of the vapours.'

Cicely hiccupped. Her grey eyes, usually lacklustre and lifeless, sparkled as she dared a quick glance back before being hauled inside.

'I think we'd better find you something to wear,' I murmured, doing my best to keep a straight face, aware that Mr Ford's chauffeur was not making the slightest attempt to disguise his curiosity. 'I'll take the basket to Cook while Alice takes you up to our rooms.'

'The back route,' added Alice in a conspiratorial whisper. 'Or you might send any one of the old duffers off with a seizure.'

They shot off to the small door at the side of the house that led to the servants' staircase, giggling like schoolgirls as they ran. I picked up Alice's basket and turned towards the kitchens.

'Mrs Helstone.' A figure blocked my way. Mr Ford's chauffeur abandoned his driver's seat and stopped in front of me. He was a small, narrow-faced man with colourless hair and pale green eyes.

'If you follow the track to the side of the kitchen garden, you will find plenty of places to park there,' I said.

His gaze rested on my face. There was a boldness in his manner and an assumption that I would listen. 'I hope you don't mind, but being the Major's wife, I felt I might approach you.'

'Oh?'

He smiled. 'I was with your husband during the Boer War. I know him to be the bravest of men, and a hero to us all.'

'Yes,' I murmured uncertainly. From the corner of my eye, I glimpsed Hugo hurrying in our direction, indignation in every step, while around us more guests were arriving.

By rights I should have welcomed my husband's old comrade-in-arms, confident Hugo would be eager to speak to him. But in truth, I could have wished him half a world away. Hugo had never confided in me about his service in the war in Africa. It was long before we married. He had friends he had served with in the army, but never any from his regiment in the Transvaal. I knew there were secrets. Whispers in corners I didn't understand. I felt forbidden from asking by Hugo's fragile pride, held together by the high walls of Hiram Hall, and the unfailing – these days not always quite so unfailing – adoration of his young wife.

Today, of all days, with so many guests arriving for Hugo's birthday, the last thing my husband needed was an unwelcome stirring up of the past, however unintentional.

I turned to make my way towards our guests. 'You must excuse me,' I muttered.

'I'm quite sure the Major relies on your judgement, Mrs Helstone,' the chauffeur continued, before I could take a step. 'I was given to understand that your Head Gardener is due to retire?'

'Yes, that is true,' I replied, my attention caught despite myself.

'Then you will be looking for expertise to run Hiram's famed kitchen garden. I have been acting as Head Gardener at

Applebourne House while Mr Turner has been indisposed. But his wrist has now healed and he will be returning to the post tomorrow.' He followed my glance towards the Silver Ghost. 'Oh, I'm acting solely as replacement chauffeur this evening, Mrs Helstone, due to the unfortunate indisposition of Mr Penhallow. The kitchen garden is my true interest. Besides, a new eye and fresh vision is always beneficial. Especially...' He came to a halt, frowning as if he had said more than he had intended. 'With things being so uncertain.'

'Uncertain?'

'All this talk of war. Which I'm sure will never happen. But if – Heaven forefend – it might, I'm sure the Major would feel happier leaving a comrade, a man he knows he can trust, to protect you and keep you safe.'

'My dear?' Hugo reached me in such a state of outrage he barely noticed the chauffeur. 'My dear, Alice has dragged in some creature in the most undignified costume. Barely decent. And now I'm informed this young woman has been invited to stay with us?'

'You must mean Lady Margaret,' I replied smoothly, moving away from Mr Ford's chauffeur. Hugo stopped. 'Lady Margaret Northholme. Didn't Alice mention her name?' I was quite certain she would have done, but since Hugo rarely listened to anything my cousin said, I was not surprised he had missed this piece of information.

The sad truth was that Hugo had grown tired of his wife's poor relation cluttering up the household. All that spring, Hugo had been on a mission. Suitable young – and not so young – men had been invited to join us with embarrassing regularity. There had to be one, I could almost hear Hugo declare, prepared to relieve us of the burden of a tall, plain-featured bluestocking without a dowry to her name.

'Lord Northholme's daughter?' Hugo showed signs of being

mollified. 'They are one of our oldest families and very well connected. I'd read in the papers that she was a wild one, but really...'

'As we were walking in, she said she has two unmarried brothers and a cousin,' I added. 'At least one brother and the cousin are coming to fetch her tomorrow. The family are immensely rich, you know,' this was a guess, but a fairly safe one, 'and if Lady Margaret stays with us they are bound to feel obliged to return the invitation. Just think how wonderful that might be for Alice?'

'Well, yes.' Hugo patted my hand. 'How very clever of you, my dear.' I was trying to steer him back towards the house, but the chauffeur was not a man to give up that easily.

'Major,' he said. Hugo turned. 'I'm pleased to meet you, Major Helstone. James Connors. I served with my uncle in the Transvaal.'

I felt Hugo stiffen. 'Indeed.'

How could I get Hugo away from this man?

'To my eternal regret, I was far too young to fight, but I worked with my uncle to take supplies to the men. My cousin Alfred was killed during the relief of Ladysmith.'

'I'm very sorry,' replied Hugo.

'He died bravely, at the head of his men, as he would have wished,' said Connors.

'Good man.' Hugo's voice was approving. He shook Connors' hand warmly. I listened for a short while, quite forgotten in the exchange of views on the heat of Africa, the barrenness of the land and the flies. I began to relax. Mr Connors had not served with Hugo, after all, and my husband appeared to be enjoying the exchange. Perhaps this might be a fortuitous meeting.

We had already lost one undergardener to one of the new factories set up along the coast, while another had left only last week to seek his fortune in America. Many of our neighbours were complaining that so few men were now willing to stay on the land. A replacement for Mr Wiltshire had yet to be found and one who had shared his experiences of the war in Africa might encourage Hugo to spend more time there and take more interest.

I glanced towards the driveway, now thronging with even more new arrivals. Hugo could not abandon our guests any longer. He could easily make an appointment for Connors to see him tomorrow. I turned back to discover the conversation had changed.

'Utter barbarity, by all accounts,' Connors was saying.

'There were atrocities on both sides,' Hugo replied quietly.

'But some of the stories we heard.' Connors shook his head slowly. 'No Englishman would be capable of such unthinkable depravity.'

Hugo was very still and very straight. He met Connor's eyes, flinching slightly. I cursed myself for my lack of attention, for not stepping in beforehand to steer the conversation back towards less painful subjects.

'We really must go in, Hugo, our guests are waiting,' I put in hastily.

Mr Connors turned. 'Of course. You must forgive us, Mrs Helstone. Old memories die hard, I'm afraid. And there are some subjects that are simply too painful for a lady's ears. Don't you agree, Major?'

'Indeed,' muttered Hugo.

Exasperation overcame me. Couldn't the man take a hint? I was not so sure his appointment would be such a good thing for Hugo, after all. 'Mr Connors came to see if there would be a vacancy once Mr Wiltshire retires, Hugo. But, if you remember, with all the uncertainties, we agreed that Mr Wiltshire would stay on until at least next spring before any decision was made.'

We had agreed no such thing, but Hugo was always too proud

to admit to lapses of memory, particularly in front of a social inferior.

'Yes, of course,' he murmured.

'Perhaps Mr Connors should come and discuss the matter with you then,' I added as Connors began to speak.

'Yes, my dear.' For once, Hugo seized on my suggestion. He sounded almost relieved. 'Next Christmas, Connors. We'll speak about this again next Christmas.'

'Of course.' Mr Connors smiled. His pale eyes came to rest on my face, as if memorising every part of me. 'I quite understand. Applebourne is only a short distance away and my post is quite secure there. I understand there are considerations to be made, Major. I can wait.'

'Brave man,' said Hugo gruffly, as the Silver Ghost disappeared in a trail of dust to the field. His voice was distant, lost in a world far away. I realised his arm was shaking. A terrible, uncontrolled jerking, like a marionette in the hands of a madman or a drunk. Over the years, I had come to know his silences, his dark moods when nothing could reach him. But I had never seen him like this before.

'Hugo?' I clasped his arm, not knowing what to do, but with some idea of comforting him.

He started at the touch, and threw me off, giving me a look of such revulsion that I leapt back, stumbling over my dress and only just preventing myself from falling.

'Hugo!'

But he was gone, striding back towards the house.

Around us more guests were arriving. I fled into the kitchen garden. The gardeners had been allowed home early in honour of Hugo's birthday and the place was deserted. I ran, my skirts catching on the twigs of beans and peas, until I reached the central pool with its trellis of climbing roses, planted long ago by Mama for their shade and scent.

I crouched on the bench, curled up, my face against my knees. I held myself tight, defying the tears that would mark my face, drawing curious glances from our guests and Alice's hastily disguised pity.

I did not know what to do. I did not know how to help him. How could I, when he would never allow me to know what tormented him? At seventeen, I had loved him with a passion. But since our marriage Hugo had persisted in treating me like a child. A delicate creature that must be protected at all costs. Not as a woman who had chosen to share his life, and therefore his pain.

No one had warned me that marriage to a man could be lonelier than a hermit's cave. I had my life at Hiram. While I could be busy, Hugo's distance was something I could bear. I kept hoping that, with patience, he might come to see me as something more than his child bride. But these last months, ever since the talk of another war, there were times when my very presence tormented him. When I did not know him at all.

After a while I grew calm. Bees hummed between the lavender in the evening light. In the distance the sea pulled quietly at the pebbles in Hiram Cove. Slowly I uncurled myself, my eyes closed, drinking in the scent of peaches warmed in the sun, the sharper hint of pears and apples, the first richness of blackberries and the soft, exotic flesh of figs. It was time to make summer pudding, and capture the flavours of summer in apple and blackberry jam. We should be preserving the rose petals to decorate winter cakes and to fill linen sachets to sweeten our clothes until next spring.

I drew the scents into me. Holding them deep within my core. Then I made my way back through the arch to the driveway. Retrieving the abandoned basket of raspberries, I took it to the kitchen.

'*Duw*, and there's a taste from the past,' said Cook, abandoning the melee of preparations to take the basket. 'There's nothing like wild raspberries. They were always your mama's favourite, Miss Elin. There's nothing quite like the Welsh ones, of course, but these will do.'

'I'm sure you will work wonders with them, Mrs Hughes,' I replied. Cook had come with my mother from the island of Anglesey, far to the north of Wales. All through my childhood it had been Mama's indulgence to spend whole afternoons with Mrs Hughes, trying out new recipes as they chatted together in their native tongue, sharing wistful memories of places far away. It was an indulgence I had now taken up, as the emptiness of my marriage settled around me. On Mrs Pelham's day off, so as not to shame Hugo – who, to my deep gratitude, turned a blind eye to my eccentricities – with talk of his wife's unseemly behaviour.

'For Heaven's sake, girl, keep stirring or it will burn!' Mrs Hughes dived to rescue her sauce from the hapless kitchen maid hired from the village for the occasion. I left them to it, making my way upstairs to join the others.

Chapter Two

AUGUST 1ST, 1914

Alice glanced quickly at my face when I reached her room, but said nothing. Lady Margaret was quite prepared to go down to Hugo's birthday dinner in her trousers and leather flying jacket and it was taking all Alice's persuasion to convince her that they were the same size and that nothing but a dress would do. Lady Margaret ran her hand along Alice's small array of outfits, choosing one without any apparent care.

'It's very plain,' protested Alice, blushing.

Margaret laughed. 'All the better. Papa is always insisting I must be trussed up like a Christmas goose to attract a husband. I'm quite sick of lace.'

'Don't you want to get married?' Alice was clearly intrigued.

'To a man who wants me for my money and a title and a stake in a large draughty mansion no one in their right mind would wish to inhabit? Absolutely not. Besides, Papa only wants to get me off his hands because he knows he can't control me and he's quite sure a husband will.' She threw off her jacket and began unbuttoning her blouse. 'And the first thing a husband would do would be to stop me flying and insist I have lots of babies.' She shuddered. 'Can you imagine anything worse? Stuck like a brood mare until I grew too old to have any fun.' She patted her hair into place, with a careless glance in the mirror. 'If there really is a war coming, I intend to have all the fun I can before it's too late.'

Hugo was waiting to greet us when we finally joined the guests. My stomach clenched as he approached, but he took my hand with his customary gentleness, lifting it to his lips. 'You look perfectly lovely, my dear.'

'Thank you,' I murmured, turning to introduce our guest. Thankfully, Hugo forgot the outrage of her arrival and was instantly under Lady Margaret's spell.

'Charming, quite charming,' he remarked a little later, as he prepared to take the General's wife to her seat. 'Northholme Manor is quite the finest in Dorset, so I've been told.' He glanced back to where Alice and Lady Margaret were standing by the fire, deep in conversation, both ignoring the scrum among the men for the honour of taking Lady Margaret in to dinner. 'Such a fortunate acquaintance, and how very clever of you, my dear.'

It was just as well he didn't look back a moment later to see Margaret brush past her admirers, firmly taking Alice's arm instead as they marched into dinner together. I hastily drew

Hugo's attention to the splendour of the table settings, the huge bowls of fruit adorned with the first grapes from the greenhouse, carefully ripened by Mr Wiltshire for the occasion.

As well as his brother Rupert, the customary small party of friends had been invited to celebrate Hugo's birthday. In pride of place sat the General and a Colonel, accompanied by wives so much older than I, and so unassailable in all their opinions, it was impossible to get a word in edgeways. Next to them were Mr Ford, who eyed Lady Margaret as if she might dance on the table at any minute, and Cicely, who was overcome by hero worship and could barely manage a word in her idol's presence, despite Lady Margaret's efforts to engage her in conversation.

There were none of the young men Hugo usually invited for Alice's benefit, just an elderly Professor of History he was convinced was in search of a wife and possibly less fussy than a younger man. So far Professor Julius only seemed interested in my husband's good wine and excellent brandy.

Everyone was a little dazzled by our unexpected guest. Lady Margaret somehow made the plain gown appear fit for a duchess just by wearing it. I felt dumpy and overdressed at her side. A string of pearls – kept in a small box beneath her pilot's seat as her one nod towards packing – were her only adornment, while I sparkled and glittered like a Christmas tree. Hugo looked pleased, as he always did when I wore the family emeralds, set amongst amethyst and diamonds. I sat up straight and did my best not to wriggle under the weight of their ornate ugliness, praying the dratted things didn't escape their fastenings and fall into the soup.

After dinner, when the men joined us in the drawing room, they continued the conversation they'd been having over cigars and brandy, as if too engrossed to let it go, even in front of their womenfolk. The mood had changed. There was war in the air, more so than usual. Little wonder, as the Austrian Empire had declared war on Serbia only days before, and rumours were circulating that the Prussians had now declared war on Russia. It was all so far away. And yet Africa, where Hugo had fought against the Boers, was – according to my childhood globe – an even greater distance.

I glanced at Rupert, who was steering Hugo into a discussion of trout fishing and grouse, and the progress of his new spaniel, who, for all his breeding, remained stubbornly gun shy. But not even Rupert could keep the frown from my husband's face tonight. And on and on they went.

'Nonsense. If it comes, it will be a local affair,' pronounced Professor Julius. 'The Balkans have been spoiling for a fight for years, and Prussia won't stay out of it for long. If they have declared war on the Tsar it will be just sabre rattling. This will be yet another Balkan scrap, you mark my words.'

'You really think the other countries will stand by and allow Europe to be carved up without them?' Mr Ford retorted. 'This has been brewing for months. There will be war across half the continent within months, that's my bet.'

Lady Margaret looked up. 'Do you think so?'

'Certain,' he replied. 'We must all be prepared to do our duty and defend the Empire. I've already informed my estate workers that I shall expect them to set an example and be the first at the door of the town hall to volunteer, should it come to it. I shall march them down there myself, the day war is declared.'

'Nothing is certain,' put in my husband, loudly. I winced.

Margaret ignored him. 'I fear you are right, Mr Ford. In Paris it feels as if it has already begun. The French Government ordered a general mobilisation while I was there. Many of the shops were already shut, even some of the cafés. The assistants had already gone, you see. When I left my hotel this morning there was not even a taxi to be had.'

'There have been general mobilisations before.' Professor Julius brushed her words away. 'The French know the Prussians won't call their bluff. It's a game of brinkmanship, my dear lady. It always is.'

'It didn't feel like it in Paris,' Margaret said. 'By the time I left every tram and train was crammed with men. It seemed the war must begin at any moment, for all the talk of it only being a precaution. I was glad to get out while I could. And it wasn't just Paris. All the way to the Channel there were trains full of soldiers and reservists, and signs of equipment being moved. In more than one place I had to make a detour in case they mistook me for a spy and shot me out of the sky.'

'Really?' Alice was round-eyed.

Lady Margaret nodded. 'I had a narrow miss at an airfield near the coast. That must be when I lost my bearings.'

'Countries tend to mobilise the cavalry at any hint of unrest,' said Rupert gently. 'It doesn't mean anything.'

Hugo looked up from stirring his coffee and smiled at me. 'Besides, there's no point in alarming the ladies, is there, my dear?'

I was so tense I said, 'If there is a war I can hardly avoid it,' before I could stop myself.

'Well, if there is, it will be over in months,' said Rupert. 'The British Empire is a civilised place. No petty war in Europe has affected us yet.'

'This will.' Margaret frowned. 'I saw several Zeppelins in the air, as well as bi-planes. I was thinking, as I approached land, it took me only a few hours to cross from Paris. The English Channel was nothing. It would be easy to fly incendiaries over. Or troops. Even spies. We're no longer protected by the sea.'

'So, what do you think to a few hours' fishing tomorrow, Ford?' said Rupert, even before Margaret had finished speaking. Lady Margaret pursed her lips in annoyance. Pointedly turning her back, she resumed her conversation with Alice.

Rupert met my eyes. I threw him a look of gratitude. He

cleared his throat loudly. 'It looks as if this settled weather will continue and the fishing is always good in Hiram Bay this time of year, don't you agree, Hugo?'

We finally changed the subject. But for all his brother's efforts, the closed expression on Hugo's face remained. The hand holding his brandy shook slightly. He placed the glass on the table beside him with care. I turned my face away, before he looked up to check if anyone had seen, and shivered inwardly.

I had been such an innocent when I married Hugo. I had known only the familiarity of Hiram Hall and the safe haven of Hiram Cove. If only Lady Margaret, with her disturbing independence and talk of war, had found another landing field. I busied myself dispensing tea. In the morning our guests would leave and the settled routine of our lives would return. Things would be as they had always been.

But I knew, even as I thought it, that I was fooling myself.

As I handed Lady Margaret her tea, she glanced over to where the men were discussing sea trout. 'You should come and try the fishing in Northholme, Major Helstone,' she said, drawing Hugo over to join us. 'The estate has the best trout stream this side of London. Or so my brother George says.' She brightened. 'In fact, we've a party coming to Northholme Manor tomorrow. Why don't you bring Mrs Helstone and Alice to visit us? I'll speak to Papa, but I know he will be delighted. It's the least we can do in return for your hospitality. My younger brother Edmund is down from Oxford for the summer, so there's bound to be fun.' She winked at Alice. 'Papa is wild for Edmund to find a wife now that his engagement to Lady Cristobel is definitely off, so there will be parties all summer with absolute bucket-loads of eligible young men and women – plenty to go around.'

'Indeed.' Hugo's voice was thoughtful. 'Thank you, Lady Margaret, your offer is most generous.'

Alice flushed crimson.

'Oh, not at all.' Margaret said. 'My brothers are always having their chums visiting, it's time I invited some friends of my own.' She beamed. 'Trouble is, I can't bear all that comparing dancing shoes and trying to bag the richest heir around, even if he does look like a sack of potatoes with the mind of an ant. I've a few girl friends who are permitted to go off adventuring, but in the main I'm seen as a bad influence. Not that I am, of course. Not in the least.'

'I'm sure no one could ever see you as a bad influence,' replied Hugo.

Margaret appeared to blush. 'Thank you, Major Helstone. There you are, you see, you'll just have to come to Northholme and be my champion.'

Hugo grunted, but I could see that in his eyes Lady Margaret could already do no wrong. I could hardly resent it, since he was equally forgiving of my grubby petticoats and the scratches on my arms from gathering plums or wild garlic, or the flour on my chin when I'd been helping Cook with a pastry.

'Of course,' Lady Margaret added, with a brief glance at the General's wife, who happened to be passing, 'I don't mind at all that no one wants to marry me except for my money. I shall just spend my life adventuring.' The General's wife retreated in a swish of satin skirts, feathers nodding violently as she whispered to the wife of the Colonel in a far corner of the room. Margaret sent them the blandest of smiles. 'And when George inherits and finds himself a nice rich wife to adorn the staterooms,' she tossed her head, 'who will of course want to get rid of me, I shall set up a flying school. For women only. There are plenty of rich women wanting to learn to fly. I shall do very well. And if not...' She gave a sharp glance towards the rest of the guests, who were all pretending to be engaged in their own conversations, although they were quite clearly hanging on every word. 'When I was a child, my Aunt Elspeth ran away from her husband and spent

her time studying butterflies in the Congo. I've always had a
hankering to follow her example.'

Alice was overcome with a fit of coughing, while Cicely's eyes
gleamed. I glanced anxiously at Hugo, but he had returned to
his chair, his eyes on the fire once more, lost in thought, beyond
hearing.

I turned to Rupert. In the flicker from the lamps, I could see
the fear in him, reflecting my own. I wasn't sure if Rupert knew
what had happened to his brother in Africa, and I had never
dared ask. I had brought peace to Hugo, Rupert had told me,
the first Christmas after my marriage. He held my hand, tears
glistening in the candlelight, as he thanked me for bringing Hugo
back to himself. For bringing them all peace of mind.

'Never again,' he had told me, as I sat bewildered and
overwhelmed and quite certain he was mistaken. Hugo was a
hero. He had seen the world. How could I have brought him
anything? 'He must never go back to the army. Heaven knows
what might happen if that is all raked up again. You can keep
him safe, dearest Elin.'

Could I?

Gradually conversation resumed. 'Yes, Mrs Harper, the roses
are very fine,' I replied to the General's wife, her dignity now
restored. 'My mother brought them with her from her home on
Anglesey when she married my father. Their scent is exquisite,
don't you think? Our Cook came with Mama and brought such
wonderful old Welsh recipes. Mrs Hughes has a way of pickling
rose petals that keeps the scent right through until Christmas.
We can pass it on to your Cook, if you would like. It's well worth
the effort, to have the memory of roses in the winter months.'

Chapter Three

AUGUST 2ND, 1914

We were still at breakfast the next morning when wheels skidded to a halt on the drive outside, far too abrupt and reckless to belong to any horse-drawn vehicle. The screeching was followed by a rush of voices.

'Really!' Hugo looked up from his newspaper with irritation. The servants had abandoned all pretence and were craning their heads to see through the windows. 'Who in their right mind makes calls this early in the day?'

'Excellent.' Lady Margaret drained her coffee and leapt to her feet. 'They'll soon have me in the air again.'

Breakfast decorum was thrown to the winds. Alice shot out in Lady Margaret's wake. Even Hugo couldn't quite hide his curiosity.

'The aristocracy have rules of their own,' he muttered, finishing the last of his ham in haste and making his way outside. Which left me free to follow.

'Shall I clear away, Madam?' asked Philips the butler, looking for once quite nonplussed. To tell the truth, I was a little afraid of him. Hugo had chosen him when Adams had finally retired. Hugo had been smug for days at luring Philips away from a much larger establishment in Hampshire. He was white-haired and impressive, and seemed to find Hiram a little beneath him.

'Better wait a little while. As they've arrived so early, I'd better offer our guests some refreshment.'

'Very good, Madam,' he murmured, lips pursed. Usually this look was enough to make me question my decisions, but today I was too impatient to join the laughter outside to care.

The sun was shining, that brilliant, newly washed light that steals across the ocean in early August, bringing a promise of long days of heat to come. The trees and shrubs still wore their fresh, early summer green. A breeze came in from the sea, bringing a taste of salt to my lips.

A sleek cream Chevrolet, its hood down and its windscreen spattered by flies, had slewed to a careless stop in front of the house. It was now propping up two young men in casual trousers and brightly coloured blazers, who were ribbing Margaret with careless familiarity. I didn't dare glance at Hugo. When he drove, he always took great pride in bringing his vehicle to a precise stop, before summoning one of the men to take it round to the garages. He always inspected the parking of the vehicle afterwards. And as for familiarity…

'Damn it all, I still don't know how you could miss it so badly, Mouse,' said the young man leaning his elbow on the bonnet, dark hair falling over his eyes.

'Yes, well, you should try it, with half of France wanting to shoot you down from the skies,' retorted Margaret. 'Even my skills were put off their stride.'

'Oh, so you admit you might have failings?' He was laughing at her, but she didn't seem to mind.

'None whatsoever. And I made it back to England. That was the bet. So now you have to pay up, Owen. Don't you dare try to wriggle out of it.'

Owen scratched his head. 'I'm a bit strapped this month, Mouse. I don't suppose a kiss would do instead?'

'Absolutely not. I don't approve of that sort of thing between cousins. Besides, I know your kisses are two-a-penny. Any pretty girl who smiles is offered one.'

'And not just the pretty ones,' put in the driver, a helmet and goggles dangling from one hand. 'Owen, I should be calling you out, pistols at dawn, for making so forward a suggestion to my sister.'

'If you could shoot straight,' Owen said.

'And if you could shoot at all.'

'Children, children.' Margaret was waggling her finger at them. 'Can we please not make this a matter of your masculinity? This is about me.'

'Isn't it always?' said her brother.

She glared at him. 'Only because I make it so. Nobody offers you anything for free in this world. You have to fight for it.'

Owen blinked. 'My dear Mouse, how very cynical.'

'Yes, well. I wasn't born that way.'

'Mouse,' said her brother, gently.

'Don't "Mouse" me, Edmund. It's all right for you. No one ever questions what you get up to.'

'Rubbish.' Owen frowned at her. 'Men have constrictions as well. No one can ever behave just as he wishes. Admitted, women are more restricted, but that's only to be expected.'

'So you think we should stay at home and remain uneducated and ignorant of the world until our chosen masters decide what we should learn?'

'I didn't say I agreed with it. I said I understood the need for extra protection.' Owen caught Hugo's expression, which was like thunder at this hint of serious impropriety, and stood up straight. 'Besides, we are being infernally rude, breaking in on the Major and his wife like this, without any warning.'

'Would you care to join us for breakfast?' I put in, before Hugo could get up a head of steam and throw them out. 'Cook always does far too much, you'd be more than welcome.' Hugo would huff and puff that this was unnecessary, but I could play the innocent and argue that as a good hostess I really had no choice. And pretend that I hadn't understood the potentially indecent turn the conversation had taken. Although, since Hugo knew better than anyone that I was no longer an innocent about the procreation of children, I didn't quite see why.

'That's very kind of you,' said Owen, squashing Mouse's

impatient protests. 'Thank you, Mrs Helstone.' His eyes rested on my face with all his cousin's frankness. I took a step back towards Hugo. Even before my marriage I had not been accustomed to the scrutiny of young men. My best attempts at social graces never quite came out right. I tripped over the hem of my best gown and my elbow collided with the hostess' most delicate glass or prized vase. Owen Northholme was a student at Oxford like her brother, Lady Margaret had told us. Was he viewing me as some kind of specimen to be studied? To see how the middle classes lived?

As if sensing my embarrassment, he gave a faintly apologetic smile and turned to join Edmund, who was thanking Hugo for taking such good care of Lady Margaret.

'I'll speak to Mrs Pelham,' I murmured, escaping inside the house.

How lively the breakfast table seemed, filled with the chatter and laughter of the newcomers. How very different from the rustling of the morning paper and requests to pass the butter that were our usual breakfast routine, even when Rupert and his wife Louisa came to stay. The laughter echoed through the building, setting the wooden panelling humming and the curtains swaying as if from an invisible breeze. The entire Hall was infused with life.

'You have a beautiful house, Mrs Helstone.'

I turned to find Owen smiling politely at me across the table.

'Thank you.'

'It looks to have a long history. I take it it's been in your husband's family for generations?'

'The original manor house is thought to have been Elizabethan,' put in Hugo gruffly. 'Destroyed during the Civil War. Of course it could do with considerable improvements. I've been drawing up plans to extend the far side and the stables. The drawings are in the library next door, if you would care to look, Mr Northholme.'

'I would be delighted, Major.' Owen turned back to me. 'I understand you have a very fine walled kitchen garden, Mrs Helstone. Mouse was telling me just now that it's far better managed than the one at Northholme Manor.'

'We do our best,' I said warily. 'My great-grandfather built the walls to provide protection from the sea winds and there is rarely any frost.'

'I see.' He smiled faintly, as if something had fallen into place.

I felt the blood rush to my face. He was not the first to see Hiram Hall as the only reason a man like Major Helstone would have proposed to me. I lifted my chin and held onto my dignity. 'If there was an original wall it was probably destroyed with the house.'

I wished he would find his amusement elsewhere, preferably with Alice, where it ought to be, but he was still watching me, as if trying to work something out. 'I'm trying to guess which side your ancestors might have been on: Cromwell or Restoration?'

'Puritan,' I returned, rather louder than I had intended, before Hugo could open his mouth. 'We always were the local squires, here at Hiram, taking care of our tenants the best we knew how. We never did hold much respect for the idle aristocracy.'

He laughed. 'Despite appearances, neither do I. You're quite the firebrand beneath that calm exterior, Mrs Helstone. So that's why Mouse was so insistent you join us at Northholme. There aren't many people she really likes.' The faint smile was back and his voice dropped lower. 'Or who aren't shocked by her, who can see beyond the bravado. You don't judge a book by its cover. I do my best not to, either.'

I caught Hugo glaring at me. For one – unnervingly thrilling – moment I thought he might be jealous of me talking to an unattached young man. Then I noted the slight nod towards Alice.

'Oh it's my wife's cousin, Miss Griffiths, who is the firebrand in this household,' Hugo said. 'Quite the scholar, too. Always with her nose in a book. As clever as she is pretty. She organises talks at our local lending library. You should tell Mr Northholme about that latest one, Alice, about that painter which caused quite a stir. Spanish, wasn't he?'

'Pablo Picasso,' muttered poor Alice, dying of mortification.

'Really?' Owen turned his smile obediently towards her. 'That was very daring of you, Miss Griffiths. I hope your audience wasn't too shocked.'

'A little.' Alice frowned. 'I'm afraid I find his distortions quite disturbing. I'm not very modern in my taste myself.'

'I felt they were intended to challenge the viewer?'

'I suppose so.' Finding he was not about to mock her, Alice relaxed. 'And I can see a painter's dilemma, with photography becoming so popular. I'm a terrible sketcher myself, but I can understand the frustration of seeing how scenes that take days – even months – to paint can be captured in an instant by a camera.'

'That's very true,' replied Owen, watching her with real interest. 'But perhaps photography goes no deeper? The eyes through which you see a scene, the passion of the application, might give a painting a greater reality?'

Mouse snorted. 'That's rot, Owen. I'm all for photography myself. If I'd had a camera with me yesterday I could have shown you what was going on below me on the ground. And that doesn't lie.'

'That's because you are always impatient, Mouse,' he replied with good-humoured affection. 'And my remarks were addressed to Miss Griffiths. I'm well aware of your opinions, you express them loudly enough.' Mouse took not a blind bit of notice of this rudeness, turning back to Hugo again as if she hadn't heard a word.

'Don't worry, Mrs Helstone,' said Edmund, catching my expression. 'Owen and my sister always fight like cat and dog, they have done ever since we were little. But I suspect they'd kill for each other if need be.' He smiled, a warm gentle smile. 'And besides, it does Mouse good to be crossed. No one else quite dares, you know.'

I watched Alice laughing and chatting with Owen and Mouse, holding her own amongst the banter, reserve forgotten. This was an Alice I rarely saw. The Alice who disappeared most mornings, striding down the path to Port Helen to volunteer at the lending library, arranging lectures and exhibitions. The Alice who had recently taken a correspondence course in bookkeeping and – according to Cook, who had her finger on the pulse of every piece of gossip in Port Helen – was working wonders with the Lending Library's accounts.

'I see Miss Griffiths isn't easily overawed,' remarked Edmund. 'I'm glad my sister has had the courtesy to invite you all to join us at Northholme tomorrow.'

'It seems very sudden,' I said.

'There may be no other time,' he replied, his eyes on Alice, who was heatedly arguing a point with Owen. 'At least, maybe not for a few months. If we should find ourselves at war with Prussia, that is.'

'You really think it will come to that?'

He looked contrite. 'I'm sorry, I didn't mean to alarm you. It will most likely blow over. War is such a medieval occupation. I can't imagine any modern state embarking on such barbarity.'

'But you think it might.'

'Possibly.' He gave a faint smile. 'There are treaties. No one can be seen to back down. Besides, no country should threaten to invade another, particularly one smaller and more defenceless than itself. No man of honour can bear to see such injustice and not act.'

'No.'

'So you see, Mrs Helstone, we must take things while we can. Everybody is, you know. I've never danced so much or drunk so much champagne as in these last months. And a gathering at Northholme is always a distraction.'

I nodded politely. I had never been a guest in a great house. I felt out of place enough amongst my own class. The thought of being surrounded by grandeur and diamonds and elaborate table manners filled me with dread. What on earth was I going to talk to them about? The best method for raspberry junket was hardly likely to be a suitable subject, any more than the best time to gather lavender. But Hugo was eager to go and Alice's eyes were alight with the prospect. I put my cowardice to one side.

'I believe my husband has already accepted Lady Margaret's invitation,' I replied with a smile.

'Good.' Edmund's serious face echoed a touch of his sister's mischief. 'It's high time new blood came to Northholme and livened it up a bit. It's a ramshackle old place, for all its grandeur. Living in the past and grown moribund, I fear.'

A burst of laughter came from further down the table. I met Hugo's eyes and smiled. But for all the laughter and the sunlight streaming through the tall sash windows, bringing with it the scent of summer and the roll of the distant sea, I could not shake a sense of desolation that had crept up on me. It remained all that day, long after Mouse and her companions had gone and our customary quiet had returned.

Chapter Four

AUGUST 3RD, 1914

Hugo chose to drive us to Northholme in the Silver Ghost himself, heading inland from Cornwall into Dorset. At last we reached a neat little village of cottages surrounding a village green. Each garden spilled over with roses, red, white and great boughs of yellow, ranks of peas and beans and the tall blue of delphiniums. Cars were clearly a novelty. Heads turned as we passed. Children paused in their games to stare. A white-muzzled sheepdog sleeping in the sun scuttled off, barking in our wake.

A shaded lane led past fields of wheat and barley to the most enormous gates I had ever seen. Before the Silver Ghost had come to a halt, a wizened gateman emerged from a cottage to one side to let us pass. As the intricate swirls of the iron gates swung open, I stared up the long straight drive to the pale façade with row upon row of tall windows glittering in the sunlight. I swallowed hard. Northholme Manor was even grander than I had imagined. Gargoyles crouched in the eaves. Grecian statues gazed down from long rows of colonnades and balustrades. Stone lions prowled beside steps leading to a wide terrace, beyond which lay a pond of water lilies, with a fountain shooting high in the air.

'It's a palace!' exclaimed Alice, as Hugo followed the driveway between banks of rhododendron.

'It certainly lives up to its reputation,' said Hugo. He manoeuvred the automobile onto the gravel in front of the house, careful to avoid the cream Chevrolet and several other vehicles parked there at all angles. As we stepped out, I could see even wider lawns behind the house, leading down to tennis courts and the distant blue of a boating lake.

The next minute Lady Margaret came hurtling towards us,

dodging between the butler and the footmen on the steps. 'Isn't this wonderful?' she exclaimed, hugging first Alice, then me, before leading us towards the front door. 'Owen and Edmund have gone for a swim in the lake, but they'll be back soon. I'll show you your rooms and then we can have tea. I can't wait to take you exploring. My grandfather had the grounds made like a proper wilderness. There's a hermit's cave and a chapel, and a secret room behind one of the waterfalls that you'd never know was there.'

We were taken up wide flights of stairs to a suite of rooms overlooking the pond. Alice had been given a bedroom a little way along the corridor from Mouse, with its own little sitting room and a view of the boating lake. The rooms were each hung with heavy brocade curtains and dark with ornate mahogany chests and dressing tables. Persian rugs covered the floorboards and every last mirror and mantelpiece was spotlessly clean.

Once we had changed out of our travelling clothes, Mouse led us down through corridors and vast staterooms, filled with portraits of ladies and gentlemen in all kinds of elaborate wigs and ruffs, until we reached the terrace. There we found Edmund and Owen, hair still damp from their swim, sprawled on garden chairs, deep in conversation with a richly dressed woman in her fifties.

'This is Cousin Iris,' said Mouse. 'The only sensible one of my relatives. And Owen's godmother.'

'By the skin of my teeth,' replied Cousin Iris, smiling. 'They haven't quite found a way of divorcing a godmother from her godchildren, however disgraceful they consider her manner of living.' Cousin Iris was tall and slender, with skin browned by the sun and deeply wrinkled at the corners of her eyes. A lived-in face, Mama would have called it.

The tea was delicious, with delicate sandwiches and the lightest cakes I'd ever tasted. I held each morsel in my mouth trying to guess at the flavours, wondering if I dared ask the Northholme cook for the recipes. And deciding probably not. She was bound to be a fearsome creature, who would regard such impertinence from the wife of a mere major with the deepest disdain. I would rather experiment once I was safely home with Mrs Hughes.

After the table had been laid and the first tea poured, the afternoon became informal, with the maids banished and Mouse airily instructing us to help ourselves.

'Papa won't be here until this evening,' she said, with mischief in her eyes. 'So make the most of it. Papa is terribly old fashioned and such a stickler. I'm afraid you'll find it very dreary. I know I always do.'

'That's because you are impatience itself, Mouse, dear,' called Owen, turning from his conversation with Edmund and Hugo on the far side of the table.

'And you aren't?' She took a piece of fruitcake and began picking at the currants. 'I wish you were staying too, Cousin Iris. Things are always much more exciting when you are here. Cousin Iris was the one who taught me to fly,' she confided. 'She's climbed mountains in the Alps and travelled all the way up the Nile on a boat and been inside a Pharaoh's tomb and a pyramid. And she's been to Africa and seen lions and elephants. One day, I'm going to have just as exciting a life.'

'Just so long as you don't make my mistakes, my dear,' said Cousin Iris.

'If only I had the *chance* to make mistakes,' sighed Mouse. 'Papa is worried about the Northholme reputation as it is.' She tossed her head. 'It's silly. Respectable mamas pull their daughters away before I can speak to them, as if I'm some degenerate hoyden and they'll ruin their chances of a good marriage by just being seen with me. While really I haven't had the chance to be in the slightest bit wicked.' She grinned. 'In fact, I'm not entirely

sure I'd know where to start. I can't see that flying biplanes and
flirting a little is so horribly sinful. I've always wanted to be truly
shocking.'

Cousin Iris laughed. 'Dear Mouse. Beneath all that bravado
you are still very innocent, you know.' Her eyes became more
serious. 'Be careful what you wish for, my dear: I'm not sure you
can imagine all the consequences. Not even your father's wealth
can always protect you.'

'Well, I'd like to be given the chance to try.' Mouse polished off
her cake and stood up. 'Come on, Alice, Edmund and Owen have
been dying for a proper game of tennis for weeks.. I hope you're
not squeamish about hitting hard when you're serving to me,
because Owen never is and I shall be serving as hard as can be.'

'I didn't know Alice played at tennis,' Hugo said, taking
Mouse's abandoned seat as the game began.

'Neither did I,' I replied, as Alice served with such speed and
accuracy Owen was sent racing to the very edge of the court. 'She
must play with her friends from the lending library.'

Cousin Iris smiled at my tone. 'Perhaps you would like to join
them, Mrs Helstone?'

I shook my head. 'I haven't played in years.' Since my
marriage, in fact. I hoped Cousin Iris wouldn't force me to admit
that Hiram was a very small kind of manor house unable to boast
a tennis court. I was certain that she'd feel this tantamount to
living in the meanest terrace.

Hugo leaned over and squeezed my hand. 'And besides, my
dear, we must remember what the doctors said.' With a final
pressure he made his way down towards the courts.

I saw the question in Cousin Iris' eyes. 'Oh! I'm not...' I
mumbled. 'And I'm not ill. Not now. It was years ago.'

'I'm sorry.' Her smile was gentle, but the question was still
there.

'I was very ill for a while. I don't really remember anything about it, but for a few days the doctors told Hugo I might not survive. And when I did, they weren't certain I'd ever get my strength back. Hugo's never quite forgotten it.'

'I see.' There was a sharpness to Cousin Iris' scrutiny that had me shifting in my chair.

'I can get away with things at home,' I added quickly. 'He's so busy and not always aware of what I am doing.' I stopped, conscious of having dug a rather large hole for myself. 'In time he'll come to see that I am recovered,' I murmured, getting to my feet. 'Shall we go and watch the game?'

We walked for a while around the tennis courts, sitting every now and again to watch. Alice, I was glad to see, was already happily at home amongst her new friends and I had no doubt Mouse had insisted on her being partnered by Owen for no innocent reason. I listened to their laughter and shouts of protest or encouragement and felt a restlessness stir. It appeared that Alice's life, against all the odds, was about to begin in earnest. Hugo had dropped any mention of that 'interesting advertisement' in the paper concerning five girls in Twickenham in need of a governess and was content to let things develop. I was happy for Alice, but I couldn't help a little twinge of envy too, a sense of being left behind.

With the game in full swing, I slipped away to wander along the shores of the boating lake. For all Northholme Manor's grandeur and secluded beauty, I was already missing Hiram. At least there I had a place and an occupation. I could escape to Cook in the kitchens or take the little rowing boat out into the clear green waters of Port Helen Bay. Here, I had nothing to occupy my hands or my mind. I had no wish to be worn down by the life of a working man's wife, her hours filled with daily washing and cleaning and the care of small children, but at the same time it came to me that I was not born for idleness.

Innocent that I was, I had never understood how separate the spheres of men and women were until I was married. His was action, decision, a place in the world. Mine was to be spent within his shadow, there to provide understanding when his day was done. The wild child in me rebelled, but I had nowhere to take my rebellion. That was the way of the world. The way it had always been and always would be. Mine was the failure if I was unable to accept it.

My mother had been the same, I realised. Papa had never welcomed visitors, and so Mama had relinquished her dreams of lively house parties for artists from St Ives and musicians and intellectuals from Taunton. I might have the advantage of Hiram Hall as my dowry, but Hiram, much as I loved it, was small and old-fashioned, tucked into the cliffs above an obscure fishing port, with little society worth the name close by. Little wonder Papa in his last years despaired of ever seeing me settled and the future of Hiram Hall secure.

Papa had been so certain I required a husband to take over the running of the Hall that I had never thought to question it. It was my destiny to be married. What other life was there, except to linger in shame as an old maid, laughed at by some, pitied by others?

I had watched as one by one the girls of my own age appeared with a fiancé, and then a husband, on their arm. I wondered if I would ever acquire the attentiveness and the sweet smile to attract a young man, until Hugo appeared at one of our summer gatherings, resplendent in his uniform and medals from the Boer War.

I had watched from a distance as a dozen or so of the prettiest girls in Cornwall fluttered their pale skirts and delicate lace parasols around the newcomer. I made no attempt to join them. And yet, as the party settled down for one of Cook's extravagant picnics, Hugo had sought me out. He was grave and he was charming. He had listened to my every word, his eyes resting on my face as if to drink in every part of me. Little wonder that by the end of the day I had been hopelessly besotted.

The voices from the tennis court no longer echoed quite so loudly. I made my way back before I was missed. As I reached the shade of a large arbour next to the tennis courts, Mouse's laughter reached me, accompanied by the thwack of a tennis racket and a resigned protest from Edmund. Near to, voices stopped, then resumed their conversation. It was Alice and Owen, sprawled out on the grass in the sun.

I should have stepped straight out and joined them, but I remained in the darkness beneath the colonnade.

'Oh, I don't know,' Owen was saying. 'It seems something of an indulgence that I'm returning to studying ancient cultures when a neighbouring country is fighting for its life.'

'An indulgence?' Alice was indignant. 'I would never call the opportunity to study at university an indulgence. I'd give up anything for such a chance.'

'Really? Even though women are not permitted to take the examinations?'

'Of course. How else are the university authorities going to be persuaded to allow women to take degrees?' She sighed. 'Papa was a Professor of Botany at Cambridge when I was a child. That's what we were going to do, if he had lived: I was going to attend the lectures and Papa was going to insist I took the examinations and then we were going to fight them until they were forced to award women a degree. But now I never will.'

'I'm sorry.'

'Oh, I expect I'll find something else to engage my energies.'

'I'm sure.' Owen sat up straight. 'Perhaps we should join the others?'

Alice didn't move. 'It's all right, you know.'

'I beg your pardon?'

'When I said engage my energies, I meant some other

ambition, not ensnaring any unattached man I come across into marriage.'

'I didn't think—' muttered Owen, colouring slightly.

'Yes you did, Mr Northholme. And you're quite right: it would be the most sensible action for me to take. But I'd rather not, if you don't mind. No offense intended.'

Owen scratched his head. 'None taken, Miss Griffiths'

I made to emerge from the shadows, but Owen sat up straight and looked at Alice with an intensity of interest so very different from Hugo's attentiveness, even in those days before we were married. It was a searching look, as if he wished to understand everything about her. Even focused elsewhere, it was a gaze I found unnerving. 'So, throwing my wounded pride to one side, is this aversion simply for me personally, or is it really your ambition to remain single?'

Alice frowned at him. 'You think a woman can have no existence unless she is a daughter or a wife?'

'No. I was brought up largely by my Godmother, who dared to divorce her husband for his ill treatment of her and neither married again nor has children. I admire her adventurous life. But that's not for everyone, and surely every man and woman wishes for a home and children?'

'Why?' Alice's frown deepened. 'Why should everyone be the same? Why should every woman who ever lived wish to be a mother? Especially when the experience is quite likely to kill her.' She hugged her arms around her knees. 'I have so many things I wish to do with my life. So many places I want to see. Oh, I love children and enjoy their company. But that doesn't necessarily mean I have a burning desire to have my own. Not when it could cost me so much. I would far rather keep my independence.'

'I see.' His tone was sceptical. 'But are you prepared to live without love, Alice?'

'Can you tell me what love is, Mr Northholme? And I don't

mean sex, if that's what you're thinking.' Owen coloured, not quite able to keep the surprise, and just an edge of disapproval at such immodesty, from his face. Alice smiled. 'It's not that I don't believe in love. Far from it. But there are so many different forms of love. Love for children. For parents. For family. For friends. I would rather say that there is an infinite variety of love. In women's lives, at least.'

'Touché.' He was watching her thoughtfully with an expression I could not quite read. I wondered uneasily if Alice had not, after all, set herself up as an irresistible challenge to a young man who, like his cousin and all those of his circle, was accustomed to getting his own way and had nothing to lose. We were so used to the small, secluded world of Hiram. The grandeur of Northholme came from another social sphere entirely: one with rules that I had an uneasy feeling were beyond our understanding and could be ruthless to those without any equal power to protect them.

'Has the game finished?' I asked, joining them hastily.

'Oh, it grew far too hot,' replied Alice, looking up at me with a welcoming smile. 'I'm afraid Lady Margaret is still insisting on wearing out her brother, though.'

Owen scrambled to his feet. 'I'd better go and relieve poor Edmund, before Mouse finishes him off entirely.'

'No, I'll go.' Alice jumped up, brushing the grass from her skirts. 'The tennis courts here are the very best. I must take advantage of them while I can.' She smiled. 'And besides, I'm sure Elin would enjoy a tour of the grounds. You should show her the kitchen gardens, Mr Northholme. Elin has a passion for growing and I'm sure would love to see them.' With a wave, she ran back towards the tennis courts.

Owen cleared his throat. 'You have a very willing guide at your service, Mrs Helstone.'

'No, please, you don't have to,' I said, awkwardly. He was being

kind to a guest, but I didn't relish the thought of that intense
gaze turned upon me. I was not like Alice. I had none of her
fleetness of mind or practice in debate. In this unfamiliar world,
my bearings had abandoned me. Alice's answers just now –
opinions I had never heard her express so fully – had stirred up
emotions I had kept firmly at bay. Somewhere deep inside I felt
my world rock. And I wasn't sure I liked the feeling.

'But it would be my pleasure.' He seemed to sense my unease,
for he stepped away, walking alongside but at a slight distance,
as we made our way back to the lawns in front of the house.

'It's very beautiful,' I muttered at last, feeling I should say
something. I wracked my brains for questions to ask so he could
talk and explain, and I would be safe in my expected role of
female attentiveness.

'Do you think so?' He met my eyes. 'I was under the
impression the last time we met that you had no time for the idle
aristocracy.'

I blushed. 'That was unpardonably rude of me.'

'Not at all. You spoke your mind. And you have principles.
That's rather refreshing.'

'Refreshing?' I frowned at him. Was he laughing at me? Or
even indulging in a little careless flirtation – no doubt amused
that the plain little wife of a country squire would be flattered
by such attention.

We had arrived in front of the fountain. Owen came to a halt.
'Your cousin is not the only orphan in the world, Mrs Helstone,'
he remarked, watching the lazy drift of large, exotically coloured
carp through the waters. 'Or the only poor relation ill at ease
with their position.'

'Oh!' I glanced at him. 'I'm sorry. I…' I stumbled to a halt.

His eyes were grey, and perfectly serious. To my shock I felt
heat begin to rise, loosening my limbs and leaving a swirl of deep
emptiness in my stomach. I turned away, cooling my cheeks in

the drift of vapour from the fountain. The air was still. My clothes clung to sweat in the small of my back. I could hear the distant hum of bees amongst the beds of roses and lavender.

Owen cleared his throat once more. 'But Miss Griffiths is right. Once I've fulfilled my duty of keeping Edmund from drink and debauchery at Oxford, I shall have my degree and be free to do as I wish.' He gave a low chuckle. 'I think your cousin has shocked me a little. Made me rather ashamed of my comfortable life.'

I kept my eyes firmly on the red and white markings of the Koi moving into my shadow.

'Is that what you wish for? A comfortable life?'

He was silent for a while. 'No. I don't think so. I don't want a half-life, cocooned in ease, while a world of suffering struggles on outside its borders.' I could feel his gaze resting on my face. 'And you?'

I bit my lip. Who was I to ask anyone that question? Whatever I answered, I could not lie to my own heart.

'I don't know,' I said at last, coward that I was, avoiding an answer at all. But it was there, my true answer, in the ripple of red and gold vanishing into the darkness of the pond, in the deep silence between us.

'I'm sure even Mouse must be tired out by now.' Owen turned back towards the tennis courts.

'Yes, of course,' I replied, falling into step beside him, as we made our way without a word.

Hugo was deep in conversation with Cousin Iris as we rejoined them, his eyes following Alice as she ran and jumped and struck the ball back to Mouse, while Edmund applauded enthusiastically.

'You must be tired, my dear,' he said with a smile, patting the empty seat next to him. 'With this heat and our long drive this morning.' His face had relaxed, as if the grand seclusion of Northholme with its columns and its statues had pushed away the shadows darkening his mind. I looked at him, the stranger I had married, and about whom – for all we were joined irrevocably as one, for as long as we both should live – I still knew so very little. It was only minutes, I realised, since Alice had run down the bank to the tennis courts. It felt as if a lifetime had passed.

'Yes,' I murmured, sitting down beside him.

Owen joined Edmund at the side of the court, calling out encouragement to Alice, while Mouse protested indignantly at such blatantly partisan behaviour. 'Now, Mouse,' he called, 'you can't always have things your own way. It does you good, you know, a little pain.'

Dinner that evening was a truly grand affair. I have to confess that it was also a little bit terrifying. Lord Northholme was a tall, straight-backed man with an austere face. Mouse's elder brother George was a slightly rounder version of his father. I was very thankful that there were several earls and countesses amongst the dinner guests, so the wife of a major was relegated to several places down from the head of the family. We rarely kept to such formality at Hiram, but here the demarcation of rank was absolute. I exchanged rueful glances with Alice, who was placed even lower and quite out of reach of Owen and Edmund, who were naturally near the head of the table. Mouse was also far removed from us, seated between a corpulent marquis and an elderly, deaf, Russian prince. Despite my distance it was clear she was scarcely bothering to suppress her yawns.

Even here, amongst the glittering chandeliers and gilded mirrors, and the opulent table centrepieces of pineapples and grapes, the talk of war crept in. Conversation died as voices were raised at the head of the table. 'Nonsense,' George Northholme declared. 'There's no question of permitting the Hun to overrun Belgium. You don't think they'll stop there, do you? Next thing, they'll be reaching the Channel ports and have a free run to London. Belgium is nothing: the Empire, now that is a prize worth having.'

Edmund placed his wine glass on the table with care. 'I'm simply suggesting that the Kaiser and his generals have made their point, now they've declared war on Serbia and Russia. The chaps in London seem hopeful the Kaiser will see sense and a diplomatic solution can yet be found.'

Lord Northholme snorted. 'You can't declare war on your own cousin. It would never have been permitted in the old Queen's time.'

'Papa, Queen Victoria is long gone,' retorted George. 'There will be war before the year is out. Everyone agrees.'

'Not everyone, George,' replied Mouse, glaring at the Marquis, who had been enjoying rather too much of Lord Northholme's sherry, to the detriment of his soup and his hands, which were tending to wander.

'Nothing is ever certain until it happens,' said Edmund mildly. 'You never know, maybe those fellows who went over as a peace delegation will have their way. I certainly admire them: ordinary workingmen making their way over to Prussia to try and bring peace.'

'But possibly naïve,' put in Owen.

'Isn't there one of those peace activists near you, Major?' said Edmund. 'I heard him speak at an anti-war demonstration in Hyde Park a few weeks ago with that mathematics lecturer from Cambridge. Lord Russell's nephew.'

'Bertrand Russell,' supplied Owen. 'Yes, I heard him too. Don't agree with them, but I'll admit that for a working man he was a fine speaker. Treeve, wasn't that the name?'

'That's it.' Edmund nodded. 'Mr Treeve. From Port Helen in Cornwall. That's near your place, isn't it, Major Helstone?'

'Indeed,' muttered Hugo. His eyes were fixed on the silver napkin ring beside his plate. His face had taken on the utterly closed look I had come to know so well. Surely Hugo wouldn't forget himself here? He would not forgive himself afterwards if he did.

At the head of the table, Lord Northholme stirred himself. 'You'd better keep an eye on the fellow, Major. Can't have troublemakers running around if there's a war. Heaven knows what they might get up to. Could be spies, or anything. Or one of those "conscientious objector" fellows, in need of a fright to buck up his ideas and make him act like a man.'

'They'll shoot him and have done with it if he refuses to fight,' said George. 'Best thing for a man like that.'

A murmur of agreement rose. Hugo looked up. I saw his lips pressed in a line so tense they turned white.

'Good man, Treeve,' he announced.

Not a voice stirred. Not a spoon moved. Even the napkins remained frozen at the side of plates. Hugo, usually so careful of his dignity, appeared not to notice. 'The best. Whatever his opinions, the very best of men.'

'Really?' It was Edmund who broke the silence. 'You intrigue me, Major. Mr Treeve mentioned he'd been in South Africa. I assumed it was as some kind of observer.'

Hugo hesitated. I wanted to scream, to tell them all to keep their idle curiosity to themselves, to leave him in peace and take his torment with them, if they dared. But Hugo had never shared his demons, and to out their existence in such company would only humiliate him. I clenched my fists tight beneath the table.

'Bravest captain I served with, Captain Treeve,' Hugo said. 'The very best of comrades. The best of men. I owe him my life.'

After a while conversation slowly resumed around us, washing over this slight roughness on the surface of the gathering as if it had never happened. But the heart had gone out of the evening. Mrs Johnson next to me, who only minutes ago had been telling me so proudly of her son, just turned twenty-one, and the sweet girl he was courting, toyed aimlessly with her sorbet. I glimpsed Edmund drain his newly refilled glass and fill it again without waiting for the serving staff to jump to attention.

I discovered Hugo at my side. 'My dear, you must not get chilled,' he said, placing my shawl more closely around shoulders. 'We must remember what the doctors said.'

'Of course, Hugo,' I replied, uncomfortably aware of Owen observing us. I touched Hugo's hand briefly with mine. 'Thank you. You are very kind.' I watched him return to his place, his retreating uniform dancing with the candle flames amidst my tears.

Chapter Five

AUGUST 4TH, 1914

Northholme Manor was vast. A world unto itself. I was thankful to have Mouse to guide us, quite certain we'd have soon been hopelessly lost without her, in corridors stretching out as far as the eye could see, lined by old masters darkened with age, and the tarnished glint of mirrors. Laughter and snatches of conversation echoed from every direction, including the stifled giggle of a pair of maids scurrying their way out of sight, their footsteps clattering away down hidden stairs into the depths below.

The following morning, Hugo was invited to join our hosts for the day's shoot.

'That leaves us free to do whatever we please,' said Mouse gleefully, watching the men make their way over the lawns towards the moorland behind Northholme Manor, a dozen spaniels and retrievers at their heels.

Many of the guests from dinner had stayed at Northholme that night. Even in their morning dress the women gossiping over tea in the drawing rooms or taking a stroll along the terrace before the heat of the day, were exquisite, trailing lace so fine I would never have dared even to touch it.

I was following Mouse and Alice towards the tennis courts, when the roar of an engine sped up the driveway before coming to an abrupt halt. Mouse dropped her racket with a squeal of delight.

'They've come. I *knew* they'd come! The only real friends I have in the world. Apart from you two now, of course,' she added, with a grin. 'Everyone else is frightfully stuffy, don't you think? And they're always far too scared of marking their skirts to do anything interesting. Come on. You've got to meet them.'

The two young women abandoned their automobile to the servants without a second glance.

'There was a frightful fuss,' the driver announced as they reached us. She was taller than her companion, with a handsome face framed by dark eyebrows and hair swept loosely away from her face. 'Papa wasn't going to allow us to come over at all. He kept muttering about war being declared at any moment, and what would Sybil's parents say and how we're responsible as she's our guest for the summer.' She wrinkled her nose. 'It's only an hour's drive, and it's not as if the whole world is going to explode at any minute.' She held out her hand to first Alice and then me. 'I'm Ginny, and this is Sybil. And we're dying for a game of tennis.'

We played for the rest of the morning. As the only married woman, I did my best to be dignified and demure and confine myself to keeping the scores. But Ginny – who was taller than all of us and even more imperious than Mouse in her actions, taking no prisoners at tennis or elsewhere – dragged me to join them the moment Sybil showed signs of flagging.

For a while I was tentative. I could imagine Hugo's eyes watching me reproachfully. But Hugo was far away, amongst the distant flurry of gunfire that erupted into the still air now and again. Within minutes I'd thrown caution to the wind, caught up in the game and Mouse's determination that she and Alice would win.

'No one told me you had such strong arms, Elin,' Mouse complained good humouredly, as we ran each other into breathlessness and paused, leaning on our rackets. 'It's not fair.'

'Rowing,' I gasped. My heart was pounding and my legs ached. After the racing and the dodging, the shouts of 'mine', and guessing where the ball would land next, I was tingling all over. I'd missed this, in the still and the quiet of Hiram, in the steady routine of my life. I'd missed the stolen afternoons with other girls when I was small, visiting, playing games and racing barefoot along the shore, as if governesses and disapproving papas and the constraints of being quiet and ladylike never existed. As if we too, like brothers and fathers and uncles, could ride off to rule the world and be anything we chose.

Mouse laughed. 'Well that's cheating, living right by the sea. I should have known.'

'I thought you'd have worked that one out, Mouse.' I straightened up at the sound of Owen's voice. He and Edmund were standing next to Sybil, watching us with broad grins on their faces. 'I could have told you to make sure Mrs Helstone was on your side.'

'Go away, Owen,' retorted Mouse crossly. 'That's hardly fair, creeping up on us like that without warning. And anyhow, I thought you were both supposed to be with Papa, proving your manhood and killing things.'

'We grew bored,' replied Edmund. 'A shoot is only ever an excuse for Papa to order everyone about and moan about how it isn't like the old days and university makes a man soft.'

'Besides,' added Owen, 'we take our chaperoning duties seriously, and Heaven knows what Ginny and Sybil might get up to without us.'

Ginny laughed, with easy familiarity. 'You're a terrible chaperone, Owen. You've no idea what Sybil and I get up to when you're not looking.'

'I should hope not,' replied Owen, looking alarmed. 'You've no idea what your brothers threatened me with if I permitted the family name to be compromised.'

'Compromised any further, you mean,' said Ginny. 'I still get the lecture each time I go home on the dangers of losing my mind if I use my brain too much.' She met my puzzled look. 'If it wasn't for Aunt Iris persuading Edmund and Owen to look after us, Sybil and I wouldn't have been allowed to attend Oxford at all.'

Alice let her racket fall. 'You're attending lectures at the university?'

Sybil nodded. 'We've just finished our first year. It was wonderful. I wish you could persuade your papa to let you join us next term, Mouse. You would love it. It's thrilling living in a house with other girls who have intelligence and passion and discuss things, and want to live their own lives. Going off and having adventures isn't the only way to be independent.'

'I suppose.' Mouse sounded uncertain. Even a little scared. I glanced at her in surprise.

'You could always suggest Miss Griffiths goes with you too, as a companion,' said Owen, turning to Mouse. 'Then you could have someone starting with you at the same time, and an additional chaperone.' He gave a wry smile. 'Although I'm not sure Miss Griffiths will thank me for the suggestion.'

'Would you?' Mouse turned to Alice. 'Come with me? I mean, Papa would pay for everything, you wouldn't have to worry about that. I'm not clever, or anything, but I know you'd make up for both of us.'

Alice hesitated. I saw pride and longing struggling in her face.

'And you wouldn't ever have to be a governess and look after horrible children,' Sybil added.

Alice smiled faintly 'It's a very big decision to make, Mouse. Thank you, but I need to think it over.'

'Yes,' said Mouse, biting her lip. 'Of course.'

'It would be fun,' put in Ginny. 'And Owen and Edmund are being modest, they're very good at protecting us really. Some of the students can be horrible. They think we shouldn't be there. Or that we're devoid of any kind of modesty and they can persuade us to do anything. I'm sure Owen had to give at least three of them black eyes before they'd keep their hands to themselves.' She pulled a face. 'The worst ones know we're just as clever as them, and do their best to treat us as if we have no brains at all. At least Edmund and Owen speak to us like sentient human beings.' She tucked her arm into Owen's. 'My dear, you can marry me for my money, any day, if the girl of your dreams should never come along.'

Owen coloured slightly. 'Thank you,' he mumbled.

Ginny's eyebrows raised. 'Well and that's not like you to be so coy. Should I be jealous?'

'Poor Owen! Do stop teasing him, Ginny,' said Mouse, laughing. 'And anyhow, if he's really in love, he'll never tell. He never did.'

I found Edmund next to me. His smile was gentle and a little shy. 'Take no notice, Mrs Helstone. It doesn't mean anything. They're always rattling on like this. We've all known each other since we were children, you see.'

'Of course.' I returned his smile. I had not envied them the grand house with its elaborate ornaments that terrified me by their expensive – and horribly fragile-looking – excess, or the grounds that stretched as far as the eye could see. But I did envy them this easy companionship. Their freedom from the social conventions that had bound me tight all my life.

Ginny and Sybil no more deferred to Edmund and Owen than Mouse. They spoke their minds with an expectation that their opinions would be treated seriously and listened to. I felt the crackle of their intelligence around me. And felt dull and grey beside them. I could see their lives – and that of Alice – opening up in front of them, following their stars without deferring to any man. I felt old within their shadow.

'Of course,' said Ginny. 'If there is a war, we most probably won't be allowed back to Oxford at all.'

'What would you do then?' I asked. 'If there is a war, I mean?'

'Fight,' said Mouse, fiercely. 'I'd fly over enemy territory and report all their movements.'

'You could try,' said Ginny. 'But I doubt if anyone would let you.' Her face had become serious. 'I'd volunteer as a nurse. Or something like that. I've got my own money and Mama couldn't stop me. I couldn't just stay at home and do nothing. That's the thing I couldn't bear, not having a purpose in life. Men think women should only be interested in them, but I believe every woman needs a passion of her own to be truly alive.' Her eyes rested on me. 'Don't you agree, Elin? However much you love your husband, I feel sure you must have a passion in your life that is quite your own.'

I blinked. Heat rushed through me. 'I don't know,' I mumbled. I could feel their eyes, watching me with curiosity. 'I don't think so.'

'But you do.' Owen was frowning at me. 'Alice said you had a passion for growing.' I met his eyes briefly. The memory of the walk to the Northholme kitchen gardens, that had taken us no further than the fountain, was still there between us.

'And for creating beautiful dishes from the results,' added Alice. 'Elin can conjure up flavours that can make your tongue sing.'

'I love you for saying so, but that's just cooking,' I protested. 'It's my invasion of Cook's territory. A childish indulgence. It's not like great art, or great music, or saving the world.'

'Isn't it?' Owen was smoothing the strings of Mouse's racket, as if their evenness was the most engaging thing in the world. 'My uncle pays a small fortune to hire a renowned Chef from Paris so that his dinners can outshine his neighbours. I would think taste and flavour was a skill and an art, and a passion. It might not be one you go to university to learn, but it doesn't mean it can't be classed as an art and isn't worth pursuing.'

'Hear, hear,' called Edmund.

I blushed. But not one of them was laughing at me. A lightness entered my heart, one that had not been there since the wild days of my childhood. I felt a grin slowly overtaking my face, reaching into every corner of me. 'Well, then I have a passion,' I replied.

'Come on,' said Mouse impatiently. 'I'm hot after all that racing about. It's our turn to go swimming.' She waved the men away. 'You'll just have to find something else to do, you two. You had your turn yesterday. And no spying on us.'

The lake was cool in the shade of overhanging beech. I exchanged glances with Alice as Ginny and Mouse pulled off every last scrap of their clothes, flinging them carelessly into a pile and jumping straight into the water, shrieking loudly.

'It should be quite warm at this time of year,' said Sybil, slipping out of her dress rather more shyly.

'It looks delicious in this heat,' I replied taking a deep breath and undoing the buttons of my blouse with as much of a flourish as I could muster. Hugo would most probably die of mortification if he ever found out, but my new companions scarcely seemed to notice their nakedness. Alice giggled and began unfastening her skirt. Within minutes, we were following Sybil, who thankfully waded in tentatively from the stony beach rather than jumping straight in from the side.

I no longer felt like an old married woman, but a girl with her whole life before her. I found myself laughing and joking with my companions. Splashing water over Alice until she plunged right under. Joining Sybil as she hovered at waist height, protesting it was far too cold, until we both took a deep breath and on the count of three sank down so that the water covered our shoulders, then set out to swim.

Out in the sun in the middle of the lake, the water was soft and warm. I could feel its silkiness caressing every part of my skin. Green tendrils of weed reached out, binding themselves to my arms and legs, then vanishing again into the depths. Ginny and Mouse raced each other, right to the far end and back, in a flurry of spray and the indignation of ducks.

'This is heavenly,' sighed Mouse, as they joined us to float lazily in the shallows. 'Whenever I'm here, I always think nothing really bad could happen anywhere.' She lay back in the water, fair hair spread out like a mermaid's. 'But of course it does.'

As the day began to fade, we fastened each other into our clothes and made our way back to the house.

As we reached the front door, I could see that the men had returned.

'They're early,' said Mouse, her step quickening. 'Something must have happened. Papa always takes it as a matter of pride that they stay out until it becomes too dark to aim.'

We entered the hallway to a scene of rush and bustle. Trunks and valises were being brought down from the bedrooms and taken outside to the waiting vehicles. In the drawing room I found Hugo looking out over the lake, a telegram in his hand. A knot contracted hard and cold in my belly.

'I have to leave,' he said as I reached him. He smiled, but the smile did not touch his eyes. 'I've been called to a meeting in London. I'm afraid it cannot wait.'

'Is it the army?'

I thought he was not going to reply, but then he nodded. 'I'm afraid so. Our government has declared war on Prussia. The ultimatum expired at midnight last night. It was only to be expected, most likely a precautionary measure, in case the international situation worsens. We must hope for the best, my dear.' His eyes didn't meet mine. They travelled back towards the fountain with its feather of water flinging itself against the blue sky.

My stomach clenched. Outside all was still and quiet, the same day of perfect sun it had been before. And yet everything had changed. I took a deep breath. 'But you left the army, Hugo. You retired.'

'They are calling in retired officers, too.'

I caught his arm. 'Do you have to go? Surely they can't force you?'

'I have a duty to my country.' I knew that tone. He had the distant, absorbed expression I had come to know so well.

'I'll pack my things.'

'There's no need. Lord Northholme suggested that you might like to stay here until my return, to keep his daughter company.'

'Alice can stay. I'll come to London with you.'

Hugo turned and took my hands in his. 'No, my dear, far better that you stay. I have no idea how long this might take, and I shall be in meetings all hours of the day and night. I've telephoned Mrs Pelham to arrange for your clothes to be sent. One of the men can drive the Rover. He'll be here tomorrow morning. I can't have you on your own in London with no attendants.'

'Alice wouldn't mind coming with me. She always loves

London. We can visit the museums and the art galleries and take in a play or the opera.'

'Better that Alice remains here. She and Lady Margaret have become great friends.' He smiled again. 'Lady Margaret's cousin is paying her considerable attention. Her brother, too. This is a great chance for Alice. Who knows? It may never come again.'

'But Hugo—' He turned away again to gaze out of the window. I bit my lip. I had failed. I could not keep Hugo safe. Hugo had loved me once, but his elaborate courtesy towards me now could hardly mask the distance that had grown, piece by piece, between us.

I swallowed, my mind racing. Perhaps this was the real reason Hugo was making no effort to resist the summons. Was it his disappointment in me that was driving him back to his old army life? Back to the demons that haunted him in the dark?

'I'll drive up with you, Helstone.' George Northholme joined us before I could speak. 'I've no doubt my regiment will be put on standby, no point in hanging around here waiting.'

'Of course.' Hugo was the brisk man of business once more. He patted my hand. 'Once the Hun sees we are serious, he will soon back down. The Empire is not to be taken lightly, after all. It will come to nothing in the end.'

* * *

They were gone within the hour. It was a subdued dinner that evening. Ginny and Sybil had driven straight home, in response to an anxious telephone message waiting for them from Ginny's mother. Most of the previous night's guests had also departed, some for home, several of the men to join their regiments. We were a depleted company around the huge formal dining table. Lord Northholme spent the meal lost in thought. Even Owen and Edmund had very little to say for themselves. Mouse defied protocol and sat by us, but with so gloomy a silence around the table the three of us found our easy conversation quite gone. Our old chatter felt frivolous, and none of us dared broach the subject heavy on all our minds.

The meal was scarcely less opulent than the night before. I hoped the servants all had good appetites as none of us did more than pick at each course. Even the raspberry sorbet, with its luxury of ice in the heat of summer, was left largely untouched, melting in a crimson tide at the base of each delicate dish.

Chapter Six

AUGUST 5TH, 1914

When I came down to breakfast the following morning, Northholme was quieter than ever. Mouse had taken her coffee out onto the terrace and was sipping it with the air of one lost in thought.

'Owen and Edmund have gone,' she announced as I approached.

'Gone? Back to Oxford?'

'No. They're both determined to sign up and do their bit.' She sighed. 'They might at least have waited to see what happens, but they've both got this romantic notion of dashing off to save Belgium from the invader. There are such horrible stories in the newspapers this morning. Atrocities and what they do to women, and all that kind of thing. Vile. So they've gone off like knights in armour to rescue them. I so wish I was going with them.'

'You don't look like a soldier,' I replied, with an attempt at a smile.

'Neither does Edmund,' she replied gloomily. 'But I can see

Owen dashing around in uniform being horribly heroic. He always insisted on playing King Arthur when we were little. Edmund isn't like that. I can't imagine him killing anyone.'

'Like Hugo said, it might all blow over and be nothing at all.'

Mouse drained her coffee. 'Yes. I just can't help thinking that's what everyone in every war must have thought. I'm sure all those villagers in Belgium were praying it never happened. And I bet the people who weren't soldiers in Troy were hoping the Greeks would just go away and it would all be all right. The worst thing is knowing there's nothing you can do about it. I'm not sure I believe in God anymore, but I know why people pray.' She shivered slightly. 'In Paris you could feel the fear and the powerlessness. It was horrible. I hope that never happens here.' Her eyes went past me to where Alice was emerging from the house to join us. She brightened.

'Come on, let's have breakfast. I'm starving. Since the men have all abandoned us and Papa is threatening to join George in London too, we might as well have fun. I'm going to keep my promise, Alice, and teach you to drive.'

'Aren't you afraid I might wreck your automobile?' replied Alice. Her step lightened and her eyes shone with anticipation.

'Of course not,' said Mouse. 'I'm a very good teacher. I'll have you driving in no time.' She grinned. 'In fact, I'll have you driving by luncheon, Alice. Then it's your turn, Elin.'

I stared at her. 'I'm not sure…'

'Go on,' said Mouse, mischievously. 'You don't have to tell Hugo, and who knows, you might enjoy it. It's all the rage nowadays, you know. Who knows where it might take you?'

* * *

All that morning I sat under the awning on the lawn pretending to read my book. However hard I tried, I was unable to keep my eyes from Alice easing the car gingerly down the drive, turning at the entrance and then making her way back – often with at least one dangerous waver towards the lawn.

After several journeys she began to move faster, until the automobile shot off at speed. Mouse shrieked delightedly as they cleared the gates and sped out onto the road. The roar of the engine faded into the distance.

I abandoned my book. I felt quite sure I would never see either of them again. But after half an hour or so the engine roar returned, followed by Alice sailing up the drive at a sedate pace.

'We went right round the lanes. That was the most exciting thing I've ever done!' she exclaimed as she brought the vehicle to a halt and jumped out. 'You've got to try it Elin. It's wonderful.'

Mouse, I realised with a slight sinking in my stomach, had not moved from her seat. Her grin was a challenge. 'You don't have to go far, Elin. We can stop straight away if you don't like it.'

I laughed. 'You are determined to have your way, Mouse.'

'Of course. I always do. Haven't you noticed? Come on Elin. I won't force you to carry on if you really hate it. Just once, down the drive. I'm dying of thirst, so we'll have to stop for a cup of tea anyhow.'

There was nothing for it. I took my place in the driver's seat. The next few minutes were the most terrifying of my life. I had never been in charge of such a huge, cumbersome machine that flew – or so it felt – from under me. The pedals baffled. The steering wheel had a life of its own. And the machinery – it was a monster raring to be let off the leash to create havoc. No wonder Hugo always insisted I sat on the back seat surrounded by cushions.

After a great deal of crashing and banging we started with a shudder. 'That's it! That's it!' cried Mouse. 'Now try the brake, just as I showed you.'

We screeched to an abrupt halt. 'Sorry!' Mouse was nearly sent hurtling out of the windscreen and my entire body slammed against the steering wheel, winding me.

Mouse laughed. 'You're doing just fine, Elin. I crashed Edmund's automobile into a hedge the first time I tried, and dented a wing.'

I glanced at her. 'Really?'

'Oh goodness, yes. I was horribly impatient. Poor Edmund nearly banned me entirely before I got the hang of it. It's so unlike anything you've ever done before. It's just a matter of getting used to it.'

I took a deep breath and grasped the steering wheel again. Mouse might always get her own way, but I never gave up. More than one of my governesses had numbered being stubborn amongst my failings. I had done my very best not to be ever since. Now I could feel all of my unladylike, dig-your-heels-in pride taking over.

'Hold on, Mouse, here we go!' By fits and starts we made our way down the driveway. At the gateway I turned it around. The steering wheel was heavy, taking all my strength to pull it over. I followed Mouse's instructions, bewildered as to which way the vehicle would go.

'Well done,' Mouse said, as I finally manoeuvred the thing so it was facing the house again.

'I don't know what I was doing.'

'Oh, that's just practice. At the moment you're trying to work it out with your mind. To really get going, you have to let yourself feel the way it moves. You'll see.'

I threw her a sceptical look, took a deep breath and set off again. This time it was easier. By the time we reached Alice I was beginning to enjoy the cool breeze and the shrubs on either side shooting past.

'One more try and you'll get it,' announced Mouse, as I brought the automobile to a stop without throwing us both over the windscreen. 'Come on...then we'll have tea.'

This time I dared to go a little faster. As we reached the front gates I could glimpse what Mouse meant. I was getting a feel for it. I was in control of the vehicle rather than the machine being in control of me. And I didn't want it to end.

I pulled up at the entrance. 'I suppose we'd better go back.'

'I suppose so,' said Mouse. Her challenge of a grin was back. I set the Chevrolet in motion again and slid through the open gates, leaving the gateman shaking his head at a respectable married woman being led so far astray. I caught Mouse's eye and we burst into laughter as I took to the road.

Staying clear of the hedgerows was the terrifying bit. The first few bends nearly did for me, but by the time we turned onto the lane between the fields I'd got the hang of it. Although I was thankful for the lack of any vehicle coming the other way.

'This is wonderful!' I cried, as the hedges shot past in the flash of an eye.

'The best thing next to flying,' Mouse called back, tucking her headscarf firmly into her blouse. 'I bet you don't dare make it to the village.'

'I bet you I do.'

Within minutes the thatched roofs of the first cottages appeared between the trees. 'Better slow down,' yelled Mouse. 'They still don't expect motor vehicles and you don't want to run anyone over.'

I slowed to a crawl. Which was as well, since the next bend took us into the path of a group of girls playing hopscotch on the road. They jumped to the side of the road squealing as we passed. I slowed even further as I took us twice around the village green. The ancient sheepdog moved unwillingly out of our way, panting too hard to bark. Windows were thrown open at the sound of the engine and shopkeepers appeared at their doors to stare. The second time around we were followed by a gang of boys who ran in our dusty wake trying to keep up with us. I didn't dare attempt a third circuit, for fear the entire village might turn out to watch, so I took the road back towards Northholme Manor, leaving the boys far behind.

We arrived back at Northholme in one piece. I pulled up in front of the lawn, where Alice was dancing from one foot to the other in an agony of anticipation.

'I told you it was good,' said Mouse, jumping out. 'We got to the village, Alice. You should have seen their faces when they realised it was a woman driving. They've got used to me and they know I'm wild anyhow, but I'm sure none of them ever thought they'd see a woman like Elin driving round the village green.'

I pulled myself out. My head was swimming, my arms ached and my legs wobbled like Cook's best blancmange, so that I could barely walk. I'd never felt better.

'I'll order tea,' said Alice, looking at me anxiously as I collapsed into a chair. 'I didn't get anywhere near the village and that was quite enough.'

I smiled at her. 'So, where else can we go?'

Mouse turned to Alice. 'Where's the place you'd like to go most in the world? And you, Elin?'

'Aunt Catrin,' I said, without thinking.

Mouse looked at me.

'Aunt Catrin has a farm on Anglesey,' explained Alice. 'We used to visit there when we were little. It's very beautiful.'

I felt an ache, deep in my heart. Aunt Catrin was the nearest thing I had to a mother since Mama had died. She had the same dark, understanding eyes. Today, more than ever, I longed for her arms to come about me and hold me tight. To be able to tell her the things I could never speak of, not even to Alice. 'Only it's much too far to go,' I admitted. 'Nearly as far as Scotland.'

'Anglesey.' I looked up at Mouse's tone. 'That's an island north of Wales, isn't it?'

'Just off the coast,' said Alice. 'You reach it by a bridge.'

'Mountains and castles and an island,' said Mouse. 'If we go after Papa leaves tomorrow, we can say we're going to visit my Aunt Mary in Cheltenham. No one need ever know.'

Alice blinked. 'You can't be serious, Mouse. It would take us at least two days to get there. Where would we stay?'

'We'd find a hotel,' said Mouse airily. She caught the look on our faces. 'Don't worry, I've got my allowance. I can easily pay for a room for us all, it won't be more than a room just for me and I'd be much more stared at on my own. We can be three eccentric lady historians in search of Celtic mysteries. Or botanists, or something. No one will notice. It will be such an adventure. With this war and everything, we might all be dead soon.' She jumped to her feet. 'Come on, if we go back now, we can start packing.'

'She'll have changed her mind by the morning,' I said, as Mouse disappeared inside the house.

'I don't think so, somehow,' replied Alice.

Panic shot through me. We had always made the journey to Anglesey cocooned in the comfort of a railway carriage. Other than that, I had barely travelled more than a few miles from Port Helen in my life. And how could we set off like this with a war erupting around us? 'But we can't,' I protested. 'You and I can barely drive, and shouldn't we be preparing in case there is a war?'

'I think that's the point,' said Alice. 'We're just expected to sit here and wait, not knowing what is happening. I think Mouse has to be doing something. Especially now her brothers and Owen could well be in the thick of it. I have a feeling nothing is about to dissuade her.' She smiled reassuringly. 'I'm not sure I want to just hang around here and wait, either, with too much time on our hands, and our imaginations running riot. And it might be our only chance to see Aunt Catrin for ages.'

'I suppose,' I said slowly, with a feeling of being swept along despite myself.

Alice jumped to her feet. 'Come on. Mouse is right. The less time we have to think about what might be waiting for us in the future the better, and I'm with Mouse: I'd rather not think at all.'

Chapter Seven

AUGUST 6TH, 1914

Lord Northholme left for London after breakfast the next morning. Within the hour, our bags were in the boot of the Chevrolet, and we were off. We took turns at driving and sitting in the passenger seat with Mouse's road map folded on our knees, or resting on the back seat.

We followed Mouse's map past Gloucester and on into Wales. Here the roads returned to lanes and the landscape grew wilder. The only vehicles we passed were the occasional tractor and the odd cart. Northholme, and even the war, felt far away.

Amidst the remote beauty of hills and moorland, the only villages we passed were small, with no sign of a hotel or boarding house. The villagers were friendly, but spoke little English. I still had a smattering of Welsh, taught to me by Mama and Mrs Hughes, who always fell into their native tongue when speaking to each other. We had spent hours in the kitchens at Hiram, Mama and I, chatting to Cook and making *bara brith* and Welsh cakes and a thick soup they both called *cawl* for the workers in the kitchen garden. My attempts now were met with smiles and nods but mostly puzzlement.

'I don't think they can imagine three women travelling on their own with nowhere to stay,' decided Mouse, as darkness began to fall. 'They probably think we are on our way to sleep in feather beds in some great castle on the next hillside.'

For a while, I thought we might end up sleeping in the Chevrolet or even a barn, but eventually we found rooms in a farmhouse set up a steep winding track next to the road. The farmer's wife was welcoming, if slightly bemused by the three of us. Her husband, I suspect, was deeply shocked, while their rosy-faced children stared at us with open curiosity. The room, however, was comfortable and spotlessly clean. There was only one bed, but we were so tired we crawled into it gratefully, giggling like schoolgirls as we sorted out elbows and knees and, despite the ridiculous squash, were asleep instantly.

The next morning we were given a hearty breakfast of bacon and eggs, accompanied by delicious bread still warm from the oven and copious amounts of tea.

'Is it north you are going?' asked Mrs Jones, in Welsh, as we went outside to put our bags in the boot of the Chevrolet.

I nodded. 'To my aunt. In Anglesey. *Ynys Môn.*' I added to her puzzled look.

'Ah,' she replied, nodding. 'Beautiful, so I've heard.' She eyed our vehicle dubiously. 'But a long way. Through the mountains.'

'We've plenty of time,' I assured her, 'and the automobile has brought us a long way already. We are staying tonight in Barmouth, before the high mountains begin.'

She smiled, gathering up her youngest into her arms, clearly wondering at our husbands permitting such a reckless abandonment of our children.

'I wonder if they know there's a war?' murmured Mouse, as she took the steering wheel.

'They soon will, if it lasts,' I added, glancing back towards the farmer's eldest boy, a lad of barely sixteen, who was gazing at us intently from one of the barns.

Alice shivered. 'Let's hope it's all blown over by then. I wish I didn't know myself.'

'And I want to forget about it for now,' exclaimed Mouse. 'There's nothing we can do and it might all be finished by the time we get back.' Watched by the children and an entire field of astonished sheep, she started the engine and we were on our way once more.

My visits to Aunt Catrin – even that last time, when I still needed to cling to Alice's arm to walk more than a few paces – had always been by train. When I took my turn deciphering the map for Mouse, I feared we would never reach anywhere I recognised. The lanes became narrower and more twisting. We lumbered over several mountain passes, barely making it over the brow before rattling down the other side at a great pace, cliffs and moorland soaring away into the distance on either side.

By evening we had reached the coast and the resort town of Barmouth, where the railway crossed the estuary on a long span of a bridge. This time we easily found rooms in a guesthouse. As the sun began to sink towards the sea, we made our way out to where fishing boats rocked gently in the harbour, waiting for the tide to turn, seagulls swerving and shrieking amongst the waiting lobster pots.

'It feels very quiet,' said Alice, looking out over the few families gathered on the beach and the couples strolling in the last of the sunshine. Despite the heat, there was a chill wind in the air, blowing in from a restless sea.

'It's real, isn't it,' said Mouse, as a couple passed us, holding each other tight, oblivious to everyone around them. 'The war, I mean. It isn't a game, or heroic, or in a land far away. It's here.' She shivered. 'This feels like it did in Paris. Horrible. With everyone waiting. Trying to look after everyone they love, knowing that some of them will die.'

'We can go back,' I said. 'Perhaps we should never have come.'

Mouse shook herself. 'No. You want to see your Aunt Catrin. Anyone could see how important that was to you.' Her eyes scrutinised me. I wondered if she was remembering Hugo's outburst at dinner. If, in her own way, Mouse recognised the man already torn apart by war, where other diners had seen only eccentricity. As if somehow, from the protection of her gilded world, Mouse had glimpsed my husband in a way so many others missed, and could sense my need of Aunt Catrin's help now that he was heading straight back towards the horrors that already consumed him.

I didn't know how Aunt Catrin could help, but I needed to see her.

We sat in silence, as the light faded and the couple walked slowly into the distance, holding each other as if they wished the day might never end.

* * *

The next morning Mouse insisted we follow the old coach road through the highest mountains. She took the wheel to coax the Chevrolet up through the unbelievably steep bends of the road past Snowdon itself. We paused to allow the engine to cool down and recover, before heading on through swathes of moorland to the green Nant Ffrancon valley, and a glimpse of Anglesey in the distance. Here, I took over the wheel, swerving down the pass, past an enormous slate mine that had eaten away half a mountainside and its little mining village of Bethesda.

Before long we were near the coast, where the land was flat and the driving became easy. We drove across the suspension bridge over the Menai Straights, linking Anglesey to the mainland, before following the coastal road to the round tumbledown towers of the ruined castle of Beaumaris.

Here the landscape gradually came familiar. I no longer needed Alice's instructions but took the steep road up through the town and into the heart of the island.

'I thought it was by the sea,' said Mouse, sounding disappointed.

'It is. Right by the sea. You'll see, we'll be there soon.' I followed the lanes between fields of crops rich as any we found at home, past lush green fields of sheep and cows, until at last we reached the tiny lane that wound past stunted trees, blown all one way by the sea winds, to Aunt Catrin's farm, with the blue expanse behind and a view of the distant mountains.

Geese and chickens parted in outrage as we arrived in front of the large stone farmhouse, followed by a collection of black and white sheepdogs barking in high excitement.

As I pulled to a halt, a loud whistle dragged the dogs away, back to the front door where Aunt Catrin was waiting for us.

'Dearest Elin.' She caught me in a bear hug the moment I stepped onto the ground. 'It really is you, *cariad*. I could scarcely believe it when I received your telegram.' Her dark brown eyes, so like Mama's they still made my stomach clench, examined my face. 'You look well.'

'I am well,' I replied, kissing her.

Aunt Catrin released me and turned to embrace Alice. 'My goodness, you've grown. You're the proper lady now, my dear.' She smiled at Mouse. 'And this must be Lady Margaret. You are very welcome.'

'Mouse,' said Mouse firmly, holding out her hand. Aunt Catrin shook it, then kissed Mouse on the cheek.

'You'll have to forgive me, my dear. Our manners are very informal here, and you have brought Elin and Alice back to me, for which I shall be eternally grateful.'

I had never seen Mouse lost for words. She blushed scarlet with pleasure. 'I wouldn't have missed it for the world,' she muttered at last.

'Aha, Fly remembers you, Elin,' said Aunt Catrin, as the smallest sheepdog slunk on her belly to my side and butted her nose under my hand. 'You will never be forgotten here, you see.'

I fussed the delicate head, tickling Fly under her ears until her brown eyes closed with pleasure. 'You didn't forget.' I looked up to find Mouse watching me. 'Fly was a pup when Alice and I stayed here last,' I explained. 'She was too young to go out with the working dogs, so she stayed with me. We became good friends. I even taught her to swim.'

Aunt Catrin chuckled. 'So that's the reason I can't keep her out of the water when we go down to *Sŵn y Môr*. You should have taught her to fish, too, *cariad*, so she could bring me a good tasty supper.'

'*Sŵn y Môr*?' asked Mouse.

'It's a fisherman's cottage right on the beach,' said Alice. 'It means "sound of the sea".'

'That's true, although I prefer "Song of the Sea",' smiled Aunt Catrin. She took my arm. 'I've made sure it's aired and the beds are made up. But tonight you are all staying with me. I don't want to let you out of my sight.' She led the way into the cool of the farmhouse, to a large open kitchen with a range at one end, and shelves tumbling over themselves with books at the other, almost extinguishing the upright piano in their midst. Siani the tabby cat was curled up on the piano stool, just as I remembered her, ready to climb into Aunt Catrin's lap as she made her way through Mozart and Chopin by candlelight after the hens and the pigs had been shut up for the night.

On a hook over the central fire a kettle was boiling, while in the middle of the large oak table a rectangular *bara brith*, rich with fruit and molasses, sat waiting. From the oven at one side of the range came the delicious scent of roasting lamb and the pungent smell of rosemary.

'Oh my goodness,' exclaimed Mouse, collapsing into a chair. 'This is heaven.' She pulled at her collar. 'I'm afraid I'm terribly grubby.'

Aunt Catrin laughed. 'This is a farm, my dear. I am in and out of here in all weathers. A little dirt never caused me any trouble. But I'm sure you can all do with a bath after all that travelling. We can boil the kettle and you can have one in front of the fire once we've eaten.'

'Oh, I didn't mean to put you to the trouble of filling kettles and bringing out a bath,' said Mouse, blushing once more. 'You must think me terribly rude. I was thinking more of a swim in the sea.'

'As you wish,' said Aunt Catrin. 'But a bath is really no trouble.' Her eyes twinkled. 'My dad wouldn't use one, however hard my mam tried. He was a fisherman. He always said he'd had his fill of water once the day's work was done.'

'Really?' Mouse gazed at her as if she wasn't certain if Aunt Catrin was joking or not. 'I can't imagine anyone growing tired of water.'

'Well, I'm glad to say I don't share my dad's aversion to washing,' said Aunt Catrin with a smile.

After we'd demolished most of the *bara brith* and several pots of tea, Mouse and Alice found their swimming costumes and headed off to the beach.

'Are you sure you won't join them, *cariad*?' said Aunt Catrin.

I shook my head. 'Maybe in a little while. It's been so long since I've seen you, and I don't know when I'll be able to be here again. I want to spend every minute I can with you.'

'Of course, *cariad*.' Aunt Catrin kissed me. 'You are here for such a little while, I don't want to let you out of my sight any more than I have to.' She sat down to mend the webbing of an old kitchen chair, grown thin with age and use. Her fingers worked swiftly and surely, her eyes scarcely leaving my face. I watched her, still dazed by the fact of us being here at all. I had so much to say, and so much to ask, I hardly knew where to begin.

'You look more like your mother every day,' remarked Aunt Catrin, at last.

'Do I?' The Mama I remembered was gentle and still. When the gatherings at Hiram stopped, she would sit for hours on the window seat overlooking the walled garden, lost in a dream as she faded, little by little, away from us. The fear that had been floating in my stomach gripped me hard.

'Your Mama when she was young, that is.' Aunt Catrin smiled a little sadly. 'She was always a dreamer, was Non. She couldn't wait to get away from here. She dreamed of living in a grand house by the sea, surrounded by artists and musicians. She was so excited the day she left to keep house for your Uncle Howard in London, before he married Alice's mama. She used to say that was the day her life began.' She took a sidelong glance at me. 'She loved you and your papa dearly, my dear, but at times, in those last years when you came to stay, she seemed a little lost. The last time I saw her, she hinted that there could be a high price to pay for following a dream.'

I bit my lip. 'I don't want to live in a dream, Aunt Catrin. Not any more. But I don't know what to do. Hugo sees me just as Papa did. He won't share anything of himself with me. Soon Alice will leave me. I will be completely alone.'

Aunt Catrin concentrated on the chair. 'You are still very young, my dear. Very few marriages are easy. You are not your Mama, *cariad*. Non used to say there was a strong spirit in you. Maybe that is what you need to find.'

I shook my head. 'I don't know Hugo any more, Aunt Catrin. Sometimes I wonder if he still loves me. And sometimes I'm not sure—' I came to a halt. There were some things I could not say, not even to Aunt Catrin. I could not expose my deepest shame, not even to one who loved me so well.

Aunt Catrin's hands stilled. 'And you want me to give you a way out?'

'No!' I started. 'No, of course not.' I met her eyes. Clear and penetrating, and piercing straight to my heart. 'At least, it's impossible. Unthinkable. Especially now there is a war and Hugo is heading straight to the fighting. I can't abandon him now.' I frowned, a realisation hitting me hard in the stomach. 'And I can't abandon Hiram and everyone who lives there, to run away to safety.'

'Good girl.' Aunt Catrin nodded. 'It seems to me you have to make your own way in life. No one will do it for you. You've found new friends. You can drive. Hugo may be troubled, but he is not a monster. Many husbands and wives live almost completely separate lives. You need to find an enthusiasm and pursue it.'

'That's what Owen said.'

'Owen?'

'Mouse's cousin. He was staying at Northholme. He said my love of recipes was my passion, and I should pursue it.'

Aunt Catrin pushed the half-mended chair away from her. Her look was severe. 'Elin, at some point or other we would all like to live our lives over again and make different choices. From the outside, they always appear more attractive, and the answer to all our troubles. Believe me, they never are. You are not a fool, my dear. Don't act the fool now.'

I was scarlet. 'I didn't! I wouldn't…'

I met her eyes. Her gaze did not waver but her smile softened the sting. 'You know I will always tell you the truth, however unpalatable, and however much it hurts. That's why you came to me.'

I nodded, swallowing hard.

Aunt Catrin made her way over to the bookshelves and took down a small brown notebook, faded and battered, its pages much turned. 'But he was right. Mouse's cousin, that is.' She placed the notebook next to me. 'That's your mother's recipe

book. It was begun by your grandmother at *Sŵn y Môr.* Your
mam always had the art of making the meanest ingredients into
a feast. Heaven knows, they were mean enough when we were
little. Take it with you.'

'I can't…'

'Yes you can. I know each one by heart. Your mother would
have wanted you to have it, especially now. Mrs Hughes will help
you with the parts you can't follow.'

I held the book in my hands. The pages fell slowly open,
revealing first a hesitant hand, one not accustomed to writing
and entirely in Welsh, followed by my mother's familiar flowing
script in both languages. Traces of flour dusted a recipe for
Christmas Cake. A ghost of a crimson fingerprint rested next to
instructions for plum jam. The paper was transparent with the
remains of butter in several places. A dried leaf of sage had tucked
itself into the central seam of one page, the shriveled brown of a
bayleaf fell from another.

'Thank you,' I murmured, closing the precious gift and
holding it close, inhaling its scent.

Aunt Catrin kissed me. 'Live your life, Elin. Whatever
happens, live your life to the full and live it your way. Don't be
swayed by those who don't know you. And don't let anyone ever
use you for their own ends. Fight for what you believe in. You'll
find a way, *cariad.* There's always a way.' She turned her head
towards the open door, to the sounds of Alice and Mouse
returning from their swim. 'My life might once have been very
different. I should have had a husband and a house filled with
children. But my Dewi was drowned in a storm, three days before
our wedding.'

'I'm sorry.' So much of Aunt Catrin fell into place. Her
toughness and her gentleness, and her truth that came, I could
see now, from having been to the darkest places and survived.

'It was a long time ago. Oh, I knew the danger in loving a

fisherman. I knew that one day I might lose him to the sea.
Maybe, if I was given my time again, I would choose never to
have met him, so I would never feel the pain of his loss.' She gave
a wry smile. 'But then I would never have known the joy that
true love brings, or the best man I ever met.' She pushed the
kettle back onto the range and reached for the teapot. 'I thought
everything was over, when I lost Dewi. But I've made a life for
myself. I have my friends, and the farm. I have my music and
the children I teach at Sunday school. It's not the life I expected,
or ever wanted. But you have to believe me, my dear, when I say
it's a happy one. Make a life for yourself, Elin, and yours can be,
too.'

Chapter Eight

AUGUST 9TH, 1914

I was up the next morning as the first light reached the
farmhouse. My mind was buzzing and I could no longer stay still
beneath the covers.

All through that restless night, slipping in and out of dreams,
I could see that Aunt Catrin was right. What a fool I had been!
A selfish, silly, indulgent fool, to believe my fairytale would come
to me without my having to lift a finger. No wonder Hugo
treated me like a child, when I still behaved like one.

A new energy flowed through me. With Hugo away, the
Hiram estate would need me to run it. Why had I always shirked
from such responsibility before? Why had I never thought to
question Papa's assumption that, as a girl, such a thing was
beyond me? I had seen Aunt Catrin run a large farm all by herself,
commanding absolute respect and obedience from the men she

hired to help bring in the harvest and the shearing of her sheep. In comparison, Hiram would be simple to manage.

If I could prove that I could run Hiram as well as any man, then Hugo would see that I was his equal and worthy of his trust. As his equal, he might finally be able to confide in me. Surely then, we would have a chance to move forward into the future together and make our marriage work.

Through the open window of the bedroom, the dawn air was edged with chill, the sky already a pale hint of blue, promising the day's heat. I dressed as quietly as I could and crept downstairs. Fly was curled up on a rug in front of the range. Her tail banged gently on the tiles as I reached the bottom step. As I lifted the latch of the front door she rose to her feet, slipping past me and out towards the sheep fields.

'Fly!' I called. She stopped instantly, glancing back. I turned towards the sea and she followed, low to the ground, nose deep in the spangled cobwebs.

We walked through a meadow of summer flowers onto the rough grass of the cliffs. A few late sea pinks still clung on, tucked in amongst the cracks of rock for protection against the wind. The cliffs were smaller than in Cornwall, but wild and jagged all the same. As the light intensified, the grey shadows of mountains across the sea on the mainland began to emerge from the morning mist, huge ranges edged against the skyline.

Before long, the grass sloped gently down to a hollow next to a sandy beach. Just above the sand stood *Sŵn y Môr*. The whitewashed stone cottage was built long and low as if to protect itself against the wild gales blowing across the sea from Ireland. Its front door opened almost straight out onto the beach, while behind a wall, also of stone, did its best to protect a tiny garden.

'Pretty, isn't it?'

I jumped. Mouse was making her way up from the beach, a dressing gown flung over her damp swimming costume, hair dripping down her back. As she reached us, she bent to fuss Fly, who promptly leant firmly against her leg, eyes half closed, nose butting her hand at any sign of stopping.

Mouse looked at me uncertainly. 'I'm sorry. Did you want to be alone? I didn't mean to come this far, but it was such a glorious morning and this is the best beach. I couldn't resist a dawn swim.'

'No, of course not. I was just startled, that's all. How's the water?'

'Perfect. It's so peaceful and clear, and the view of the mountains is like something from a fairytale.' She glanced towards the cottage. 'Is that where Aunt Catrin grew up?'

Fly had shuffled on her hindquarters and was now leaning against me, gazing up with liquid brown eyes. I crouched down to fuss her ears. 'Yes, and my mother. It's where we used to stay every summer when we came to visit Aunt Catrin, when I was a child.' I looked up at Mouse. 'Thank you for bringing us here. It's meant more to me than I can possibly say.'

'Oh, that's all right,' replied Mouse awkwardly, colouring slightly. 'And anyhow, I probably only jumped at the chance to go off on one of my wild adventures while I still had the chance. I told you, I'm hopelessly selfish.'

'I don't believe a word of it,' I replied, kissing her cheek. 'I bet, given the choice, you'd have dragged us off to some mad parties in London or had us sleeping under the stars on the Lizard.'

Mouse grinned. 'Oh, well that's what we can do next.' She pulled a face. 'I keep on forgetting. Everything feels normal, and then I remember there's a war, and all the things I saw in France with the men leaving to fight and everyone scared. And now they're all happening here and who knows what might happen next.'

We sat on the sand dunes without speaking for a while. Fly settled down between us, one eye on the seals sunbathing on a rocky outcrop next to ranks of oystercatchers waiting on sandbanks for the tide to turn.

'Don't cry, Elin. It will be all right. I know it will.' She jumped to her feet. 'Here's Alice. Come on, I want to see everything inside the cottage, and then I want breakfast. I'm starving.'

* * *

Swˆn y Môr was just as I remembered it. A simple kitchen with an alcove for a bed downstairs and a narrow flight of stairs leading to the main bedroom tucked under the eaves.

I stood by the ancient range, listening to Mouse exclaiming over the sloping roofs and the beams upstairs, where there was scarcely room for the three of us to stand at one time. Through the open door I could see the soft sweep of sand, leading between green samphire and tall fronds of sea grass down to the sea. In the distance came the honk of seals squabbling over the best places to catch the warmth as the sun rose.

The house was rich with memories, not only my own, but everyone's who had lived here, since the first fishermen had built the cottage close to the sea. My memories were happy ones, but now, with adult eyes, I understood there had been grief here, too.

Once the summer had gone, *Swˆn y Môr* could be a bleak place, racked by bitter winds that reached into every nook and cranny. Sand scattered against the windows, while the sea roared, its breakers surging ever nearer to the house, as if determined to sweep it away in the night.

There were memories here of babies who had never grown into children, shrivelled by the cold and the damp air. Of children who had never lived to have families of their own and now lay, with the generations of young and old in the churchyard along the coast. And the grief was there too for the men who, like Aunt Catrin's Dewi, had no grave but the sea.

I turned my attention back to getting the fire in the range going, so we could boil the kettle and cook the bacon Alice had brought with her. As the fire took hold I placed the heavy kettle on the hook balancing on a metal arm and swung it into position.

'It's so much prettier, even than the Mediterranean,' Mouse was exclaiming as she and Alice clattered down the stairs to join me. 'It's perfect.'

A strange feeling overcame me, with the echo of footsteps and the breeze coming in from the sea. *Swn y Môr* had been my mother's refuge. The only place where I remembered her laughter unconstrained, as she and Aunt Catrin chased each other along the beach, like the children they had once been. Something – a sense, a reverberation – hung in the air with the griefs and the memories, just outside my grasp.

I wonder if, even then, I knew, deep inside, that one day *Swn y Môr* might be the only refuge I had left, when the storms and the winter winds would come to claim me too.

Chapter Nine

AUGUST 16TH, 1914

All too soon we were back at Northholme Manor.

Our return was barely noticed. No maid or footman rushed out to take our bags, and there was no sign of the butler at all.

'They can't all have vanished,' exclaimed Mouse, as we paused in the great hallway. From the direction of the kitchens there came the reassuring clatter of a pan being dropped, accompanied by the roar of the Northholme Cook. A door was flung open, and the sound of sobbing and the scent of roasting beef drifted up to us.

Footsteps creaked on the stairs above. 'Oh, my goodness!' It was one of the undermaids, face scarlet, her arms filled with bed linen. 'I'm so sorry, Lady Margaret. We weren't expecting you so early today. The beds are nearly made up. It won't take me a minute.'

'Don't worry about that,' said Mouse. 'There's plenty of time. Rose, where is everyone?'

'Oh, miss.' Rose's eyes filled with tears. 'They've gone.'

'Gone?' Mouse stared at her. 'They can't *all* have gone.'

Rose sniffed loudly. 'All the men, miss. At least, all the men who aren't married who are old enough to fight. And some of the married men volunteered too.'

'What on earth possessed them?'

'Lord Northholme, miss. When he came back from London he said men were volunteering all over the country, he wasn't going to be seen lacking in his duty, and all the men on the estate should march down to the village together and volunteer.' She burst into tears. 'Some of the labourers went straight from the fields.'

Alice and I gently removed the sheets from the poor girl's arms, while Mouse led her to a chair. 'Did your brothers go?'

Rose nodded. 'Yes, miss. Both of them.' She blew her nose. 'Don't get me wrong, Lady Margaret, I know they are wonderfully brave and I'm so proud of them, and they were so excited to be going. And I know they say this war won't last long, but it's such a thing. My poor mother won't stop crying, and Dad is at his wits' end to know how they are going to get the harvest in.'

'I'm sure they'll all be home soon,' said Mouse firmly. 'Besides, it doesn't make sense to send the farmhands. They'll have to send them back. If there's no one to get in the harvest we'll all starve and that won't win anything.'

A shout echoed up from the direction of the kitchens. Rose jumped to her feet. 'I must get the beds done. Cook is in such a temper with the kitchen maids being directed to do so much of the work in the house, she's said I'm to go and help her as soon as the rooms are ready.'

'Don't worry about the beds, Rose,' said Alice. 'I'm sure we are capable of making them up.'

'And Cook need never know,' I added, as Rose began to protest.

'Go on,' said Mouse, shooing Rose downstairs.

As we made our way up to our rooms, I could see dust already gathering in the corners of the stairs. On one of the landings, a vase of flowers was fading, surrounded by a drift of pink rose petals on the windowsill.

Mouse and I made up the beds and neatened the rooms in silence, while Alice disposed of the dying flowers, replacing them with fresh roses from the gardens.

'I'd better go and talk to Papa,' said Mouse gloomily, as the sound of Lord Northholme's automobile returning drifted up through the silent house. 'He can't send off half the staff and expect all our comforts to carry on as before. We can at least make poor Cook's life easier.' She sighed. 'Not that he'll listen. I do so wish Owen was here. He's the only one who can make Papa see sense.'

An uneasy quiet hung over Northholme that day. From the windows we looked down over fields still rich with golden corn, where nothing moved. Machinery lay abandoned by the hedgerows. A cart stood idle beside one of the estate cottages, where baby clothes hung unmoving on the washing line.

Hugo sent a message that he would be coming to take us back to Hiram the following morning. I couldn't help feeling thankful. I felt sorry for Mouse, who was stomping around like a bear after her earlier attempts to speak to her father, but I wanted nothing more than to return home. I needed action. I needed to talk to Hugo and learn as much as I could about the essentials of running the Hiram estate while I could. I was impatient to set my resolution, and my new life, in motion.

Hugo was as good as his word, arriving straight after breakfast in the Silver Ghost. He was not in uniform, I was thankful to see. Perhaps he would be given some kind of administrative post. Perhaps he would never even need to leave England. Perhaps I would not be running Hiram completely alone after all. A touch of disappointment went through me. But of course, on reflection, that would be the best solution: Hugo and I working together, him safe and well. He would still be preoccupied with his official duties, and I would have the opportunity to prove myself in his absences.

On the drive back the three of us spoke little, and nothing of the war. It felt unreal. Very little had changed. Flags had appeared in the villages, and in one we passed a small group of volunteers marching to the train station. We heard cheers from the car as they passed. But flowers bloomed in the gardens and the hedgerows. Men still worked in the fields. As we reached the coast, families were picnicking on the sand and children playing in the water's edge. I had never been so thankful to see Hiram's familiar outline as we reached Port Helen.

'They are sending me to Belgium,' announced Hugo, when Alice had retreated to her rooms and I joined him for tea on the terrace.

'Belgium?' I did my best to keep my voice even. 'Isn't that where the fighting is?'

'We are only there to assist the Belgians. I shall not be on the front line. They need experienced officers to keep the supplies moving. They say on the quiet it's a shambles out there. They need men like me.'

'Of course,' I murmured, ashamed of my selfish sense of relief and afraid that Hugo was not telling me everything. He was still going where fighting was taking place. He would still be in danger.

Before I could open my mouth to ask a hundred questions, Hugo forestalled me. 'You needn't worry: I'm not going to leave you on your own, my dear. I've been arranging to hire a Steward to take over the running of the estate while I'm away.'

'A Steward?' I stared at him, my plans and my dreams slipping through my fingers before they had even begun. I struggled to gather my scattered thoughts. After all, a Steward, like any employee, would be under my command when Hugo was not present. If Aunt Catrin could gain the respect of the farmers of Anglesey, who had refused to even speak to her when she had first taken over the farm, then I could gain the respect of a Steward. It might even work in my favour. If Hugo heard praise of me from a man he respected, it could only further my case.

'Yes, my dear. A most excellent man. James Connors. He was working for Ford.'

I stared at him. 'I thought he was a gardener, not a Steward?'

Hugo frowned. 'He's very capable. He'll be much in demand now.'

'But we agreed to speak to him after Christmas.'

'Things have changed.' Hugo's tone was defensive. 'Mr Connors came to see me a few days ago. I told him I would think the matter over. But, on consideration, I feel it is for the best.'

'Mr Connors came to ask you take him on as a Steward?' I could barely hide my astonishment.

'It was an excellent suggestion.' He was refusing to meet my eyes. 'I would have thought of it myself had I not been certain Ford would not wish to release him. But Applebourne has been requisitioned by the War Office to be a hospital for the wounded. I thought they might decide on Hiram, but Applebourne has more rooms and is nearer Portsmouth, so far more suitable. Ford has relatives in America and is taking his family to stay for the duration. We really must be grateful.'

'Yes, of course.' Could the government really take over a house like Hiram, without the occupants having any say? A shiver ran through me. There were already hospitals. All those London hospitals within a few hours of the South Coast. Were they really expecting enough wounded to fill a large house like Applebourne?

'It will all be settled before I leave. I'll speak to Mr Connors tomorrow. I can't get through to Applebourne on the telephone, I expect they are busy with the arrangements. I'll drive over there in the morning.'

I pulled myself together. I had never fought Hugo's decisions before, but I was going to be heard for once. I was not going to remain a child, helpless and useless while a war raged and those I loved were prepared to put themselves in danger. 'Hugo, I'm not sure Mr Connors is the right person.'

Hugo paused in helping himself to a slice of Cook's best fruitcake, an expression of astonishment on his face. 'How can you say that? You've barely met the man.'

'I'm not sure Mr Connors would respect me.'

He bristled. 'Good Heavens, Elin. What evidence do you have for such a statement?'

'His manner.' Even without my plan, if this war was going to last for months – a year, even – the last thing I needed was to be in daily contact with someone who would not listen to me. At least Hugo, in his own way, was fond of me. He could not bear to see me unhappy. Whatever lay ahead, I would need someone who was at least on my side. I took a deep breath. 'Could you not leave me to interview various candidates, including him. So I can be sure that Mr Connors is a man who could respect a woman's point of view. Otherwise, I fear that, whatever the reality, he would see himself as the master.'

Hugo snorted. 'Good grief. You sound like Alice after one of those infernal lectures on rights she's always taking herself off to. You forget, my dear: Connors will be the servant. He will respect you as *my wife*. We must all do our duty in this war. You must put aside these sensitivities, which are down to your imagination. Connors is highly regarded, and you will feel the same once you get to know him.'

A sense of injustice shot through me. Did Hugo have no respect for my opinions at all? I might not have seen much of the world, but I had known my fellow creatures all my life. I'd tried to smooth over first impressions before. Sometimes I was wrong, but often that instinctive like or dislike had been based in something concrete, something I could only explain when I got to know that person better.

Hugo straightened his shoulders. 'This question of supplies is urgent. I am needed at the front directly. I have been given so little time to make arrangements. Connors is a blessing. Heaven knows how long it would have taken me to find a Steward at such short notice, with so many men volunteering.' He reached across the table, taking my hand and raising it to his lips. 'My first concern is for you, my dear. I could not bear to leave you without knowing you were safe.'

'Yes, of course,' I murmured. I glanced at his face, but it held the closed expression I knew so well. I could hardly forget that Connors' presence had caused Hugo so much distress in that first meeting, and yet he was prepared to put it aside. I gritted my teeth. It seemed that I must learn to do the same.

* * *

Hugo was out early the next morning. 'I'll bring Mr Connors back with me, my dear. Then we can go over matters together. That will put your mind at rest.'

After the sound of the Silver Ghost faded into the distance I found I could not settle to anything. I concentrated on ensuring Hugo's bags were packed and ready for his departure the following day. Then I helped Cook and Alice with the cold meat and pies Cook was preparing for Hugo to take with him.

I was almost relieved when I heard the sound of an engine from the driveway. 'They're early,' I remarked, looking up from wrapping a cold apple pie.

Alice ran to the window. 'That doesn't sound like the Silver Ghost,' she said. There was a swirl of gravel as the vehicle screeched to a halt. We met each other's eyes.

'Mouse,' we said in the same breath.

A battered army truck was slewed in front of the house. By the time we reached it, Mouse had jumped out of the driver's seat and was racing her way up the steps towards us.

'Hello, you two,' she called, with a kind of brittle cheerfulness that wasn't cheerful at all. 'I managed to cadge a lift with Owen. He and Edmund are busy in Portsmouth, something to do with the mobilisation stuff. So I borrowed this and came over while I could.' She hugged us. 'I've missed you both. Northholme isn't the same without you.'

'Come and have some tea,' I said.

Mouse shook her head. 'I can't stay long and I don't want to waste a moment on tea.' Her face darkened. 'Papa's forbidden me to fly. He says I could be shot down as a spy, or an enemy. He's insisting I'm only being selfish and my bi-plane could be better used by the army. It's being taken away tomorrow. I'll never see it again.'

'Oh, Mouse,' exclaimed Alice. 'I'm so sorry.'

Mouse sighed. 'It's so utterly stupid. I'm not allowed to do anything. I could have gained information for the army. I could have flown over Prussia and taken photographs of their mobilisation.'

'That sounds dangerous,' I said.

'No more dangerous than being shot at or hand to hand combat. I could have been out of there before anyone noticed.

I'm quick. I could have dodged their aircraft and been back over the channel before half of them were in the air. And anyhow, I've friends in France. I could have easily hidden in a barn and flown at night. And now Edmund is saying they may have to ration petrol for civilians if this carries on for much longer, so much is taken up already with moving troops and equipment. So I might not even be able to use the Chevrolet. I had to come and see you both. Who knows when I might have the chance again?' Her eyes lit on the bags in the hallway.

'They're sending Hugo over to Belgium to supervise supplies,' I explained.

'I'm sorry, Elin.' Mouse hugged me close. 'This must be so awful for you. I never think, do I? I don't want to intrude.'

'You're not intruding. Hugo has business to attend to and won't be back for a while. And to be honest, I'm rather glad of the distraction. I'm not sure parting is such sweet sorrow, after all.'

'You can say that again. Edmund and Owen came back with George just after you left. The way they talk, as if the war is some great adventure. Like King Arthur, or Shakespeare, or those adventure books they were always reading as boys. They keep on saying if they don't go now they'll never get a chance before it all blows over. They'll all be off to France in a few days' time.'

'I'm sorry,' I said quietly.

Alice said, 'I'm sure they will be back in a few months.'

'Well it's unfair,' said Mouse. 'That's what it is. They want people to join up, yet they won't let me do my bit. It's so stupid. Papa spent so much money sending me to that tedious finishing school in Paris so I could snare some French aristo. He was so cross when I got bored and went off exploring the villages and the chateaux instead. How many men are there who can speak French like a native and have driven miles through the countryside round Paris, and flown over it all, too?'

'You can't really want to go and fight?' said Alice.

'Why ever not? I wouldn't mind being a nurse, or anything. It's rotten that I could do so many useful things and they won't let me. And of course Papa is hopeless. He just says I should find a husband and start breeding before the best men start disappearing off to the front. He's quite convinced it's all going to last for ages, like the Balkans, wherever they are. Apparently they've been fighting amongst themselves for years.'

There was a moment's silence. Mouse was biting her lip. Alice had begun to look deeply thoughtful.

'Come on,' I said hastily. 'Let's walk along the cliff path. It's so beautiful today, and I can watch for Hugo.'

But as we reached the kitchen garden, I could make out the dust clouds of an automobile approaching, accompanied by the familiar roar of Hugo's Silver Ghost.

'I'd better go,' said Mouse, her eyes following mine. 'Owen and Edmund will be wondering where I am.'

'We'll find a way of meeting up with you,' I said. 'Hugo's still got his old Rover in the barn and he always keeps fuel there. We could meet halfway. And there are bound to still be trains. They can't always be full of troops, surely.'

'Of course,' said Mouse, kissing me and hugging Alice tight. 'We won't be beaten.' Her eyes darkened again. 'And, whatever it takes, I'm not going to be stopped from doing my bit by Papa and all those horrid, stupid old generals. I'm not giving up. Not when Owen and my brothers and more than half the men I know are going to be out there, any day now, risking their lives. I can't just stay here and do nothing. I just can't.'

Chapter Ten

AUGUST 18TH, 1914

Hugo was furious. He stomped past me with scarcely a glance. 'Damn the man.'

'Has Mr Connors been delayed?'

'Worse than that: he's in Portsmouth and won't be back for at least a week.'

'Oh?' Well, it was a week's grace at least.

'Ford sent him to make the arrangements for the family's passage to America and insists he can't be spared.'

'At all?'

'It is most inconvenient. I've no time to wait for his return, or interview anyone else.' He slumped down at his writing desk. 'Damn this pen. Will nothing work today?'

'I'll mend it for you,' said I, quietly, picking it up from the desk where he had thrown it. I fiddled with the nib for a while. My mind was racing. 'Here.' I handed the pen back to him. 'It will work now.'

He took it, frowning. His hand closed around mine. 'I cannot leave you here on your own, Elin, without any kind of protection. I cannot be easy in my mind unless I know you are safe.' He released my hand and began to write. 'If Connors is not back within the week, we must place an advertisement in *The Times*. There are bound to be replies from at least some suitable candidates. You might have to interview them yourself, if I am unable to return. You will need to get references for anyone who appears suitable from their previous employers. And if they don't suit, we'll just have to get rid of them and advertise again when I am back on my next leave.'

'Perhaps there might be someone nearer at home? Someone

who knows Port Helen well. Someone you know you could trust.'

'There are no overseers or stewards I know of, my dear, with so many men volunteering.'

'What about Mr Treeve?'

'Treeve?' The pen paused in mid flow.

'Yes. Didn't you say he was the best of men?'

'True.' He put the pen down. 'But Ford will never release Treeve from Applebourne. I could see for myself there are only a few old men left, too old to sign up, to prevent the place from going to rack and ruin while the army hospital is there. The hospital will need to keep what gardeners there are to feed its patients.'

'He's been dismissed.' I met Hugo's eyes. 'His mother worked as a seamstress for Mama when I was a little girl. Mrs Hughes is still friendly with the family. She was saying only yesterday that Annie Treeve was distressed that her son had been dismissed without notice and without any reason given, and now no one will employ him.'

Hugo grunted. 'Damn fools. Ford knew Treeve's views when he took him on, eight years ago.'

'At your recommendation?' It was a guess, but from Hugo's wry smile I could see it was the correct one.

'A man's conscience is his own, there's no point in making him suffer for it. Ford should know better than to bow to the white feather brigade. Jack always was a hard worker. He speaks his mind, but he's never been in any trouble during all that time.' He glanced up. 'So, you think you might get along with Mr Treeve despite his firebrand ways?'

'I don't know. I've never spoken to him. But you said he once saved your life. That's good enough for me.'

Hugo smiled. He raised my hand to his lips and kissed it gently. 'Treeve may refuse, of course. He's an infernally proud man.'

Well, it takes one to know one. For a moment I worried about bringing into the house a man who had fought with Hugo in the Boer War. Would he have as many demons as my husband? But I pushed this aside. 'Mr Treeve has an invalid mother to support.'

'That is very true.' Hugo released my hand and picked up his pen again. 'I'll write a note to him. Should he refuse, we can still put the advertisement in *The Times*.'

'I'll take it to his mother myself,' I said hastily. 'I'm sure she will help to persuade him.' I had seen Hugo's notes. They were woefully abrupt and quite likely to give offence, however unintentional. Far better that I spoke to Mr Treeve and his mother first.

'Of course, my dear,' said Hugo, writing away. His frown had eased a little and his shoulders had relaxed.

I felt a thrill that I had had an idea and Hugo had agreed to it. This was the new beginning I had hoped for. I didn't give Mr Connors' disappointment a thought.

* * *

The morning after Hugo's departure, I came down to a house that appeared unchanged. Breakfast was laid and there was a mild air of bustle. The usual sounds of floors being swept echoed through the house. It was Hiram as I had always known it, and yet nothing was the same.

'How quiet it is,' said Alice, pouring coffee.

'Yes,' I replied. 'That must be it.' It wasn't so much that there was less noise, but that there was an absence of joy. There was no shriek of laughter from the maids, quickly hushed. No footsteps running along the gravel outside. It was as if everyone in the house had their minds elsewhere. Even Mrs Pelham was listless when she appeared to go through the day's menus. I nodded in agreement with her with barely a glance, impatient to have the morning's tasks done so that I could escape to the village with Alice and speak to Mr Treeve before my courage failed me.

'Very good, Ma'am.' Thankfully Mrs Pelham had not noticed that dinner could have consisted of hay and crabs' claws for all I knew. 'And what is to be done about Elsie?'

'Elsie?'

Mrs Pelham sniffed. 'I've had a word with her already this morning. More than one. It's no good. She's not doing herself any favours and she's upsetting the other maids.'

I sighed inwardly at this further delay. 'Very well, Mrs Pelham. Leave it to me, I'll speak to her.'

I arrived in the kitchens to find Cook in a state of irritation and Elsie sniffing quietly as she peeled vegetables.

'For Heaven's sake, child,' exclaimed Cook as I reached them. 'You can't carry on like that. Go and help Martha in the garden. And blow your nose.'

'What is it?' I asked, as Elsie fled.

'Poor girl. Her young man is leaving today with the rest of the volunteers from Port Helen and she's breaking her heart over it. She's asked for the afternoon off, but with so few of the staff…'

'We can manage.' Elsie was only sixteen. My heart went out to her. 'After all, it will only be myself and Alice tonight, and I've told Mrs Pelham we should keep everything as simple as possible while Major Helstone is away, especially with so many of the staff leaving. I'm going into the village with Alice. We can take Elsie. There must be some errands we can say she needs to do.'

'If you're sure, Miss Elin. I think it would put her mind at rest to see him off.'

'Of course.'

It was a beautiful afternoon as Alice and I, accompanied by a slightly more cheerful Elsie, walked down into Port Helen. When we reached the village, we abandoned all pretence of errands.

'Go on, Elsie, off you go,' I said.

'Thank you, Ma'am.' She ran, a single red rose from the gardens clutched in her hand.

Alice turned to the lending library, while I followed the road out onto the far side of Port Helen until I came to a row of thatched and whitewashed cottages built just above the shoreline, where the river made its way down to the sea. How much simpler an advertisement in *The Times* would be, or to wait until Hugo came home on leave. I stood there, tempted to run away. Finally I knocked at the door of the last cottage, set a little aside from the rest.

After a minute or so it was opened, slowly, by a woman in her late sixties, her face gaunt and far older than her years. 'Mrs Helstone!'

I took a deep breath. 'Good afternoon, Mrs Treeve. May I come in? I would like a word with your son, if I may.'

Her eyes narrowed. 'We've no need of a white feather, if that's what you're thinking.'

I stared at her. 'No, of course not. That was the last thing on my mind. How could anyone give you, of all people, such a thing?' I followed her glance towards a tuneless whistling drifting in from the garden. 'They are the cowards,' I said. 'And my husband would say the same if he were here.'

Mrs Treeve gave me a sharp look, then led me through small, but immaculately neat rooms, into a long garden at the back. Either side of a brick path lay neat vegetable beds. At the far end were grouped a selection of wizened apple trees, branches bent inland where the winds had left them. Halfway down the garden, digging energetically with a spade, was the source of the whistling.

He straightened as we approached, watching us – or at least me – with an air that could hardly be described as welcoming. I'd seen him in the village, of course. Port Helen was far too small not to have passed him at some time or other. As both an unmarried girl, and then a wife, I'd hardly had the leisure to stare. He was taller than I remembered. Broader in the shoulders. Older. Reason had told me that he must be about the same age as Hugo, but I had never noticed before the lines on his face, the trace of white at his temples.

'Jack?' Mrs Treeve sounded anxious. 'Jack, dear, Mrs Helstone has come to have a word with you.' She glanced from me to him. 'Now listen to what she says, dear. I'll put on the kettle for some tea.'

She hurried away back towards the house, leaving an uncomfortable silence behind. If I could have fled with dignity, I'd have been back at Hiram in the blink of an eye.

The gardener leant on his spade. 'Mrs Helstone.'

'Mr Treeve.' I'd spent the last few hours working out what to say, but now I didn't know quite where to begin. I cleared my throat. 'It's a beautiful garden you have here.'

'It was my brother's,' he replied. 'He grew the fruit bushes and the vegetables so we would never want for anything. The least I can do is to carry it on.'

'Yes,' I murmured. 'I was so sorry for your loss.'

His eyes were less than friendly. 'That was a long time ago. So what was it that you wanted, Mrs Helstone? I've had enough lectures on my patriotic duty to serve my country and protect the Empire. I can do without another.'

'I didn't come to lecture you. Your convictions are your business. Besides, I am not a political creature, Mr Treeve. I came…' His eyebrows were raised. I rushed on. 'I came to offer you a post.'

'A post.'

'At Hiram Hall.'

He straightened, and appeared taller than ever. 'And why would you do that, Mrs Helstone?'

'Because I cannot manage the estate alone.' His look was withering. I squared my shoulders. 'At least, I can manage the house and the grounds, but I am going to need help with the kitchen garden. So much food is currently imported from overseas. If this war lasts, there may be shortages and we may well have to grow as much as we can. Both for the house and the village. The only gardeners not leaving to be soldiers retired years ago. They have the knowledge and will help where they can. But I can't ask them to take on the responsibility, let alone the hard physical work of so many. Besides, if the kitchen garden is to be made as productive as possible, it will need to be done in a new way. And that means someone who has not worked there in my father's time.'

'And Major Helstone?'

'Is on his way to Belgium.'

'I see.' A shadow crossed his face.

I found myself oddly defensive. 'I couldn't stop him. He's a very proud man.'

The smile was back, wry this time and oddly gentle. 'So he is.'

'My husband left before he could speak to you. But he left you a note.' I held out the envelope. As Mr Treeve opened the folded paper inside I could see a bare two lines of writing. High-handed orders, I had no doubt. Mr Treeve might have recognised Hugo's pride, but he had not mentioned his own. I dug my heels in and prepared for a fight.

Mr Treeve cleared his throat. 'Major Helstone seems to be of the opinion that you need looking after.'

I felt my chin rise. 'He feels guilty at leaving me on my own, that's all.'

'Really?' His voice was dry. 'It seems to me, Mrs Helstone, that you can look after yourself.'

I eyed him uncertainly. Was that a compliment? Or some statement that his old comrade-in-arms had landed himself a perfect harridan of a wife and no wonder he couldn't wait to escape? I gritted my teeth. 'So do you accept the post or not?'

'Mmm.' He pulled a dock from the earth at his feet. 'Have you considered that my being at Hiram might bring you some of my notoriety? And if conscription starts – which it may well do if this war continues – that I may be called up?' He'd a gleam in his eye.

'What will you do?'

'Refuse, of course. I won't back down on my principles. I have no war with the working man in Prussia. I will not kill my fellow workers for the pride and the greed of the ruling classes. Even though they shoot me for it. You won't be able to avoid the political then.'

What on earth was I getting myself into? 'I understand that, Mr Treeve. And you can get yourself shot if you want to. But I'd rather you did something useful. Something that saved lives instead.' I saw his eyes flash. 'I don't mean that standing against war isn't useful. But you haven't been able to stop it yet. And what about your mother? She has already lost one son to a war. Are you asking her to lose another?'

'If the fighting continues, she won't be the only one. There are plenty of mothers saying goodbye to their sons this afternoon who will never see them again.'

'I know. Don't forget I've only just said goodbye to my husband. I don't need a lecture on the subject, thank you. I can't stop the fighting, however much I would wish to. But this is your mother. Who has no other family to look after her. Are you proposing to sacrifice her for your principles?'

He leant on his spade again, his eyes on mine. 'Do you ever give up?'

'No.' I was breathless. 'Perhaps you object to taking orders from a woman?'

'Not one I could respect and whose opinions I valued,' he replied, quick as a flash.

I swallowed. 'I'd better go.'

'Have you such a poor opinion of yourself?'

I turned back. There was such an undisguised challenge in his voice it disturbed me.

Now it was my pride that was not about to give an inch. 'Of course not. But I can't help what other people's opinions are. And men generally do not see a woman's mind is one to be respected. However much the evidence to the contrary.'

He grinned. 'Well then, Mrs Helstone, you clearly missed my lecture on the injustice of denying women the vote. "No man can be truly free unless women are too," was the closing line. I gained almost as many cheers as insults, and not all of them from the women present.'

'Oh.' That was the wind well and truly taken out of my sails. I stood there nonplussed.

Mr Treeve cleared his throat. 'I should warn you that Ford informed me in no uncertain terms he would not be giving a man who shirked his duty to his country any kind of reference.'

I blinked. 'You intend to accept?'

'If you will take me without a reference.'

I met his eyes. 'I have the only reference for you I need, Mr Treeve.'

'Very well, then.' He held out his hand, as if I was indeed a man. I took it hesitantly. His grip was firm: roughened by manual work, strong but gentle. I pushed my doubts to one side. If I was going to take charge at the Hall, then I was going to have to get used to dealing with men. I returned his clasp firmly.

'I'll expect you next Monday, Mr Treeve.'

His eyes travelled beyond me, to where his mother had appeared at the back door to say that the tea was ready on the table. 'Very well, Mrs Helstone. And thank you.' He turned away so I could barely hear his next words. 'Let's pray that neither of us will regret it.'

Chapter Eleven

AUGUST 19TH, 1914

The sun was sinking as I walked back to Port Helen. The stone curve of the little harbour was warmed by evening light. The tide was in, lapping gently against the harbour walls, sending the fishing boats' masts rattling into the still air. In the houses along the front, washing barely moved. Even the seagulls appeared lulled to sleep in the sun.

'I've never seen the sea so calm,' said Alice, as she emerged onto the steps of the lending library, a small parcel of books in her hand.

'Nor me.' From the direction of the town hall, a band struck up.

'That will be the men leaving,' said Alice. 'There's a train waiting for them at the station. Poor Elsie.'

'Poor Elsie,' I agreed, with a shudder. I frowned out over the sea, wondering if Hugo was out there somewhere, heading for a battleground. I fought down sickness as I hurried behind Alice towards the main street that led to the station.

'They're all so young!' said Alice, as we joined the small crowd lining the streets. People leant from every window, shoppers stopped and turned. Some cheered, some wept. Children ran alongside, caught up in the excitement of the ragged march of men still in their working clothes.

Most were younger than I. Men I had known all my life; the familiar faces that surrounded my world. Boys from the farms. The lads who rode their bicycles delivering parcels of meat from the butcher's. Fishermen's sons from the row of cottages along the harbour front. Some beamed with pride, while a few showed a touch of dawning fear on their faces. Most, I knew, had never left Port Helen, apart from fishing at sea or visiting relatives in another village along the coast. Soon the train would take them away from everything that was familiar, to a new existence of training and battlefields, from which some might never return.

'It's as if it's a great adventure,' said Alice. 'A chance to get away.' She sounded wistful.

I glanced at her. 'Would you go, if you were a man?'

'Maybe. Life never changes here. You know exactly what you are going to be from the moment you are born. I think maybe I'd seize the chance to see the world, away from the observation of my family and the neighbours. Wouldn't you?'

'I suppose. But I hate the thought of fighting.'

'Let's pray it never comes to that,' said an elderly woman next to me. 'I lost two sons in the Boer War. I never thought to see my grandsons march off so eagerly.'

'Look, there's Elsie.' Alice pointed. The parade turned up the hill into a narrower street, forcing Elsie to lose step with the fair-haired young man with a crimson rose in his lapel, who lingered at the end of the line. As they vanished into the shadow of the buildings, he turned back, face pale in the darkness, then was gone.

Alice ran over and pulled a sobbing Elsie towards her, holding her tight. 'We'd better get her home.'

In the distance came the whistle of the engine preparing to leave. The street had fallen silent. Even the children seemed to have caught the mood and clustered tight around their mothers or big sisters. Small groups of people were making their way home, more than one with a handkerchief held to their eyes. Faces vanished from windows that were pulled shut, but the shopkeepers and their customers stayed at the open doorways as if not quite able to resume the business of the day.

We waited with them until, with a final great whoosh of steam, the train began to make its slow way out along the line. We watched it go, heading along the coast, before turning inland, until at last even the sound had faded away.

Afterwards, the three of us walked back along the cliffs, Alice and I holding Elsie between us. The poor girl had stopped her sobbing but walked head down, as if lost in grief. When we reached the Hall, she could scarcely walk with exhaustion. We took her to the kitchens for hot sweet tea and a place by the fire. Alice fetched a shawl, for although the evening was warm Elsie could not stop shivering.

'She can stay there, poor child, until she is ready to go to bed,' said Cook, shaking her head.

'I wish there was more we could do,' sighed Alice.

'Back to her usual routine will be the best.' Cook bent over the pastry she was rolling on the long wooden table in the centre of the kitchens. 'Besides, Miss Elin, with so many of the men gone, we'll need every hand we have left.'

Even now, Cook could never quite forget the child I had been. She slipped so easily into calling me 'Miss Elin'. But I was not a child. With Hugo gone, I was responsible for the Hall and everyone in it.

'At least I've found someone to take charge of the kitchen garden,' I announced. 'I've offered Mr Treeve from the village the position. The garden hasn't been used to its full capacity for years.'

Cook looked at me askance. 'Annie Treeve's son?

'Yes. Have you any objections?'

'Well, no, miss. Jack always was a pleasant young lad, as I remember, and Annie has been a good friend to me. But since he lost his brother, he has turned a little wild.'

'Mr Treeve speaks up for what he believes in,' said Alice.

'Which is not always wise, miss, especially not in time of war.'

'I thought we were supposed to be fighting for our freedoms, Mrs Hughes, not silencing them?'

'Alice,' I said gently. Cook had turned away to deal with the pot on the stove. Alice should know better than arguing with Cook when she knew she could not answer back. We were a tight family in Hiram, but it only went so far, and it was unfair to push at the fences that kept us all in our place.

Alice subsided. 'I suppose we will all need to pull together,' she murmured. She stared out of the window. 'I still can't believe there will be a war just across the water. Those poor French and Belgians fighting to keep their farms and villages, and those boys who've never held a gun in their life going off to help them.'

'They won't be sent straight over,' I said. 'They'll need to be trained first, like Edmund and Owen. It might be over before they're finished.'

'Maybe.' Alice's voice was far away.

I picked up a knife and began chopping the pile of carrots ready and waiting on the table, glad of something to distract me.

Alice took a deep breath. 'But I can't just wait here and do nothing, Elin. I've been offered a post.'

'A post?' I stared at her. 'You've volunteered as a nurse?'

'No. Well, not exactly. I did put my name down at my First Aid course to be trained as a proper nurse. Lots of the women who attend the lectures at the lending library have already left to become VADs.' She looked up. 'But when I went in today the Matron at the new hospital at Applebourne House was there. Their administrator has signed up before he even started, and they can't find anyone else. She knows I've been doing the library accounts recently and arranging the lectures for years. So she suggested I might take it on. It's nothing heroic. Just keeping accounts and ordering supplies for a few days a week. But it's something.'

'You should definitely take it,' I said, squashing an ignoble wish that she should do no such thing. 'But how on earth are you going to get there?'

'It's only a few miles. I shall use my bicycle. And there's a room

I can use if it snows. I'll still be here for some of the time, and I'll help in any way I can.'

Cook turned from her stove. 'Well, well,' she said with a faint smile. 'It seems that both of you have been busy.'

Alice jumped forward and hugged her. 'I'm sorry, Mrs Hughes. I didn't mean to be rude just now. I shall so miss your pies when I'm not here. I expect the meals at the hospital will be horrid.'

'I very much doubt it,' replied Cook, but she looked pleased all the same. 'And there will always be something waiting for you when you get home.'

Alice kissed her. She glanced at Elsie, who appeared to have fallen asleep in the armchair, cup teetering perilously on her lap. She retrieved the cup, placing it safely on the table. 'Poor girl. Can she even write?'

'Her name, and very little else, Miss Alice.' Cook, who'd put her three children through school and was now making sure her grandchildren attended their lessons, sounded disapproving. 'I've tried to teach her letters of an evening, but she has no interest. She doesn't seem to see the point.' She wiped her hands on her apron, looking down at the blotched and swollen face. 'Perhaps now she has a reason to write letters, she will. If he survives that long,' she added under her breath.

* * *

Later that evening, I walked out onto the cliffs alongside Hiram Hall. It was a strangely quiet world. No machinery clanking and rumbling in the fields along the coast, scarcely a boat returning from the day's fishing. Even the usual laughter of a Friday night, which would drift up towards us from Port Helen, along with the scent of stews and wood fires, had been silenced.

Seeing the men go, and feeling the silence and a sense of unease left in their wake, seemed to have woken us all up to war.

Until then, it had seemed unreal, for all the talk in the newspapers and the posters calling for volunteers. Now this silence in the soft gold of evening, the light slowly extinguished over the sea, felt like an ending to the world.

The whitewashed curve of cottages around Port Helen quay gleamed in the dusk. How many there, I wondered, were eating meals without their menfolk this evening, the women and children and the old gathering around the kitchen range together with only a creeping fear for company?

I felt my stomach turn. All my life, Hiram and Port Helen had been the responsibility of Papa, then Hugo. Now that responsibility was mine. Since I was a little girl, I had taken baskets of bread and meat, along with fruit and vegetables from the garden, to the poorest in Port Helen: from the old soldier, lost in his mind, who tramped by on some endless journey each spring, to the families of fishermen who had been lost at sea. But this was different. It was not just the servants at Hiram, but their families, who relied on the Hall for food and shelter, while the poor in Port Helen would be the first to starve if food prices rose even a little.

And supposing there was an invasion? Over the gold of the sea, I could make out the shadow of land on the horizon. The land from which it had taken Mouse only a few hours to cross. The crossing my ancestors had reputedly made regularly in tiny craft, smuggling casks of brandy from France, sailing in without lights into the caves in Hiram Cove. An army would have ships. Huge ships.

What would I do if the grey fleet of an invading army appeared on that tranquil sea, heading for Port Helen, as an army had come crashing into those Belgian villages somewhere over that horizon, with all the unspeakable horrors hinted at in the newspapers?

The light had faded. Port Helen was in darkness. There was

no friendly flicker of a candle amongst the silent streets. I looked back at Hiram. A light was burning in my room. One of the maids went across, pulling the curtains shut. The only other light was stealing around the edges of the shutters in the drawing room, where I had left Alice reading. Since the electric lighting had been installed, just before my marriage, Hiram had always been a welcoming beacon of light calling me home from my evening rambles along the cliffs.

But no more. As I watched, a curtain was drawn there, too, covering the light behind the shutters. I looked up at the sky. It was a clear, moonless night. There had already been rumours in Port Helen of Zeppelins haunting the coastline at night, looking for the best landing places for an invasion. Tonight the rumours appeared to have spread around the entire coast. It had always been one of my pleasures on a warm summer evening to sit at my window watching the faint twinkle of light from the villages around the bay gleaming in the darkness, the reassuring glimmer of lives continuing as they had always done and always would do, until the end of time.

Tonight the light was extinguished.

Part Two

Chapter Twelve

The telephone woke us. I was out of bed like a shot, racing down the stairs without even a wrap to cover my nightdress. As I reached the bottom stair the ringing stopped. I heard a voice speaking quietly. The lamp next to the telephone gleamed in the darkness. Alice had arrived first, a shawl half flung over one shoulder, the rest trailing forgotten on the floor.

'Yes, yes of course,' she was saying. 'I understand.'

I almost grabbed the receiver from her. 'Is it Hugo? He's not hurt? Or…'

Alice shook her head. 'No, it's nothing like that. It's the hospital,' she mouthed, still listening intently. 'Yes, of course,' she said into the receiver. 'I'll set off immediately.'

'Miss?' Elsie had reached the landing above us. 'Miss, it's not…'

'No, no. There's nothing to worry about. It was Applebourne Hospital. They've been told to expect ambulances with wounded evacuated from France. After all these months I thought we'd never see a patient. I suppose at least now the hospital will be of some use. They've been told to expect quite a few casualties. They're calling everyone in, just in case. I'd better get dressed.'

'But it's the middle of the night,' I said. 'Can't it wait until it gets light?'

'They're expecting the first ambulances in a few hours. The roads will be clear at this time. It won't take me long to cycle there.'

'I'll drive you. It will take even less time.'

'There's no need.'

'Yes, there is. I'm not having anyone I love racing through those lanes in the pitch black. Hugo bought in stocks of petrol before he left in case there might be shortages and Applebourne isn't far. Besides, I haven't left Hiram for weeks.'

'Thank you.' Alice sounded relieved. 'To be honest, they were a bit panic-stricken. They've only treated a few blisters and a broken arm. I don't think they expected an entire fleet of ambulances bearing down on them.'

'Surely there must be hospitals that are closer to the ports?'

'There are,' replied Alice. 'They've put every hospital for miles on standby. And they said the London hospitals are all ready too.'

I felt slightly sick. But this was no time for an over-active imagination. I dressed quickly, in the warmest and most practical clothes I could find. There was no fire to make even a cup of tea, so I flung a few apples into my pockets and went out to the barn.

I didn't glance at Hugo's beloved Silver Ghost, but pointed my flashlight at the solid old Rover instead, familiarising myself with the controls, which were thankfully not so different from Mouse's Chevrolet. Careful not to scratch Hugo's pride and joy, I manoeuvred the Rover out onto the driveway.

Alice arrived in time to shut the barn door, then jumped into the passenger side. I set off slightly gingerly down the drive and onto the cliff road. I had never driven by night before and it was unnerving. In the headlamps, hedges rose up on either side. Rabbits darted away at our approach, and once a fox stood stock-still, eyes flaring in the sudden light, before slinking back through a gateway into a field.

At first I was worried I wouldn't be able to keep to the centre of the road and might swerve into the ditches on either side. I was glad Alice was next to me; she made no comment on the crunch and squeal as I tried to change gear and the jerks when I experimented with the pedals, which nearly sent us both through the windscreen. After a short while, the hours I had driven the Chevrolet on the way to see Aunt Catrin came back, and I began to enjoy myself.

I'd forgotten the sense of freedom in speeding along, entirely my own mistress. I could understand why Mouse's letters for the past weeks had been full of her frustrations of not being able to fly and being constrained to the Northholme estate and charity events in the village. Poor Mouse. Even the automobile had been forbidden to her since September and her exasperation crackled though every word.

We reached Applebourne to find the first ambulances had already arrived. 'Oh my good Lord,' breathed Alice, as we drew up onto the gravel in front of the imposing façade of Applebourne House, lit up like a stage set in the light from thirty or so ambulances crowded around the front door. 'I know they were expecting a number of casualties, but nothing like this.'

Three more ambulances edged their way past us, followed by vans and several automobiles, their lights strafing those already waiting. I took the precaution of turning the Rover around while there was room to manoeuvre still. Only just in time. As I pulled up on to grass at the side of the driveway, another ambulance came past, followed by a butcher's van. A bus that coughed and spluttered stopped next to us with every appearance of never moving again.

A young nurse was supervising a stretcher as it was lowered from one of the vans. When we stepped out of the Rover, she turned and ran towards us. 'Miss!' she called, with relief. 'Miss Alice, thank goodness you've arrived. You speak French, don't you?'

'A little,' said Alice, surprised.

'Oh thank goodness. We thought they were going to be our lot, but they're all French and Belgians and no one can understand a word they're saying. Poor lads, they've had to abandon their villages and their families to the Hun. They are in a terrible state. They've had no food and their wounds haven't been dressed for days. You can smell the gangrene the moment they open the ambulance doors.'

'I'd better go,' said Alice to me. She glanced back to where yet another group of ambulances were arriving, almost crashing into the fenders of the Rover in their haste. 'And you'd better get out of here, Elin, while you've still got a vehicle left.' Alice vanished between the shadows of the crowd.

I hesitated. I knew a few words of French, not nearly as much as Alice, who had regularly attended lessons at the lending library, but I had picked up some phrases while helping her practise. In the streams of light from headlights, men passed us on either side. A few limped on their own or were supported by colleagues, but many more were carried on stretchers, heavily bandaged, faces white with pain. The stench was overwhelming: mud, dirt and unwashed bodies, and rotting, dying flesh. There were cheerful encouraging calls from amongst the men, but also the most terrible cries.

'Mrs Helstone!'

I blinked into the dark.

'Mrs Helstone.'

A small group of officers had been in fierce discussion beside one of the ambulances. The tallest broke apart, making his way to me, pausing to allow a van to pass, then dodging between the walking wounded and the stretchers. 'Mrs Helstone, I thought that must be you.'

I peered into the darkness at the familiar voice. A headlight flared, briefly revealing a well-built man in a sergeant's uniform, his face white and strained. 'Mr Killick?'

'That's right.' Mr, now Sergeant, Killick, owner of the largest grocer's shop in Port Helen, had volunteered on the first day of the war. Each time I'd been in there for sugar and spices to turn Hiram's apples into chutneys and plums into jam, Mrs Killick had been proud, but almost equally exasperated at being left in sole charge of five boys and an elderly mother, and the sudden responsibility of a shop to run.

Sergeant Killick coughed. 'I couldn't ask a favour of you, could I, Mrs Helstone? We're in a bit of a fix.'

A truck rattled by, nearly extinguishing his words, but not the edge of panic in his voice. 'Of course,' I said. 'I'll help in any way I can.'

'Thank you.' His relief was unmistakeable. 'I'm sorry to trouble you, but Miss Griffiths said you'd be on your way back any minute. The thing is, we need ambulances. My men have been detailed to collect several more from the army base just the other side of Port Helen. There's a repair workshop there. The ambulances are ready for us to collect, but there's another ship due from France and all these vehicles are under instructions to get back as soon as possible. Given the state of the poor wretches just brought in...'

'Of course,' I replied. 'I'll take you there.'

'Thank you. It'll be just myself and two of my men. The base is only a couple of miles inland from Port Helen, it won't be much out of your way.'

'We can go this minute,' I said. I led the way towards the Rover. Sergeant Killick beckoned to his men, who fell in behind.

'Will your driver be long?' he demanded, as the two corporals piled into the back seat.

'There is no chauffeur,' I replied, shouting above the squeal of brakes as a truck halted next to us. 'I drove Miss Griffiths here myself.'

'You drove—' Sergeant Killick choked over the words. He grasped the handle of the driver's door. 'I'll take you back to Hiram, Mrs Helstone, and then drive on from there.'

I could have cheerfully hit him. 'I'm perfectly capable.'

'And I have the safety of my men to consider.' The panic was back in his voice. 'This is an army matter, Mrs Helstone, I have every right to seize your vehicle.'

'But not to be so infernally rude.' I turned as a figure jumped down from the passenger side of the truck, signalling it to move on.

'I have my orders, Captain Northholme.' Sergeant Killick sounded defensive.

'Yes, I know you do, Sergeant,' replied Owen. 'And we are all under strain in this dreadful business. You ensure your men get something to eat and as much rest as they can. Heaven knows how many journeys it will take before all those poor wretches in Calais can be evacuated. I'll go with Mrs Helstone.'

Sergeant Killick hesitated. He glanced at me, evidently remembering, rather belatedly, that I was Major Helstone's wife and his most valuable customer.

'It's quite alright, Sergeant Killick,' I said, 'Captain Northholme is a friend of my husband's.'

'Very well.' His relief was palpable. Owen flagged down an approaching ambulance, and Sergeant Killick was safely deposited inside.

'Thank you,' I murmured, as Owen returned. 'But shouldn't you be getting some rest too?'

'There will be plenty of time on the crossing back.' He moved to the passenger door. 'Besides, Mouse would never forgive me if I left you to be browbeaten and insulted at the side of the highway.' He fixed the two corporals in the back with a glare. 'And anyone who objects to a woman driving can get out and walk.'

The next few minutes were terrifying. I urged the Rover between the flow of cars and ambulances, attempting to swerve through without crashing into an oncoming vehicle or landing in a ditch. Owen gripped the dashboard as I swerved this way and that while, judging from the curses and sharp intakes of breath from the back, my passengers were convinced their last hour had come.

Finally we reached the main gate and escaped into the peace and emptiness of the road. Owen sat back in his seat again. My heart was pounding, the exhilaration of having survived the last few minutes rushing through my veins. Forget Wales, I could have driven all the way to Africa, seabed and all.

Over the horizon, the first light of dawn was lessening the darkness. We drove for a while in silence. The two corporals lit up cigarettes. I could hear them sucking the smoke into their lungs for dear life, having survived trusting life and limb to a woman. By the time we approached the familiar curve of Port Helen Bay, they had finished their smoke and, from their gentle breathing, had fallen asleep.

I glanced at Owen. In the grey dawn light, his face was thinner than I remembered. There were lines on his forehead and shadows under his eyes. He had the look of a man who had not slept for days. Weeks, even.

'Was it very terrible?' I asked. He was silent for a few minutes, as if gathering his thoughts together. 'I'm sorry.' I concentrated on the road again. 'That was a foolish thing to ask. I saw the injuries those men had and the state they were in. I know I can't possibly imagine it, and you wouldn't want to tell me, if I could.'

Owen leant his head back against his seat. 'You're right. I don't know what to tell you. I don't know where to even begin to describe what it's like out there. I can't believe it myself now I'm back here in England, however briefly.' He turned his face away, as if gazing over the sea. 'I never thought I'd see Hell – not wake up each morning to face it, hour after hour, day by day.'

'I'm sorry.' I slowed to a halt as a herd of cows appeared in the road ahead, making their slow way towards milking, backs steaming in the chill morning air, followed by the farmer's boy shouting and whistling and slapping the haunches of any lingering too long over a tasty morsel in the hedgerow.

'We were treated like heroes by the villagers when we first

arrived.' Having begun, the words spilled out of him. 'They couldn't do enough for us. They were so relieved we had come to save them. It felt as if we had already won. All we needed was to be there, fight the odd skirmish or two to show we were serious, and it would all be over. Then the real fighting began.' He turned to meet my eyes. 'This isn't about right or wrong, it's about machinery tearing men apart. We're not proper soldiers, any more than those wretched labourers and farmhands we brought back just now. A few weeks' training is no preparation. It's not heroic. I can tell you that, Elin. All I can do is to try and keep my men alive, and do the best for those that are wounded.'

I didn't know what to say. Instinctively, I put my hand over his. 'I'm sure you do the best you can. Isn't that all anyone can do?'

He gave a faint smile. 'It never feels enough. Not for one moment does it feel enough.'

'I'm sure it doesn't to the doctors fighting to save those men's lives back there either. But if they weren't there, and if you hadn't brought those men to be treated, then none of them would have survived.'

His hand turned beneath mine, clasping it tightly. 'I thought it was my imagination, when I saw you in the headlights. I have such strange dreams. At times I could swear I'm back at Northholme, swimming in the lake.' He gave a grunt. 'Or rather eating every morsel of my uncle's dinners then starting again all over. I'm glad it was you.'

Ahead, the cows had disappeared into a group of farm buildings. I gently disengaged my hand and set off again. Owen gave a hasty glance towards the back seat, as if suddenly remembering our companions. From their breathing they were still sound asleep. We drove on without a word.

Chapter Thirteen

OCTOBER, 1914

We reached the army base as the sun rose. From what I could see, it was mainly a workshop. In lighted hangars, men bustled around and under ambulances, automobiles and trucks. There was an urgency about the entire place. By the look of things, they had worked through the night.

I parked outside the nearest hangar and followed my passengers inside. Owen and his men vanished as soon as we were amongst the mechanics. Most of the workers tried not to stare, but I couldn't miss the side-long looks and the slowing of spanners, even one sent clanging to the floor. No woman set foot inside this domain, it appeared. Unless she came hotfoot from the music halls to boost the morale of the troops, of course. I stood my ground, increasingly uncomfortable but determined not to lose my dignity and flee.

I was glad when Owen reappeared. 'The ambulances are all ready. They're just filling them with fuel.'

'I'd better go.'

'Come and have a cup of tea first,' he said. 'I'm sure you're in need of one and the least we can do is escort you home. There's a telephone in the office you can use to let your people know.'

I hesitated, but the offer of tea was too good to refuse. I'd had nothing but a sip of cold water since we'd set off in the middle of the night and I was beginning to feel dizzy.

The canteen was cheerful and spotless and thankfully almost empty, so I was saved from curiosity and stares. I took the mug of tea gratefully, warming my hands as I drank. When hot buttered toast appeared, I fell on that too. The apples were still in my pocket, forgotten, and I was famished.

I'd only just finished the last mouthful when it was time to go.

The men had filled up the Rover with petrol, and the container in the boot, as I discovered later. Even the windscreen had been cleaned.

We made a strange procession, winding through the lanes that morning: a dusty Rover followed by three shiny ambulances. At the turn into the lane to Hiram, I saw two of the ambulances continue. The third followed until I finally drew up in front of the hall. It was only a few hours since I had left, but as I clambered stiffly out, it felt more like a year.

Mr Phillips appeared at the top of the steps looking scandalised. Mrs Pelham was peering from the front drawing room window. I could feel their eyes boring into me as Owen jumped down from the ambulance.

'Thank you for seeing me home,' I said, awkwardly, trying to ignore our audience.

'It was the least I could do.' He took a quick glance towards the house. 'Thank you for your help, Mrs Helstone,' he said, loudly. 'I apologise for putting you to so much trouble, but we'd have had a devil of a job without it.' He shook my hand. A firm, business-like handshake. He was about to open the door of the ambulance, when his eyes focussed on the archway into the walled garden. 'Good grief, Elin, are all your employees so fierce?'

I followed his gaze. Jack Treeve was leaning against the wall watching us, arms folded, a deep frown on his face.

'It's our gardener,' I replied. The severity of Jack's gaze made me step hastily away from Owen, my cheeks reddening. 'I'd quite forgotten we were supposed to be going through the planting of the kitchen gardens for next spring this morning. So if you'll excuse me, Captain…'

Owen was still watching him, eyes narrowed. 'Treeve, isn't it?'

'Yes.'

'I hope you know what you are doing.'

Jack was looking more severe than ever.

'That's none of your business,' I returned.

'I remember your husband spoke highly of him when you were at Northholme, but I'm surprised at you employing a man like that in his absence.'

I blinked. What on earth had got into him? 'Mr Treeve is employed to produce food for Hiram and Port Helen. He has an elderly mother to support so he is hardly likely to jeopardise his post here. He isn't the only pacifist to choose to work on the land, and since he preaches peace, he's hardly likely to murder us all in our beds.'

'I wouldn't bank on it, that look he's giving us now.'

Then I understood. 'The look he's giving you, you mean.'

Owen coloured. 'I hope you are not governed by your employees' views of your friends,' he growled.

'Of course not. But Mr Treeve considers himself entrusted by my husband to look out for my interests.' Owen scowled. 'Oh, for Heaven's sake!' I whispered in exasperation. 'Do you really mean to insult me even more than Sergeant Killick? Are you suggesting that I'm about to fall in love with any man I have any kind of dealings with? That I have no capacity for being anything else? A friend? A colleague? Besides, Mr Treeve is nearly old enough to be my father.'

Owen shot me a withering look. I felt myself crimson from head to toe.

'Hugo may be older than me, but he is still my husband,' I snapped. 'And I could never betray a man who is away risking life and limb to keep safe everything I love.'

Owen gave a faint smile then. 'No. You would not be yourself if you did.' He gave a curt nod towards Jack Treeve and pulled himself into the driver's seat. When he spoke again, his voice was deliberately loud and formal.

'Goodbye, Mrs Helstone, and thank you once again for your

help. I'll be sure to give your message to your husband when I
see him.'

I shot him a grateful smile. 'Goodbye, Captain Northholme.'
His face was pale within the shadow of the ambulance. I thought
of Hugo, and all the partings there had been over the past
months, each one holding with it the possibility that it might be
the last. 'And good luck.'

He gave a wry grunt. 'By the look of those poor devils at
Applebourne, we are going to need it more and more.' With the
briefest of waves, he was gone.

Wearily, I turned back to Jack Treeve. 'I'm sorry for the delay
to our meeting, Mr Treeve. My cousin was called in to the
hospital at Applebourne. Casualties came over from France and
Belgium.'

'So I heard.' His eyes rested on my face. They didn't have
Owen's intense gaze, but there was a question there, none the
less.

'Captain Northholme is the cousin of my friend Mouse – Lady
Margaret Northholme,' I said, sounding defensive even to my
own ears. 'He and his men are bringing the wounded over to
hospitals in England. They needed a lift to fetch additional
ambulances to take back to France. I could hardly refuse, having
seen the state of the wounded brought back to Applebourne.'

Jack's shoulders relaxed a little. 'A wretched business, by all
accounts.'

I nodded, fighting down tears that sprang unbidden to my
eyes. I was back instantly amongst the stench and the screams
and the horrors half-glimpsed in the light from the ambulances.
There was no one with whom I could share what I had seen.
Every family I knew had a young man – however distantly related
– heading for the front. It was too painful, too dreadful even to
mention. I could understand Owen's despair. He had been
amongst so much more. He was right. This was not the heroic

glitter of knights in armour saving the helpless from some nameless evil; this was the wretchedness of men broken against the grinding of some remorseless wheel.

Until Alice came home, no one could know the shadows haunting me. But in Mr Treeve's eyes I saw their reflection, and glimpsed the shadows haunting him. I was grateful he tactfully turned away until I had recovered.

'So?' I said at last. 'Shall we make a start, Mr Treeve?'

He cleared his throat. 'We can discuss the planting of the gardens tomorrow, Mrs Helstone. Or this afternoon, if you prefer.'

I shook my head. 'No. Please. I'd rather keep busy. I'd rather keep the pictures out of my head.'

'Of course.'

Over the weeks he had been working in the gardens, I had kept any conversation between us strictly to the subject of autumn clearing and planning for the next year. Now, I couldn't help asking him as we made our way into the garden, 'Do they ever fade?'

His gaze was straight ahead. 'The things you have seen? A little. Like all things, with time you grow accustomed. But hopefully never hardened.'

'No, I would never wish for that.' I came to a stop, aware of the silence heavy between us. All Jack – and Hugo – had seen in previous wars. The questions I did not dare ask. Did I understand my husband better after what I'd seen last night? Or did I just feel the gap between us even more?

'The plans I drew up for the spring planting are in the house,' I muttered. 'I'll fetch them.'

I fled through the house, avoiding the butler and the housekeeper, and the curious gaze of the maids. My flesh felt raw, as if the protective skin had been scraped away, and Hiram no longer held its power to hold me safe.

I made my way to my mother's rooms at the top of the house. Papa had always kept her little bedroom and sitting room just as it had been when Mama was alive. Her brush, its back embroidered with flowers, still stood on her dressing table, with her bottles and her jewellery. Papa had removed the more expensive items, but there were still the simple chains and the glass beads that caught the light with azure blue and the deep green of her eyes, just as I remembered as a girl.

Hugo had once talked about turning the rooms into a nursery. He had spent weeks making endless plans. The brand new rocking horse he had had imported from France still stood there, saddle gleaming, its mane untouched. But those plans had long ago been forgotten and the room left much as it had always been.

I leant against the rocking horse, desolation consuming me. Seeing the horrors that night, my old grief had been stirred. I shut my eyes, gripped once more by the agony of those long hours when the midwife and the doctors had fought to save me, and the child struggling, too early – far, far too early – to be born. The child I should now be holding on the rocking horse, crowing with delight, but had been too small to ever breathe the air, or open her eyes to see the sun rise on the day she was born.

Hugo had never forgiven me. He had never spoken of it. He had turned away when I had reached out for the comfort I had so desperately needed. It was Alice who had sat by me, hour after hour, willing me to live. In those first weeks, when I was finally strong enough to leave my room, I did not understand. Hugo had been my protector, the man who worshipped me and could not bear to see me come to harm. I had thought grief was for sharing, that it might bring us closer, and that one day, when I was strong enough, there would be other children to fill the emptiness of our loss.

But Hugo avoided me. He was barely able to look at me. My presence made him uneasy, my touch was unbearable to him. He had found me bleeding, he had heard me scream, the fairytale he had married had been lost and he could not bear my crude physicality. It frightened me when he pushed me away. But my loneliness and my hunger for a single touch had, over the years, eaten away at me slowly, day by day.

I shut my eyes tighter. My every sense was on alert, tearing at my exhaustion. I could still feel the pressure of Owen's hand where it had clasped mine. The earthy damp of his mud-stained jacket surrounded me, with a faint edge of cigarette smoke and the elusive smell that was the essence of him. I was back in the lake at Northholme, with the sunlight breaking through the soft water to ripple on my skin, while the slow curl of weeds trailed themselves around me. The heaviness of the room settled close around me, until I could not breathe.

I straightened, forcing my eyes open. The window overlooking the kitchen garden was slightly ajar. I pushed it wide, drawing in the cool air, deep into my lungs until the sense of suffocation passed. In the gardens below, Jack Treeve was methodically cutting down willow seedlings and the stranglehold of brambles. He had already cleared a considerable patch of ground, but there was far more to be done. We were going to need help. My mind steadied, returning gratefully to the practicalities of life. Despite the boy hired from the village, and the hours Alice and I had spent weeding the vegetable beds – scandalising Mrs Pelham with our muddy boots and wind-swept hair – there was still an impossible amount of work to be done.

When I was a child, the garden had provided the Hall with almost all its needs, with enough to spare to take to the poorest families in Port Helen. But over the years, with the convenience of the grocery in the village, with the innovation of tinned fruit and meat, alluring bags and packets of goods from all over the Empire, whole sections had fallen into disuse. Even before the war, the old ways were changing, with fewer lads staying to work on the land, when there was better-paid factory work to be had. And now they were all gone. Mr Wiltshire had finally retired to live with his daughter in Kent, when the rest of the garden staff had been among the first to volunteer.

I pulled myself together. The price of many foods had gone up and there had been plenty of hoarding by those who could afford it. For many of the poorer families, with the men away, there was not even the odd rabbit, poached from Hiram Woods, to stew. Along with the bottling of fruit and the gathering of rosehips to make into cordial and jellies against the winter months, I had already begun to work with Cook making additional loaves of bread, pies rich with mutton and the last of the year's vegetables, to take each week to the families struggling the most. If this war continued, we were going to need to grow more.

Mr Treeve placed an armful of brambles onto the bonfire. A thin spiral of smoke lifted into the air. A breeze sent a flurry of dried and twisted leaves to the ground. Soon the trees would be bare and the icy rains and snow arriving. I needed to make sure there was enough coal to keep the fires in Hiram burning through the winter months, with some to spare to help any family that needed it. There were drains in the lower fields that Papa had always been anxious should be cleared of leaves to prevent flooding when the rains and the snow melt came. And no doubt a hundred things I had not yet considered besides. There was no time for grieving, or even for thought.

Still mulling over the problem of extra help for the garden, I collected my plans for the spring planting and headed downstairs.

Chapter Fourteen

CHRISTMAS, 1914

Elsie's young man was the first.

I stood in the kitchen on Christmas morning, with the warmth of steaming pudding and a rich scent of goose taking me back to every candlelit, magical Christmas I had known at Hiram, and I could not believe it.

I had heard of casualties amongst our own men, of course. One of the boys from the next village had been shot through the leg and spent time in Applebourne to recuperate. I'd seen the endless casualty lists in the papers and consoled Mouse when the brother of one of her school friends was killed. Like others, I lived in dread of a familiar name amongst the dead or missing. But this was the first time I could see in my mind's eye the face of the man who had died: the first time I knew him as a living, breathing person, with a mother and sisters and a sweetheart for whom a world had ended.

A cold shiver went through me. A selfish one. Hugo, too, might be lying cold in a distant field instead of racing home for Christmas as he had promised in his telegram.

'Apparently it happened two weeks ago,' Cook gave her sauce a vicious stir. 'But the telegram only arrived yesterday. She was in such a state, poor girl. I told her mother not to even think of sending her up here today. She needs her family about her. So it won't be so many courses as usual, Miss Elin, but we'll manage.'

'It will be delicious, as ever, whatever you do,' I said. 'It hardly seems right gorging ourselves when there is so much grief.'

'Nonsense, Miss Elin. You're no different from anyone else, and you should be celebrating when your husband is home.'

I helped Cook with steaming the Christmas pudding and preparing Hugo's favourite junket, flavoured with last season's bottled raspberries reserved for today. Then I joined Molly in attacking mounds of vegetables, much to the silent indignation of Mrs Pelham at the lady of the house stooping so low as to wash cabbage, war or no war. I was glad of the occupation and ignored her.

Hiram was eerily quiet, the excitement of Christmas Day vanished into whispers and subdued footsteps, our preoccupation with our loved ones and the ever-present dread of our own telegram at the door. I was thankful for the distraction when Rupert and Louisa arrived with their two young sons, who raced noisily round the house and the kitchen garden, bringing the exuberance of childhood to the lacklustre day.

As daylight began to darken, there was still no sign of Hugo. I did my best to entertain our guests. After all, Hugo's telegram had said he'd only managed to get leave at all at the last minute, and he would be crossing on the first boat that had room for him. Dickie and Charles returned inside red-cheeked and breathless and loudly famished.

'I suppose we'd better begin,' I said hesitantly to Mrs Pelham, who looked cross and more than ready for her own Christmas dinner downstairs with Cook and Mr Phillips. It felt like a defeat not to wait any longer for Hugo, and I was afraid he might be hurt by this treachery. But on the other hand, Rupert, Louisa and the boys were our guests and I could hardly leave them to starve on Christmas Day.

'Very well, ma'am,' returned Mrs Pelham primly. 'I'll inform Cook.' As soon as she had disappeared, the telephone rang. I raced into the hallway, grabbing the receiver from Mr Phillips' startled hands.

'Yes?' I demanded.

'There's no need to be so fierce.'

The knot in my stomach burst apart so abruptly I sat down. 'Mouse.'

'Am I interrupting?'

'No, of course not.' There was something about her tone. I waved Mr Phillips away. 'Mouse, is everything all right?'

'Yes. Yes of course. Well, as much as it can be, due to this beastly war. Edmund's been wounded.'

'Oh Mouse, I'm so sorry.'

Mouse snorted. 'Don't be. It's not serious. He came home yesterday. He'll have a fearful scar down one arm, but that will only make the girls go wild for him.' Her voice grew more serious. 'And it means he'll be safe for a while at least. He's at home, and being as spoilt as can be. I've never seen anyone eat so much. Or sleep!' She sighed. 'I keep hoping that it will all be over by the time he's well enough to go back, but Edmund doesn't think there's a hope in hell. He says this might last for years and years.' Her voice regained its excitement. 'For which I'm thankful, of course, because otherwise there wouldn't be any point.'

'Point?'

'In going over to France.'

I heard my own sharp intake of breath. 'You're really going over there?'

'Oh yes. As soon as Christmas is over. Ginny and Sybil managed to get their hands on a truck that was too old to be requisitioned. We've done it all out, with a woodburning stove so that we can cook. Ginny's built amazingly clever shelves and I've done the mechanics. Once we've filled it full of bandages, medicines and food, we'll be off.'

'But Mouse, you can't just drive into a battle and pitch up!'

'Just you stop me. Edmund says it's absolute hell out there and men are hungry and dying from cold and sickness and infection just as much as from being wounded. I'm not going to stay here and be nursemaid to Edmund and look in the paper for the next friend to be killed. Owen's regiment is stationed near Lille. We're going to start there. Owen'll help me. He always did.'

I experienced a twinge of sympathy for Owen. I admired their courage. A small part of me envied their unswerving sense of purpose. But the thought of three elegant young ladies with their clipped accents and assumption of servants attending to their every whim jumping into a dilapidated truck and setting off into a war zone was as terrifying as it was incongruous.

Fear gripped at my heart. What Mouse was planning felt like something from another time. I thought of those wretched men arriving at Applebourne only weeks before, and the bleak horror I had seen in their eyes. I could not imagine those two worlds clashing.

'It's all right.' Mouse could read my thoughts, even down the line of a telephone. 'Ginny's a VAD and Sybil's been working as a volunteer nurse for months. Besides, from what Edmund said, it's hot food the men need most of all. We've got huge pans and bags and bags of vegetables from the Northholme gardens. We'll be cooking up hot soup in no time.'

'Mouse…'

The roar of an engine filled my ears as a vehicle sped up the driveway. 'Hugo is here. I must go,' I said. 'I'll speak to you later, Mouse.'

'If I'm here,' she replied, cheerfully. 'I'm aiming to get out of this place as soon as I can. Papa's found another husband for me and is quite determined we should be married before he goes to the front. Which is all very well, and he's terribly rich, but suppose he survives?'

'Mouse!'

'I'm sorry. I know you've a husband who has been out there, and I wouldn't have anything truly awful happen to George or Edmund or Owen for anything. But I'm not taking the risk that

I might be saddled with some boring stockbroker, or whatever he is, for the rest of my life, just so Papa can say I'm a married woman and my husband can get blown to pieces a happy man.'

'Mouse, that's a dreadful thing to say.'

Mouse gave a short laugh. 'Yes, well. I never did have the makings of a good Society wife. I have a feeling I shall be much more suited to dodging bullets and tending wounds.'

The automobile had drawn up in front of the house and Mr Phillips was busily opening the front door, taking up his position impressively on the steps. 'Promise you'll speak to me before you go.'

'If I have time. But I'll come and visit you when I come back for supplies,' called Mouse. 'That's a promise.'

Through the open door I could see Hugo unfolding slowly out of the passenger side of the army truck, as the driver removed the luggage from the boot. He handed the bag to Mr Phillips, who, scowling at the indignity, handed on the battered and grubby article to Molly, who had just arrived, dishevelled and distinctly flustered from trying to do both her job and Elsie's.

I stood on the steps, a tight knot twisting in my belly. Even in the dusk I could see that he must have managed to wash and change on the way. He appeared smaller, his spotless uniform hanging from his frame as if it had been made for another man.

As the truck returned down the drive, I went down to meet him.

'You managed to get away,' I said, feeling shy and uncertain what to say.

He nodded. 'Close thing. There was some panic on as usual, but I managed to sort things out before I left. Nothing was going to keep me away, my dear.' I could make out the strain in his face. Exhaustion drew shadows into his cheeks and deepened the lines around his eyes. He took my hand. 'It's good to be home,' he said, with a slight tremor to his voice. The sound of the boys' laugher spilled out from the house. As if recollecting himself, Hugo cleared his throat and stepped away.

'Good to have you home, sir,' said Phillips, from the steps. There was a heartfelt tone to his pomposity. The Major was back, the house was no longer run by females and all was right with the world his thin smile announced, as he led the way into the house.

Chapter Fifteen

CHRISTMAS 1914

Christmas was subdued, however much we tried to make it the same as it had always been, for Hugo and for the boys' sake. But it was no good. Wherever we turned, the shadow of Elsie and her grief hung over the household, stirring up thoughts of all those we knew who remained in the fighting.

I missed Alice. She had chosen to stay at Applebourne, volunteering to work on Christmas Day to allow nurses to return to their families, and, if they were lucky, to brothers and sweethearts home from the front. I had barely seen her since October. That first rush of casualties had been followed by a constant stream, until she saw little point in returning to Hiram at all, staying instead in a room in the nurse's quarters. I understood, but I missed her.

Even my thankfulness at Hugo's safety was tempered by the knowledge that within days he must go back. There was no more talk anymore of an easy victory and the men coming home. We laughed and chatted and played games with Hugo's nephews, but each adult knew that this might well be the last Christmas we would spend together. Each hour I spent with Hugo was tinged with the pain that I might never see him again.

Hugo was more subdued than usual, but he took pleasure in seeing his nephews and taking long walks around the estate with Rupert. In so many ways, nothing had changed. The old distance was still between us. He spoke with affection in his voice, but treated me with his familiar courtesy, so that at times if felt as if he had never left. If I tried to talk seriously to him about matters concerning the estate he smiled and changed the subject, as if doing so would banish the fact that I was running it in his place. So much for my dreams of him ever respecting me as his equal or of us running Hiram together. But at least he was glad to see me. As each short day ended, he liked to have me sit by him next to the fire, so that he could see me each time he looked up. He did not speak of the war, and I did not ask. He would sit in his favourite armchair, gazing into the fire, brandy glass in hand, as we talked quietly of the antics of the boys, and memories of the Christmasses that had passed. For all his pleasure at being home and us all gathered around him, a terrible weariness held him in its grip. If I left the room, or just turned away for a few minutes, his head would sink onto his chest, and he would not stir when I gently prised the glass from his hand in case it dropped.

'I wish I had longer,' he muttered late one evening, rousing himself.

I refilled his brandy glass, placing it in his hand. 'I wish you never had to go back.'

He smiled, his hand remaining in mine. 'Dear Elin. I could wish to spend the rest of my days in Hiram.' For once, his sense of his own dignity had gone. His gaze held a wistful affection I had not seen since the early days of our marriage. My heart twisted inside with all the hopeful love that had once consumed me, but which he had over so many years pushed to one side.

I had never asked for his affection. I had not the right. I did not know the words. Tonight I held him a little closer. 'Stay with me?' I murmured tentatively.

He released my hand, placing the brandy glass on the arm of his chair. 'I see Treeve has done great things in the gardens, my dear. That was an excellent suggestion of yours. I am glad that it has worked out so well. Jack is a man you can trust with your life, you know.'

I gazed at the profile of his face, turned away from me, shutting me out. Whatever I had done to lose his love, there was no way back. Not even now, when each moment together might be the last. I pushed down my humiliation and my despair.

'Yes of course Hugo,' I replied quietly. I sat with him for a while as he drank his brandy, then excused myself and made my way upstairs.

On the last day of Hugo's leave, Mr Treeve resumed his work in the kitchen gardens. I returned from a walk along the cliffs with Louisa and the boys to the sound of voices echoing amongst the greenhouses. The men turned as the boys rushed up to them, their faces cheerful, warmed by the bonfire they were building. I met Rupert's eyes and smiled. The faint crease of anxiety that had remained on my brother-in-law's face had eased.

'At least he is away from the worst of the fighting,' he said, joining me as Hugo helped his nephews gather more sticks to stoke up the fire. 'As he says, at least he knows he is making a difference out there, ensuring an efficient line of supplies.' He smiled. 'I might well have been mistaken, saying he should never go back to the army.' He glanced back towards the fire, where Hugo was helping Dickie place the dead trunk of a diseased pear tree into the centre of the flames. 'This seems to have given him a sense of purpose. Perhaps it might have been for the best, after all.'

* * *

That last evening, Rupert and Louisa retired early, leaving me alone with Hugo in front of the fire.

Hugo's tendency to fall asleep had abated over his days at Hiram, but now he gazed into the fire, too preoccupied to respond to me. It felt as if he was already back amongst the soldiers, his mind working on the problem of keeping regular supplies coming over from England. More than ever, I couldn't reach him.

I took a deep breath. I deliberately hadn't asked about his life in Belgium during his leave, sensing that he wished to put it as far away as he could. Perhaps I could ease a little the darkness deep within his face, and attempt to bridge the gap between us that had only widened in his absence. I should at least try.

'I took Alice to Applebourne Hospital, the night the first casualties arrived there.'

'That was very good of you.' My words barely registered.

I tried again. 'I know it's not the same as actually being in a battle, but the things I saw—'

'I've a gift for you.'

I blinked. 'A gift?'

He reached behind the decanter of brandy on the table beside him and pulled out a small object wrapped in a cloth, holding it out towards me. It was heavier and more solid than I had expected. I looked at him.

'Well, go on,' he said.

I laid the parcel on my lap and unfolded the wrapping. My fingers touched cold metal. I recoiled. 'A gun?'

'Pistol. Small. Suitable for a woman's hand.'

'But Hugo—'

'Captain Treeve will teach you to use it.'

I felt very cold and still inside. 'Hugo, I don't want Mr Treeve to teach me, and I'm certain he wouldn't agree.'

'Nonsense, my dear. I've already spoken to him.' He leaned

over and squeezed my hand. 'He's a good man. I know he has some strange ideas, but when it comes to it, he'll always do the right thing.'

'He's our employee, Hugo. I don't want to put the poor man in such an impossible position.'

'I've also instructed him to have a look at the rowing boat in Hiram Cove.' Hugo frowned at me intently. It was clear he hadn't listened to me.

'The boat?'

'To make sure there are no leaks and it's securely tethered. And to put some supplies in there, and in the caves along the edges of the beach. Tinned food. Stuff that won't perish.'

The cold had reached my brain. I could feel it creeping beneath my scalp. I searched his face. There was an expression there I'd never seen before. 'Please Hugo, you're frightening me.'

He took both my hands in his. 'Listen, my dearest. If we can't hold them and they reach the Channel, there will be very little warning. They will land all along this coast.'

'I thought the army was pushing them back.' I faltered. 'That's what it says in all the papers.'

He shook his head. 'You won't have much warning, but at least they'll land at Port Helen first and there's a clear view from up here. You must keep a watch. And the servants must watch through the nights, too. You must insist on it.'

'But…' My protest that Molly was so exhausted she could scarcely keep her eyes open in the day, however much help we gave her, died on my lips. Hugo's concentration had deepened, blocking out all else.

'If the way is clear, you must get down to the boat in any way you can. Follow the coast away from them. Get as far as you are able.' His hands tightened. 'And if you can't, if you are trapped here without any hope of rescue…' His eyes burned. I lowered my gaze to the pistol in my lap. 'It's an honourable way, Elin.'

'Honourable?' I stared at him in horror. What madness was lurking beneath that calm surface of the past days?

'War – there's no civilisation left. If you'd seen the things I've seen, my dearest, you would know that this is the only honourable way out. I pray with all my heart that it will never come to this. But if it does, I would rather lose you than think of you…' His voice trailed into silence.

In the intensity of his grip, my sense of reality was beginning to waver. Practicalities. I clung to my old friends, practicalities. 'But what about Elsie and Molly? And Alice, too.'

'Treeve will take care of them. The only important thing, my darling, is you.'

That wasn't what I meant. If there *was* an invasion, could I really leave all those I had known and loved all my life to face whatever horrors? I shut my eyes. Was my husband seriously giving me instructions to end my own life?

His grip tightened again. 'Elin, you do promise me, don't you?'

My eyes flew open. I searched his face, uncertain which of us had lost their minds. Or maybe I was simply being naïve. How could I ever have imagined that the glimpse I had caught of the wounded soldiers at Applebourne equipped me to understand this war? I was safe here in England. I had never been on a battlefield. Hugo had spent the last months in Belgium. As a senior officer he must know more than an ordinary soldier. I swallowed. There had been whispers in the village that the newspaper reports of great victories in France were not victories at all. I'd taken no more notice of such gossip than I had of continuing rumours of spies lurking in each bush and abandoned outhouse.

'Promise me.'

I was just one woman. I could not fight an entire war. All I could do was to give the husband who was going back into a hell I could not imagine, to fight to keep me and all those I loved safe, the peace of mind he so desperately craved. What else could I do when within weeks, days, hours, he could be just another name on the casualty list?

'I'll arrange time with Mr Treeve for him to teach me, the moment you leave,' I promised solemnly.

His body relaxed a little. He kissed my hands. 'I'd do anything to protect you, my dearest.'

I was shaking. 'I'll go and see about your bath,' I murmured, overwhelmed by the need to breathe in the fresh air. 'And I need to see if Cook has packed the pies and cakes she made for the morning.'

He let me go without protest. When I turned back at the door, Hugo had settled back into his armchair. Flames danced through the glass in his hand, turning the brandy gold as he stared deep into the fire. His face had relaxed a little, but he still held the look of a man gazing into the flames of Hell.

Mrs Campion, the seamstress in Port Helen who had made my wedding dress, had been spoken of as one of the fortunate ones when her son was returned to her. I remembered Cyril Campion from before the war, loud and rude, always at the heart of any pranks in the village, and yet who'd turned out to have a miraculous way with horses. I'd seen him only a few days before Christmas: a wizened shell of a man who shook and mumbled and leapt cowering into a ditch at the sound of a passing automobile.

I began to tremble in earnest, remembering Mrs Campion's words when the vicar of St Helen's Church reprimanded her for ceasing to attend Sunday service. Should she not be giving thanks to the Lord for the miracle of her son being restored to her, after being pulled only half alive from the mud in no man's land?

'There are other ways of losing those you love,' she had said, her voice uncompromising, 'than in a grave amongst thousands in a land far away.'

* * *

The driver arrived for Hugo early the following morning.

I kept my face calm and cheerful until the automobile had left the drive. The others made their way inside, tactfully leaving me alone for a while. But I could not stay still. There was something I had no intention of putting off a moment longer.

Mr Treeve was in the stable block. Snow had fallen in the night, obliterating the garden. I found him sorting out gardening tools and cans of paint and wood preservative. I had a suspicion he was expecting me.

'Good morning, Mrs Helstone,' he said, straightening up from a can of foul-smelling liquid.

There was no point in beating around the bush. 'I understand, Mr Treeve, it's not against your principles to show me how to shoot.'

His face was carefully neutral. 'It's not against my principles to give peace of mind.'

I frowned at him, nettled. 'For me or for my husband?'

'Would it bring you peace of mind?'

I squared my shoulders. 'Major Helstone seems to be under the impression there might be an invasion. If there is, I'd rather fight to the death than put a pistol to my head. And you can forget about doing the job for me, if that was also part of your instructions.'

He started slightly.

'Oh my dear lord,' I whispered, sitting down heavily on a wooden barrel. 'He didn't really ask that, did he?'

Jack cleared his throat. 'Your husband doesn't mean it, Mrs Helstone. Any of it. You must understand he feels unable to help you, if the worst should happen. I think that, in his own mind, he has done his best to protect you.'

'Protect me!'

'He doesn't want you to end your life in fear and degradation.' He cleared his throat again. 'The newspaper stories of what happened in the villages taken by the enemy may be exaggerated, but they do also contain truth.' His eyes were focussed on the frost etched on the windowpanes. 'The violation of women and children...' He hesitated. 'There can be some terrible ways to die. If you have seen them, you would not wish them on anyone, least of all on those you love.'

'Oh.' I digested this. I felt sick. I twisted round to look at him. 'But you still wouldn't, would you?'

He met my eyes. 'That would be a choice only you could make.'

'And you told him that? He was once your commanding officer, after all.'

'I didn't argue. If Major Helstone chose to take that as acquiescence and it gives him some peace of mind, then that is for him.'

'I did just the same,' I said. 'When I knew straight away that I never would.'

We sat in silence for a minute or so.

'War is the world gone mad,' said Jack quietly, lifting rusting cans from the shelves. 'All you can hope is that one day some kind of sanity will be regained.'

'It can't come too quickly.' I stood up and moved away a little. The air in the stables had become oppressive.

'We should start planting soon,' I said. I saw his shoulders ease at this return to normality. 'You are going to need help if it's to be done on time. Papa had at least six gardeners in his day, and we are planning a far more ambitious growing schedule.'

'The problem is finding anyone capable of heavy work.'

'It can be solved. If you're not too proud to work with women and children, that is.'

'Children?' He sounded alarmed.

'Schoolchildren. My friend Mouse was telling me there are places in London where children are helping to grow vegetables, so I don't see why we shouldn't be doing it here. They can do routine work like planting and weeding, which would free you up to concentrate on the tasks that take strength and skill. I've spoken to several young women in Port Helen also willing to try. I suggest they help with the heavy work. When you've carried pans and pails up and down stairs half your life you're as strong as they come, if you're thinking they might be too weak.'

'Not at all. It sounds the only practical solution to me.'

'Good. I'll speak to the teacher at Port Helen School and see if some of the women I spoke to will agree to the work.' I coughed. 'This is a respectable house, Mr Treeve…'

'Don't worry, Mrs Helstone,' he replied. 'I'm not in the habit of luring young women into temptation for my own amusement.'

I turned towards the door. But the silence between us, which would always be between us when it came to Hugo, was something I could not quite let go.

'Mr Treeve?'

'Yes, Mrs Helstone?'

'Mr Treeve, how did your brother die?'

Jack was very still, his hand resting on the broken handle of a spade. 'The Boer War was a long time ago.'

'His death had something to do with Hugo, didn't it?' He was silent. The answer hung there in the air. '*Captain* Treeve?'

'It was just after the first news of the appalling conditions in the camps where the women and children had been placed. We had word one night that a dozen or so of our men had been captured by a group of Boers. Heaven help us, we had no idea when we burned the Boers' homes and destroyed their crops and forced their families into the concentration camps that we were sending so many of their women and children to their deaths.'

His face was turned away from me. 'You must understand, feelings were running very high.'

I swallowed. 'And Hugo was one of those captured.'

He nodded without turning. 'He was the only one still alive by the time we managed to get to them.' He bent over a rusted knife. 'War truly is the world gone mad.' He seemed about to continue, then walked to the far end of the shelves so that I could barely hear him. 'Human beings can do the most terrible things to each other.'

'What things?' I demanded.

But he was stacking bottles and boxes at a great rate, as if he had not heard. 'And yes, you are right, Mrs Helstone. My brother was one of those who died saving your husband's life.'

Chapter Sixteen

JUNE, 1915

'It was Zeppelins, Mrs Hughes. Hundreds of them. My cousin Lily is chambermaid for a hotel on Richmond Hill, and she said the sky was black with them and the noise was something terrible. They all ran out into the road in fear for their lives, and there was London, all ablaze in front of them.'

I paused on the steps from the hallway. In the kitchen below Molly sounded petrified.

'I don't think London could all have been on fire,' said Cook. 'Your cousin must have been mistaken. Oh, I'm sure it must have seemed like it at the time,' she added as Molly began to protest. 'It said in the newspapers there were people killed, and even more injured. But there was nothing said about it being hundreds.'

'But suppose they come back? They bombed that other place, that one along the coast. They could bomb anywhere.'

'Port Helen isn't like Great Yarmouth or London, child. We're far too insignificant here for the Hun to have heard of us.'

'Well, I'm not sleeping up there in them top rooms. It takes an age to get downstairs. And suppose there's a fire?'

'That's all right, Molly,' I said, hearing Cook's exasperated intake of breath. Threatening to tan the poor girl's hide wasn't going to help matters. And we could not afford to lose her. Apart from Cook, Molly was the only help we had in the house and with two land girls now living with us and people traipsing in and out from the gardens, it was hard enough to keep the place clean and the grates swept as it was. What Hugo would have made of his wife scrubbing floors and hauling buckets of coal up the back stairs, before settling accounts with the local shop keepers and supervising the mending of fences, Heaven only knows. Not to mention threatening to tan the hide of young Timmy Hams when he was caught, yet again, with half a dozen of Hiram's eggs in his pockets, and with such conviction he still blanched if we passed each other in Port Helen.

It was with relief that I turned each evening to scouring my mother's battered recipe book for instructions on making pies and bread and making the cheapest cuts of meat as tasty as the finest. Not to mention her miraculous permutations on the uses of potatoes and kale with a handful of beans. Hugo would have been mortified at my preoccupation with the braising of cabbage and the best way of preserving of eggs, but to me they were a comfort and a return to a realm that was familiar when I had so many new things to learn.

Elsie had returned only briefly to Hiram after her fiancé was killed. I think the memories were just too painful for her; by Easter she had found work in a munitions factory along the coast.

Mr Phillips left shortly afterwards, lured by the promise of a much larger house in Kent and a family who knew how to keep up standards, war or no war, and didn't have half-dressed women running round the grounds calling everyone by their first names and without a skirt between them. Nor would they permit the wife to bark orders at him and expect him to supervise the humblest of deliveries with strict instructions to keep an eye out for any attempt to push a shortfall in quality or number past him, just because it was a woman in charge.

Mrs Pelham had been equally scandalised by the arrival of the land girls, Charlotte and Bethany, and their insistence on wandering around in trousers and blouses at all hours, not only when they were helping Jack in the garden. She was mollified for a while because Charlotte was the niece of an earl and a debutante in the last Season. Even Bethany, the daughter of 'Trade' was acknowledged as generally respectable, despite the trousers. Kitty, a mere fisherman's daughter from Port Helen working alongside them and joining us in the dining room for meals, however, sent her stalking the corridors in silent indignation. But the last straw came when I finally lost all patience and insisted she took her turn at the household chores, along with the rest of us. When I presented her with a mop, I might as well have asked her to personally clean out the latrines. My dismissal of dusting as a waste of time was like suggesting we turn the place into a hotbed of sin.

There were few tears shed at Mrs Pelham's outraged departure to help her sister run a hotel in Bath. I had, I'm afraid, put aside what Hugo might think. He wasn't here. He might have a war to fight, but this task, running a large house and an estate with a fraction of the workers it had taken through all the centuries of Hiram's existence, was mine.

'Besides,' I remarked to Cook, 'it means two less mouths to feed, and everyone else gets far too hungry to be half as fussy.'

I'd never understood the mysteries of stocks and shares, and neither Papa nor Hugo had sullied my existence with the balance of rents and repairs from the cottages on the Hiram estate. Now

I spent my evenings poring over figures, until I was forced to face the fact that Hugo's investments – though sound at the time – had suffered along with so many others, due to the war, and our income was now considerably reduced.

Hugo, like Papa, had been a good landlord, and the rents on the Hiram cottages had never been high. With money tight for everyone, and many of the families facing the loss of their breadwinner, I could scarcely put up the rents now.

We were not poor, not by any means. We would never go short, never go cold. And we would certainly never starve. But I looked back with astonishment to the years when I had never considered money. Although we lived on nothing like the scale of Northholme, I had never questioned that everything I might need, and more, would instantly appear. I thought of presents carelessly bought and instantly disregarded. Of more boots and shoes and ball gowns than I would wear in a lifetime. Of necklaces left in their cases, earrings lost in the bottom of my jewellery box, brooches and hairpins never worn.

Most of all, when I set out in the Rover, using precious petrol in the hunt for sugar – which had become expensive and sometimes hard to find – or tied endless rows of growing beans and peas to their supports, I remembered the extravagance of mealtimes. Every time we sat down there had been more meat than we could eat and enough courses to jade any palate. Even Cook's finely spun baskets of sugar and delicate towers of different coloured jellies had been something we had taken for granted. So much had been left for the servants, or even thrown away, I recalled with shame. Not one of us had ever let it enter our minds that such abundance was not our natural due, and that one day it might end.

I liked the spirit of informality Charlotte and Bethany had brought with them: a welcome breath of fresh air danced its way with their laughter through the dusty corridors of Hiram. Now the fine weather had returned, they preferred picnics on the lawns to formal courses in the dining room.

Besides, while the work in the gardens was endless, and the upkeep of the house and the estate drove me to distraction, there was very little to employ a housekeeper or a butler. Hugo had not returned home since Christmas, and Alice was worked off her feet with the casualties that now poured in daily. She visited occasionally, and then for only a few hours at a time. I didn't attempt dinner parties or gatherings. Besides the extra burden on Cook – and the unwelcome distraction of making Hiram spotless from top to toe – there seemed no point. How could I invite anyone to an evening of merriment when each day news came of more men lost? So many families already wore a black armband, and who knew where the next loss would strike? There were rumours of U-boats, great underwater vessels that stalked a ship like a cat with a mouse and could sink it instantly with terrible explosives, destroying the cargo ships carrying food and other vital supplies. With the stocks of fruit and vegetables preserved from last year almost exhausted, we were too busy laying down more to consider the extravagance of a dinner party.

Molly I could not afford to lose. Without Molly's good humoured willingness to help me clean and mend, wash and iron, haul coal and chop vegetables all day long, while playing occasional lady's maid to Charlotte when they both thought I wasn't looking, I didn't know what I would do. Without Molly we would fall into chaos.

I smiled soothingly at her. 'It doesn't make sense you staying up in the attic, Molly. There's a room a little down the corridor from mine, just across from Charlotte and Bethany. Once the bed is aired it should be very comfortable, and it will mean that we are all close together in case there ever should be an emergency. I don't know why we didn't think of it before.'

'But Miss Elin…' Cook shook her head in disapproval. Clearly hordes of barbarians were about to start battering at our gates.

Molly gazed at me with round eyes. 'Really, Mrs Helstone? That room next to Miss Alice's?'

'It makes sense. Then if there are any Zeppelin raids we can help each other find safety. We can go to the caves in Hiram Cove, or if there's no time for that, to one of the cellars.'

'Oh my goodness.' Molly was looking scared again. 'Yes, ma'am,' she whispered.

'But as I said, there's nothing here in Port Helen to interest anybody, and we're far too small to be worth terrorising. So we shall be safe enough.'

Cook shook her head as Molly rushed upstairs to sort out her belongings. 'Well, I can't say I'd ever see myself agreeing with that Mrs Pelham, but once you starting breaking down the natural order, the more impossible it is to get back,' she muttered.

'We've got to survive this war first, Mrs Hughes. I'd rather worry about all that once I know I might live to an old age. For now I'm afraid I don't have the energy.'

I left Cook to her mutterings and took the first of several trays of tea and cake into the walled garden. The fresh green of new growth burst around me as soon as I stepped through the archway. For the first months of the year, the garden had been a wilderness, followed by an emptiness of mud with just the occasional green shoot poking through. If it hadn't been for the energy of Charlotte, Bethany and Kitty, supplemented by the children from the school, we would never have cleared the neglected parts, let alone planted. Many of the seeds had gone in late, but now they were speeding along as if determined to make up for lost time.

I placed the tea things on a wooden table next to the central pond. Jack looked up from wrestling with tomatoes and cucumbers in the nearest greenhouse and nodded his appreciation. Kitty and the children were still collecting seaweed from the beach to be turned into fertiliser, but Charlotte and Bethany dropped their spades instantly.

'Oh thank goodness. I'm parched.' Charlotte brushed her hands on her trousers. Her fair hair was caught up in a tousled mop on the top of her head and her jumper was covered in earth, yet she somehow (possibly not unconnected with bribery of Molly) managed to retain an air of slender elegance that would not have shamed tea at the Savoy.

'It's all right, Elin, I'll fetch the rest,' called Bethany, pushing her chestnut curls back behind her headscarf with equal cheerfulness and equally grubby hands.

'Thanks,' I smiled in reply. I still found it strange that not so long ago Charlotte and Bethany would have been vying with each other to bag the nearest duke. But the dukes, along with every other Prince Charming, had ridden off to war. Bethany had discovered an enthusiasm for rooting out brambles and docks wherever they might hide, while Charlotte demonstrated a flair for wielding a saw on unwanted saplings that had impressed even Jack, who had at first viewed the exquisitely tailored coats of his new assistants with the air of a man about to take to the barricades. He'd since relented, and was unstinting of his praise for their boundless energy and willingness to learn.

'I'm sure those tomatoes have grown in the night,' I remarked, as Jack joined us, handing him his tea.

'In a bid to take over the greenhouse, I don't doubt,' he agreed with a grin. 'Thanks, Mrs Helstone.'

'Oh for heaven's sake, Jack!' Charlotte folded herself on a bench, sitting cross-legged as she fished out her cigarettes and sipped her tea with an air of bliss. 'I don't see why you don't call Elin, Elin. Everybody else does. All that formal stuff is such rot. It's what old people do.'

'You forget, I *am* old,' he replied. I hid a smile. Charlotte was used to men falling at her feet. She had been perplexed from the first that Jack's praise of her skill with a saw was impersonal and her flirtatious banter was met with unrelenting gravity.

'You're not in the least old,' she said.

'I'm nearly old enough to be your father: that makes me old.'

'Rot,' she snorted. 'You're not in the least like Pa. He's stuffy and plays bridge and is only interested in working out who is richer than him and falls asleep after dinner and snores.'

'I don't play bridge,' he replied solemnly, 'but as for the rest, I'm guilty as charged.'

Charlotte eyed him over the rim of her cup. 'I never know when you are being serious or not.'

Jack smiled. 'Oh, I'm always serious. Can't you tell? And I'm very serious about your reputation. All your reputations. Gossip flies around in small places like this, and whether you like it or not, your reputation can be your only real protection.'

Charlotte busied herself with lighting a cigarette. 'I don't need protecting.'

'I agree. Particularly if you take care to protect yourself.'

'Here's Bethany,' I said, seeing Charlotte beginning to pout. As Bethany returned with her laden tray, the gate leading onto the cliffs was flung open for several wheelbarrows pushed by Kitty and the children.

'Oh Lord,' said Charlotte, wrinkling up her nose. 'Rotting fish. I can smell the stench from here.'

'It's your imagination,' laughed Bethany, helping herself to a large slab of cake. 'It's only seaweed. Don't be so squeamish. And anyhow, Kitty is going to show us how to catch fish, remember? And I'm going to gut, cook and eat mine, so you'd better not be so fussy then.'

We were instantly surrounded by boys and girls heading for the cake.

'I'd better fetch more,' I said as the slices vanished and every last cup was taken. As I reached for the tray, the sound of an automobile came from the driveway.

'That sounds military,' said Jack, looking up from a large conch shell proudly presented to him by one of the boys for his admiration.

'Hugo,' I murmured. The world slowed. A Red Admiral butterfly floated past, taking an eternity to settle on one flower, then another. A spider poised in its web between the branches of a pear tree. The roar of pebbles in Hiram Cove retreated to an infinite distance away.

Abandoning the tray, I rushed full speed to the front of the house.

Chapter Seventeen

JUNE 1915

The vehicle arriving at Hiram was military all right. Some kind of ambulance. Dirty and battered, pockmarked along the sides with what even I recognised must be bullet holes. Sickness clenched my stomach as I raced towards the driver, who was enveloped in a filthy greatcoat and was stepping down as if barely able to move from stiffness.

'Is it Major Helstone?' I demanded, my voice thin. 'Is he badly hurt?'

The driver turned. 'Well, not unless he snuck in unnoticed at Calais.'

Relief shot through me. I hugged the greatcoat, for all it stank of mud, engine oil and general filth. 'Mouse!'

'Hello, Elin.' Mouse was grinning. She hugged me back. When she released me, I saw tears in her eyes. She turned away as if to look at the house, blinking hard. 'Hiram seems much the same as I remember. I thought it would have changed. I was afraid it might have been requisitioned by the army, or not even be standing after I heard about the incendiaries being dropped on the coast.'

'We're all quite safe. I tried to reply to your letters, but you never said where you were.'

'Oh, the censors would never allow it, in case the enemy got hold of it and worked out where our soldiers are based.' She hugged me again. 'Look, Elin, I'm awfully sorry to be a nuisance, but I managed to get back with Owen, bringing the wounded over. I've got a job taking the ambulance for repairs and picking it up with supplies when it's ready. Owen said there's a place for me to stay near the base, but I'm tired of soldiers. If I can get someone to drive me back, could I possibly stay with you for a few days?'

'Of course, Mouse. That would be wonderful! I'd love to have you here. I'll telephone Alice to see if she can get away. She'd love to see you. But what about your family? Don't you want to spend some time with them?'

'No,' said Mouse. 'Papa will only forbid me to go back, and there will be terrible rows. Edmund's on his way back to the front and George hasn't been back home since the war began. So there's nothing for me there.'

'I'm sorry. But don't you want to see your father?'

She shook her head. 'Oh Elin, what's the point? I can't be the daughter he thinks I should be. I never was. It's not that I don't love him. I do, desperately.' Her eyes were wistful. 'Perhaps more than I ever did. But I can't go back and pretend everything is the same as it was before. Most of the boys I grew up with are dead. Or missing. Or so horribly injured they wouldn't be allowed in Papa's polite society.' She turned back as a second ambulance began to make its way up the drive towards us. 'You will tell, him, won't you? That I can stay?'

The ambulance drew up in a flurry of gravel, followed by Owen jumping down from the driver's seat. 'Do you have to drive that thing as if it's a race?' he demanded. 'I gave my word you were a responsible driver, Mouse.'

Mouse stuck her hands in her pockets. 'Oh, don't fuss, Owen. We're here in one piece, aren't we? And Elin says I can stay with her until it's ready to drive back.' She frowned. 'Anyhow, I thought it was supposed to be one of your sergeants driving that thing?'

'He has a wife and children he hasn't seen for months,' returned Owen shortly. He was thinner than ever. The sleeve of his jacket was torn, and there was a streak of blood – not his own, by the looks of things – on his cheek. He looked like a man in the last stages of exhaustion. His eyes met mine. He gave a faint smile. 'Hello.'

'Hello,' I replied.

Mouse was chewing her lip. 'I thought I was helping.'

Owen glared. 'If you'd told me you were going to just abandon the ambulance when you felt like it, I'd have found another driver.'

'And deprived me of the chance to have a hot bath, a decent meal and a good night's sleep? No fear.'

Owen looked as if he was about to explode.

'I'll follow you in Hugo's Rover and drive you back, Mouse,' I said quickly.

'You don't have to do that, Elin. She is being inordinately selfish. I'll borrow an automobile and get her back here – if that's what you insist on, Mouse.'

'I'm sure you were meant to sleep too, before you return to France,' I replied, glancing at Mouse, who was beginning to look sheepish. 'I could do with getting out of here for a few hours and the old Rover could do with a run before it seizes up completely. Give me a few minutes. There's cake and tea in the garden.'

'If you're sure…' Owen was still uncertain.

'Completely.'

Mouse vanished in pursuit of cake. 'She means well,' he said, watching her disappear beneath the archway. He sighed. 'To be honest, I hoped this would encourage her to remain in England. But of course she won't.'

My stomach had constricted at the closeness of him. I could scarcely breathe. 'You can't save everyone.'

He smiled. 'And especially not Mouse. Old habits die hard, I'm afraid.' His hand grasped mine. 'Elin…'

'Not here.' I shook my head, pulling myself free as Molly appeared, heading for the gardens bearing a laden tray. I fled upstairs to change my trousers for a skirt and clean blouse, hastily brushing my hair. Mrs Hughes shook her head in despair when I informed her of my mission.

'Don't worry, we'll be back before dark.' I raced round to the stables to retrieve the Rover, before joining my guests in the garden.

It wasn't clear who had wolfed down the most, the schoolchildren or the new arrivals, but a general air of contentment reigned. I found Owen being quizzed by Charlotte and Bethany, while Kitty looked on in awe at a real officer from the front.

'So you're a hero then,' Charlotte was saying, with her most winning smile, gazing up at Owen with large blue eyes.

'Hardly. I just do what I'm told and try my best to keep my men alive and their feet from rotting.'

'Oh, but that makes you a hero,' purred Charlotte, sending a sideways glance to where Mouse was sitting on a log pile next to the greenhouse talking to Jack, who was listening with more attention than he had paid to Charlotte the entire time she had been there.

'It's the civilians I feel so sorry for,' Mouse was saying. 'I mean,

I feel awfully for the soldiers and it's vile how they have to live in all that mud, with the shells going over and being killed and injured all the time. But at least they know if they survive they'll have homes to go back to.' She sighed. 'I used to go to Lille before the war. It was so like here, the fields, the villages and the church steeples. All so green and rolling and peaceful. Now the villages are just ruins and everyone who can has fled. The only ones left have nowhere to go. I don't know how they survive, especially the poor children. We end up feeding them as much as the soldiers. I used to think fighting was very heroic. But it seems now to come down to boiling potatoes and scrounging a few beans.'

'Which makes it truly heroic,' said Jack. 'Sometimes it can be just as hard to do the things that go unnoticed and never get a medal, but make all the difference.'

'I suppose,' said Mouse, looking at him intently. 'I hadn't thought of it like that. But you're right.'

From the corner of my eye, I saw Owen stir. 'Don't be a fool,' I said quickly. 'Mr Treeve is only being polite, and Mouse can look after herself.' I made my way over to join them. 'I'm sure we have some vegetables we can spare, Mouse. It's still a bit early in the season, but we've the preserves from last year and Cook and I can make pies and cakes for you to take back. Cook's nephew has just been sent to join the troops in Gallipoli. I'm certain she'll wish to do all she can to help those who are fighting. I feel so helpless here. I'd love a chance to do something.'

'Would you mind?' Mouse beamed. 'Getting anything is hellish out there. That would be wonderful. Don't feel you have to collect lots of vegetables or things for me, I can do that. You should see my garden next to the field hospital. It's not like here, but I can coax anything to grow, so I certainly know how to dig up potatoes and harvest greens.'

'Time we left,' said Owen gruffly. 'I'm sure you don't want to be driving back in the dark.'

Mouse jumped up. 'Oh my goodness, yes. Of course. We should go now.' She shot through the archway before anyone had time to reply. The two men nodded coolly to each other as I followed Owen towards the vehicles.

* * *

It was a beautiful evening as I drove behind Mouse, taking care to keep the ambulance in sight. We passed the occasional horse and cart or tractor, but mostly the roads were empty. I breathed in the clean sea air and revelled in the lack of responsibilities, feeling the speed in the hedges flying by and the exhilaration of freedom.

The base was obviously expecting us. Once we reached the hangars, Mouse drove the ambulance straight inside. I turned and parked, ready to leave, before joining her.

'I think it's a fault in the fuel line,' Mouse was explaining to the overalled mechanic bending over the engine. 'They got trapped when one of the battle lines shifted. Some of the patients and two of the ambulance crew were killed, they said. We managed to get it back from near Lille with a bit of coaxing, but it felt like touch and go at times.'

The mechanic straightened, revealing a mass of auburn curls framing a round and pretty face. 'Yes, that's what it looks like to me too,' she said. 'There's a couple of other things I'd like to have a look at as well. Don't worry, we'll be able to patch it up.'

As Mouse and the mechanic inspected the rest of the ambulance, I let my eyes stray around the hangar. The last time, the workshops had been full of young men. Now any men were grey-haired and wrinkled. Amongst them shone brightly coloured headscarves, as women of all ages bent over engines or crawled underneath huge trucks. I shivered slightly and returned outside to the Rover. There was something eerie about those missing faces and the inevitable thought: where are they now?

I found Owen leaning against the bonnet, cigarette forgotten in his hand, his gaze on the sweep of fields and hedges, the blue expanse of sea beyond. He started as I joined him, as if dragged back from far away.

'I didn't mean to disturb you.'

'That's all right.' He busied himself retrieving his matches, cupping the cigarette against the breeze as he relit it. The glow briefly warmed the pallor of his face. The streak of blood had faded from his cheek, leaving the barest shadow. I could see the filth engrained in his hands. A half-healed cut ran along the side of one thumb.

'Have you somewhere to stay?'

He nodded. 'They're putting a camp bed up for me in one of the offices.'

'You are welcome to stay at Hiram. I can bring you back tomorrow morning.'

He stubbed out the butt of his cigarette beneath his heel. 'I don't think that's a good idea.'

'No,' I murmured. 'Probably not.' Mouse was still nowhere to be seen and the air was growing chill.

'Come on,' he said, leading the way towards the ruins of a manor house, surrounded on one side by an orchard of wizened and neglected apple trees. As we reached its broken wall, he came to a halt.

'I lied,' he said abruptly.

'Lied?'

'When I said I allowed Mouse to drive the ambulance back because I thought it might make her stay in England. I knew she wouldn't. They think the world of her out there, and she's in her element, despite the danger. But I thought – I hoped – that she might find her way to Hiram, so that I might come with her. It might be my only chance.'

'Oh.' The breath had gone from my body and my stomach

hollowed. In the distance, metal clanged on metal. An engine choked into life, then stilled.

'I had to see you one more time, Elin. Even if it's the last time.' He grasped my hand, pulling me through a tumbledown gap in the orchard wall, in amongst the sweet, cider-edged scent of rotting apples. 'I lied last time I saw you, too. It's not the lake in Northholme I see in my dreams, Elin. It's you.'

'You shouldn't,' I muttered feebly, with a vague sense I should be expressing outrage and running from him as fast as I was able. But I'd always known I couldn't lie, not to him. Instead I took a step closer, feeling his warmth through my blouse.

Owen's arms came around me. 'I only wanted to see you again, Elin. Just one more time. I don't expect anything. I just want to be with you. Just for a little while.'

'I'm glad you came,' I replied, leaning against him and feeling the rapid beat of his heart. 'I thought I'd never see you again.' I held him tight, dreading the call of voices from the hangars, returning us back to the world where I waited the return of a husband, and Owen returned to the bombs and bullets of a war that would almost certainly kill him.

'Do you love him?'

I look up to meet his eyes. 'Don't ask me that. You know I can't answer.'

'Yes you can. All right, not to me, but to yourself... Because if you love him, truly love him, then I swear I will never trouble you again.'

I bit my lip. 'I made my choice, Owen. I can't ever undo that. I won't betray him. And I'm not as brave as your godmother. I couldn't bear to lose Hiram and become an outcast and be shunned and despised by everyone I know. At least I have a life at Hiram. Others are content with worse.'

'Are you content?' His gaze bore into me, stripping all the hiding places away.

'When I first saw you, Elin, I thought I saw a woman who was resigned to exist within her husband's shadow. I couldn't understand why Mouse had taken such an instant liking to you. And then I saw the real you, passionate and brimming with life. A woman who was treated like a child – a toy. I couldn't bear to see such vibrancy stifled and invisible.' He held my face gently between his hands, preventing me from turning away. 'No, listen, Elin. You can't stay with him. I never understood until now how precious life is. How infinitely fragile, lost between one breath and the next, and how exquisitely precious. Even if I never live to see it, I couldn't bear the thought of you living and breathing for the rest of your days, with your spirit extinguished.'

I met his kiss, lost in its intensity until I could scarcely breathe. 'I can't leave Hiram, Owen. Not now. I can't just run away when so many people depend on me.'

'I understand that. But this war will end. One day, it has to. Heaven help me, I feel sure I won't see it. Go to your Aunt Catrin. Set up house with Alice in London. Have wild affairs with artists and dance until dawn. Anything. You'll find a way to start your life over again. My godmother will help you, if no one else will. However little you have, at least it will be a life.'

From the far distance, a world away, a voice was calling.

'Mouse,' I said. Owen heard it too. I held him tight. 'Come back,' I said fiercely. 'Whatever you do, Owen, come back to me.'

His kiss was gentle this time. Lingering. Regretful. A silent goodbye, with no promises uttered. Then he was gone, striding back up the path, a shadow in the evening light.

I leant against the gnarled and twisted trunk of a fallen tree. My legs shook. My breath came in great gasps. I tried to steady myself amongst the skeleton branches and the fallen walls.

Chapter Eighteen

JUNE 1915

Owen had gone by the time I reached Mouse. I smiled at her vaguely as I appeared next to the Rover.

'Owen said he'd seen you go for a walk,' said Mouse. 'I knew you wouldn't have gone far.' She looked back at the workshops. 'I hope he's all right. He drove all the way through the night. He looks exhausted. I thought he might come back with us to Hiram. He said you'd invited him. But he won't. I don't know why.'

'I'm sure he'll be comfortable,' I murmured, settling myself at the wheel. We set off in silence. Within minutes, Mouse's head was nodding. By the time we reached the coastal road she had propped herself against the door and was fast asleep.

I was glad of the silence, as I drove through the gathering dusk. My mind was in a whirl, darting this way and that until I didn't know what to think. I could be free. I need never face Hugo's distance and the loneliness of his courtesy towards me. I could be loved. I *was* loved. And I could love, with all the hunger that had consumed me, a real woman's love, not the empty dreams of a girl.

But never to see Hiram again. To lose everything I had know all my life. My friends, the cheerful greetings in Port Helen. To leave a husband was unthinkable. It meant utter disgrace. Hugo would never go through the humiliation of the courts, for all to see and laugh at, to grant me a divorce. Despair returned. It was impossible.

I urged the Rover over the steepest part of the road. The last light was disappearing from the horizon, but it was only a few more minutes until we would be in Port Helen. As the automobile reached the highest point, a light flared at the corner of my eye.

'Look out!' Mouse woke instantly, as I swerved us away from hitting a farm gate and into the ditch. Mouse broke the silence. 'Bloody hell.' I saw her looking at me anxiously. 'Are you all right, Elin?'

'I could have sworn there was something up there.' I peered to where the field sloped down to the sea. The sky had cleared to blue, a few wispy clouds touched by the last rays of sunlight. 'It must have been my imagination. I should have been paying more attention to the road. I hope we can get out of this.'

Mouse jumped out of the car. 'It isn't too bad. Just go slowly.'

I revved as steadily as I dared and with Mouse pushing with all her might, we eventually managed to get the Rover back on the road.

'Not too much damage done.' Mouse inspected the side. 'A couple of scratches. We can get those out. Hugo will never know. Come on, it'll be getting dark soon, and I'm starving. Let's get back to Hiram.'

We set off, but an alarming bumping from the back wheel announced our worst fears.

'There's another gate here,' I said. 'At least we can get it off the road so vehicles can pass.'

'Damn,' muttered Mouse. 'Last thing we need is a puncture. Any good at changing tyres?'

I shook my head. A night camping in the large barn in the centre of the nearby field seemed to be in store.

'Luckily I am. I'm a wiz. Plenty of practice.' Mouse was out and taking charge in a moment. Under her instruction, we managed to change the wheel for the spare. But Mouse was used to patching up army trucks and ambulances not the pride and joy of a gentleman at leisure, and I was woefully ignorant. It was a slow, heavy job.

'We'll have to drive in the dark,' I said, as Mouse tightened the last nut. 'It's all right, it's straight from here.' For the first time I looked at our surroundings. Night had settled around us while we worked. Stars shone in the emptiness above. There was not a sound, except the distant crash of waves and the call of an owl from a nearby wood. We had reached the highest part of the road before it dipped down to the sea. Below us, I could make out the shadow of Port Helen tucked within the bay and Hiram Hall on the cliffs above.

'It's beautiful,' breathed Mouse. 'As if it's just you and me awake in the whole world. I've never seen so many stars.' We stood for a while entranced, watching the arch of the Milky Way and the patterns of the constellations. A shooting star burned briefly over the sea. Mouse tucked her arm into mine. 'I could stay here forever.'

'You don't have to go back to France. Stay with me and work in the gardens. Or help Alice at the hospital. I'm sure they need drivers and mechanics.'

'I could be a mechanic,' said Mouse. She sounded wistful. 'I wish I could do more out there. But it's all so horrible. So hopeless. A mechanic sounds good.'

'And you'd still be doing your bit for the war effort.'

'I suppose so.' She sighed. 'I need to take the ambulance and the supplies back. I promised.'

'But you could make it your last time. Who knows how long this could go on for? We're fighting the war here, too.'

'Yes.' Her voice was distant. I felt my heart sink. Not even the magic of the night could not hold her long: restless, adventure-seeking Mouse was back.

'Come on,' I said. 'I'm getting cold. There's hot soup on the stove at home.'

'Mmm. That sounds like bliss. I'm ravenous. I'll drive.'

We turned back towards the Rover. As we did, something

caught my eye once more. Not a flare this time but a glint of light in the sky. Not a shooting star, but moving steadily high over the sea towards us.

I grabbed Mouse. 'Don't!' I hissed, as she moved to start the engine.

'What?'

'Look. Look over there, right over the sea. It's an aeroplane.' I felt slightly foolish. 'It could be one of ours.'

Mouse followed my arm, just a shadow in the dark. I could hear it now, a low hum.

'Come on!' Mouse pulled me out of the Rover, huddling us both into the shadow of the hedge. 'That sounds like a Gotha.'

'A what?'

'One of theirs. They're always sending them over. Horrible things.'

We crouched as low and as still as we could. I could hear the drone of engines coming closer. Starlight glinted every now and again on metal high above.

'They might be able to make out the metal of the automobile,' whispered Mouse. 'I don't want to be near all that petrol if they decide to throw a grenade.' She grabbed my hand. 'Come on. We can make a run for it now, before it gets too close and can spot us. If we can make it to the barn, we can stay there as long as we need to.'

The gate wasn't padlocked. She opened it just enough for us to slip through, and into the shadow of the hedge on the other side. I followed her, crouching low as I could. The patch of field between the hedge and the solid structure of the barn was a chasm. I could hear the Gotha drawing closer.

'Sounds like it's beginning to circle,' whispered Mouse, stopping in her tracks and pressing herself as far as she could amongst the leaves. 'Either it's lost, or it's looking for something. Keep still and keep your face covered. Faces stand out in the dark.'

I obeyed, lying flat amongst the grass, my head buried in my arms. Above us the bi-plane circled slowly. At times it sounded so low I expected it to crash through the branches of the trees.

'There aren't any big ports or military installations here, are there?' whispered Mouse, as the engines began to move slowly away.

'Not that I know of.'

'Then it might just be lost.'

I risked a glance upward. The bi-plane was silhouetted against the stars, banking low as it turned as if to come round again. 'It'll go behind the trees in a bit.'

'Good. Then it won't be able to see us for a few minutes. We can make a run for it. Who knows how long it might be hanging around, and there might be others. If we get to that barn, we can stay there all night. And we can see what it does.'

We clambered slowly to our feet, braced to race across the open ground the moment it disappeared. As the Gotha began to sink beneath the trees a breeze drifted in across from the sea, cool on my face. I smelt cigarette smoke, harsh-edged and unfamiliar.

'Now!' hissed Mouse.

I grabbed her hand, pulling her back. 'I think it's going. Come on, let's get out of here.'

I turned and ran back along the edge of the field, trusting Mouse would not abandon me. Sure enough, as I reached the gate she caught up. 'It's coming round again.' We pressed ourselves into the hedge again, as if trying to disappear inside altogether. I could hear my breathing rasping, loud as could be. My heartbeat was like a drum, echoing round the field.

I heard the Gotha turn slowly. The engine was like a pulse all around us. I could have sworn the ground itself shook. All I could think of was the Rover on the other side of the gate, with its tank of fuel so thoughtfully filled to the brim and the cans of spare in the boot. Just as I felt my head might burst, the engine faded away. By the time I dared turn to look, it was making its way along the coast.

'Come on!' I shot through the gate, pulling Mouse behind me. Within minutes I was easing the Rover carefully down the lane.

'It could come back,' said Mouse, feeling around her feet and retrieving her tobacco and papers.

'I thought so. You left your cigarettes in here.'

'Of course I did! I was hardly likely to light up with that thing right above us. It's bad enough being able to see Port Helen in the starlight, without the encouragement of any lights. I suppose at least he didn't bomb the village.'

'I don't think it was here on a bombing raid,' I answered as we reached the edges of Port Helen. I pulled the Rover to the side of the road. I was shaking. 'Didn't you smell it?'

'What?'

'Cigarette smoke.'

'There can't have been. No one would have been mad enough to be smoking with that thing overhead.'

'Unless they knew it was coming. Unless they were waiting inside that barn, maybe to give it some kind of signal.' I turned towards her. I could just make out the glint of her eyes. 'I could have sworn that's where the smell was coming from. There's been so many rumours about spies in the papers and in Port Helen. I never for a moment thought it might be true.'

'If there *was* someone in there, they would have heard us,' said Mouse.

'And wouldn't have made the signal. Which could be why the Gotha circled and then went away.'

Mouse lit her cigarette, crouching under the dashboard to minimise the flame. I could see the slight shake of her hands in the brief flare of the match. 'So if we'd tried to get in there…'

'Don't think about it.' I glanced in the rear mirror. 'At least no one seems to be following us. Thank goodness it was dark. We could have been anybody stopping to mend a puncture. If there was someone in the barn, it doesn't mean they realised we knew they were there.' I moved the automobile forwards again. 'All the same, I'm going to take the back roads. If there was someone there, I don't want to lead them straight to Hiram.'

* * *

The Hall was silent when we crept in a few hours later. I parked the Rover under the trees at the edge of the grounds. From the driveway, we could still make out the field and the silhouette of the barn on the opposite side of Port Helen Bay. If there was someone up there scouring the countryside for any sign of an automobile, I had no wish to signal one arriving back at Hiram Hall.

Charlotte and Bethany had gone to bed hours ago. Cook had waited a little longer before doing the same, leaving Molly with instructions to telephone Constable Jones at the Police Station if I didn't return before midnight. Molly set about making tea and heating up the soup Cook had left, but she could barely keep her eyes open, so I sent her off to bed too.

At least there was hot water for Mouse to have a bath. I found a dressing gown and a nightdress for her, along with some clean clothes for the morning. The clothes she had been wearing were almost rigid with dirt and stank to high heaven. While she sat by the range in the kitchen to dry her hair, I placed everything – greatcoat and all – into the bathwater (which was filthy enough with just having had Mouse herself in it) to soak for as long as they could. Her underclothes didn't get near the water. They looked and smelt as if they hadn't been changed for months, so I threw them in the fire. My clothes might not fit her, but I had recently bought new vests and camisoles to give to Alice for her birthday. I was quite certain that under the circumstances she wouldn't mind giving them up.

'That feels good,' said Mouse, stifling a yawn as I made my way back into the kitchen. 'I feel civilised again.'

I fried up potatoes and carrots left over from last night's meal and added a handful of early peas from the garden, still in their pods, as Mouse whisked up eggs. I scattered the omelette with chopped ham, with a sprinkling of sage. As it cooked, I spooned out the soup, accompanied with bread and butter and a slab of cheese. I fetched a bottle of wine from the depths of the cellar, which I struggled to open until Mouse took it from me and uncorked it with the professionalism of a waiter.

'Another skill I've picked up,' she said airily. 'I can cook, too. I'll never be as good as you, Elin. But I can feed myself. I never thought preparing food could be so much fun. I can see why you love it so much.' We drank from cups, not bothering to find glasses, as we ate. 'That tastes wonderful,' sighed Mouse, finishing her omelette and ladling a third portion of soup into her bowl. 'And cheese. I've so missed cheese.'

'You sound half starved.'

'Food isn't exactly plentiful, and it's very tedious most of the time. There's been so much destruction over there it's hard to get hold of anything. I don't know how the civilians survive at all.'

I shivered. 'I'd hate Hiram to become a battlefield.'

'Me too.' She demolished her slice of bread and cut herself another.

'Do you think that's what that Gotha was doing? Finding the best places for an invasion?'

Mouse shrugged. 'Who knows? They were more likely to be trying to find a port like Portsmouth or Southampton.' She paused, knife half through the bread. 'If there was someone in that barn, it could be someone from the village.'

'Of course not!' I emptied my glass. 'It couldn't be.'

'No, silly idea,' said Mouse hastily. She tore her slice of bread in half, ladling it with my damson jam as if she would never have the chance again.

* * *

For all my tiredness, sleep eluded me that night. I sat by the window, looking over Port Helen to the barn on the hill, my body braced, as if expecting an entire fleet of Gothas and Zeppelins to appear in the sky. Every owl screech had me holding my breath. The snuffle of badgers on the lawn sent alarm shooting down my spine. The distant hum of an engine from the coastal road made me wish I kept Hugo's pistol close at hand. I listened to the engine noise growing nearer, half expecting a vehicle to slink up the drive, or for the slow tread of footsteps to pad over the lawns to the house, their owner testing each shuttered window for weakness.

I was thankful that before he went away, Hugo had insisted we checked twice over each night that every lock and window was secure. But all the same, I couldn't shake the sense, deep in the core of me, that the very air around Hiram Hall hung heavy with waiting.

Chapter Nineteen

JUNE 1915

Mouse slept for most of the following morning. When she finally emerged, bleary-eyed and tousled, she headed straight for the kitchen. I found her there when I returned with the new potatoes I'd dug from the garden, a coat flung over her nightgown, chatting away to Cook, as she demolished a huge plate of eggs and bacon accompanied by thick slices of toast.

'This is *so* delicious,' she exclaimed as I reached them. 'I dream of butter, you know. Toast dripping with butter in front of an open fire, piled high with your wonderful raspberry jam. It's the taste of England.' She laughed. 'Don't look at me like that, Elin. It's true. I'd never been properly hungry before I went to France. Not that kind of hungry when you're not sure where your next meal is coming from and knowing when it does it's likely to be cabbage with the odd potato floating in it. This is bliss.'

'I shan't need to take you to Claridges for tea, then?' I replied with a smile, washing the delicate, translucent skin of the potatoes, while Mrs Hughes cleaned and rolled herrings, ready to place in with the potatoes and dried rings of last year's apples to create my mother's delicious herring pie.

'Absolutely not.' She gave a contented sigh. Her eyes followed me as, potatoes done, I returned to the making of seed cake, collecting jars of caraway seeds and the candied peel we had made last Christmas from the pantry, along with a bottle of orange flower water. 'Your cakes are something I dream about, too, Elin,' she added, as I began to beat eggs, one by one, into the sugar and butter mix. 'And puddings. Apple crumble with custard. Even semolina.' She caught Cook's eye. 'You must think I've gone quite mad, Mrs Hughes.'

'Not at all, miss.' Cook took the boiling kettle from the range and filled the teapots, which had already been warmed and the correct amount of tea spooned in. 'But surely the army must have supplies?'

'Oh, yes. But they don't always get there, and the front lines shift and everything gets stuck in the mud. You've never seen such mud. I'm mostly driving around, picking up men and supplies for a field hospital. Nurse Spedding, who set up the hospital, is a real nurse. And utterly wonderful. I don't know how she manages to source supplies, but she always does. That's why I stayed there when Ginny and Sybil decided to go back to the trenches in Belgium. It seemed unfair to leave her, when I know the roads so well.'

'You are driving around in a war zone?' I asked, shocked.

'Oh, no. Not really. The hospital is away from the main fighting. They all know us. The Germans as well. It depends who they are, but they usually promise not to shoot.'

Cook practically dropped the kettle. 'You've *spoken* to the Hun?'

'Oh, yes.' Mouse calmly took a large bite of toast. 'Not so much now I'm away from the trenches. But when I was with Ginny, driving an ambulance for a hospital on the front line, we'd meet them quite often. The trenches are so close, you see. If you stand in the middle you can easily hear conversations on both sides. That's what makes it so horrible.'

'And I trust you did no such thing, young lady,' said Cook, severely.

'Sometimes. When there'd been fighting. We'd arrange a time to go in and pick up any wounded we could find, and remove any…' She caught the expression on Cook's face and came to a halt. 'Sorry,' she muttered. 'You get used to it. Well, not *used* to it. But it's strange how quickly you forget that life can be any other way.'

I watched her. 'So what are they like, the enemy?'

She shrugged. 'Some of them are horrible. They arrested me a few weeks ago as a spy. They didn't have any evidence of course, and when Owen heard he made the most terrible fuss and told them Papa was very important and that I was Queen Mary's cousin, which isn't in the least bit true. They soon let me go. Their tea was terrible. Where I'm working now, where villages have been overrun and then taken back by the French, you see things and hear things that make you think they're all monsters and you just want to shoot them. But it can't be all of them. We got to know some of them in the trenches quite well. They were all so young, and so cold and wretched and frightened and homesick. Just like our fellows, really. Sometimes we felt so sorry

for them that when we were taking hot chocolate to our boys we
took it to them, too.'

'Well, I never,' breathed Cook, sitting down heavily on a chair.
'Well I never.'

Mouse bit her lip. 'I'm sorry, Mrs Hughes. I should have
remembered. Elin told me you had a nephew in the army. He's not
in France or in the trenches in Belgium, is he?' Cook shook her
head. 'Good.' Mouse eyed her in contrition. 'I'm sorry. Rattling
on like that was thoughtless. I forget people here are always waiting
for news. It's so different out there in the thick of it.' She grimaced.
'At least if I go to hell, as the minister at Northholme is always
threatening, I know I'll feel reasonably at home there.'

Cook shuddered. 'Don't even joke about such things, miss.'

'Come on.' I placed the first teapot on a tray. 'Finish your
breakfast and get dressed, Mouse. You can help me get lunch.
The herring pie is for later. The girls are always ravenous. It's a
lovely sunny day, we can have a picnic outside.' I glanced up at
the sounds of Molly cleaning out the grate in Bethany's room.
'And it leaves so much less washing up to be done.'

Mouse was dressed in double-quick time. Alice's blouse was
too big for her, but at least her trousers were dry and her boots
reasonably clean. She joined us carrying a large tin of Cook's best
shortbread biscuits in her arms. Having deposited them on the
old tea chests we were using as a table, she made a beeline for
Jack, shamelessly taking advantage when Charlotte was unable
to withstand the call of nature any longer and forced to retreat
to the latrine.

'I want to learn all there is about growing things,' she
announced.

Jack watched her with the severity he reserved for Charlotte
when her attempts to flirt became too marked. 'I'm learning
myself, Lady Margaret. I'm not sure I'm the best person to help
you.'

'Well of course you are. And call me Mouse. Everybody does, and Lady anything sounds *so* stuffy. Especially when I'm covered in mud.' She looked at him seriously. 'I don't want an expert, Jack, I want someone who's growing things now and finding out what is the best way to go about it when you don't have knowledge or skill, or time.'

Jack hesitated. A faint smile appeared and his face lost its gravity. I caught Kitty's eye. Wonders would never cease. After all Charlotte's smiles and careful washing and brushing of her hair, it was Mouse firing questions at him, writing down each answer carefully without giving him a second glance, that had finally brought a faintly mesmerised look to Jack's eyes.

Well, at least with Mouse he was safe. She was bent over her notebook, completely engrossed in the finer points of cabbages. I was just about to return to the household accounts when Mouse paused, pencil resting on her bottom lip. 'I've met plenty of Conscientious Objectors out there, you know. Driving ambulances, carrying stretchers and helping Nurse Spedding with the heavy work. They're all terribly brave. But none of them have been soldiers.'

'It's not a requirement,' he replied, dryly.

Mouse blushed. 'You think I'm just playing at it, don't you.' She sounded hurt. 'You think I'm a bored rich girl who's used her money and her connections to get herself out there so she can think she's heroic while not understanding anything.'

'I would never think so little of anyone putting their lives at risk to help others.'

'But you think I'm a spoilt little rich girl.'

He smiled, his slow serious smile. 'More to the point, Mouse, do you?'

'Oh.' Mouse chewed on her pencil, brows creased in concentration. 'I never thought of it like that. Well, yes, I suppose. I've never had to think about money and I always knew I only had to say my name and people would treat me like royalty.' She met his eyes. 'My life always felt like it should be a fairytale, except it wasn't. At the heart of it, the bits that matter most, weren't like a fairytale at all. Maybe I was trying to find something real.' She gave a wry grunt. 'Well, I've found that all right and I'm not sure I like it. Perhaps I shall agree with my brother Edmund and declare the human race is done for and we're not worth saving.'

He frowned. 'You don't believe that.'

'No. I don't suppose I do.' She smiled. 'You have to have some hope, just to carry on. Some people can be vile beyond belief, but I also see others being incredibly kind and caring, ready to brave anything to help someone in trouble. I want those people to win and I don't care what it takes.'

Jack's eyes were still resting on her face. 'You have a great deal of courage.'

'Oh, not really.' Mouse's voice faltered a little. As if suddenly aware of his gaze, her cheeks turned pink. She pulled at her jacket, as if conscious of its well-worn shabbiness. 'I'm not really brave, you know. Not really.'

Charlotte, who arrived back in time to observe Jack's smile and Mouse's confusion, loudly poured herself another cup of tea and scowled in their direction. Bethany and Kitty had already returned to building wigwams of birch twigs for the next peas and runner beans. The schoolchildren would be here soon to plant out the seedlings from the greenhouse and ensure the stems were secured against their frame. I could see Charlotte bracing herself for an assault on Mouse's monopoly of Jack. I was very glad to see a familiar figure arrive through the cliff gate.

'Look, Mouse, here's Alice,' I called.

Mouse ran instantly to hug Alice tight. 'I was afraid I might miss you, until Elin said you were coming over today.'

'I managed to get away a little earlier. Elin telephoned Applebourne to tell me you were here.'

'I'm glad.' Mouse slipped her arm through Alice's. 'It's so strange – I keep on hearing your name mentioned in France. You're quite famous, you know.'

'Me?' Alice laughed. 'I'm only an administrator. I'm not even a nurse.'

'Ah yes, but you can get anything. That's what Nurse Spedding says. She's so angry when she can't get hold of things to help the men. And she always says she's going to write to Alice Griffiths at Applebourne Hospital because she knows you won't rest until you get what is needed. Apparently you can be quite terrifying.'

'I suppose I can if I need to,' replied Alice, smiling. She looked up at the house. 'Funny, isn't it. All my life I've been dependent on others. Now I'm pestering and outwitting even the most bullying suppliers and I'm like a dog with a bone if I can't get the bandages and the morphine we need.' She pulled a face. 'I wish it hadn't been a war that taught me what I was capable of, or the satisfaction of earning my own living.'

'Well, I think you're wonderful,' Mouse declared, hugging Alice tightly. She glanced back at Jack. Charlotte was asking him random questions about soft fruits. His face had returned to its customary severity. He quickly excused himself and escaped inside the greenhouse. I couldn't help but see the way Mouse smiled, before turning back to join us.

* * *

I left Alice and Mouse to sit on the cliffs exchanging their news, while I finished the accounts and helped Cook dish out large helpings of herring pie (a particular favourite with the schoolchildren) for the workers in the garden. After everyone had been fed, Mouse and I walked Alice down the cliff path to the railway station so she could catch the train back to the hospital.

By the time Mouse and I made our way back, the garden

was deserted. A soft haze settled over the sea as the sun sank beneath the horizon, its warm glow reflected on the walls of Hiram Hall.

Mrs Hughes must have been looking out for us. She met us on the steps, a look of profound disapproval on her face. 'There's a Mr Connors from Portsmouth to see you, Mrs Helstone.'

'Connors?' I stared at her in astonishment. 'I heard he was delivering medical supplies. What on earth is he doing here?'

'I told him to come back tomorrow, but he insisted on waiting.' She sniffed. 'I've put him in the library. I trust he used the time to acquire some manners.'

I glanced up at the library window. A shadow stood there, watching us, with no attempt to step out of sight or slip behind the curtains. 'Thank you, Mrs Hughes. I'll see him now.'

I found Connors standing amongst the palms and the ferns, turning his hat in his hands. 'Mr Connors.' I smiled as best I could. 'I'm afraid my husband isn't here. What can I do for you?'

'It's you I wished to speak to, Mrs Helstone,' he replied. He ducked his head slightly, but his eyes had lost none of their insolence.

'I'll ask Cook to make you a cup of tea.'

'That won't be necessary. At least not on my account.'

'So what can I do for you, Mr Connors?'

He coughed. 'It's a delicate matter, Mrs Helstone. Major Helstone spoke to me the last time he was in Port Helen. Before he returned to the front.'

'He never mentioned it.'

'He suggested that I meet him here to discuss a position.'

'A position?'

'Yes.' He was watching me, trying to gauge how much my husband might confide in me. 'The position of Steward.'

He sounded so confident. Had Hugo really promised him such a thing without consulting me? It was more than possible.

I took a deep breath. 'I'm very sorry, Mr Connors, but you have to understand that your original conversation with my husband was some time ago. The position has since been filled. I know the Major thinks highly of you and would write you an excellent recommendation.'

He put down his hat. 'I understood from the Major that the position was still open. Should I want it. I had an appointment with him today.'

Now I was sure he was bluffing. 'The Major is still in Belgium and has not mentioned any appointment to me. As I said, we already employed a man to oversee the gardens and there is little else to run on the estate these days that I can't manage myself. I can write to my husband and see if he had any other position in mind.'

'Oh, it was the position of Steward. To run the estate. Collect the rents from the cottages in Port Helen. And to oversee the gardens. The Major quite clearly indicated as much.' His fingers were playing with the inner lining of the cuff of his jacket sleeve. I didn't believe a word. Why on earth was he suddenly interested in Hiram again? His suit was an expensive one, the gold ring on his finger large and ostentatious. Mr Connors was doing well for himself delivering medical supplies to the hospitals along the south coast.

I took a deep breath. 'I'll write to my husband to clarify the situation. But in the meantime I have to tell you that our current arrangements are perfectly satisfactory, and there's no need to change them.' I turned. 'Now, if you'll excuse me…'

He stepped in front of me, blocking the half open door. His face was white, his lips a thin line. 'That Treeve fellow, he isn't altogether what he says he is.'

Despite myself, I paused. 'I beg your pardon?'

'You'll see.' A pleased expression appeared. It didn't improve his features. 'There's many things you don't know, Mrs Helstone.

Strange things happen in times of war.' His voiced lowered. 'You'll see, soon enough.'

The door was pushed wide, nearly knocking him off his feet. 'Well, that's stupid,' said Mouse loudly. Connors started at the sound of her voice. His pale eyes fixed themselves on her. 'Anyone can tell that Jack wouldn't do anything to harm anyone else, and there's no good in trying to say otherwise.' She sent me a smile. 'Mrs Hughes sent me up. She didn't like the thought of anyone being impertinent.'

Connor's eyes never left her face. 'As you wish.' He ducked his head slightly. 'Lady Margaret, isn't it?'

'To my friends,' returned Mouse pointedly.

He smiled. A pale, thin-lipped smile. 'Of course. Mr Treeve is fortunate in his friends, it seems.' His eyes travelled back to my face. 'Thank you for your time, Mrs Helstone. You have put my mind at rest. Good day.'

'Good day,' I replied. As he passed, a faint smell of cigarettes reached me.

'What an unpleasant man,' said Mouse, as his footsteps clattered away down the stairs. 'I hope he never comes again. What on earth did he want?'

'I'm not sure,' I replied slowly.

'Well I'm certain you ought not to be alone with him. In fact, I'd give orders that he wasn't to be admitted at all. I'm sure he would never have spoken to you in that way if Jack was here.'

'Yes, of course.'

Would things have been different, if I had spoken aloud what was in my mind? I should have shouted out for all to hear that I was sure the smell rising from Connors that day was the same brand of harsh-edged cigarette smoke that had come from the barn while the Gotha circled. He might have wanted to take Jack's job, running Hiram was a powerful position in the community, but perhaps he was also investigating if we'd seen anything last night, whether we suspected him. I was relieved that it hadn't occurred to me till he was leaving, so hopefully I'd done nothing to give my thoughts away.

But I put it from my mind. I had no proof. I still saw Connors as a small man – not someone who could do me any real harm.

* * *

Mouse stayed with me for three more days. By the end of the second day I knew she would go back, whatever I said. Already she was itching to be in France.

We fetched the patched-up ambulance from the base, driving the longer route that avoided the barn. Back at Hiram, we packed the back with sacks of vegetables and a trunk full of pickles and preserves and all the pies and cold meats I had managed to prepare.

The following dawn, I watched Mouse set off on her way to meet Owen for the drive back to France, picking up her consignment of medical supplies from Applebourne on the way.

'You will write to me,' I said. 'Even if the army won't permit me to write to you? And you will take care.'

'Of course.' She kissed my cheek and pulled herself into the driver's seat. 'This war can't last forever. You'll see, Elin, we'll soon be having picnics on the beach again with Alice, as if none of this had ever happened.'

With a jaunty wave, she made her way down the drive, the ambulance enveloped by mist clinging to the grass with a gossamer of jewelled spider's webs. Then she was gone.

Chapter Twenty

OCTOBER 1917

You cannot live with fear forever. Over the two years that followed I learnt that. The fear never goes away, but you have to find a place to parcel it in your mind so that you can get on with living. As the war dragged on and the loss of men grew more terrible, a kind of numbness settled. With the talk of shortages and even possible rationing, with more and more ships destroyed by enemy U-boats, work continued in the garden more urgently than ever.

Cook and I worked hard to preserve what we could. In the summer months, the kitchen steamed as we bottled fruit from the garden and made jams with the blackberries from the hedgerows. Rings of apple and pear hung drying in the sun. We pickled everything from onions to walnuts to rose petals. Sacks of potatoes lurked in corners. Apples rested on shelves in the old barns, overhung by strings of onion and garlic. When we could find enough sugar, we candied peel and nuts and the bright green of angelica. When eggs were plentiful, we pickled and preserved them and made thick lemon curd.

We began to grow medicines, too … the old plants and herbs that had been half forgotten. Cook said it was the old ways, the country ways of understanding the land when no one had anything, that would get us through. We made soap with lard, sweetened with rosewater and orange blossom, and face creams with elderflowers. We created cough mixtures from honey and syrups for colds from elderberries and rosehips.

My hands grew rough with picking fruit and spending much of their time in vinegar and water. But I never tired of gathering lavender on a sunny day, or experimenting with violets preserved in jelly and the aromatic bubbling of elderflower champagne and herb beer.

Hugo came home rarely and always very briefly. A terrible exhaustion consumed him, so unlike him it frightened me. He no longer made his tour of the grounds and showed little interest in how the estate was being run in his absence. He spoke briefly to Jack and, as if that were enough, returned inside to sit by the fire as if barely able to move. I did not ask him about the fighting and he no longer asked me about Hiram.

I had the occasional letter from Mouse, who sounded angry and despairing behind the cheerful talk of the fine garden she was developing amongst the destruction. A stray shell had destroyed her cabbages, but they would grow again and at least the potatoes had been left intact. From Mouse I also heard news of Owen. I did not dare write to him and he did not attempt to see me again. I knew he was alive. I tried not to think of the future.

Alice now rarely left Applebourne Hospital. The casualties sent over were never-ending. Even there medicines were in short supply. I could see the lines of her own particular battle on her face on the brief occasions when she came for tea.

Mostly, I was tired. We always seemed to be tired these days, with the long hours of work and a diet consisting increasingly of vegetables and grains. Even in quiet Port Helen, there were moments of terror, when a Zeppelin sailed over the sea towards us, or a small fleet of bi-planes, ready to drop their incendiaries.

Sometimes, we would hear them being dropped on ports along the coast and see the glow of flames in the far distance. On bad nights, half the village sheltered in the caves above the tide-line under the cliffs. Some of the villagers had taken in families from London, who told terrible stories of whole streets flattened and fires raging day and night.

And there were the losses. So many losses. There did not seem to be a family left untouched. I knew them, of course. Not always to speak to, but by sight. For the youngest, I remembered their births. The baby who had hovered between life and death for days, and the joy when he survived. The child who had been longed for, for years. I remembered their faces at school. The boys growing into men laughing at the corner of the streets at the end of a day. All of them lost. I still could not believe it.

Like everyone I knew, I was waiting. Waiting for the waiting to be over. Waiting for the boy with the telegram. For the knock at the door.

When at last it came, it came with neither.

I was stirring vegetables for the next day's stew for the gardeners one evening when I heard footsteps outside the kitchen door.

'Alice,' I cried, with pleasure.

'I thought I would find you here.'

I could not make out her face, thrown into shadow by the low sun behind her. But the thin tone of her voice had me dropping my ladle in an instant.

'Oh dear Lord no. Not Hugo?'

She put her arms around me. 'No Elin, I have no news of Hugo.' She was holding a piece of paper in her hand. I could see it was a letter. Not a telegram. Not an official communication. A letter.

Then I knew. 'Mouse.'

'She's alive,' said Alice. 'At least, as far as I know she still is. The letter is from Nurse Spedding. Mouse has been taken prisoner by the Germans. She's accused of being a spy.'

'A spy? But that's ridiculous. And anyhow, I thought they'd arrested her once before and let her go?'

'Nurse Spedding says that there had been a change of officers at the front. These are not the ones they knew before. The ones who knew Mouse. They were all warned not to go out after the battles to collect the wounded, but Mouse wouldn't listen. Nurse Spedding thinks they want to make an example of her to frighten the others away.'

'But if she's been arrested as a spy…'

'They could shoot her. Yes.'

'But that's impossible.'

'It happened to Edith Cavell – the nurse. There was all that coverage in the newspapers and pleas to save her. But they still executed her.'

'By firing squad.' I remembered the newspaper articles all too well. I felt sick. 'When was the letter written?'

'Nearly a week ago.'

A week. A week of sunshine and laughter in the walled garden. A week of watching the sun set over Hiram Bay. And all the while Mouse was languishing in a cell. Perhaps enduring torture or the wait for execution. She might already be dead.

'No one's heard anything else since?'

'Not unless there is a letter on its way. I came over as soon as this arrived. I wanted you to see it for yourself. Oh Elin, I'm sorry, I can't stay. I have to get back by the next train. With all the casualties and more expected from the front tomorrow, I have to. We're running dangerously short of morphine.'

'Yes of course.'

'You know her family. They might listen to you. They won't listen to someone who's just an administrator in a hospital. But you've spoken to them before, you know Edmund and Owen and you can speak to them as Hugo's wife – at least it's worth a try. Their connections might have influence to get Mouse out.'

I nodded. 'Yes, of course. I'll telephone them now.'

I pushed the kettle onto the heat for it to boil while I tried to get through. At first there was nothing. On and on the ringing went, until at last the butler answered.

'His lordship is not taking calls today.'

'But it's about Lady Margaret,' I began.

'His lordship is not taking calls today. With no exception.' He explained. I put down the receiver after he had finished speaking, making my way slowly back to the kitchen.

Alice handed me a cup of tea, her eyes on my face. 'Did you talk to them?'

I shook my head. 'Only the butler. He wouldn't listen or let me talk to anyone. George has been killed at the front. The news arrived just half an hour ago.'

Alice gasped. 'I'm so sorry. That's terrible for them. But surely when they hear that Mouse's life is in danger and could be saved…?'

'I tried to explain, but once he had said about her brother he put the phone down. I've tried calling back but they are not answering at all now.'

'We could drive to Northholme and insist on speaking to them. I understand how they feel, believe me, but surely the last thing they want is to lose Mouse too. We've got to do something.'

I shook my head. 'That will just take more time. If Mouse is still alive, every minute will count.'

I saw Alice's face turn pale. 'Elin, you're not thinking…'

I swallowed. 'I've got the Rover and I've kept more than enough fuel to get me to Anglesey again, in case it was needed, so it can surely get me to France. I can't wait here and not know. I always feel so useless. Hugo and the others could be killed at any minute and there's nothing I can do. I can't just let Mouse die.'

'I'll come with you.'

'No. Your work is too valuable. Didn't you just tell me you're needed to find morphine and medical supplies? You can't walk away from the hospital, not when people need you.'

Alice grabbed my hand. 'You are needed too, Elin. You are feeding Port Helen and giving fresh vegetables, preserves and all kinds of good things it's really hard to come by to the patients at

Applebourne. What would Hiram do without you? Or Hugo? Everyone who loves you?'

'Hugo might be killed any day. Any of us might be. We all know that. And there are plenty of others who can carry on my work here. How can I pot jams when Mouse might be dying? I can't just leave her.'

Alice argued for a little longer, but I wouldn't give way and soon she would be forced to leave to catch her train. I retrieved the Rover from its barn while Alice hastily filled a canvas bag with salad leaves for her patients, and I drove her to the station.

'You will look after Hugo and Hiram if anything should happen to me,' I said, as the train began to move.

'Hugo would never let me. You know what he thinks of me.' Her smile was watery as she stood at the open window of the carriage. 'So you'll just have to come back, Elin.'

'But you promise?'

'Yes. I'd do anything for you, Elin. I'd look after Hiram the best that I can. I just pray I never have to.'

Slowly the train pulled away. I watched until the trail of smoke vanished around the headland, then drove back as fast as I could to Hiram Hall.

I hadn't changed my mind, but now fear was pulling at my belly. I would pack tonight and leave at first light tomorrow morning. I had Alice's directions to Nurse Spedding's field hospital. I would start there. Maybe Edmund and Owen would be stationed nearby. Nurse Spedding would know, and surely she would help me. I didn't know what I was going to do, but I had to do something.

I pulled the Rover up in front of the house, and made my way down to the kitchen. I had provisions to pack, and a note to leave for Cook. I could not go empty handed into a war. I found an old hamper in one corner and hurried into the garden. It was dusk. Charlotte and Bethany had been invited to eat with Kitty and her family, and had left several hours ago, bearing gifts of swede and carrot. As I expected, the garden was deserted. I went immediately to the store to find a spade.

'There's no need.' I swung round at the voice. Jack was sitting on a stool just inside the greenhouse, watching me.

'Jack! I assumed you had left with the others.' I paused. 'This is none of your business.'

He stood up. 'I mean it. There is no need. It's already done.'

At his feet stood several large sacks. A haversack lay on the potting table next to him. His face had a look of stubborn determination. I should have known. 'Alice. She told you about Mouse.'

'Yes.'

'I can't ask you to come with me. It's a wild goose chase. I can't ask you to risk your life for that.'

'You didn't ask,' he replied. 'How are you going to find Mouse?'

I faltered. 'I don't know. I'll find a way.'

'Then let me help you. I speak French, and a little German –'

'German!' I stared at him.

'Just because I'm a working man doesn't mean I haven't had an education. Thanks to the libraries and evening classes. Perhaps if we ever get back, you'll consider supporting education for the masses.'

I had an urge to throttle him. 'Yes,' I replied.

'Not all Prussians are blood-thirsty imperialists. In truth, there are plenty who are just as horrified as you and I at the world going mad. There are plenty who agitated long and hard for peace before the war came.'

'Oh.'

He smiled, gentler this time. 'And thanks to them, I've driven through Lille. At least I'll know the area a little. Though heaven knows if it's recognisable.'

He swung the haversack over one shoulder and lifted the first canvas bag. 'I'll put these in the boot. With two of us driving, we'll make much better speed.'

It made sense. I'd been running around like a headless chicken, desperate to do something. At least with help I stood a chance of achieving something useful. I nodded, and ran back towards the house.

I made mental lists as I packed as many jams and preserves as we could carry, along with the last store of coffee I'd been saving for Hugo. There was bound to be at least one black marketeer from whom I could buy more, if I ever returned. I put that problem out of my mind.

As Jack packed the provisions – to double up as bribes if need be – in the boot, I ran upstairs. All it took was a few necessities in my mother's old carpetbag. I changed into a sturdy pair of boots and the most hardwearing skirt and jacket I possessed. From the heavy iron safe in Hugo's office I took money, and every precious earring and necklace I could find, which I stashed half in the carpetbag and half in a small bag I could hang around my neck hidden deep inside my clothes. I hesitated over my mother's pearls, the only thing I had that I remembered her wearing. I put them on, under my blouse.

My hand hesitated over the last item in the safe. The pistol. Next to it lay a packet of bullets. I shoved them inside the carpetbag and ran downstairs to write a note for Cook telling her not to worry and I would be back in a few days.

Jack was placing bottles of a spirit – I wouldn't exactly have called it vodka except for purposes of bribery – we had made with the glut of potatoes last year, when I reached the Rover. I placed my bag on the back seat next to his haversack and all the spare blankets I could find.

When I straightened, Jack was next to me. 'You don't have to go,' he said. 'Let me go and find Mouse. You have your life here.'

I shook my head. 'I'm not afraid. Well, I am, but it doesn't matter. I'm tired of feeling useless. You don't have to go, though. I'm quite capable of doing this on my own, whatever you might think.'

'I never doubted you were,' came his wry reply. 'But when it comes to it, I find I can't quite bring myself to let you ride off in your shining armour to rescue the damsel in distress without some help.'

'Well, I have to confess I'm quite glad to have it.'

'We will find Mouse,' he said, firmly. 'If it's the last thing I do. We'll find her and bring her home.' I pushed the pistol out of sight beneath the passenger seat. 'Let's hope we never have to use that,' he said when he saw me. But there was no disguising the bleakness in his voice.

Part Three

Chapter Twenty-One

I took the wheel for the first part of the journey. It made sense. Here the roads were familiar to me, even in the dark. I would be only too glad to hand over to Jack once we arrived in France.

I drove carefully, dreading a collision or a puncture. Several times we were stopped by patrols of local men, who were suspicious we were spies, but thankfully they accepted my story that we were patriotic volunteers with supplies for our boys at the front.

We went first to Applebourne Hospital, where Alice was waiting for us with bandages and medicines for Nurse Spedding's field hospital.

'What are you planning to do when you get there?' she asked, as we fitted the supplies into every available corner.

'Find out where Mouse is. I'll ask and badger and bribe whoever I can. Nurse Spedding must know which Germans are holding Mouse. If we can find out where she is, we can persuade them to release her.'

'Elin, you can't just walk into an enemy camp and demand to speak to them!'

'Can't I?' A flutter of sheer terror appeared in my stomach. I squashed it. 'From the way Mouse described them, they're not monsters. It's obviously a mistake. They've nothing to lose by letting her go. And her family is rich and knows important people who might have influence. If we can make enough fuss, they'll decide it's easier to let me take her home. Even if I have to make her swear she'll never set foot in France again. At the very least we can try to find Edmund or Owen and make sure they know. They'll know what to do. All I can think is to be as much of a nuisance as possible.' It sounded weak to my own ears as I said it, but I felt this burning need to do something. Over there, *maybe* I could help. Here I certainly couldn't.

'But are you even sure they are in France?'

'No,' I admitted, 'but that's a chance I have to take.'

'Wait here.' Alice disappeared into a storeroom for a minute, returning with a bundle of clothing in her arms. 'Here, you might find this useful.' She handed me a nurse's uniform.

'I'm not a nurse!'

'You've tended ailments at Hiram and you've got common sense.' Her eyes were serious. 'It will give you neutrality, Elin, and a little more respect. It will also give you a reason for travelling around the countryside while there is a war raging. Soldiers on both sides, as well as the civilians, will be used to medical volunteers moving from place to place. The last thing you need is for either of you to be mistaken for a spy. It could be the best protection you can have. There's a doctor's uniform for Mr Treeve. You told me he's been a soldier,' she added as I began to protest. 'He'll know enough about wounds to do the basics, if you're ever challenged.' She coughed. 'And it will mark him out as a non-combatant. It will help to make sure he isn't arrested by our own side as a deserter.' She handed me a large envelope. 'There are papers in there that identify you both as volunteers from Applebourne taking out supplies and relieving volunteers. It's something we do regularly, and I'm the one they'll speak to if anyone should check. There's a letter in there to Nurse Spedding requesting her to do the same for when you return. Those should get you through without any questions, from either side. You are quite likely to come across Germans as well. Nurse Spedding is always telling me how the battlelines move from day to day, so it's impossible to tell who you are likely to have to deal with.'

'Thank you,' I whispered. 'You've thought of everything.'

'Come back,' she said, hugging me tight. 'I hope you find Mouse. But whatever you do, come back.'

'I promise.'

I stepped into the driving seat as Jack arrived at the passenger door.

* * *

We drove through the night in silence. Jack pulled his coat over him and leant against the window. I could soon tell by the regularity of his breathing that he was asleep. At first I was faintly irritated. I had so much excitement – and more than a little terror – running through my veins I felt I would never sleep again. But I remembered something Hugo had told me once, that a soldier learned to switch off and get rest in the most terrible places knowing that some kind of recovery of body and mind – however slight – might be the key to the next few hours' survival. My foolish pride threw itself out of the window. I didn't want attentiveness from my companion. I wanted survival. Already, a part of me had changed.

I drove on, concentrating all my attention on the darkened road. We passed through villages, eerie like shadow villages with their lights hidden. Occasionally a door opened as we passed, showing a silhouette of someone entering or leaving, and the warmth of distant light hidden deep within the house behind the blackout blinds. It was like a glimpse, a camera photograph, of entire lives caught in an instant. I was aware of heads that turned to watch our vehicle making its way through the night, containing its own lives being led in secret from everyone else in the world.

For all its conflict, it was a peaceful landscape. I knew then I was different from Jack. I didn't care what it took. I had no fine principles. I would fight with any weapon that came to hand to keep the clock towers chiming and the people in their houses, safely crouched around a meagre fire and the last morsel of light.

Why should the big and powerful who didn't care win? The smallest child in those houses had a life that was worth just as much as a head surrounded with diamonds.

At last Jack stirred. 'I'd better take over.'

'I'm not tired.'

'No, it's not that. Look, can you see the outline of the ships down there? We've arrived. I have a feeling it might be better if I appear to be in charge, for now at least. If we are going to get a passage tonight, or at all, we'll have to appear to be something they can understand. Alice was quite right: being a volunteer doctor and nurse on their way to deliver supplies to the front line will stop us from being shot as spies if we are questioned, and give us the best cover story for getting through with our supplies. Every lie is more convincing if it is at least partly the truth.'

I glanced at him. I'd not prayed since I was a little girl, but I was praying now. Praying for myself and for Mouse. I didn't even care if I still believed in a deity to help us. I just prayed.

I brought the Rover to a halt next to a field. While Jack pulled on his doctor's coat I slipped behind the hedge and changed into my nurse's uniform, much to the astonishment of a flock of sheep all settled down for the night, who to the last lamb paused in their chewing to observe my every move.

'Are you a good sailor?' Jack said, as I pushed my discarded skirt under the packages in the back and took my place in the passenger seat.

'I think so. I was brought up by the sea.'

'Good. It's calm here, but there's a swell on the water. It could be rough out there in the English Channel. I suppose at least that means there are less likely to be Zeppelins or Gothas waiting to firebomb us.'

That seemed the smallest mercy. Luck could come in the strangest fashions.

With Jack at the wheel, I did not follow his example and try to sleep. My stomach was too knotted. If we couldn't persuade a ship to take us, our mission was over before it had begun.

Several troop ships were embarking as we reached the dock. I stayed in the background and remained demure, leaning against the bonnet looking vaguely helpless, hiding my impatience as Jack negotiated and charmed his way onto the last boat, to much waving of hands and shaking of heads from the officers.

As the last group of men made their way on board, Jack sprinted back towards me. 'Hurry,' he hissed. 'They've found room for us. Let's get on there before they can change their minds.' I swung myself into the passenger seat and we set off in the wake of a lorry and what Jack described as some kind of large field gun. 'Last chance to turn back,' he said, as we approached the ramp. 'We can still turn out of line and disappear into the night and no one will ever know.'

'You can, but hand over the wheel first.'

'Yes, I didn't think you would.'

I heard excitement and suppressed fear in his voice.

'Nervous?'

'Terrified,' I replied.

'So you should be. There's no point in being brave from now on. Forget what anyone ever told you about heroes. Once we reach the other side, it's fear that will keep you alive.'

We were the last vehicle on the ship. As the bows closed behind us, I struggled to the front of the men on the deck. Seeing my nurse's uniform in the dark and hearing a woman's voice, they let us through to the railing. We were already moving. The edge of the harbour wall loomed up, as we passed out into open sea. A wind swept through, buffeting my coat and painting my lips with salt. I could feel the sway, and see the crash of white as spray broke against the bow.

'There's the white cliffs,' said one of the soldiers in the crowd. He sounded young, scarcely old enough to be out of school.

'Shining in the dark,' said Jack, standing behind me.

'Long time before we see those again, eh, Doc?' came another voice. Older. With a cockney sharpness.

'Hopefully not,' said Jack.

The boy – for he was no more than a boy – standing next to me was shaking. He laughed and bantered with the rest of them, but I could feel his body trembling uncontrollably next to mine. I suppressed a shudder, remembering the first volunteers I'd seen marching so eagerly to join up, before the stories and the wounded and the endless lists of those dead or missing appeared.

In the darkness, I sought the gleam of Jack's eyes in the shadow of his face. 'We'll be seeing the white cliffs again before long, Nurse,' he said, moving slightly closer, so his shoulder rested reassuringly against mine. I could not say it, not in front of the men, but I was glad he was there. I dreaded the thought of having to face this on my own.

As we sailed further into the English Channel the men on deck fell silent. I could feel the weight of thoughts around me as the salt wind blew in our faces and we watched the white cliffs fade away, the long white trail of our wake leading tantalisingly back towards them, like a ribbon we all prayed would never be severed, but could pull us back again to its reassuring safety.

I thought of Mouse, and the young men around me. Of all of those, the soldiers, the doctors and the nurses, who had made this journey. And all those who had passed this way and would never see their homes again.

Chapter Twenty-Two

OCTOBER, 1917

Once we left the boat, the nightmare began.

I could never have made the journey alone. It took two of us with our full attention on the road to make any progress at all. Jack drove while I looked out for potholes. Craters. Great holes filled with mud. As dawn broke, we found ourselves in a blasted landscape. We passed by ruined and abandoned villages in a great desert of mud, with scarcely a tree standing and that a skeleton, as if poisoned by the very air we breathed.

Wrecked vehicles of all kinds lay abandoned by the sides of the roads. Some were military, others the poor remains of carts and cars whose owners had tried to flee. I soon learnt to concentrate on the road ahead and not to look one way or the other. There were some things I did not wish to see. What I saw before my mind closed down for its own survival's sake will haunt me forever.

Jack drove unerringly, despite the lack of signs and the altered landscape. He hesitated at a couple of turnings but kept going. At last a chateau stood on a small hill above us, with the ruins of a small village, its church tower still standing, scattered beneath. A little way from the village stood an ancient farmhouse, its red-tiled roof painted with a cross, declaring it to be a hospital.

Jack pulled up into a large paved courtyard. A girl of about eight, with tousled black hair and a grubby face, looked up from the pump where she was filling a bucket with water. She watched us open-mouthed, neither joyful or afraid, but transfixed as if we had come from the moon.

'I've come to speak to Nurse Spedding,' I said. 'Do you know if she is here?' She looked blank. '*Madame* Spedding?'

'*Madame* Spedding?'

'*Oui. Madame Spedding. Elle est ici?*' said Jack. The girl smiled at our attempts at French and nodded. She ran like a rabbit over the cobbles on bare, dusty feet, then disappeared through a window with no glass, its shutter crudely patched.

'Looks as if they had a narrow miss at some point,' said Jack. He looked around uneasily. 'I thought this was supposed to be several miles from the front line?'

The woman who opened the door was wary. She was tall, in a nurse's uniform, and appeared to be in her early forties, with high cheekbones and piercing green eyes. She stepped beneath the lintel, her body barricading any view within. The little girl peered from behind her skirts.

'Nurse Spedding?' I said.

'We have had no notification of a new nurse,' she said, frowning. Her voice sounded more suited to handing out prizes at a village fête than standing in a bleak field on the edges of a battle. Her eyes focussed beyond me and her frown deepened. 'Or a doctor.'

'Oh, we're not,' I said. Her eyebrows rose. She looked about to shut the door. 'I mean, we're dressed like this to make it easier to get through.'

'Then I suggest a better solution would be for you not to have come at all.' She fixed her eyes on Jack. 'And what are you doing out of uniform if you are not a doctor, young man?'

'We've brought supplies,' he replied. 'From England.'

'Bandages, medicines and food,' I added.

'Morphine?'

'Some,' Jack said. 'As much as Applebourne Hospital could spare.'

'Applebourne.' Her eyes travelled from Jack to me and back again. 'Never heard of the place.' But she didn't slam the door.

'Then my cousin Alice must have been mistaken,' I said.

Her hand relaxed from the door. 'You are Alice's cousin?'

'Yes. Elin Helstone from Hiram Hall.' I reached into my pocket and brought out the papers Alice had given me as we left. 'If you are Nurse Spedding, then there is a letter in here addressed to you.'

'You'd better come in, Mrs Helstone,' said the nurse, taking the note. 'And...' She looked at Jack and hesitated.

'Mr Treeve is a friend who has come to help.' Her look was severe. 'I mean, to help find Mouse. Alice told us she'd been arrested. You haven't heard anything more, have you? Do you know if she's all right?'

'I'm afraid I don't.'

'I think we should unload the automobile,' said Jack.

Nurse Spedding nodded. 'You've been lucky. There's been a lull in the fighting over the past few days. It's all come too close for comfort. We're thinking we might have to move the hospital elsewhere if it comes any closer. Especially after that last mortar hit.' She glanced towards Jack as if weighing him up. Then she nodded. 'I'll get some of the more able men to help you. The supplies will be safe in the basement. Lisette...' She turned to the little girl speaking rapidly to her in French. Lisette nodded and vanished inside.

'Have you heard anything at all about Mouse?' I asked, once Lisette had vanished out of earshot. 'She once said her cousin was stationed near here. I was hoping to find him to let him know. But I know he might be anywhere. Or even back in England.'

Nurse Spedding lit a cigarette, sucking in the smoke deeply. 'Captain Northholme came a few days ago.'

Relief flooded through me. Owen knew about Mouse. He would do anything he could to release her. I began to feel slightly foolish. My mission had been worthless, after all. Nurse Spedding watched the smoke of her breath curl outwards into the air. 'We sent a message to him as soon as we knew what had happened. I didn't think it had got through, but he managed to get permission and drove over here almost straight away. But it was already too late, of course.'

I stared at her in horror. 'Too late? You mean she's dead?'

'Good Heavens, no. At least, I hope not. Didn't you know she escaped? I sent a letter to Alice as soon as the Captain told me. He'd managed to speak to one of the German officers holding her. I assumed Alice had received it with a great deal more speed than usual, and that was why you were here.'

'No. I hadn't heard. It must have arrived after we left. So is Mouse here?'

Nurse Spedding shook her head. 'I'm afraid I don't know where she is. No one does. And that's the truth. She just vanished. She won't come back here. She knows German soldiers will be looking for her and she'd be re-arrested or shot – as we would be too – if they find her here. So she won't come back. I wish she would. Or at least get word to me. I heard she was wounded in her escape. Heaven knows what state she is in now. At least if I knew where she was, I could patch her up and let her cousin arrange for her to get out of here and back to England.' She frowned intently at me. 'She can never come back to the fighting. You understand that, don't you? This new German Colonel clearly wants to make an example of her. And frighten us into the bargain. They say the war won't last much longer and that the allies are prevailing now America has joined them. But then they've been saying that since war was declared. I'm not sure I believe anything I'm told anymore.'

'And Captain Northholme?'

'His men left yesterday for England, on leave at last. He accompanied them to Calais, but he said he'd be coming back to search for Mouse. He's promised to help find us a safer place for the field hospital at the same time. Although I'll be loath to leave this building. It's the best we've had – Mouse's garden is thriving. Heaven knows how she does it. Our patients haven't been so well fed anywhere else. I never thought anything would survive in this soil. But if it comes to it, we'll just have to take what we can and pray we can start again.'

A young nurse came hurrying towards us. Nurse Spedding drew deep on her cigarette, carefully extinguished the rest and placed it in a little box. 'I'm sorry, I have to go. You are welcome to stay with us. And we'll do everything we can to help. The world is going to need determined women like Mouse once this war is over. And, to tell you the truth, we've all grown very fond of her.' Nurse Spedding turned and followed the nurse back inside.

'Anything?' said Jack, returning with packages of bandages.

I told him everything Nurse Spedding had told me. 'And you?'

'Nothing. No one seems to know anything.'

'I wish Owen was here. He might be able to pull strings.'

'Then let's hope he's back before long.'

'Maybe this was a wild goose chase.'

'Nonsense. We're here and we'll find her, if anybody can. Come on, I need a hand unpacking these.'

At least the things we had brought were useful. The nurses fell on the medicines and the food as if they were caviar and diamonds.

Mist came down that evening, accompanied by a strange, eerie silence.

'Looks like they're preparing for a new offensive,' said Nurse Spedding, as we stood in the open door as night fell.

'I can imagine Mouse here.'

'Yes. She was in her element. I miss her. She's a good worker. Come on in,' she called to Lisette, who appeared through the mist to join us.

I watched the child skip over the flagstones and into the hospital 'Does Lisette live here, then?'

'Yes. For the past six months or so. She has nowhere else to go. Mouse found her in the ruins of Lavanc, the village you must have seen on your way here. It was caught by mortar fire and completely destroyed. There were still some villagers living there. Mouse went to see if she could help any survivors. She found Lisette in the ruins of a basement. All I can get out of her is that her mother died several months ago and her father was killed in the war. She was living with her grandparents. They were both killed in the cellar where she was found. It's a miracle the poor child is alive at all.' She ushered us both inside. 'Come on, I don't like standing still for too long. You can never tell where a sniper might be hiding, and they are not all respecters of our calling. They forget that the day may well come when they might need our skills themselves.'

* * *

The next morning there was still no sign of conflict. Nurse Spedding, however, was growing increasingly uneasy. 'The warning from the army was as clear as they could make it. It's bound to start soon.'

For days we searched ruined barns and farmhouses surrounding the field hospital, along with the remains of hamlets almost completely deserted and engulfed in mud. As we tried to help soldiers struggling through the squelching ground with supplies or stretchers containing the sick or wounded, or found the last remaining villagers, haggard and despairing, with nowhere to go, we pleaded for any scrap of information they might have. But there was no sign of Mouse. I was persuaded not to go further afield until Owen arrived back. I assisted in the tiny and very basic kitchen, while Jack helped ferrying the men. Without Mouse, they were short of volunteers to drive the ambulance, and all the real doctors were needed.

'I've offered to go and pick up some of the wounded,' said Jack one afternoon. 'Since it seems we can't do much until we have more news, it feels like the least I can do.'

I nodded. A knot of anxiety caught my belly. There was an unmistakeable air of anticipation, of waiting for something. Whether it meant an offensive was imminent or not, I had no idea.

After Jack had left in the ambulance, I carried on cooking in the empty kitchen. At least attempting to create something edible from unpromising ingredients was a task I could tackle, and it freed up the others to tend to the wounded. As the afternoon drew on I was joined by Lisette, a scraggy puppy of indeterminate parentage in tow; both creeping into the warmth of the kitchen as if they didn't want to be noticed. I politely ignored them for a while.

'Here.' I handed her the end of a loaf I had baked from the Hiram flour. She took it eagerly, nodding her thanks. She fed a few mouthfuls to the puppy, who was painfully scrawny, and took a small portion for herself. Out of the corner of my eye, I saw her put the rest in her pocket. She didn't try to hide the fact. She met my eyes as she placed it there. The world went very still.

'I'm Mouse's friend,' I said carefully, as I turned back to cleaning carrots. 'I've come to find her. To make her safe. To take her back to England. Home.'

'England,' repeated Lisette.

I nodded. '*Angleterre.*' How I wished my French was better. '*Ami,*' I said, pointing to myself. 'Like family. *Famille?*'

'*Famille?*' She looked puzzled.

'*Grande ami. Comme famille. Comme soeur,*' I explained, wincing. She was bending down over the puppy, but I saw her cheeks creasing. A stifled giggle emerged.

I held out the rest of the small loaf. 'Mouse. *Mademoiselle.* Do you know where she is? Can we take her some food? *Du pain? Pour Mademoiselle?*'

Lisette watched me warily. She glanced round as if listeners might be at every corner. From the far distance came a gigantic roar. It shook the earth, setting the pans on the stove rattling. She jumped and pressed her hands over her ears. I caught her. She was trembling.

'What is that? The guns?' I had no idea what a gun was in French. '*Soldat*?'

'Yes, soldiers. Big guns.'

'*Ça commence*? The fighting. *La bataille, elle commence*?'

She nodded. 'Yes. It begins. Always so much noise.'

As if to make her point, the field guns roared out once more. Lisette began to shake violently.

'Come on,' I said, grasping her hand and leading her down to the cellar where Jack and I had earlier taken the precious supplies. 'We'll be safe in here.'

The wounded men who were able to move under their own steam were already there arranging mattresses on the floor. I ran to help the nurses carry those who were bedridden. For several hours we crouched there as the ground shook and explosions erupted, sending rivulets of dust and mortar slithering down the bare walls of the cellar. Every bone in my body was shaken. I braced myself against each tremor in the walls and the ground beneath my feet. My stomach was a hard knot and my legs were trembling. The very noise seemed to be blasting me apart.

'How long will this last?' I asked a young nurse, crouched by the side of a man whose face was almost completely swathed in bandages.

'It varies,' she replied. 'It depends if it's a skirmish or a full-scale assault to try and capture more ground.' She glanced up towards the room above where Nurse Spedding had remained with a patient too close to death to be moved. 'At least they don't seem to be firing this way. For now, at least.'

I stared at her, horrified. If this was the result of guns aimed away from us, Heaven help us if they should be turned in this direction. I couldn't see how anyone could survive, even without a direct hit.

The shells did not reach us, but the firing went on throughout the night. I thought of Jack, Mouse, Owen somewhere out there, perhaps holed up unable to move. Perhaps dead. And I knew that we were too late. After everything, we were too late. If a full-scale battle was erupting around us, the last thing on anyone's mind would be the fate of one fugitive Englishwoman.

As dawn came, the firing ceased. A deadly hush fell over the hospital and the valley. Not one of us had slept, but at the ceasing of immediate danger, the hospital rushed into action. Everything that could be was moved down into the cellar in a practiced manner – clearly this had been done many times before. I lit the stove and heated the soup, which we all ate in silence, before work resumed once more.

Under Nurse Spedding's instructions, I filled every vessel I could find with water in case it became too dangerous to reach the pump. Finally I went out to fill the large kettle to provide some hot water while I could. As I had done each time before, I peered along the road while I pumped water in case I saw an ambulance making its way towards us. As before, nothing moved. An eerie stillness reigned. Even the birds were silent. From the little copse behind the house I could hear the sound of spades breaking through the earth. I could have been back at Hiram, except that this was the digging of a grave for the man who had died last night, with Nurse Spedding holding his hand to the very last.

I shut my eyes, willing myself back to the lavender beds of the kitchen garden, with laughter all around me and the crash of the sea in the distance. What if I never saw Hiram again?

I felt a light touch on my hand. '*Madame.*' It was Lisette. 'Madame 'elstone?'

I smiled down into the child's anxious face. 'It's all right, I'm coming now.'

Lisette shook her head, her hand preventing me from moving. '*Mademoiselle*,' she whispered slowly. 'Mouse. *Blessé*. Hurt.'

'Yes. I know.' I did my best to sound cheerful. 'We'll find her and take her away. Make her better.'

She struggled to find the words. 'If they find, they kill her.' There was something about the intentness of her face.

'That's why we came to get her away.'

She shook her head. I hadn't understood. 'And here. *Tout le monde.*' She waved around the building.

'You mean that if they find her here they will kill everyone?' She nodded. '*Oui, oui.*'

I crouched down until I was at her level. 'I understand that, Lisette. I know that when we find her we can never bring her here. We came to take her away. To England. In the automobile.' Listette's brow creased. I mimed turning the wheel as I made the noise of the engine. 'Back to England. *Angleterre. Maintenant. Aujour'dui.*'

Slowly, she nodded. She pointed to the automobile, imitating my mime. 'Now,' she said, 'before the battle. Or she die.'

My heart had begun to race. So she did know something. I pointed to the Rover. 'We should take that now to fetch Mouse?'

Lisette nodded. I glanced back towards the house. But I did not dare call out to let them know where we were going in case Lisette took fright and I lost my only chance to find Mouse. I took a piece of paper to write a note, but I could see Lisette backing away.

So instead I hastily returned to the kitchen and put the kettle to boil. I grabbed a hunk of bread and a piece of Port Helen cheese, wrapping them up in a cloth. Lisette grabbed the puppy. I started to protest that Jojo would be far safer here, but there was a stubborn look on her face and every word of English miraculously eluded her. I took a deep breath. If Lisette had been planning to take the bread she had pocketed yesterday to Mouse, then the hiding place could not be far. It was within walking distance. Her insistence on the Rover must be because she knew Mouse could not walk that short distance. If she was still alive at all. Fear clenched my stomach.

But there was no time to lose. Heaven knows when the bombardment might begin again, and a battle start in earnest. I bundled Lisette and the puppy into the seat beside me, and we made our way carefully out through the gates and back onto the road towards the village.

I'm certain that by foot the journey would not have taken us more than ten minutes, but by road it was slow and tortuous as I wove my way between potholes and abandoned vehicles.

After a while, ruined buildings rose up ahead. A quick glance at Lisette's face told me that this was Lavanc. She must know it like the back of her hand. She directed me down the main street, lined on either side by broken walls and the smashed remains of shop fronts, awnings shredded, shutters lying on the ground amidst broken glass and blackened remains of timbers.

'*L'église*,' said Lisette, pointing ahead.

'The church.' The tower I had glimpsed from the road when Jack and I had arrived appeared in front of us. Holes gaped in one side, but it was mostly intact. 'Mouse is in the church?'

Lisette nodded. As she did so, the silence was broken. I pulled the Rover to one side as the roar of the guns began. This time closer than last night. A mortar exploded just beyond the outskirts of the village, making us both gasp.

There was no time to lose. I grabbed the bag of food and bandages, lifted Lisette and her wriggling burden down out of the car, and followed her up a short flight of steps and into the church.

Chapter Twenty-Three

OCTOBER, 1917

The church was deserted. While the tower was almost intact, in the main body of the building the roof had been blown in and timbers lay crisscrossed over the aisle.

Lisette moved without hesitation, picking her way between the timbers, until we reached a side chapel, which miraculously seemed almost intact. Even the stained glass window had remained unbroken, sending a glow of blues and reds over the ruins.

Behind the little altar, something stirred. Lisette called out in a whisper and pointed. I followed her, and there, hidden away in a bed of straw was a pale and drawn face I would know anywhere.

'Mouse,' I murmured in relief, sinking down beside her.

'Elin,' she replied, opening her eyes. She seemed unsurprised to see me, as if we had just come from a swim in Hiram Bay. Fear clutched at me. Not the fear of never finding her this time, but the fear of losing her now she was found. The fear that we were, after all, too late.

Mouse attempted to pull herself upright, but fell back, her breath coming through her teeth in a hiss. Beneath the rough blanket that surrounded her, I could make out her arm crudely bandaged.

Another mortar fell, closer this time. I heard the crumble of stones as a building fell. 'Can you walk?' I said. Mouse opened her eyes again. They glittered feverishly. Her clothes felt damp, and there was the sour smell of fever sweat. I pressed a small bottle of water to her lips. She shook her head, turning away.

'It's clean. It's from Hiram,' I said, wishing I'd brought the brandy instead.

'Hiram,' whispered Mouse. Her voice was hoarse, but she drank the water, which seemed to bring her to her senses a little. She grabbed my arm. 'Elin! Elin, what on earth are you doing here? Don't you know it's dangerous?'

Behind us, the earth shook. 'I have an idea,' I replied. 'Come on, we need to get you out of here.' She frowned and shook her head. 'It's all right, I'm not taking you anywhere where you can put people in danger. I'm putting you in Hugo's Rover, and we're taking you straight back to Calais. I'm taking you home.'

She was very weak, but between us Lisette and I managed to get her onto her feet. I grasped her good side and half supported, half carried her between the fallen timbers and masonry. I did not dare stop to inspect the extent of her wound. She had survived this far without bleeding to death or succumbing to infection, I just hoped she could survive a little longer.

As we reached the door of the church, I could feel that Mouse could not go a step further. I settled her down on the steps, pulling the blanket around her. Her eyes were closed again, this time with a crease furrowing between her brows. She was slipping in and out of consciousness. In the daylight, her face was thin and drawn, pale as if it had not seen the light for months, her cheekbones sharp beneath the skin, her collarbone jutting from the neck of her blouse. I pulled the blanket up close, covering as much of her as I could.

'Stay here,' I said to Lisette. I pointed to the automobile and gestured bringing it from its hiding place to the steps of the church. Lisette nodded, buttoning the puppy into the bodice of her dress, ready for action.

I worked my way around the side of the church, staying in the shadow of the buildings for as long as I dared. The bombardment seemed to have stopped. I took a deep breath and stepped out into the middle of the street. I had almost reached the Rover when a huge explosion shook the ground, knocking me off my feet.

Instinctively, I glanced behind me as I scrambled to my feet. The church tower was still standing. I could make out Mouse crouched on the steps, with Lisette beside her. But Lisette was no longer sitting. She was standing up. I could see her lips move and see the wave of her arm. A movement caught my eye. I jumped back, just in time, as the side of the street next to me folded in on itself, an avalanche of brick and roof tiles landing next to the Rover. A half burnt beam leant over, then slammed onto the bonnet, flattening it with a sickening crunch of metal, one end smashing through the windscreen.

The beam was huge. Try as I might, it would not budge. A mortar crashed further away, followed by the roar of an engine – or maybe many engines – coming closer. I pushed with all my might. Desperation gave me a strength I didn't know I had. The beam began to move. Slowly but surely, it moved across the bonnet, screeching loudly as it inched across the metal. The bonnet was almost completely crushed. But at least if I could get it free of the debris we might stand a chance.

Out of the corner of my eye, there came a glint of metal as a vehicle emerged from the main street, making its way towards us. A few minutes and they would see us. We would all be lost. I pushed. The beam moved a little more, and then with an almighty squeal slid to the ground. In front of the bonnet. I made for the driver's side as the vehicle pulled up directly behind me, blocking me in. It sounded as if there was only one. I reached beneath the passenger seat and pulled out the pistol.

'Elin!'

I paused, pistol in my hand. I must be dreaming. Next to me stood an old-fashioned Ford, that must once have graced the driveway of a great house but whose back section had been covered in canvas to form a miniature ambulance. 'Owen,' I breathed as his familiar figure swung down from the driver's side.

I was caught up into his arms. 'Owen. Thank God it's you. How did you find us?'

'Treeve told me you were at the field hospital and your mad idea of finding Mouse.' His arms tightened. 'I couldn't believe you could be so reckless.'

'You've seen Jack?' Despite a mortar falling in the next street I could have jumped for joy. 'He's alive?'

'He was the last time I saw him. Heading back to Nurse Spedding with an ambulance of patients. I came ahead. A nurse saw you and the young French girl heading this way. I followed the tracks. Didn't take much to work out where you were going. This is the only destination. Elin, there's an entire German division heading this way. We only have a few minutes.'

'Mouse is here. I found her.' I motioned to the church step.

'Thank Heaven.' He released me, pulling the door of the Rover open. 'We need to get you out of here. The army could only spare this old thing. Yours will be faster, if it still goes.' He tried the engine. Nothing. 'Obviously not.' He jumped out again. 'Come on.'

'But we can't just leave it.'

'With an entire German army advancing and about to take over this stretch of countryside, we can.'

'But that's how we were going to get Mouse home.'

'We'll just have to work out something else. Elin, there's no time to unpack,' he exclaimed, as I pulled free and reached for the boot.

I pulled out the cans of spare petrol. 'There is for this.'

'Sorry. I should have thought. Best put them where we can get them out easily if we are hit.' I pushed the cans inside the canvas at the back and ran the short distance to Mouse and Lisette, while Owen drove to the base of the church steps. He left the engine running as he followed me, scooping up Mouse in his arms. I held Lisette's hand fearful that she might run back into the church at the sight of a stranger, but she watched with large eyes, as he motioned her to follow. As we reached the Ford, he placed Mouse in the back, reaching for Lisette.

'No animals,' he said, frowning at the small nose peering at him.

'If Jojo doesn't go, Lisette won't either, and she was the one who saved Mouse's life,' I replied, lifting them both next to Mouse. I flung in my shoulder bag and crawled in after them.

We were saved from any further argument by the crash of a mortar, even closer this time. I heard Owen run towards the driver's seat. We swerved backwards, then moved forwards, the canvas around me swaying as we made a circle of the little square and set off down the main street once more, back towards the field hospital.

If I'd thought the journey to the village was frightening enough, this was a hundred times worse, unable to do anything to help myself, trapped in the closed darkness, thrown this way and that. After a while, my eyes adjusted. In the faint light creeping in through tears in the canvas I could make out that the division between the back of the makeshift ambulance and the wooden driver's cab had been torn away, and was now only covered by an old blanket. A quick tug and the blanket collapsed, allowing in more light and a glimpse of Owen, peering through the hole in his shattered windscreen.

As Owen speeded up, I concentrated on steadying Mouse and Lisette as best I could. Lisette clung to me. The snuffling of her little dog reached my ear with the warm lick of a tongue. Mouse, perhaps thankfully, was beyond knowing where she was. I could feel her burning flesh and hear her low muttering as the delirium took hold.

'We'll have to go past the farmhouse,' called Owen. 'They were starting to move the patients out as I left. I warned them this advance was going to take place. They were directly in the line of fire.'

'Where have they gone?'

'The abandoned chateau should be far enough, at least for now. They should be out of range there. You'll be safe there for tonight.' I began to protest. 'Don't worry, the last thing on anyone's mind now will be an escaped prisoner. But we'll need to get Mouse out of here as quickly as possible. The front line shifts so much round here, it's hard to know where it will end up. If Treeve manages not to wreck that ambulance we might be able to get you to Calais.' He swerved violently. 'Heaven knows why you risked your life like this.'

'To find Mouse. Just as you are doing.'

'You were the one who was supposed to live, Elin,' he muttered. 'Not go throwing your life away on some quixotic mission.' He concentrated on the road. 'How is Mouse doing?' he asked at last. I could hear him trying to sound as if it were merely a cold he was asking after.

'She has a fever. The wound must be infected.'

Owen swore under his breath. I could feel us bumping faster over the ruts and rubble of the road.

At last he slowed. 'Well, at least the farmhouse is still standing. We'd better see if there's anyone else needs moving out. It won't take a minute.' I felt him turn, the tires rattling more than ever as he followed the short drive. I heard a mortar fall at a short distance. Owen swore again, urging the vehicle towards the shelter of the courtyard.

The next minute, a great burst of lightning lit up around us. A violent explosion rocked the Ford. It swerved, then came to a halt.

'Owen?'

Through rising smoke I could make out his figure slumped over the driving wheel. He made no sign of hearing me. A smell of burning rubber filled the air and through the shattered windscreen I could see flames licking around the bonnet. I pushed my way through the canvas at the back. 'Quickly,' I said to Lisette, who was braced in terror in one corner. 'Get out.' She did not move. I lifted her, sliding her past Mouse and onto the mud. I pushed the cans of petrol out with my feet. At least Lisette had the presence of mind to grab them and place them as far away as possible, as I pulled Mouse out and to the shelter of the walls, away from the petrol cans. 'Stay,' I commanded, placing my bag next to Lisette. *'Reste ici.'*

Flames were rising high from the bonnet as I reached the driver's cab. I pulled the door open. Owen's eyes were closed. His face and body were streaming with blood and the stench of singed flesh filled my nostrils. I tried but I could not move him. The flames licked higher, reaching towards the engine. In their light, I saw his foot was caught by the pedal. Swearing, I manoeuvred it free, then pulled Owen out of the seat onto the ground, dragging him as far away as I could. We'd scarcely gone a few paces when the engine exploded. Heat reached all around us as the flames shot into the sky.

'Wake up!' I screamed. We had to get further away or fire would be raining down on us. The burning vehicle would be a beacon to anyone looking for a target. I began tugging him along the ground, inch by painful inch, waiting for the explosion that would consume us all.

'You've done it. It's all right. I'll take him now.' I'd never been so glad to hear Jack's voice. 'Quickly. Get Mouse and the child into the ambulance. There's room with the men. We need to get out of here.'

I ran ahead, with Jack following, carrying Owen in his arms like a baby. Mouse seemed a little more conscious in the cool air. I supported her as she stumbled with me towards the ambulance waiting on the cobbled courtyard.

'Here you go, miss,' said one of the men, helping me lift Mouse inside with his one good arm. Inside, two other wounded men placed her on a rough mattress, pulling her blanket around her, settling Lisette and her wriggling burden next to her. The first man went to help Jack. They soon had Owen on a stretcher on the floor of the ambulance.

'Come with me in the front,' said Jack, as we finished lifting Owen inside. 'The men will look after them, and I need someone to watch the road.' I pulled myself up into the passenger seat and we were off.

Jack swerved around the still-burning Ford, bumping over the grass. He took a side road just past the farmhouse, heading through a forest. As we reached the trees, I looked back. A mortar crashed through the roof of the farmhouse just as the engine exploded, sending an enormous wall of flame that lit up the sky.

Chapter Twenty-Four

OCTOBER, 1917

We arrived at the chateau some twenty minutes later.

It was a scene of utter chaos. Outside the grand façade stood trucks hastily filled with all the supplies they could carry and ambulances bursting at the seams with wounded men. Nurse Spedding was directing operations with a remarkably unflustered air.

'Oh, my dear, we were so worried,' she said as I jumped down from the ambulance. 'I had a feeling Lisette might know where Mouse was. When Nurse Pearson saw you driving off, the only place I could think of was Lisette's village. I sent her cousin on to find you both.' A gun roared in the distance, making us both jump. 'Thank heaven for Captain Northholme,' she added. 'If it wasn't for his warning we might still be in the midst of that.' Her eyes met mine. 'And Mouse? Did you…?'

'Yes.' I nodded.

'Thank Heaven.'

'But we can't stay here and risk your lives as well as Mouse's. The Germans may still be looking for her. And I think she's been badly hurt.'

'At least she's safe now and we can look after her.'

'And the captain was hurt, too.' I did my best to keep my voice steady. 'I think badly.'

'We'll do our best for them both,' she said gently. Men came out with stretchers, taking both Mouse and Owen inside. 'You stay with Lisette,' said Nurse Spedding, as I tried to follow them. She ushered us into a large kitchen, where a fire was already roaring in the grate. 'You get some rest, that's the best way you can help your friends for now. We need to get you out of here as quickly as possible. At least one of you is going to need to be reasonably rested if you are going to make it back to Applebourne.'

'Come on,' I said to Lisette, who was pale and shivering. 'Let's find you something to eat.'

There was a kettle boiling on the fire and boxes of foodstuffs placed hastily on the table. Despite the fire, the kitchen was cold. The deep cold of walls that have not been lived in for some time. Around us boots clattered over flagstones and creaked on floorboards. Distant voices echoed, followed by the creak of shutters being opened to let in much needed light and air.

A kettle was boiling over the fire. I could not find the tea and coffee we had brought, but a mint bush grew just outside the kitchen door. A handful flung into hot water made a warming drink for us both.

This was something I could do. I worked my way methodically through the boxes on the table, sorting out tins, vegetables, fruits and dried foods to go on the shelves around the kitchen walls. In the second box I found some bread for Lisette – making sure that most of it went into her own stomach, despite the pleading brown eyes of little Jojo. Having satisfied myself that she had eaten, I left a second piece of bread to her own devices while I located a container of tea and made a fresh pot. My hands were shaking.

'How are they?' I asked, as Jack joined us. I pressed a warm cup of tea with several spoonfuls of sugar in it into Lisette's hands.

'As well as can be expected. Nurse Spedding says Mouse's arm doesn't appear to be too badly infected, all things considered. At least there's no sign of gangrene. You got to her just in time. They're working on getting her fever down.'

'Thank heaven.' Every part of me was rigid. 'And Owen?' I saw him hesitate. 'He's not—'

'No. Nothing like that. He'll be strong enough to make the journey back. He needs proper treatment, and quickly. There are bad burns to one side of his face and body, and his right arm is broken. They think he might have several broken ribs.'

I began to cry. I didn't mean to, but by the time Jack had finished I was sobbing quietly, turning my face away so that Lisette couldn't see. 'If I hadn't rushed off like that he wouldn't have followed me. This is all my fault.'

'Nonsense.' Jack grasped my hands, holding them tight. 'You must never think that, Elin. Ever. I went up to the top of the chateau just now. You can see right across the countryside from there. The shelling has been directly on Lavanc. You can see the church has had a direct hit. The tower is flattened. If you hadn't got Mouse out when you did, she would have been killed. Owen wasn't far behind you, even if you had never gone at all. If you hadn't found Mouse so quickly, he could have been there still looking when the first shell fell.'

'He saved us,' I said, sniffling. 'I'd never have got that Rover started.'

'And you risked your own life dragging him out of a burning

vehicle. I'd say you were pretty much equal, when it came to saving.'

I smiled in watery fashion. 'I'd like to go and see them.'

'Of course. Drink your tea first, though. Mouse was asleep when I left, and they were still attending to Captain Northholme.' He took the dainty cup I handed to him filled with tea. 'They are both in the best hands, Elin. And we need to work out what to do next.'

'Yes, I know.' I deliberately kept my voice light. I found a blanket for Lisette and Jojo. Two small stomachs filled, they were both curled up together next to the fire, eyes drifting, heads nodding, jerking as they tried to keep awake. I wrapped the blanket around them, and they were both fast asleep in an instant.

Jack looked up from his tea as Nurse Spedding came into the kitchen. I poured another cup and handed it to her in silence. She looked tired and worn.

'Thank you, my dear.' We looked at each other. 'Well, this will do very well. There's a wine cellar that goes deep into the rock and a patch of ground beginning growing again. But we have to get Mouse away from here, and as quickly as possible. If the Germans were to find her here, I dread to think what might happen to our men.' Her eyes strayed to Lisette, who stirred, as if even in her sleep she could catch the anxiety in the nurse's voice. 'To all of us.'

'And now because of me destroying the Rover, we can't,' I said.

'It was hardly your fault,' said Jack.

'Vehicles are destroyed all the time,' added Nurse Spedding. She was watching both of us. 'There is a solution. If you are both willing to take it.'

'Anything,' I said.

'At the next lull in the fighting, you take the older ambulance with the men who need to be evacuated back home – those who are most likely to survive the journey, that is. Along with Mouse and Captain Northholme.'

'Yes,' I said quickly, before Jack could speak.

'I'll give you a letter from me to the head of the hospital as Alice suggested. It's a regular occurrence. So if you do get stopped, either by our side or by the Germans, that should get you through without too many questions.'

'And if not?' said Jack.

Nurse Spedding sighed. 'We will have to ask for volunteers amongst the men. It's not fair to send them into that much danger without telling them. If you are stopped and searched, or if the Germans have any suspicion you have Mouse with you, they could well shoot the lot of you.'

'I understand,' I said. 'And I'd rather take that risk than wait here.'

'It's their best chance of survival. Both Mouse and Captain Northholme,' said Jack, as if that settled the question.

'Yes,' said Nurse Spedding. She hesitated again. 'I've thought long and hard about this. There is no easy answer.' The three of us turned to watch Lisette, her head tucked under the blanket. 'This is no place for a child. She has seen too much already. Heaven knows how much worse it will get. And if anything should happen to me, or to the rest of us, she is the most vulnerable of all. I have seen what happens to children who are left to fend for themselves in a war zone.'

'Doesn't she have any family?' said Jack.

Nurse Spedding shook her head. 'Not as far as we can tell. We have tried our very best to find out. I had hoped she might have relatives on the coast, or somewhere in the countryside. But those who could had already left the village before the bombardment started. There was some talk of an aunt in Paris, but how on earth we would track her down in all this chaos, I don't know. Even if we could find a way to get to Paris in the

first place. And we don't know if an aunt would be willing to
take in another mouth to feed, with things as they are. What
that child needs is a safe home until this war is over. And if no
family can be found…' She paused and gave a wry smile. 'My
children are all grown. I would be more than willing to adopt
her. If I ever get home, that is.'

I looked at Jack. 'Whatever we do, she has to take her chance
with everyone else.'

He nodded.

'It won't be easy.' Nurse Spedding's gaze was serious. 'You'll
have to get through the lines and make your way to the coast.
And I can't guarantee that you won't break down in that thing.'

'But we have to try,' I said. I looked pleadingly at Jack.
'Whatever the risks, we've at least got to try.'

Across the room, he slowly nodded.

* * *

We left at dawn. The guns had fallen silent as first light came. As
the patients were carried or helped into the back of the
ambulance I was glad to be moving at last. Mouse was growing
more feverish by the hour, while Owen was drifting in and out
of consciousness.

'I've done what I can,' said Nurse Spedding, as she
accompanied us out into the grand drive of the chateau. In the
early morning mist, the abandoned fountains looked eerie, the
cherubs' hands upraised as if expecting a rush of water to appear
with the sun. She handed Jack a small bag. 'There should be
enough morphine there to help them all.'

'Jack's not a doctor.'

'I've done enough first aid in my time. I can administer
morphine.' Nurse Spedding glanced towards the ambulance.
'Carols and Edwards are the weakest and the ones we could not

consult. I hope they make it back. Their injuries are too serious to be dealt with properly here. It really is their only chance.'

'We'll send you word as soon as we get them to the hospital in England,' I said.

She nodded and hugged me tight. 'Good luck. Good luck to you all.'

We set off down the driveway of the chateau, following the river towards the main road. There was a strange silence as we passed. Occasionally a gun carriage loomed out of the mist, pulled by horses. Now and then a truck supplying provisions rumbled past. I sat at the front next to Jack, to watch out for potholes and any sign that the bombardment might start again.

Corporal Smith, the least injured of the men, tended to the wounded in the back. Lisette lay next to Mouse, holding her hand. She had refused to be parted from Jojo, so the little dog was curled up next to her.

We travelled hour by hour through the pale excuse of daylight that came through the fog. As the light began to fade, we reached the turning to the coast.

'It looks as if we're past the worst of the battlefields,' said Jack, the tension relaxing in his voice. A few minutes later he swore under his breath.

'What is it?'

'Roadblock. It doesn't look like one of ours.'

'Let's see.' Corporal Smith peered out. 'Yes, that's the Hun all right. They must have retaken this bit. There's a road that goes further round to the coast.'

'Too late,' said Jack. 'They've seen us. If we take another way that will only make them suspicious.'

'We're an ambulance,' I said. 'They've got to let us through.'

'Let's hope so,' said Jack.

We were waved to a halt. As Jack wound down his window in obedience to the gesturing, a head peered through, followed by a rapid bark of German. Soldiers collected on my side of the ambulance too, preventing me from opening the door.

I glanced back. Jack was replying. He spoke without hesitation, but he didn't seem to be getting anywhere.

'They insist on searching the ambulance,' he said at last.

I swallowed hard. 'Why?'

'They won't say. Not hard to guess.' The *leutnant* on Jack's side of the ambulance was listening intently as if he understood every word.

'Well, since there's only wounded men there, who are gravely ill and could die at any moment, I hope they won't hold us up too long. Every minute counts.' I pushed the door open and swung down, doing my best to sound outraged not scared. The sergeant next to me grinned, but a couple of the men behind him looked uncomfortable.

I pulled the back doors open and climbed inside, followed by the lieutenant.

'Don't move them,' I pleaded as the officer approached Carols. He looked down at the man with a great gaping hole in his face, his breath coming in painful rasps. Next to him, Owen was hunched partially upright. The bandages no longer covered the burns on his arms and face, raw and angry in the German officer's flashlight. I didn't need Jack to translate. As the *leutnant* bent over them, Owen groaned loudly, 'For Heaven's sake!'

Terrified the man would be angry with Owen, I practically pushed the German away, my voice filled with all the fury I could muster. 'Can't you see the man's dying? Leave him in peace.' To my relief, he nodded, turning his attention to the next.

Our men barely moved. Even Smith managed to give off the air of a man defeated, too lost in his own suffering to be a threat to anyone. The searcher was losing interest. A question was shouted from the road. He shook his head as he replied. I held my breath. I could feel all those around me – those conscious enough to know what was happening – holding their breath too. From outside came another shout. One of impatience this time.

The *leutnant* obeyed the summons. He had one hand on the lintel, ready to step down, when the muffled figure next to the door moved slightly, muttering under her breath.

There was nothing for it but to bluff. 'One of my nurses,' I said, pulling the blanket down from Mouse's sweat-streaked face to show the uniform Nurse Spedding had found for her. 'She was caught by shrapnel while helping the wounded. Your shrapnel,' I added for good measure.

The soldier bent a little closer. 'She will live?' he said under his breath in English. It was such a curious question. I glanced at him. He was young. Pale and drawn, fair hair plastered with mud to his scalp. His grey eyes met mine.

'I hope so.'

He nodded. He gazed down into Mouse's unconscious face, as if to keep the image of it with him.

A second man crawled in.

'Influenza,' said the fair-haired *leutnant*. It was not a question, but I nodded instantly in reply. He spoke urgently, to his companion, who scuttled out as fast as he had come. Even my utter lack of German could catch the cursing as he half fell out of the door in his haste.

The fair-haired soldier gave the faintest of smiles. He pulled the blanket back over Mouse's uniform and gave a cursory glance over the ambulance, before jumping back out again, shaking his head.

I wriggled out after him, barely daring to move. No one stopped me as I closed the doors and began to walk around to the passenger side. Just as I reached it, there was a shout. I turned round slowly. The sergeant beckoned to me. He pointed to one of the men, who had slumped down against an overturned car at the side of the road. One shoulder, I could see, was roughly bandaged with what looked like the remains of a shirt, and dripping with blood. From his face he was in agony.

I froze. They were expecting me to treat him. This was no minor wound. The moment I tried they would be bound to realise I was not a nurse hardened to such sights. Perhaps this would prompt them to make a second, more thorough search of the ambulance, and its patients.

I took a deep breath. None of them looked like a doctor. So long as I moved with confidence, they would have no reason to question me.

Jack pulled out the medicine bag from behind his seat and thrust it into my arms as he jumped down. 'They've given us little enough, Nurse,' he said. 'But see if there's a bandage that will be suitable.' As I rummaged through the bag, he inspected the soldier's shoulder. He cleaned it as best he could before applying the bandage and giving the man a precious shot of morphine.

I caught the eye of a small, half-starved looked man who was limping hesitantly towards us. He looked so wretched I nodded and beckoned to him. His feet were in a terrible state, but cuts and blisters I could deal with. There had been enough amongst the gardeners at Hiram. I quickly found myself surrounded by a group showing me similar ailments. I did what I could, trying not to betray my anxiety to escape. Next to me, Jack was attempting the same.

I was in a growing agony of terror that another officer might take this opportunity to search the ambulance again, when we were relieved by an ambulance arriving from the opposite direction, a German one this time. It was flagged down to much heated discussion on both sides. Eventually, the man with the shattered shoulder was supported to the doors. The soldiers gathered around me appeared uncertain whether to stay in line, or try the new arrival. I caught Jack's eye. Maybe we should just walk away and make a run for it while the rest of the roadblock was occupied.

I was still hesitating, when the fair-haired *leutnant* reappeared, directing those still waiting to the German ambulance, waving us impatiently to leave, as if we had become an obstacle. I swung hastily into the passenger seat, stashing the bag at my feet, as Jack pulled himself up on the other side, his mouth set in a line. Within minutes, we were pulling slowly away from the roadblock. No one spoke a word as we travelled along the straight road beneath the broken remains of trees on either side. I braced myself, nails digging into my palm, waiting for a shouted command to stop followed by the strafe of bullets.

When we were safely out of sight, Jack steered the ambulance off the road behind the remains of a small farm. I wriggled my way into the back.

'You're an idiot,' I growled at Owen, starting to replace the bandages as best I could. 'You could have got yourself killed back there.'

'At least I'd have been in good company,' he replied. 'Besides,' he added, 'every risk has its reward.' His lips brushed mine with the barest touch, twisting my heart inside. I longed to hold him, but did not dare even return the kiss, his lips and cheek looked so raw. A ragged cheer went up around the ambulance, breaking the tension. A ripple of conversation started up. I briefly clasped Owen's good hand, then busied myself pulling away the cushion of blankets between him and the wall of the ambulance, where Lisette still lay unmoving, Jojo clutched in her arms.

A wave of nausea overcame me. I wriggled back, just making it out of the door in time to throw up the remains of my breakfast – meagre as it had been – into the nearest hedge.

There was no time to lose. I settled an ominously silent and passive Lisette next to Mouse and clambered into the passenger seat. In the light of the torch he was using to check the map, Jack's face was grey beneath the dirt and the stubble.

'That was far too close for comfort,' he murmured as he pulled back onto the road and we set off at a discretely sedate pace once more. 'We were lucky.'

'Yes,' I replied. Into my mind came the young soldier, looking down so intently into Mouse's face. I couldn't help but wonder just how deep our luck had run. I had a feeling that if we came up against another roadblock, we might not be so fortunate.

Chapter Twenty-Five

OCTOBER, 1917

Thankfully, there were no further roadblocks. Behind us the guns had begun to roar once more, shaking the ground beneath our wheels and sending the equipment rattling. I looked back in the darkness to a display like fireworks, which lit up the sky with a terrible beauty that will haunt me forever.

At last we found ourselves surrounded by English soldiers, who waved us on to join the queue of battered trucks and ambulances filled with wounded men waiting for the next boat to take them back to England. There was a hospital next to the port, but even in the darkness it was clear it was overflowing.

I glanced at Jack. In the passing lights from vehicles, his face was drawn with exhaustion. We had changed out of our uniforms as soon as we reached the first British soldiers and were now plain volunteers, from Applebourne, amongst the many who had risked their lives to bring the injured home. The dress Nurse Spedding had found for me (my own clothes having gone up with the Rover) was ill-fitting and worn but its wool provided a kind of warmth as I huddled beneath my coat. Behind us I could hear the injured men growing restless as the effects of the morphine wore off.

'I'll find a doctor,' I said, swinging myself stiffly out of the ambulance. 'It looks as if we could be here for hours.'

When I opened the back door, Corporal Smith was dispensing the last of the water as best he could. He paused over Carols, who lay unmoving, his breath shallow and laboured. Corporal Smith met my eyes and shook his head. I swallowed hard.

As I clambered inside, Mouse stirred. She looked at me, but without any recognition, before drifting back into unconsciousness again. Her face was damp with sweat, and when I touched her forehead it was burning. I smiled reassuringly at Lisette, who was huddled up next to Mouse, her eyes anxiously watching me.

'She'll be fine,' I said, pushing down the fear curling around my belly.

Owen had pulled himself upright and was leaning against the wall of the ambulance, a deep frown of pain between his brows. 'She's spoken a few times,' he said. 'But she doesn't seem to know where she is. Which is probably as well.' I followed his glance around the ambulance at the men attempting not to disturb each other and contain their own private agony. His gaze came to rest on Carols. 'He hasn't moved for hours,' he murmured.

'I'm going to fetch a nurse or a doctor if I can,' I said. 'A real one this time,' I added as I passed Corporal Smith.

He grunted. 'That was a close one. I thought we were all gonners then, miss. I never did like the sea, but I can't wait to be on it now.'

'You could always make a swim for it, Bob,' called one of the muffled forms swathed in bandages. 'You could do with a wash, I can tell you.' A ragged chuckle rippled through the ambulance.

'And miss the caviar and champagne on our cruise liner home?' replied Corporal Smith.

'A hot cup of tea will do me,' added another voice.

'Forget the tea,' retorted the first man. 'It's a pint I could do with. And then a bloody good—'

'Ladies present,' cut in Corporal Smith, to an eruption of coughing and 'ssssh'ing. I grinned and wriggled out of the ambulance into the darkness of the fish-smelling port.

I found the hospital easily by following the slow-moving line of ambulances. Even in the darkness, in the flicker of lamps and the occasional electric lightbulb, I could see it overflowed with wounded men. I passed injuries that a few days before I could not have imagined and would have sent me heaving. But survival had taught me to focus on the task in hand, pushing all other considerations to the edges of my mind, to haunt my dreams at night. Nurses and VADs rushed from one patient to another with barely a pause in between, calling doctors to the most desperate cases. For a long time I despaired of finding anyone, but eventually a young doctor took pity on me and followed me out to the ambulance.

He was quick but efficient, summing up each man's needs, dispensing morphine to the worst. He paused over Carols, examining him gently. 'Really, he shouldn't be moved in this condition,' he said. 'But, to be truthful, getting him back to a proper hospital in England is his only chance. I'll do what I can. But he is barely alive as it is.'

When he came to Mouse, he clucked with annoyance. 'This should have been properly seen to days before. What on earth were they doing leaving it so long?' It was a rhetorical question, born of frustration and the hopeless nature of his task. I didn't attempt to answer.

His eyes fell on Lisette. 'Good grief! What on earth is that girl doing here? This is no place for a child.' I saw Lisette shrink at the tone. She looked braced to run.

Before I could reach her, Owen put his hand gently on her arm. 'Leave her alone,' he muttered. 'Do you honestly think the nurses back there would have let her go if they had had any choice?'

'At least the kiddie's safe here,' put in Corporal Smith, limping back from a foraging expedition of his own with a container of milky tea and several loaves of bread. 'I've three daughters of my own at home not much older than this one. I'd want them out of that hell-hole she was living in, whatever the chances.'

'She'll have a safe home in England, I can guarantee that,' I put in. The doctor looked sceptical, but within minutes he was called away as another ambulance lumbered its way into the hospital grounds. I left Corporal Smith persuading Lisette to help him dish out the tea in any tin mugs we could find amongst the battered equipment, with hunks of bread for those able to eat, and took a tea to Jack, who was leaning against the driver's door watching the organised chaos before him with the glow of a cigarette and the pale swirl of smoke rising above his head.

He straightened, dropping the butt onto the ground, crushing it beneath his heel. 'Thanks.' We drank in silence, warming our hands on the tin mugs.

After a few minutes Corporal Smith appeared at the window behind us, winding it down until he could reach through. 'Bit more tea left,' he announced, pouring the dregs into our mugs. 'No sugar to be had, but there's this.' There was a clink of glass and the smell of brandy as he poured into my tea. He held out the bottle towards Jack, who shook his head.

The unfamiliar spirits ran through me like fire, catching the back of my throat.

'Steady,' said Jack, as I was convulsed by coughing. He caught my mug just in time to prevent it from spilling.

'I see why you don't like alcohol,' I said, catching my breath. I felt him tense slightly. 'Unless it's one of your principles,' I added hastily.

'Not at all.' He released the mug. 'It's not principle. It's necessity. I once liked a drink far too much.'

'Oh.' I glanced at the silhouette of his face.

'I was a touch wild when I returned from Africa, I'm afraid.' His voice was wry. 'The rumours about me are quite true.' He returned to his tea, pushing himself away from the door as if to join the men inside. He hesitated. 'War really is the world gone mad. There are very few who come out entirely unscathed. I mean in the mind, as well as the body. Drink was my way of shutting it all out. All the things I had seen.' His voice was distant. 'The things I had done. The unforgiveable things I had been a part of. And that includes the death of so many women and children in those hellish concentration camps.'

'You weren't responsible for that.'

'But that doesn't stop me from feeling it. I didn't ask. I didn't choose to see. For that I could not forgive myself. Drink was my refuge. It cost me my career in the army and my fiancée before I saw the light.'

'I'm sorry.'

'Oh, don't be. It was my own foolish fault. Marianne found a much better husband than I would ever have been and has two sons of her own now. It was a long time ago.' He finished his tea. 'I was lucky. I wandered into an anti-war lecture while I was living in London. I had so much beer inside me I could barely stand. To be honest, I only went in to shout abuse at the speaker. He was the kind of man I most despised: lecturer at Cambridge, the grandson of an earl. Yet the moment he began to speak, his mind was so clear and his arguments so logical, it was like being hit over the head. You could say that Mr Bertrand Russell saved my life.'

'Why did you say you were lucky?'

I thought at first he wasn't going to reply. 'Because I saw so many of my comrades who did not find a way back.' He sighed. 'I loved Marianne with all my heart. I don't remember a time when I didn't love her: we were childhood sweethearts, you see. The hardest thing I ever did in my life was to let her go. But the man who returned from Africa was not the one she had fallen in love with. How could I hold her to the promise she had made to the boy who went away? There are more ways than one of never coming back. My hell was my own hell. I could not drag her in there too. You can't lead people's lives for them. You can't take on their grief or their weaknesses. And no one should ever ask you to. Believe me, they never thank you. Living your own life is hard enough. And Hell is the most private place of all.'

I had never heard such despair in his voice. 'There is always hope,' I said. 'You've made a new life for yourself.' I hesitated. 'Surely you must believe that there is still a possibility of happiness?' I tried to make out his face. 'And of love?'

He gave a grunt. 'I could not ask any woman to share my demons.'

I frowned at him. 'Without even giving her that choice?'

'She wouldn't want to,' he said gloomily.

There was a loud clanging around us as the doors of ambulances were shut and engines coughed their way into unwilling life.

'We're on our way, Doc,' warned Corporal Smith. I emptied my tea and took Jack's empty mug to stash under the seat.

'Come on,' I said, as Jack got to his feet stiffly. 'We're nearly home. We've rescued Mouse, that's the important thing.' I touched his shoulder briefly. 'Don't ever give up, Jack. Who knows what the future might bring?'

Chapter Twenty-Six

OCTOBER, 1917

The crossing was uneventful, thank goodness. No Zeppelins or Gothas to firebomb us. No U-boats to sink us. As the white cliffs loomed up ahead in the soft haze of pre-dawn, it felt a lifetime since I had left, not just a few days. I felt the deep tug of a long-lost traveller finding home. '*Hiraeth*' my mother called it, the Welsh word for an inexpressible longing I had not understood until now. I shivered in the cold salt wind, swearing to myself I would never leave the familiar comfort of these shores again.

Carols barely survived the crossing. As I took the wheel as we arrived on the other side, a strange silence had fallen among the soldiers in the ambulance. They must have been through this a thousand times, waiting hour by long hour for a man to die. At least Lisette was fast asleep, worn out by the journey across the sea. She barely stirred when, at a whisper from Corporal Smith, I pulled up as gently as I could into the entrance of a farm track at the side of the road. There we waited in the dawn, each of us in silence, until the last slow, harsh, painful breath finally ceased.

We set off again without a word. I felt numb. I could no longer feel sorrow, or grief. I simply focussed on the road in front of me. By the time I finally pulled the ambulance to a halt in front of Applebourne, I could barely move with exhaustion. As the shrouded figure of Carols was quietly removed and the rest of the men taken off towards the wards, Alice ran down the steps, just as Mouse was being lifted from the ambulance, followed by Corporal Smith carrying a sleeping Lisette in his arms, wrapped up tight in a blanket.

'You found her. You found Mouse. And you came back.' Alice hugged me tight, tears flowing down her cheeks.

'Thanks to Jack,' I said, as he stumbled round the side of the ambulance in the chill morning light, limbs so stiff he could barely move. 'We could never have got back without him.'

'I knew you would.' Alice flung her arms around Jack, and hugged him too, leaving him startled. In the blush that suffused his face I caught a fleeting glimpse of the shy, sensitive boy who had never travelled outside Port Helen until he left to fight a war in Africa. The boy who had once been Jack, and who had never come back. I pushed a deep sadness away from me to deal with the practicalities at hand.

We were fed hot soup and toast and copious amounts of tea in the kitchens before being led to Alice's rooms in one of the estate cottages a few minutes' walk away. Lisette was now wide awake. She curled herself in an armchair next to the fire, cocooned in her blanket and looking around silently with large eyes at this new world the dawn had brought.

Jack was nodding over his tea and I could barely keep my eyes open when Alice appeared at the door.

'How is she?' I demanded.

'She's doing well, all things considering. Did you know she had been shot?'

Jack looked up, tea forgotten and spilling onto the ground. 'Shot?'

'She was lucky. The bullet went right through her arm. The doctor thinks there's no real permanent damage.'

'Thank Heaven,' he muttered.

'So she's not in any danger?' I said.

'You got her out before infection really took hold. A few more days, and it might have been a very different story. She's sleeping now. You'll be able to see her when she wakes up.'

I met Jack's eyes. 'We still have to tell her about her brother.'

He frowned. 'There'll be plenty of time for that.'

I turned back to Alice. 'And the others?'

'Alive, thanks to the two of you.' She hesitated. 'I'm afraid Owen's burns are quite severe. I'm not sure how aware he is of their extent, and the doctors can do amazing things nowadays. The broken ribs will heal, but he's going to carry scars on his face and body for the rest of his life.'

I put my head in my hands. 'If only he hadn't come after us.'

'Nonsense,' said Jack. 'If he hadn't been with you he'd have been worse off. You risked your life to pull him from the driver's seat before the fuel tank exploded. You kept your head and found a way to get him out. And I'll break his other ribs if he ever tries to deny it.'

Alice stared at me in horror. 'It's all right,' I said. 'We survived.'

I shut my eyes: there was heat on my face and the stench of oil as the fire crept closer to the tank. I felt my body explode into a myriad pieces as the flames surged, until there was nothing left. I forced my eyes open again. I was cold to the very core, my hands clenched into fists to stop their shaking. 'I need to get home.'

'Out of the question.' Alice was firm. 'One more night away from Hiram won't make much difference. You're exhausted, Jack is practically dead on his feet, and that poor child looks as if she has been through quite enough for one day. Neither of you are in any fit state to drive that ambulance. You're all staying here until tomorrow.'

I was too tired to argue. A place had been found for Jack with one of the hospital orderlies. Alice made up a bed for me and a mattress for Lisette in the room of a nurse on leave. As we settled into our new home, Lisette brightened at finding someone who spoke her native tongue with something like fluency, and was soon chatting away to Alice as if she had known her all her life.

I curled on the bed with a coverlet over me, listening to their voices fade into the distance as Alice took Lisette for a further inspection of the hospital kitchens, with the promise of cake and a glimpse of Mouse if she and Jojo were very quiet and didn't disturb anyone on the wards. I was still shaking, unable to get warm. I was filthy and every part of my body ached. Yet a sense of peace enveloped me as I listened to the singing of birds outside the window, accompanied by the crunch of feet to and fro and the cheerful conversations of nurses. I could smell the grass on the lawns. A door opened deep within the house with a burst of laughter, stilled instantly as it closed. My shaking stopped and I fell into a deep sleep.

For all my exhaustion, I woke several times, my body bracing itself for the sounds of screams or for shells exploding. Once, I was back at the German roadblock again, with the men searching the ambulance. I shot upright, my body trembling, as I thought of what might have happened, frightened even to shut my eyes again.

* * *

I was able to see Mouse before I left. She looked tiny, almost like a child amongst the coverings. As I reached the bed her eyes opened. She held my hand tight.

'Elin. Dearest Elin. I thought I'd dreamed you.'

'I'm no dream,' I replied with a smile.

'No,' she replied quietly. 'No.'

I took a deep breath. 'Mouse…'

'I know.' Tears glistened in her eyes. 'That is if you were going to tell me about George. I knew before you found me.'

'I'm so sorry.'

'There are so many dead.' There was a despair in her voice that was so unlike Mouse. 'On both sides. Why should my family be spared?'

I squeezed her hand. 'I'm sorry, but I have to go. I need to get back to Hiram. But I'll come back and see you when I can. Lisette is staying here with Alice so she can be near you.'

Mouse seemed scarcely to have heard. 'Can't I come back with you?'

'As soon as you are stronger and the infection is gone.'

'Then I can stay?'

'Yes, of course, Mouse. And Lisette too, until we can find a permanent place for her to live. For as long as you wish. But what about your family? Can I speak to them? Arrange for you to go to them? They must want to see you. Especially now.'

She shook her head. 'No. I can't see them. Especially not now. You won't telephone them. You promise?'

'But I need to let them know you are safe.'

She bit her lip. 'Then write. Write to Edmund. He's stationed in France, near Calais. Owen will know where to reach him. That way they can't question you.'

'Very well. You get some rest. You might feel differently about it later.'

'No, I won't. Not ever.'

'She'll change her mind once she feels better,' said Alice as I turned to make my way to the ward. I tried to match her certainty.

The wounded men who had shared our journey were almost unrecognisable, having been bathed and their wounds dressed. I fought back tears as they greeted me as if I were a comrade rather than a visitor.

'You made a much prettier nurse than this lot,' called Corporal Smith with a grin, as I passed him sitting on his bed reading a newspaper.

'Covered in dirt and in the dark maybe,' I returned.

He chuckled. 'At least you had no time to patch me up ready to be shipped out there again.'

'Surely that will be a long time yet.'

'Not nowadays,' he replied, gloomily. 'They're running out of men. So us poor sods will be sent back as fodder as soon as we can walk. I might have been better if I'd lost a leg.'

'There'll be no talk like that on my ward,' said Sister, bearing down on us. Corporal Smith vanished behind his paper.

'Take no notice,' said Owen, who was lying in the last bed, his face and arm heavily bandaged. 'They're all glad to be home, however long it lasts.' He motioned to the chair next to the bed, set on his good side.

I looked down at him, almost completely muffled. The skin I could see was raw and angry. 'I'm so sorry,' I blurted out.

'What? For saving my life?'

'But if it wasn't for me—'

'I would never have found Mouse in time. I could have been in the church with her when it was hit. I could have been killed on the way.' His unbandaged hand clasped mine. 'Don't ever blame yourself, Elin. You saved Mouse. It was the bravest, and the most foolish thing you could do. Almost as stupid as pulling me out of that burning vehicle and acting the nurse to those soldiers at the roadblock.' He gave the faintest of smiles, wincing at the effort. 'Although I still think you would have been safer following my suggestion of having wild affairs with mad artists.'

'I wouldn't have been anywhere else,' I replied, returning the pressure of his hand. 'You get well and get out of here, do you hear me? Mouse is going to need you.' I swallowed. 'We all need you.'

Silence, I realised, rather belatedly, had fallen on the ward, laced with a considerable dose of curiosity. 'I have to go,' I muttered as a nurse arrived with an air of purpose. Whether to protect her patient's virtue or dispense medication, I was not quite sure. 'I'll be back to see Mouse.' The nurse was making no bones about wishing me anywhere but there. 'I'll visit you all, as soon as I can,' I said, making a hasty exit.

Chapter Twenty-Seven

OCTOBER, 1917

I had never been so glad to see the familiar gates of Hiram Hall. Every swirl, every flower of the metal design seemed to have been imprinted on my heart. I felt as if my whole life hung there, my memories, the life I had always known, welcoming me home.

Jack pulled up as we reached them. 'I'll take this on to the base,' he said. 'I'm sure they'll want to patch it up enough to send back.'

'Like the men.'

'Like the men.'

I glanced at him. 'How will you get home?'

'I'll find a lift. Or borrow a vehicle. I'll need to get a message to my mother to reassure her I've returned. She's probably waiting to give me a clip round the ear for running off like that with only a message from a schoolteacher to warn her.'

'I'm sorry. I never thought…'

'Don't be sorry. Don't ever be sorry.' He gave the faintest of smiles. 'Whatever happens in the future, I will never be.'

'Promise you'll come with me, when I go back to Applebourne,' I said, as I returned from opening the gates to let us through. He frowned. 'Mouse will want to thank you for all you've done. I know she will. And the men we brought over will be glad to see you, too.'

'I'll think it over.'

The land girls came rushing out of the walled garden, followed by the children, as we lumbered up the drive in the ancient ambulance that sounded as if it was about to give up the ghost at any second. Their eyes widened at the sight of the bullet holes and the dents and the mud of a real battle.

As we drew up at the main door, I slid stiffly out of the

passenger door. Cook pushed her way through the others, flinging her arms around me.

'Miss Elin!' She kissed me soundly as if I were a long-lost child. There were tears streaming down her cheeks. 'We've heard such reports in the newspapers of new fighting. We were so afraid we'd never see you again.' She scrutinised my face. 'You look exhausted, *cariad*.' She hesitated. 'And Lady Margaret…?'

'She's safe.'

'Thank Heaven.'

'She's been hurt but she's with Alice at Applebourne and she's doing well.'

Cook gave a relieved chuckle. 'I should have known. Indestructible that one. It will take more than a few Boche to finish off Lady Margaret.'

I turned back to the ambulance, whose engine was still running. 'I'm sure you could do with something to eat before you carry on, Mr Treeve. Both Mouse and I have a great deal to thank you for.'

Jack shook his head. 'Thank you, Mrs Helstone, but the army base is expecting me and if I stop I have a feeling the vehicle might not start again.'

'I'll send a message to your mother to say that you are safe and on your way.'

'Thank you,' he replied. I watched the ambulance make its noisy and slightly halting way down the driveway. Despite the hunger crawling through my insides and the utter exhaustion settling on my limbs, I waved away Cook's insistence on food and a hot bath and went inside the walled garden. The workers had disappeared into the stables in search of hot soup and fresh bread. I could hear their excited voices in the distance. It was a normal, comforting sound. I walked through the little door at the far end and out onto the cliffs.

There, I breathed in the solitude and the peace. It had only been days since we had left, but it felt like years. A lifetime. I looked at the little bay with new eyes. I looked up at Hiram Hall as if I had never seen it before. It seemed smaller than I remembered it. And yet at the same time impossibly old and grandiose. A place from a time long gone. A time of knights and ladies watching over the little village at their feet. A time long gone. If it had ever even existed at all.

For the first time I felt I understood Hugo and his need to stomp around the grounds when he returned from the front, as if to regain his world again. I felt alien in my old surroundings. In France, every nerve had been stretched, every sense had been used. I could feel them buzzing around me. How could I settle into the old life again? And the things I had seen… Even if they asked, how could I ever tell them? How could I tell mothers and sisters of the hell their loved ones were living through. Already, I wanted to block it out. Not to forget. But not to relive it.

I wanted to march like Hugo round the estate, marking my boundaries, as if that would bring back the way things were and block out the things that had been.

But I had changed. Even then, I could feel it. Before I left, I had thought that coming home alive would be the end of it. Standing on the cliffs, looking down into the little bay, with its turquoise swell of sea and the little boat bobbing gently in the tide, I remembered Jack's words and understood that the protected girl who had left Hiram just a few days ago would never return. My life was changed forever.

* * *

Over the next few weeks the threads of my old life knitted together again, bringing with it a semblance of normality.

A brief letter was waiting for me from Hugo to say that he was safe and was hoping to get leave at the end of the summer. Meanwhile, there was a more pressing problem. Everything we needed for everyday life was in even more short supply. Rumours flew through Port Helen of U-boats sinking all the merchant ships bringing supplies from America. The work in the walled garden doubled. When I was not planting or weeding, Cook and I attempted to make tasty meals from a very meagre stock so that we had some fresh greens to spare for the hospital and the poorest families in Port Helen. The huge rise in prices had left so many families looking thin and cold. I looked at our own diminishing coal stocks and dreaded the winter ahead. Years of war meant we all had very little resilience left.

I was itching to get back to Applebourne, but, having destroyed the Rover, I did not quite dare to take Hugo's pride and joy, even on such a short journey. Explaining the loss of one automobile would be enough. Luckily the ambulance – by some miracle – was soon restored to some kind of use. Like the most badly wounded men, it would never return to the front, but it could ferry injured men to and from Applebourne. I informed Jack in no uncertain terms that as a respectable woman I couldn't possibly be seen racing round the countryside in an army vehicle – even an ambulance – on my own. After a few minutes' protest, not entirely convincing, he gave in.

When we arrived in front of the hospital, Mouse was waiting on the steps. She looked pale and tired, her arm still in a sling, dressed in a skirt and blouse that were too big, making her seem smaller than ever.

'Are you sure you are well enough for the journey?' I asked anxiously as I jumped out to hug her, while Jack took the ambulance to join the rest of the little fleet, tucked safely out of sight in a barn a short distance from the house.

'Completely. Just get me out of here, Elin. I'll go mad if I have to stay another minute.' Which at least sounded more like the old Mouse. 'And Lisette can't wait to see you too. She's thriving and her English has come on like anything. Alice is trying to find her aunt in Paris, but she's had no luck so far. Are you sure we can come and stay with you?'

'Of course,' I replied, kissing her. 'You'll always be welcome, and you must stay as long as you like. And Lisette, too.'

'Thank you. Dear, dear Elin. Thank you.'

'Shall we go and find Lisette?'

'Of course. She's dying to see you, and she can't stop talking about the chateau she is going to live in.'

'Hiram is hardly a castle. I'm afraid she'll be horribly disappointed.'

'Nonsense,' said Mouse. 'It'll always be a castle to Lisette. And to me too.' She bit her lip, her eyes gleaming with tears. She seemed about to say something else, but then she tucked her good arm into mine. 'But first you've got to come and see Owen. He says he won't see you, but he's not thinking straight. You saved his life. And anyhow…' She smiled, sending a disregarded rivulet of tears escaping from the corner of her eyes. 'Well, I think Owen should tell you that bit himself.'

She dragged me to a flat terrace where those well enough were sitting in every kind of chair, drinking in the sun. Owen sat in a wheelchair to one side, still heavily bandaged, gazing over the garden. He barely looked up at our approach.

'Come on,' said Mouse, 'we've come to get you out of here. A turn around the gardens will do you the world of good. Aren't the nurses always telling you about the benefits?'

'I'm not sure,' he began, turning his chair away from us.

'Oh, forget your dignity. Besides, no one will notice you being pushed around by two women in this place.'

Between us, we guided the wheelchair out onto the lawn under the shade of an oak tree. He was pale and subdued, barely meeting my eyes as we settled on a bench next to him. At the edges of his bandages I could make out the raw, half-healed burns. He seemed to have aged by years.

'Good,' said Mouse, jumping to her feet. 'I'll fetch some tea.'

'There's no need…' I began, but she was already disappearing into the distance. An awkward silence fell. 'Mouse seems much better,' I said at last.

'Physically,' he replied. I glanced at him. His face was turned away.

'Surely the rest will come?'

'Maybe. She won't say what happened to her out there. But then none of us do.'

His voice was distant, as if to shut me out. I could not bear it. 'And you, Owen? How are you?'

'They're going to try skin grafts. So I'll at least have some excuse for a face. Mustn't frighten the horses.'

'Owen.' I took his hand. He did not return the pressure. 'Owen, no one will ever be frightened of you.'

He grunted. 'I'm afraid fellows like me are a bit too visible a reminder of what the rest are going through. A nice neat bullet to the leg, a broken arm, and you can be a hero. Missing limbs or disfigurement and you're shuffled off into a corner. I suppose at least I should be grateful that after three long years in the thick of it, they're unlikely to send me back to the front. Bad for morale.' I heard in despair the bitterness in his voice, not knowing what to say. He turned himself a little more towards me. 'I'm sorry, Elin. Take no notice of me. I'm just feeling sorry for myself. Heaven knows, there are plenty far, far worse off than me.'

'You've got every right,' I replied. 'But I can only be glad that you came back to me.'

'Don't say that.' He turned away again. 'You were right, that day in the apple orchard: you have a husband, and people who depend on you at Hiram. I was a selfish fool to attempt to lure you away from that. I never thought I would survive. And never like this. You are better off without me.'

'Never,' I replied fiercely. 'Whatever happens, that will never be true.' He raised my hands to his lips, kissing it gently, then held it tight, as if overcome. I did not dare touch him. I could see even the slightest movement was agony. I stood there helpless, not knowing what to do, or how to help him, aching to hold him in my arms and kiss the hurt and the grief away.

'I have something for you,' he said at last, sounding more like his old self. He let go of my hand and reached into his breast pocket, pulling out a large cream envelope.

I opened it cautiously. 'A letter?' I blinked at the impressive notepaper with its embossed heading and prominent coat of arms.

'I called in a favour,' said Owen. 'Or maybe I should say used my uncle's name in vain. Nothing like a lord to impress.' I pulled out the letter. Something jingled beneath it. Owen cleared his throat. 'Not exactly a Silver Ghost. Or even a Rover. But it's the best they could find to replace your husband's vehicle I, ah, requisitioned. And in such a cavalier manner. It was a life or death emergency.'

I frowned at him. 'You don't have to do that, Owen. I can sort out my own mess.'

'I don't doubt it.' His good eye met mine. 'But it might prove a slightly more tactful explanation to a husband than his wife riding around in an ambulance in foreign parts, however heroically, unchaperoned and in male company?' A faint smile appeared. 'Open to the odd stolen kiss.'

'Very well.' I returned his smile. 'But on condition that I use it to visit you here.' He turned his head away again. 'I won't take no for an answer.'

'There might be talk, Elin. You know what people are like. I don't want to be the cause of any trouble in your life. I've caused enough of it as it is.'

'Don't you dare be so self-sacrificing,' I exclaimed. 'There's nothing to stop me visiting Alice, and I'm sure the gardens here are struggling to feed so many patients. It might not be much, but I'm sure we can find something at Hiram to spare.' His face was still turned away. 'Mouse can come with me, while she's staying with me. And surely I can call in while I'm here to see how the cousin of a friend is recovering?'

He was silent. Then he nodded slowly. 'I would like that.'

'Good.'

He turned to face me again. The smile was back. 'Nothing will ever change, Elin,' he said. 'Nothing will change how I feel.' His good hand clasped mine, pulling me closer. 'It may be selfish, but I'll be counting the days until I see you again.' He released me hastily. 'Here's Mouse.' His gaze lingered on the figure racing towards us over the grass. His voice sharpened. 'There's something wrong.'

I turned as Mouse hurtled towards me, flinging herself into my arms. She was sobbing wildly.

'Mouse!' I held her. 'Mouse, what is it?'

'It's Edmund.'

'Edmund?' Owen grasped her arm. 'Has he been hurt?'

Mouse nodded. 'The ambulances just came. He wasn't in Calais, he must have gone back towards Lille to try and find me.' Her voice was shaking. 'He's with the men who were the worst injured.' She began to sob once more. 'The ones who aren't expected to survive.'

'At least they sent him back,' said Owen firmly. 'They only send men back who they think will survive the journey and have at least a chance. Come on, let's find out if we can see him.'

Mouse nodded. She wiped her eyes roughly on the back of her sleeve as I pushed Owen back towards the hospital.

We waited throughout the night, and most of the next day. When we were allowed to see Edmund, he had been placed in a side ward, barely conscious. I hesitated at the edges of the room, unwilling to intrude as Mouse and Owen gathered round. Edmund's face was untouched. It was pale and waxen, as if the blood had been completely drawn from the skin, but there was not a cut, or even a bruise, to mar the Edmund I remembered so well. His eyes lit up as they focussed on Mouse. His voice was a whisper, so low I could not hear the words. Every breath, I could see, was an effort.

'Save your strength,' said Owen urgently, as Edmund struggled to speak again. But Edmund would not rest. His eyes searched, a slight frown of distress creasing his brows, until they fell on me.

'It's all right, Edmund, I'm here,' I said, joining Mouse at his bedside. A faint smile stirred his lips. His hand, cold and scarcely with the strength to move his fingers, reached towards mine. I took it as gently as I knew how.

'Thank you,' he whispered. There was a pause as he struggled for breath. 'Mouse,' he managed at last.

'I'm glad we found her and brought her home safely,' I replied. Edmund smiled again, his hand tightening a little. I bent down and kissed him, as he lapsed back into unconsciousness.

'He's too weak to operate on,' said the doctor, arriving a few minutes later. He looked down at the heavily muffled form. 'Internal injuries are always the tricky ones, I'm afraid.' He was not unkind, just already moving on to the next hopeless case, the next grief and despair. 'We'll see how he is in the morning.'

There was nothing I could do. Sometimes I sat with Mouse and Owen, at the side of Edmund's bed. At others, I stayed with Lisette, who was too accustomed to death and dying not to understand Mouse's distress, playing quietly with her and Jojo, or reading to her as she sat between me and *Monsieur* Jack.

I read on through the night. It did not matter that neither of them were listening to the troubles of David Copperfield, I knew my voice was enough. Lisette curled up against me, gazing out into a space that I could tell was haunted by memories of Lavanc and Nurse Spedding's field hospital, and all that her young eyes had seen. Jack stared at the floor, his face closed in on itself. I did not dare think of the sights he might be remembering, of the faces passing in front of him while we waited.

Around midnight, Lord Northholme arrived. I glimpsed his expression, bleak and set, as he passed us on the way to the ward. I could not bear to think what he must be feeling.

The next day, Edmund was no better. The doctor came in as I was handing round cups of tea to the silent figures around the bed, who each gripped its warmth without drinking.

He shook his head. 'I'm sorry,' he said. 'I'm very sorry.'

Lord Northholme rushed out after him to remonstrate, but there was nothing that could be done. It had become just a matter of time. Three other men died that day. Many more were brought in, filthy and broken. A young woman passed us, sobbing inconsolably. Another, clinging to an older woman, who appeared to be her mother, rushed towards the wards with dread on her face.

I thought of Edmund and his gentleness and kindness. Of his light-hearted banter with Owen, that first morning when they came to Hiram to fetch Mouse. Of the sadness in his voice when he told me he'd never danced so much or drank as much champagne as in that brief desperate time when we were all dreading the start of war while hoping beyond hope that such barbarity might never happen. Of the echoes of laughter amongst the tennis courts at Northholme Manor. Of the books and the chandeliers, the elegant ripple of a piano in a world that was organised for every comfort and without any care. And I read on through *David Copperfield*, until I, too, no longer heard the sound of my own voice.

Chapter Twenty-Eight

NOVEMBER, 1917

Edmund's funeral was held a few days later. Mouse, deaf to all argument from her father, rather than travel home with him, had chosen to stay at Applebourne, to be near Owen. I caught a glimpse of them, sitting close to each other, utterly inconsolable, and let them be, not wanting to intrude.

I drove them to Northholme on the morning of the funeral. Mouse next to me, and Owen in the back. Neither of them spoke a word. Mouse leant against the window, with all the appearance of one asleep. I could tell from the rigid set of her jaw and the flicker of emotion over her forehead that she was awake.

As we finally reached the gates of Northholme Manor and were waved through by the gateman, Mouse adjusted her coat with trembling hands and tugged at her hat. 'I wish I had a proper mirror.'

'You look lovely. And the perfect lady.'

Mouse snorted. 'That I'll never be.' She caught my eye. One gloved hand reached over to press mine. 'But I can play the part for a few hours. Can't I, Owen?

'Of course,' he replied, as if too lost in thought to hear her words.

'Don't take any notice, dearest Elin. I'll be fine once we get there.'

As we reached the front of the house, others were arriving. Magnificent automobiles, chauffeurs in attendance, were disgorging black-coated inhabitants, to make their way slowly up the steps. I had never seen so much fur and finery in all my life. The diamond earrings alone would probably have bought Hiram twice over.

Mouse squeezed my hand again as we came to a stop. 'Don't

worry. They don't bite. The old fossils.' She sniffed loudly, as we stepped out onto the gravel. She had turned very pale and she swayed a little, as if utterly overcome with emotion.

'Come on,' I said. 'You must be exhausted. We've been travelling for hours. Let's find you a cup of tea before we go to the church.'

'Good idea,' said Owen, impatiently shaking off the footman who was attempting to help him as he emerged painfully, leaning heavily on a stick. 'You've hardly eaten for days. They are bound to find you something.'

Mouse shook her head. 'No. I don't want to trouble them. They'll all be in a flap as it is. Even Papa has difficulty finding servants these days and they're bound to be worked off their feet.' She straightened her shoulders. 'At least Cousin Iris is here.' She rushed over to hug Owen's godmother tightly. 'Oh, poor Edmund. This is unbearable. How I do wish this was over.'

'There, there, my dear,' said Cousin Iris gently. She indicated to a grey-haired man in a smart overcoat, who had appeared pushing a wheelchair. 'Dr Allen thought you might find this useful, Owen.'

'I'm fine as I am,' muttered Owen.

'Yes, I'm sure you are, my dear. But it won't help Edmund and it won't help anybody else, either, if you collapse halfway through proceedings.' To my relief, Owen – who already looked as if he could barely stand – allowed himself to be manoeuvred into the wheelchair. As he was pushed away, with Mouse clinging to his good hand, he glanced back. 'Don't worry,' called Cousin Iris. 'I'll look after Elin. I've arranged that she is to come with me.'

I watched them go. 'I hope they will be all right.'

'They'll bear up. At least they have each other.' Cousin Iris scrutinised my face closely. 'I understand from Owen that without you we might be mourning more than poor Edmund today.'

'Oh.' I looked at her uncertainly.

'It's quite all right, my dear. Owen has sworn me to secrecy. I'm not even to tell Lord Northholme. I understand how difficult things might become for you if the story should ever get out.'

'Thank you.' My eyes slid away from her gaze.

'Hmm.' She appeared lost in thought for a few minutes, then she began to guide me towards a large automobile at the back of the waiting procession. 'Dr Allen is a very fine surgeon,' she remarked. 'He's been specialising in the treatment of burns since the beginning of the war. He is considered the best in his field.' She slipped her arm through mine. 'I know that Applebourne will do their best, but I want Owen to be under Dr Allen's care. I shall insist that he stays with me tonight and goes with Dr Allen to London. I hope you don't mind.'

'No, no of course not,' I replied. 'I'm sure Mouse will wish the best for Owen. And he's been so despairing, I'm sure being amongst specialists will at least give him a focus and something to fight for.'

'Indeed.' Iris' arm tightened against mine. 'Although, from the way he was speaking, it seems to me that he already has much to live for. Even though he is quite determined not to say so.'

'I'm sorry…' I hesitated, uncertain what to say.

'No, don't be. And never live your life with regrets.' She smiled gently. 'I spent half my youth thinking that if only I was more solicitous to my husband, less selfishly interested in my own happiness, that I could make everything right and all would be well. I was wrong, of course. And by the time I realised it, I had thrown away my one hope of love.' She sighed. 'Real love and true happiness comes but rarely, Elin. Don't ever make my mistake and believe that you must always put another's happiness before your own.' She stopped and faced me. 'I know it is impossible under the present circumstances, but one day this war will end. And then, my dear, you must choose your own future. I think you will find that the woman who set off into the midst of a war to rescue a friend, who braved mortar fire and kept all those in her care safe from enemy soldiers, will not sleep or disappear.

'Owen is the nearest thing to a son I shall ever have. A woman who can risk her own life to save him from a burning vehicle deserves to soar like an eagle, whoever might try to hold her back or shoot her down. If you are ever in need of a friend, Elin…' she paused, 'or a refuge, you have only to call on me.'

'Thank you,' I murmured, overcome by her kindness.

'Good.' Iris set off again towards the line of automobiles. 'Don't worry, the lecture is over. It will be for you to ever speak of this again.'

In front of Northholme Manor, the hearse, strewn with white lilies and drawn by black horses each crowned with jet-black plumes, began its slow journey, followed by the largest of the automobiles. Iris shook her head. 'Poor Edmund. He was such a kind and gentle soul. We shall all miss him dreadfully.' We watched as the rest of the dark-clothed figures made their way into the waiting vehicles, which set off, one by one. 'They are a dying breed,' said Cousin Iris quietly. 'Facing a future that has no place for them. And each time they meet like this, to bury one of their young men, you can tell they sense it. It's you and Mouse who are the future now, Elin. And don't you forget it.'

I watched the remaining mourners waiting on the steps through a scattering of sun and showers. Most were elderly. White hair and fragile features, clothed in fashions that had been cast off decades ago. A breeze tugged at their black garments, setting them flapping like a collection of mournful ghosts attending their own funeral.

I fought back the tears. But inside, I was weeping. Weeping for Edmund, and for all those that had been lost and that we were still to lose.

* * *

It was a gloomy day, both at the church and at Northholme Manor afterwards. As the afternoon wore on, I found Owen sitting on his own in his wheelchair in a patch of sunlight. He looked exhausted and as if he could barely keep still for pain.

'Are you staying with your godmother?' I asked, tentatively.

'It makes sense. Dr Allen appears to know what he is talking about.'

'Good. I'm sure they will do their best for you.'

'We'll see.' He stirred slightly. 'Take no notice of me, Elin. I'm a bit tired, that's all. Thank you for bringing us. Mouse is determined to go back with you. She has Lisette to think of.' He stared out into the distance. 'I shall miss your visits while I am in London. But perhaps it is for the best.'

'If you can be treated by the best men in their field, it must be.'

'That's not what I meant.'

'I know.'

His face was turned away from me. 'You have your own life to lead. Your own responsibilities. I would be a selfish soul if I demanded you add me to all those in your care.'

'You would never be a burden to me, Owen.' I looked at him in despair. 'You came back. You are safe. That's all I care about. Get yourself well.' Across the lawns I could see Dr Allen making his way towards us with purpose in his step. Within minutes Owen would be swept away. Terror shot through me that I would never see him again, and before I knew what I was doing I said, 'Fight this, Owen. You have to fight this. Men are making their way back from injury all around you. I know you can too. And when you are well enough to travel, come to see me. Promise that you'll come to see me.'

For a moment he was still. Then slowly, without turning to face me, he nodded.

* * *

Mouse and I barely spoke all the way home. I was exhausted by the long day and a tumult of emotions that threatened to overwhelm me. Whenever I glanced across towards Mouse, she was staring out into landscape, as if searching for an answer she despaired she would ever find.

Chapter Twenty-Nine

DECEMBER, 1917

We fetched Lisette from Applebourne the very next day.

'Welcome, little one,' said Cook, as we arrived back at Hiram, Lisette still open-mouthed with awe at the sight of the 'chateau', and clutching a wriggling and inquisitive Jojo. 'I don't suppose she understands any English?'

'A little,' said Mouse. 'Lisette was with the nurses in the field hospital in France before she came to Applebourne. She's learning fast.'

'Ah well.' Cook patted the thin little face. 'Then we'll get along just fine. I could barely understand a word of English myself when I came to Hiram with Miss Elin's mama. But I soon learnt enough to get along.'

Lisette frowned at her in puzzlement, then glanced up enquiringly at Mouse. '*Comment?*' Lisette appeared even more bewildered that there was more than one language spoken in '*Angleterre*', while '*Pays de Galles*' might as well be the moon. But she understood that Cook was motherly, and that was enough.

'Good hot soup,' pronounced Cook firmly, smoothing Lisette's dark hair with her large hand. 'And there's bread in the oven.'

This needed no translation. Lisette placed her hand in Cook's. 'And I expect we can find something for your little friend. There's enough soup for all of you,' Cook added, glancing back towards me. 'And enough water for several baths. Especially for that creature,' she added under her breath, as Lisette carried a happily barking Jojo into the kitchen.

Later that afternoon, I went to the kitchen garden on a mission to collect potatoes and onions to line in layers with the last of the bacon to create my mother's *Tatws Pum Munud*. I discovered Lisette surrounded by curious children, all pretence of weeding forgotten. They were smiling and nodding at each other, fussing over Jojo, who had grown sleek and distinctly potbellied during his stay at Applebourne, and was licking hands with cheerful enthusiasm. For the first time since I had met her, Lisette had lost that grey, strained look. Her thin cheeks appeared rounder as she nodded and smiled, both eager and wary at the same time. I could see how painfully thin she still was, her new clothes hanging from her frame. But surrounded by the children, she had become a child again.

For a few weeks, things settled back into their previous routine. There was once more talk of the war ending soon, but in the meantime, food and medicines were in even shorter supply.

At first Lisette did not settle. I heard her troubled dreams echoing through the corridors at night. Whenever I went to her room, Mouse was already there. Sometimes Lisette was awake, hugging Mouse tightly, but more often she had already fallen back to sleep, Jojo – much to Cook's outrage – curled up next to her on her pillow. Gradually the nightmares eased. She was a bright little thing. Without any formal tutoring, her English came on day by day. At first she was a little shy of the village children, but her natural curiosity soon led her towards their voices each time they were working in the garden. The land girls treated her like a pet. On the third day, Jack handed her a trowel.

I found her weeding with the other children. She was solemn at first, but after a few hours she was chatting away.

'Did you like that?' I said, as she came rushing into the kitchen at the end of the day, Jojo at her heels.

'Yes.' She put her arms around my waist and leant against me, looking up. '*Madame*, can I go to school? Mouse says I must ask you.'

'Would you like to?'

'Very much. With *mes amis*? With my friends?'

'I'll make enquiries.' I caught Cook frowning. 'No promises, but we'll see.'

'Are you sure that's wise?' said Cook, after Lisette had rushed off to change out of her earth-covered trousers, the only dressing for dinner we had these days.

'School sounds the best place to me. She needs something to occupy her mind, and a sense of normality again.'

'But before we know where she is to go? You don't want her to put down roots and then be torn away again.'

'Her home is here. With us.'

'And her family?'

'Nurse Spedding is trying to contact the aunt in Paris, but there's been so much movement of people it's proving impossible. Hopefully she'll be found. But she may well be dead. Lisette has to get on with her life now.'

'And when Mr Hugo comes home?'

'He'll understand. He's seen what it's like out there. He'd know that we couldn't leave her there to die. I'm sure he'll grow very fond of her.'

Cook was scraping at a pan. 'I hope you are right. But forgive me, Miss Elin, men don't always welcome children that are not their own. Or, come to that, their wives' friends.'

I blinked. 'I can't just throw Mouse out. Besides, Lisette is far too old for there to be any whisper that she might be—' I felt myself blushing. Such things were never talked of. Whispered in corners maybe. But never spoken aloud. 'Of a scandal.' I looked round at the toys that already seemed to have collected, and the chewed bone belonging to Jojo. 'I like having a child at the Hall. It brings it to life.'

Cook squeezed my hand. 'It does indeed, *cariad*.' Perhaps she understood without my saying it aloud how bittersweet it was hearing a child's voice echoing through the corridors, seeing her face glowing in the firelight, rosy after a day running around in the cold.

The school in Port Helen accepted Lisette without question. Of course they would take a poor refugee child. When she started the following day, the Hall felt quiet. I began to look forward to her running in, Jojo at her heels, to tell us eagerly about her day.

Lisette was soon making further friends at the village school. Now on the days they came up to us to work, she would wait impatiently to greet them, running out to meet them as soon as she heard their voices. It stirred the old emotions in me. Grief, and maybe regret. And maybe also a little fear. For I could see how she was settling with us. How the half-starved urchin with the hurt look, always wary, always fearful, had become a child of the village. More than that: a child of Hiram Hall. Within weeks, Hiram had stirred out of its stupor, sending out tendrils of life into the still air. The dust no longer settled in the upper rooms. The wainscot no longer whispered as dusk fell, a gathering of all the ghosts of Hiram's past, greedily clinging on. The shrieks of hide and seek and the hushed voices of the fairy stories Charlotte would whisper in the dark had banished their greediness – for now.

To move Lisette, I told myself, and take her security away, would be simply cruel. The thought nagged at my mind. I pushed it away, but it was always there, ready to stir in my dreams. I couldn't forget how keen Hugo had been to marry off Alice.

Mouse was pale and tired, but with enough glimmers of the old Mouse for me to hope that she would regain her spirit. Her arm was regaining its strength, and she cheered a little when she found she could begin weeding in the gardens.

'I don't cook, except under extreme duress,' she announced, brushing away my attempts to involve her in gentle stirring in the kitchen until her arm grew stronger. 'I never want to see cabbage soup again. I'll be much more useful outside. And besides, it's the best way to build up my muscles again, I'm sure of it.'

'You'll make sure she doesn't overdo things,' I said to Jack as I gathered greens to fry up with eggs and potatoes for the day's lunch.

'Of course, Mrs Helstone. 'His eyes twinkled. 'I've grown quite accustomed to marshalling women and children. I can't say it's that much different from regular recruits.'

'You enjoy making them obey you, you mean,' said Mouse, looking up from her weeding.

'I was about to add "apart from them answering back",' he said.

'I'm not a slave,' retorted Mouse, sounding cross.

'I was told slavery was a state of mind.'

Mouse snorted. 'Then you've clearly never been a slave.'

He scratched his head. 'Touché.'

'Really?' Mouse stared at him. 'You're not going to lecture me on the shallow arrogance of the aristocracy and the suffering of the poor?' Charlotte let out a nervous, high-pitched giggle. 'Or threaten me with the guillotine,' added Mouse, her tone irritated.

'Maybe tomorrow, after you've finished weeding the potatoes,' he replied. Even Mouse joined in the ripple of laughter. She was scarlet, but smiling.

'I'm glad you're not shocked by me, Jack. Most people, and definitely most men, think I'm far too opinionated for my own good and quite a hopeless case.'

He gave a gentle chuckle. 'Well then, more fool them, I'd say.'

Mouse smiled, bringing the colour back into her cheeks, as she returned to her weeding.

* * *

At first I thought all would be well and that Mouse had recovered fully from her captivity and her escape. But as the weeks went on it seemed to me that shadows were still haunting her. She was cheerful in front of Lisette, but after a while she no longer worked in the gardens and kept herself to herself. Without the excitement of her work in France, she seemed to have lost all sense of purpose.

'Perhaps you could volunteer with Alice when you are fully recovered. Or with another hospital?' I suggested one morning. 'Or become a tram driver. Or a driver to one of the military. I'm sure you would be welcomed with open arms, with your skills and experience.'

'Are you asking me to leave?'

'No! Of course not… I'd never do that, Mouse.'

'Because I don't blame you, with the talk of the war ending now the Americans have come in on our side, and your husband coming back on leave soon.'

'Mouse!' She sounded so bitter. So unlike Mouse. 'That's unfair. Of course I'm glad that Hugo is coming home on leave in a few weeks. But that doesn't mean I want to change my life. Or disregard my friends.'

'I know. I'm sorry. That was unfair of me. And you are right. I can't stay here forever. But I can't go back to Papa and his expectations. I need to make a new life for myself. If only I knew how.'

'Speak to Cousin Iris. I know she would help you. Why don't you go and see her? You could see Owen, too, now he's back with her in Chelsea. She said in her letter that his first operation was a great success and he is coming along very well. I'm sure he would love to see you.' I reached for the telephone receiver.

'No!' Mouse grabbed it from my hands. She tugged so violently it sprang from my hand, the wire pulling the base from the table, sending it crashing to the floor.

I stared at her. 'Mouse, what is the matter?'

'You can't speak to Owen. Or Cousin Iris. Nobody must ever find out. Ever.'

Something went very still and cold inside me. Of course I'd known. I hadn't wanted to know. I'd hoped beyond hope it was all my imagination. But the pieces had all been there, ready to fall into place.

'Oh, Mouse…'

'Don't you *dare*.' She flung the receiver away, throwing herself on the nearest armchair, where she curled up, arms around her knees, crouched like a creature cornered. 'Don't you dare pity me. And don't you dare judge me. Don't you dare.'

'I'm not, Mouse. Surely you know me better than that. All I want to do is to help.' Now I was frightened. Mouse began to rock herself to and fro on the chair. 'How long have you known?'

'A few weeks. At first I thought it couldn't be possible. Not after all that time in the church and nearly dying and everything. I thought nothing could have survived that. Then I hoped I might be mistaken. But I'm not. I can't be.'

'Have you at least seen a doctor?'

'And have half the south coast gossiping? No, of course not. Besides, what could a doctor tell me that I don't already know?'

She had at least ceased to rock and was quiet.

'And that is the reason you can't go back to your family?'

She nodded, face hidden. 'Not even Owen. Especially not

Owen. He'd be the one who'd understand. And no – he could never tell Papa. I couldn't burden poor Owen with that secret. Besides, I know him. It would bring out all that stuff about justice. It would send him back to the front again, the moment he was half well enough. He'd lie and pull strings. And he'd be killed. I know he'd be killed. And I couldn't bear it. Not after Edmund and George, and all the rest. I couldn't bear to lose Owen. And neither could you. You'd never forgive me, I know you wouldn't.' She looked up and caught the look on my face. 'You don't think I chose this do you? That I'd be that stupid?'

'I don't know. I've never lived in a war zone.'

'For all it was so horribly, horribly awful, being out in France was the best time in my life. I was doing something. Being useful. I didn't want a man. Especially not one that could be killed at any moment. Besides, I meant it when I said I don't even like children. I never wanted a baby.'

I felt sick. How could I not have known? How could she not have told me? But then, such things were never spoken of. Even loving relations between man and wife were never mentioned. Let alone... The thought of what she must have been through was unbearable. I grasped her hands.

'Mouse, you mustn't blame yourself. It's not your fault. And you have friends who can help you.'

'But it *is* my fault.'

'Of course it isn't. You were a prisoner. You were forced. You had no choice.'

Mouse began to laugh, a harsh, bitter laugh. 'But I did have a choice. That's the whole thing. I made that choice.' She bent her head between her arms once more. 'Papa was right. I'm utterly, utterly selfish. I was only thinking of myself and my own survival.'

'But—'

'How do you think I escaped? One of the soldiers guarding

me, he said he'd help me. Keep the others away, and make sure I didn't face a firing squad. They were so sure I was this spy they were looking for. They said they'd had information from a source they trusted, and they had all the proof. Which was rubbish, of course. They were going to take me out and shoot me, even without a trial. And they'd do whatever they wanted first. I could hear them discussing it. I didn't understand everything, but enough. *Leutnant* Schäfer said he'd help me. Keep the others away and give me the chance to escape if he could. And that was the price. I wasn't even sure if I could trust him. But it was a chance. It felt like my only chance.' She wept into her arms. 'Hardly noble. I never thought I was afraid of dying. But when it came to it, I found I wanted to live. I didn't care what it took, or how small a chance it might be, I wanted to live.'

'Don't blame yourself, Mouse. You did what you had to do to survive. I'd have done just the same in your place.'

'Papa will never understand. He'd much rather I'd grabbed a pistol and shot myself, or swallowed a cyanide pill. I had one, in my boot, after that first time the Germans arrested me. Just in case. I didn't use it.'

'I'm glad you didn't. And Lord Northholme need never know. We can make up some story…'

'No! I'm not going to pass off some Prussian bastard as his grandchild so that if it's a boy he can make it heir to Northholme. Besides, Papa might never guess, but Owen would know. He's not stupid. He knows I was a prisoner. And he can count. He can't ever know. None of them can. Not even Cousin Iris. I wasn't going to tell you… I was going to go away and find a place to get rid of it – but I couldn't even do that. I wasn't brave enough.'

I put my arms around her and held her close. 'There's always a solution. Between us, we'll find one. It'll never be your problem alone.'

Mouse wept into my coat until she could weep no more. As

her sobs quietened, I helped her onto the couch, where she curled up like a child. She was shivering. I laid my coat over her and sat with her, holding her hand until I could tell by her breathing that she had fallen into the deep sleep of exhaustion.

Quietly, I made my way down into the kitchen. Cook was sitting in a patch of sun with Lisette, preparing vegetables for the midday meal. My stomach was in a tight knot, even the faint lingering of peeled onions threatened to send me retching. I wasn't certain I could school my face into normal cheerfulness yet. I put the kettle on to boil as quietly as I could, trying to gather my thoughts.

In the distance, I could hear the cheerful voices from the walled garden. From further away, a train hooted as it rounded the headland. Gulls screeched above, fighting over a scrap of fish. All familiar noises, just as I had heard them all my life. I had thought I'd seen all there was to see. As I reached for the jar of tealeaves and the pot, I realised that I knew nothing. I had only glimpsed the horrors possible on our ride through the war-torn French night, heading for safety and the sane, civilised world of home. How thin that civilisation seemed now. How cruel the world, and how precarious the life all of us clung to as best we could.

I pulled myself together. There would be plenty of time to think of that later. I needed to plan, not to think. To work out a way to give Mouse a safe place to have her baby and to make whatever choices she would need to make.

Whatever she chose would mean heartbreak. But at least if she had a place where she was safe, where she didn't have to worry about discovery, she could make the choices that would have to remain with her for the rest of her life. Hell, as Jack had said, was the most private place of all.

I toyed for a few minutes with the prospect of telling Iris. Of swearing her to secrecy and asking for her help. But I knew instantly that Mouse would never forgive me. And that she was right. Owen would be bound to find out.

As I stirred sugar into the tea – both Mouse and I were in dire need of it, luxury though it might be – the answer came to me. So utterly simple and so perfect. A place of safety. A place far away, with people she knew who would accept her and help her and never judge.

I placed the cups and saucers on a tray, along with a slab of carrot cake from the tin, and hurried back up the stairs unseen. I would let Mouse sleep for as long as she could. When she woke, we could plan.

The room was silent as I slipped in through the door. I placed the tray on a side table and took my cup to the armchair next to the mound of coat that covered Mouse, as quietly as I could so as not to disturb her.

It was only as I reached the couch that I saw that the overcoat lay crumpled and empty. Mouse had gone.

Chapter Thirty

DECEMBER, 1917

I ran down the stairs. There was no sign of Mouse. In the hallway I called her name. Again and again. The sound echoed around the building, fading into nothing. At last the footsteps came running towards me.

'Miss Elin?' It was Cook, out of breath, a concerned look on her face.

'Have you seen Mouse, Mrs Hughes?'

'No.'

'She was upstairs. She must have come this way…' I turned as Lisette came racing into the hallway.

'*Madame?*' The frightened look was back in her eyes. Dread spilled into my stomach.

'Mouse?'

Lisette nodded.

'Did you see where she went?'

Lisette pointed to the cliffs. 'Steps,' she said. 'The path. To the beach.'

To the beach. To the sea. I met Cook's eyes.

'Lisette, take Cook and fetch Mr Treeve from the garden,' I said. 'Don't alarm the others. Just make sure *Monsieur* Jack goes to the beach.' Lisette nodded, her face pale but calm. She knew all about action, poor mite, and there was no hiding my fears from her.

I kissed her. 'Good girl. We'll find Mouse and bring her back, don't you worry.' I pulled on a coat from the rack by the door. 'Bring the child back here and keep her distracted,' I said in a low voice to Mrs Hughes.

The wind on the cliffs was chill as I raced to the steps. I made my way down, boots clattering on the stone. It was a grey sea beneath a dark sky. The tide surged against the beach, a vivid green streaking through as the waves rose, crashing against the rocks to send spray shooting wildly up into the air. Gulls rose, shrieking in outrage, blown like falling paper this way and that.

'Mouse!' My voice was torn from me, drowned by the waves' roar and the howl of the gale through the caves. 'Mouse!' I slipped on the pebbles down to the sea. Foam was flung at my feet, with splintered sticks of driftwood. 'Mouse!'

The boat was not there. Before I reached the little jetty, almost engulfed in spray, I could see the rowing boat had gone. In dread, I scanned the bay, praying that she had not yet left the shelter of the cove. That the wild spray beyond the natural harbour entrance had dissuaded her from going any further, whatever her purpose.

A huge wave flung itself against the rock in the centre of Hiram Cove. It crashed down again, the white breaker racing towards me. Water swirled around my ankles. A mist of salt bruised my face. But I felt neither. Beyond the rocks, close to the passage to the treacherous sea beyond, I could make out the dark shape of the boat, tiny and fragile, being thrown this way and that.

'Mouse!' There was a thin figure in the boat, oar bent to pull the little craft around to face the next wave head on. The boat rose, standing almost upright as it crashed through the spray. It landed safely, but, pulled around by the force of the wave, it was now side-on to the larger surge following. In the lull between rollers, the boat began to turn, slowly, painfully slowly, to face the next break of spray bearing down.

It almost made it, but the wave caught the side before it had fully turned, carrying the boat helplessly back towards the shore. Above the roar, I heard the sickening screech as it hit the rock. Side panels peeled away like a child's toy. The force had wedged it in, but at any moment it could be swept off again, this time to sink, taking Mouse down with it.

Then I saw her. At least she hadn't resigned herself to be crushed with the boat. Mouse was fighting for her life. She had pulled herself out onto the rock, holding on tight as the waves passed her by. The storm had eased a little. I could feel it; the wind was calming as the tide began to turn. But she could not hold on for long. She would be chilled and exhausted from her fight this far.

I pulled off my boots and my skirt, throwing off my coat as I stepped into the water. I was dragged back to the shore more than once, but I dived through the waves until I was out into the deeper water, swimming as strongly as I knew how towards the rock.

I reached her just as another wave powered down on us. Grasping her by the shoulders I pulled her against me. Mouse was weak and barely conscious.

'Come on,' I cried, 'it's not far. Ride on the next breaker. The waves will carry us to safety.' Mouse nodded. I steadied her until there was a break, then pulled her with me. She barely had the strength to swim, and I was terrified of losing her. The short distance to the shore seemed so far. The closer we got the wilder the sea became, as surf broke around us. I could feel the tug on my legs as the tide turned. Already it was harder to ride with the waves. Within minutes we could be dragged out into deeper water again.

We almost made it. My feet had touched solid ground and the beach was so close, when a wave grabbed Mouse, pulling her away from me, dragging her under.

'Mouse!' Something brushed against my legs. Instinctively I grasped at the material. It tore, but my other hand reached Mouse's wrist. I dragged her up to the surface. She was limp, arms moving helplessly with the waves. I pushed again for the beach, chest burning, mouth full of brine. A breaker crashed over us, nearly tearing Mouse from me again. Another came, this time practically stunning me with its force. I felt Mouse being dragged from my arms once more.

'I've got her.' Mouse was lifted from me, but with a sense of purpose no wave could bring. As I struggled, I watched Jack with Mouse in his arms, carrying her towards the beach. My feet touched ground again, then were swept away from beneath me. I was buffeted this way and that in the water. Jack was back again. This time he reached for me, pulling me out of the waves and onto the shore.

I crouched for a moment, retching, attempting to catch my breath. When I could lift my head, I found Jack bent over Mouse, a look of utter despair on his face.

'Is she…?' I scarcely dared ask the question.

'She's still breathing.'

'Thank Heaven.' A fit of coughing overcame me as I threw up seawater. My chest was burning.

'Are you all right, Elin?'

'Yes.' I sat up. Jack was shivering, but he had not been so long in the water and still had the use of his fingers. He put on his boots. We were only a few steps from my mound of clothes. I threw my skirt over my head and fastened my boots as best I could. We wrapped my coat around Mouse. She had lost her boots and her skirt was torn to shreds. Jack swept her up in his arms again and set off towards the path, making sure I was following.

The steps had never seemed so high or so long. I dragged myself up, one by one, following Jack as he hurried towards the house, where Cook was waiting.

'Oh my dear Lord,' she exclaimed, as we stumbled into her kitchen like refugees from an undersea prison. Lisette sat small and wide-eyed, the cake she had been making with Cook entirely forgotten, a wriggling Jojo clutched tightly in her arms.

'She's all right, we're all safe now,' I said quickly. Despite the climb, the cold had not eased in my blood. My hands and feet were numb and my brain felt slow.

'Plenty of hot bricks and hot water bottles,' said Cook, 'and she'll be as right as rain. Now Lisette, you go and show Mr Treeve where to take Mouse. I'll get her bed nice and warm. And you go and change this minute, Miss Elin, or you'll catch your death, and that won't do any good to anyone.'

Lisette nodded. '*Içi, monsieur* Jack.' With a quick tug on his arm, she set off. I followed them. Mouse was cold and pale as we reached her room and Jack laid her on the bed. I could scarcely feel her breathing.

'If you could keep Lisette occupied,' I murmured as he straightened. He nodded. 'Lots of hot water bottles,' I said aloud to Lisette. She hesitated, glancing down at Mouse's unconscious face. 'That's what we need. If you can show *monsieur* Jack the way back so he can help too.'

Lisette brightened. She grabbed Jack's hand, pulling him

towards the door. Within minutes I could hear their feet clattering down the stairs.

My fingers would hardly obey me, but I managed to unpeel Mouse's wet clothes and pull her into the warmest nightdress I could find before Cook arrived with the first hot water bottle. She helped me ease Mouse under the covers, carefully placing a couple of extra eiderdowns over her.

'Go and get yourself changed, Miss Elin, before you catch your death,' she said, shooing me away. 'I'll look after Lady Margaret.'

By now I could barely stand. Cold burned my scalp, while the very core of me was ice. I hurried to my room. I was still shivering as I made my way down to the kitchen, where Jack was helping Lisette with warming bricks and water for the hot water bottles.

'Here.' I held out a parcel of clothes. 'They're Hugo's. They won't fit, but they'll do while your clothes dry.' He hesitated. 'Don't be silly, Jack. You must be frozen. They're old ones. Yours will dry faster if we can hang them up. It won't help Mouse if you perish of pneumonia.'

He nodded, and disappeared, returning a few minutes later with his soaked shirt and trousers in his hand.

'How is she?' he asked, watching me anxiously as I hung his wet clothes over the range.

'Asleep. She regained consciousness for a bit. Cook said she managed to get some hot tea inside her, just now. Lisette has just taken some more up. Mouse is a survivor.'

He took the cup of tea I held out towards him. His hands were shaking. 'I'm glad. I don't know what I'd have done…' He coughed, turning his face away.

I put a hand on his arm, all the comfort I could give. 'Thank you,' I said. 'For me and for Mouse, thank you. Once again we owe you our lives.'

'Oh, I don't know. You seemed to be doing very well on your own,' he replied, turning back towards me with a faint smile.

'I'd never have got Mouse back onto the beach. I wasn't strong enough after fighting the waves for so long.'

'You would have been. But I'm glad Lisette found me.' He stared down into the depths of his untouched tea. 'Do you know what on earth Mouse was thinking, taking the boat out in such weather?'

'No.' I met his eyes briefly. 'I'm not sure. I need to talk to her.'

He bent to place a new brick in the oven to heat, his face hidden. 'As you said, Mouse is a survivor.'

The clatter of footsteps and the murmur of voices came towards us as Cook and Lisette made their way down the stairs.

I fought back tears. 'Yes. Yes of course.'

* * *

I left Jack being mercilessly fussed over by Cook, an indignity he took with good grace, and carried the next batch of hot water bottles up to Mouse. She was sleeping peacefully. I sat in the armchair beside the bed, meaning to watch until she woke, but as warmth slowly and painfully returned to my limbs I could feel my eyes closing, my head nodding.

When I awoke, Mouse was still asleep. The sun had come out, slanting through the window. As I gazed out into the peaceful afternoon Jack, returned to his own clothes, crossed the yard into the walled garden.

'Is it morning?' Mouse was watching me from her pillows, frowning slightly.

'No. It's late afternoon.'

'I feel as if I've been asleep for days.'

'That's good. It means you must be rested.' I adjusted the sheets and pulled the eiderdown back into position. 'Are you hungry? Cook is heating up more vegetable soup than both of us could eat in a week.'

Mouse shook her head. She reached out and clasped my hand. 'I'm sorry.'

'Hush. There's no need. You go back to sleep.'

'Yes there is. I was stupid. I didn't think. I had this wild idea I was going to sail away so the sea would swallow me up and I would never be found. I was utterly, utterly selfish. I never thought you might come after me, and I'd put your life in danger. And Jack's. After all you did to save me…'

'It doesn't matter now. You were upset.'

'Yes it does.' She sighed. 'And it hasn't changed things. After all that, it hasn't changed things.'

'I'll call Dr Harris in the morning.'

Mouse shook her head. 'No. Please don't. I don't want anyone to know.'

I sat for a while as she dozed again. As the light began to fade, Cook brought up a tray of soup and toast. This time Mouse ate a little. Slowly and stiffly she got out of bed, pulling an eiderdown around her.

'You needn't watch me so closely,' she said, joining me on the window seat. 'I've learnt my lesson. I'm not about to do anything stupid.'

'Let me talk to Cousin Iris.'

'No. I haven't changed my mind about that, at least. This is my mess. I need to deal with it in my way.'

'You know you can stay here for a long as you wish.'

She shook her head. 'Not when your husband returns. I don't want to hurt your feelings, Elin, but I think we both know he won't be so understanding. About me or Lisette. And especially not now. Not with this.'

There was nothing I could say to that. 'Then we'll find a place for you to go. Where you and Lisette can be safe. Where you can decide what to do next.'

Outside the storm had died down, leaving just gusts to pull at the curtains of the half-open window every now and again.

'I thought war was glorious,' said Mouse abruptly. 'I thought it was about dying for freedom. When I was working in Lille and some of the other villages that had been occupied, I was just like the rest. I pitied the women who were raped and I thought it could never happen to me. I didn't understand how the pregnant ones could keep their babies. Many didn't, of course. But some did. And most of all I despised the women who made compromises. Who sold themselves to survive. I saw things in black and white. It wasn't until afterwards I understood.'

'I'm sure I'd have done anything to survive, too,' I replied.

'Those women weren't doing it for themselves. It's simple to die yourself for what you believe in. But when it's your children, your mother, your sister, your brother who will be raped and tortured and killed, and when it's a choice of watching those you love starve...' She hid her head in her hands. 'I saved myself. They did it for others.'

'But you survived. Mouse, I'm glad you survived. Whatever it took.'

'But what on earth am I to do now?' She gave a bitter laugh. 'I don't want a child. I never did. I just want it taken away.'

'You might feel differently later.'

'No I won't. Ever. Whenever I look at it, I'll remember. I'll remember that man's face. I'll remember every minute of every time.' She shuddered. 'I'll hate it. I know I will. I'll hate it all my life. There were women out there who killed their babies. Maybe I'll be the same.'

'You don't know that. Not when you see it. It's a child. And it's yours. Once it's born, you won't feel like that at all.'

'You don't know that,' snapped Mouse. 'How can you know that? Or perhaps you just want me to have it so I can hand it over and you can pretend it's yours because you can't have children and at least that way you'd have something.'

'Don't say that.' I slid from the window seat. 'You don't know me. You don't know anything about me.'

I saw the stricken look on her face. 'Oh, Elin,' she whispered. 'You never said. I never thought. I'm so sorry.'

I couldn't bear her. I couldn't bear her pity, her tears or her self-pity. It reached too deep, and broke something inside. 'Leave me alone,' I heard myself hiss, as I ran as far away from her as I was able.

Chapter Thirty-One

DECEMBER, 1917

I found myself in the walled garden. The short day had ended and the workers had gone. Jack too. The storm had cleared to a calm, still evening with scarcely a cloud to be seen. As the sky turned to indigo, fringed with the deep gold of a distant sunset, I walked between the beds of winter vegetables to the pond at the centre. I sat on the bench beneath my mother's favourite rose. A few blooms remained, lured out by the unseasonable warmth of the past days. The scent, though faded, still filled the air, sweet and heavy, holding memories of playing around her feet when I was a child.

I did not look up when Mouse came to join me. We sat for a while in silence.

'I'm so sorry,' Mouse said at last. 'I told you I always was thinking only of my own troubles. I feel as if I've passed half my life being utterly blind. Why didn't anyone tell me?'

'We never speak of it. Besides, only Cook is left to remember. It was the first year Hugo and I were married. It's never been mentioned since.'

'You mean…' I could hear Mouse being careful in a most un-Mouse-like way. 'You mean the baby died?'

'It – *she* – died before she was born.'

'Oh, Elin.' Mouse hugged me tight.

'She was so tiny. So unbearably tiny. Scarcely a baby at all. They didn't want me to see her. They wanted to take her away. But I insisted. I only held her for a few minutes, not long enough to say goodbye.'

'Poor Elin.'

'I don't really remember much. I was very ill, you see. They thought I would not survive. Hugo could never talk about it; it was Alice who told me. I was very weak for months afterwards. I didn't step outside the house for a whole year, and when I did I could barely walk to the garden and back. The doctors weren't sure if I would ever fully recover, or if I could have another child. They advised Hugo that we shouldn't try again for some time.'

'So that's why… I did wonder. But you're strong now. You're brave and resourceful and amazing. You've saved my life at least twice. You could still have lots of babies.'

I turned my face away. I could not tell her. I had never breathed a word to anyone, the secret my husband and I held between us. The spell that had been broken that day he found me, terrified and in pain, the blood flooding around me, creeping through the silk of my summer dress, turning its pale flowers crimson. His horror. Since then, his unwillingness to touch me… As if his dream of a fairy-tale princess, safe in her castle unsullied by the world, had evaporated into nothing. Into the empty shell that our marriage had become. I knew there were other ghosts haunting him, apart from our baby. But that terrible day had destroyed any chance I'd had to reach him.

Alice was the only one who had guessed. But I had avoided her questions, too shamed by my crude physicality that my husband could not bear to see. I think that that last year before the war, Hugo had begun to sense her silent understanding too. My husband's pride would never have permitted Alice to stay. Once she had gone, he would never allow anyone else into Hiram who might prove a mute witness to the darkness inside him I could not touch.

To the world outside, our marriage seemed perfect. The handsome hero and the dutiful wife. The brave soldier taking protective care of his fragile lady. The story as it should have been. The story of long ago – a lifetime ago – when he had smiled at me as if I might be his salvation.

Something hit me, in the pit of my stomach. All these years, I had believed it must be my fault, and that it was for me to make it right. All my life I had been told it was for a wife to be her husband's support and his helper. Her first duty was his care, her only interest to preserve his happiness. I had failed. I was some kind of unnatural woman, unworthy of any man's love. The failure must be mine.

I shut my eyes. I was back in the ruined orchard, held within Owen's arms and the passion of his kiss. He had not seen me as unnatural. He had loved and desired me as a woman. He had not been repulsed by the eagerness of my response, my own desire, rising to match his.

It was a revelation. A falling away of my shame. Cousin Iris had left a husband who beat her. I had seen at Northholme the sideward glances she still attracted as a woman who had dared to divorce her husband, who had dared claim that no man had the right to use violence against her or to humiliate her. Hugo had never been violent, but he shut me out. He stifled me, even in his kindnesses, as a living, breathing human being with a mind and a will of her own … with a life to lead.

I took a breath. My world rocked on its axis and steadied again. But the pieces would never be the same. Somewhere inside I'd changed.

'Dear Mouse.' I kissed her cheek. She looked so remorseful I could not help but smile. I wasn't sure it would last. I didn't want it to last. A meek and thoughtful Mouse wasn't quite Mouse at all, and I loved the old Mouse too well to wish to change her now.

She was still watching me. 'But you do love Hugo?'

'He's my husband.' I pulled the dying bloom next to me, peeling away the curling petals into my hands, releasing their scent.

I should never have married him. That was as clear as daylight to me now. I should not have married him, any more than Cousin Iris should have married the husband who took out his own inner demons on those who loved him. I remembered her regret, for all her rich life, of allowing her chance of true happiness slip through her fingers.

'I thought...' Mouse was hesitant. 'I wondered if maybe you had grown to love someone else.'

'Then I'd be a fool, wouldn't I?' I replied quietly, scattering the rose petals onto the black waters of the little pond, where they swayed in the faint breeze, setting off, a pale Armada, into the dusk.

Mouse said nothing. She curled up close to me and held me tight. We sat there, with the dusk growing around us, until the last reflected light had gone from the sky, and we stumbled back through the shadows of the trellises, to the dark shadow of the house waiting beyond.

Chapter Thirty-Two

JANUARY 1918

As the weeks passed and Mouse grew stronger, it became clear there was only one solution. I came into her room one day, an open letter in my hand. 'This is the answer.'

'You haven't written to Papa? Or Cousin Iris? Not after you promised?'

'No one on Anglesey knows who you are. This is from Aunt Catrin. You can stay with her, she says, or at *Swn y Môr*, if you choose. It's perfect.'

Mouse looked uncertain. 'I love your Aunt Catrin, and *Swn y Môr* was heaven. But will she want me?' She reddened. 'Now, I mean.'

'Aunt Catrin understands. Besides, she always needs helpers on the farm. The men have left, much as they have here. Hugo isn't back from Belgium until the end of the month. I'll come with you and we can stay for a week or so until you settle. No one here need ever know.' I hesitated. 'Whatever you decide.'

Mouse was silent for a while. 'But you'll come and visit?'

'Of course. Whenever I can. All Hugo ever need know is that I am visiting Aunt Catrin. And I know Alice will visit you too. And if you don't feel happy, we can find another solution.'

Mouse was silent for a few minutes, lost in thought. 'But what about Lisette? I can't just abandon her.'

'Aunt Catrin says that she is welcome, too. Jojo might even learn to herd sheep. A dog needs an occupation. She might not have any of her own, but Aunt Catrin loves children, and at least Lisette will be with you. I know it means dragging her away from her friends and everything she knows here, but maybe it's better now…'

Mouse met my eyes. 'Rather than when Hugo comes home.'

'I'm afraid so. I'm so sorry Mouse, but Cook was right.' I swallowed. 'I'm not sure Hugo could bear to see a child in this house. Not a little girl that wasn't his. Please understand.'

Mouse hugged me tight. 'Of course. Dear, dear Elin. And I'll never do anything ever again to hurt you, or Hugo, or cause you unhappiness.' She smiled. 'I love Aunt Catrin and, if she'll have me, I can't think of a better place to go than *Swn y Môr*.' She bit her lip.

'At least talk to Jack before we go. He knows there's something wrong. He saved your life, Mouse. At least speak to him.'

Mouse shook her head. 'I can't. I couldn't bear it. He'd know. The moment I told him I was leaving, he'd know.'

'And would that be so bad?' I asked gently. 'Surely Jack, of all people, would be the one to understand.'

But Mouse shook her head. 'I couldn't bear it.'

* * *

We left a few days later on the London train, changing at Plymouth, where no one would know us, for the journey north. We told everyone Mouse and Lisette were going to stay with family while Mouse helped the war effort by driving trams in the city. I was going to stay with them until Lisette was settled and we had found her a suitable school. It sounded reasonable, and Mouse insisted, so there should be no trail to Anglesey and Aunt Catrin. If Mouse was ever to return it was to be her choice.

The journey was uneventful, with only a few delays as trains carrying conscripts passed on the journey south. Much of the time was spent entertaining Lisette, who had grown anxious at the prospect of yet another move. But she was soon telling Jojo all about his new home and the sheep. By the time the mountains appeared, with the hint of ruined castles, she had forgotten her trepidation and was too excited to sleep.

When we finally reached Llanarthur station, Aunt Catrin was there waiting for us with a pony and trap to gather us up to the safety of the farm and all the hot tea and Welsh cakes we could manage.

* * *

The days passed quietly. Mouse was more settled than I had seen her in a long time. She took long walks across the fields and along the coastline, sometimes with Lisette and Jojo, sometimes on her own, returning ravenously hungry, cheeks glowing in the candlelight each evening.

On the last evening, after Lisette was safely tucked up in bed, I sat with Mouse amongst the sand dunes, overlooking the beach. 'You don't have to stay,' I said. 'You can come back with me in the morning. You could find a flat in London for you and Lisette.'

Mouse shook her head. 'I like it here. I like Aunt Catrin. She has a clear mind and an honest view of things. I trust her.'

'If you ever change your mind…'

'I know. Thank you, Elin. I don't know how I'll ever repay you.'

'You don't have to repay anything, Mouse.' I looked at her. 'Won't you at least write to your family? You don't have to explain. If you give me a letter, I can post it when the train gets to London. That way they won't know where you are, until you are ready.'

'Yes.' Mouse nodded. 'Yes. I'll do that.'

I hesitated. 'And Jack? Won't you at least let me say something to Jack when I get home?'

She shook her head. 'No. Especially not Jack.'

'He would never judge you. He's bound to wonder why you rushed off like this without saying goodbye. You must know how much he cares for you, Mouse. I'm sure you don't want to hurt his feelings.'

'No, of course not.' She chewed her lips. 'When the baby comes. I'll tell him then. When I've got used to the idea.' She sighed gloomily. 'I don't expect I'll ever see him again.'

'You never know, Mouse. Jack is an unusual man. He may well surprise you.'

She put her arms around her knees and placed her chin on her arms. 'I don't need saving by Jack, or avenging by Owen. It happened. Nothing can change it. I've got to deal with it. And I'm the only one who can. I suppose that's what I couldn't face: the fact that my life will never be the way I planned it to be. But I'm not giving up. I won't be his victim. That soldier will never know. It's nothing to do with him. And he's probably dead by now, anyway.'

The face of the fair-haired lieutenant at the roadblock came into my mind with an instant clarity. The soldier who had looked so intently at Mouse and then let us through. Who had most probably saved our lives. And maybe even risked his own by doing so. I hesitated. Should I tell Mouse or not? Would she think I was just comforting her? Maybe it would destroy her fragile peace of mind. And anyhow, who was to say it was the same man. It could be a coincidence: my imagination running riot. Besides, given the horror of that landscape and the roar of the guns, she was most probably right. 'I expect so,' I said.

'Then it's mine. *All* mine.'

I looked at her in alarm. 'Mouse?'

'Don't you see? No one can tell me what to do. Or take it away. If the baby survives.' She gave a slight shudder. 'And if *I* survive. Then the baby is mine.'

'Yes, it will be.'

'I'll find a way to live, somehow. I've thought about it. I've got Mama's legacy. It's not enough to live on, but it's a start.' She looked at me, her eyes earnest. 'All those widows of the men killed in the war, they are going to have to look after children on their own on much less than Mama's money. If they can, I can.' She hugged her knees tighter again. 'Oh Elin, why did I think I was so special?' She sighed. 'Those poor women I saw in France. I saw them with children they were trying desperately to love. Some did. Because they were children.' She smiled. 'Like Lisette. Like anybody. You get to know them, and you love them. And if it's a child, you'd do anything not to see them hurt. That's not weakness, or being a victim.'

'I know you'll find a way through this, Mouse,' I said. 'And I'm glad you're alive.'

Mouse smiled. 'I'm glad I met you, Elin. I'm so glad my bi-plane missed its route that day.' She looked up at the sky. 'This war won't last forever. And when it's over, I'm going to get my bi-plane back. I'll make one with my own hands, if that's what it takes. And I'm going to fly.' She grinned. 'I could even start a school for women pilots. Then if we're flying all over the place, just like the men, they'll have to give us the vote.'

'That sounds like a brilliant idea to me.'

The old Mouse was back. Who was planning for the future… I was anxious, of course – there were so many women who died in childbirth – but Mouse was no longer in danger of taking a small boat out into the ocean. I'd warned Aunt Catrin, just in case, but Mouse had the fight back in her, and Mouse with the fight in her could survive anything.

I thought of Jack working diligently away in Hiram's gardens, never asking after Mouse, but listening so intently to every last morsel I told him. I wouldn't break my word to Mouse. But I'd find a way. Somehow, however long it took, I'd find a way.

I looked out over the sea, the salt wind whipping into my face. Mouse had not done anything wrong. She had not chosen any of this. All she had done was to be brave and bold and risk her life to help others in the most terrible need. She should never, ever, have to feel shame or fear. Why should she feel unable to take her chance of happiness, just so that the world could go on as if nothing like this ever happened?

Why should anyone?

Why should I?

I sat very still. The question had burst into my head as if it had always been there, waiting its moment. Why should I stay in a life that stifled and negated me, so that the world could maintain the polite pretence that marriage could never lead to unhappiness? That a woman must always put her husband first, bending herself to fit to his wishes, as if she had no existence or desires of her own.

Anger shot through me. I'd seen the looks of disapproval Iris had been given at Northholme. I understood now why Mouse would never choose to go back. Those looks had declared that the violence meted out to Owen's godmother must have been of her own provoking, and it would have been better if she had been found with her throat cut than to bring the truth out into the open. Better that she had never existed at all than to choose to live her life in freedom.

I took a deep breath. If this war was indeed to end soon, I had a choice to face. And, when it came down to it, I found it was no choice at all.

* * *

Aunt Catrin took me to the station the next morning. Mouse and Lisette sat on either side of me, holding me tight.

On the platform, Mouse slipped a letter into my pocket. 'For Cousin Iris,' she whispered.

'I'll post it as soon as I get to London.'

'And you promise you won't tell her where I am?'

'Of course. Except if you are in trouble.'

'Or if…' The gleam of fear was back in her eyes. 'If anything happens to me.'

'It won't.'

'But if it does?'

'I promise. With all my heart.'

She hugged me tight, tears streaming down her cheeks. 'I might never see you again.'

'You will,' I replied, brushing the hair away from her damp face with my hand. 'I swear that you will.'

Aunt Catrin kissed me soundly. 'I'll look after her,' she said in Welsh. 'And if anything is not going smoothly, or if it looks as if there might be problems, I'll let you know.'

'Thank you.'

'And you, *cariad*, you take care of yourself. And remember, there is always a place here for you, should you need it. We have farms and gardens here too, you know. Plas Caradoc Farm is lying empty.'

'The farm by the sea?'

'That's the one. Both their sons and their son-in-law were killed at the front. Their daughter went to live in Canada with relatives after her husband was killed. Talk is they'll join her. I can't see them wanting to come back here. Too many memories. Better to start again. They've been trying to rent it out for months. I did wonder…' She glanced over at Mouse. 'But time enough for that. She doesn't want to be taking on a big old house in her condition. Some of the fields are let, but the farmhands have all gone. Something to think about for the future.'

I watched them, as the train pulled out. They looked like a mother with her daughter and granddaughter, standing there on the tiny station. A pang of envy went through me. And something else. A touch of grief, maybe? As I settled myself to watch the countryside fly by, I couldn't help thinking of my mother, all those years ago, setting off for a new life at the other end of the country, with only Cook to remind her of her old world and her mother tongue.

I did not post Mouse's letter when I reached London. Instead, I found my way to an elegant little cottage on the riverbank at Chelsea.

Cousin Iris was expecting me. 'My dear,' she said, kissing me soundly. 'I was so thankful when I received your telephone call. I was so worried when I telephoned Hiram and no one would say where you had all gone. I knew Mouse couldn't have just vanished from the face of the earth.' Her face was anxious. 'She is quite safe, isn't she?'

'Yes,' I replied. I handed her Mouse's letter, and sat with her while she read it.

'Poor, dear Mouse,' said Iris quietly, as she finished reading it through a second time. 'What she must have been through. I thought there was something, the day of Edmund's funeral. But then with so much suffering...'

'She is quite safe now,' I assured her.

'I know she is, my dear. I wish she would let me help her, but that's Mouse all over.' She squeezed my hand. 'Now don't you look so anxious. Mouse will write to me properly when she's ready. The least I can do is respect her wishes.' She rose. 'Thank you, my dear. You must be exhausted after all that travelling. Mrs Brigge is preparing tea for us all.' She smiled. 'There's someone here who would like to see you.'

Owen was sitting near the window overlooking the river, a book lying forgotten on his lap. 'Elin!' He rose to greet me, steadying himself against the windowsill. 'Iris said you might call today.' He glanced past me. 'No Mouse?'

'No, not today. She's quite well. I saw her this morning and she sends her love.'

'Good.' He smiled. 'Good.' His bandages were not quite so all encompassing, and he appeared stronger.

'Iris said your treatment at the hospital is going well.'

'Yes.' He grimaced. 'I'm afraid I was a self-pitying fool when I saw you last, Elin. Seeing the state of some of those poor fellows makes me realise I got off lightly. At least I can see and hear and have a mouth to speak with, and my hand is improving day by day. You'll be glad to know that I'm resigned to a lack of admiring glances. It will probably prompt me to do something useful with my life instead.'

'You don't need beauty Owen. You never did. Not for me.' I could make out more of his face. He was still the same Owen, despite the scars and the bandages. There was a troubled look in his eyes. I wanted to take him in my arms and smooth it away, but not until I'd said what I'd come to say. 'I wanted so much to see you.'

'Did you?' His voice was wary.

I took a step closer. 'Of course I did.' I took a deep breath. In the distance came the clatter of tea being prepared. It was now or never. 'Owen, I am going to leave Hugo.'

There was a sharp intake of breath. 'Leave?'

'Yes. Not now, of course. I couldn't leave Hiram now, and I couldn't hurt Hugo while he is still risking his life. But afterwards. When the war is over and things are back to normal.'

'If they ever are,' he muttered.

I ignored this. 'I'm not asking anything from you, Owen. I'm not doing this for you, but because I can't stay with Hugo. Not anymore. I can never go back to being the girl I was when I met him, and I can't pretend. I *won't* pretend. I wanted you to hear it from me, and I wanted to tell you that I'm not asking you to make a decision of any kind. I don't want you to think that this traps you in any way. I am going to do this, whatever you decide.'

Slowly, he leant his head on my shoulder. I held him as gently as I could. 'Elin, I can't ask you to do this,' he said. 'I have no means of supporting you. I don't know if I will ever be strong enough to support a family of my own. It wasn't meant to be like this. I was supposed to die, and you were supposed to go and live your life in freedom.'

'If you'd died, a part of me would have died too.' I lifted his head so his eyes met mine. 'You are not asking me to do this. I don't want you to support me, Owen, or look after me. I can look after myself.' I kissed him as lightly as I could. 'And I certainly don't intend to play nursemaid. So, you see, you will just have to get yourself well.'

He laughed. A slightly painful laugh that ended in a sharp intake of breath, but a laugh all the same. His lips rested gently against mine. 'You know that all I want is to be with you.'

I returned his kiss, feeling him wince with pain under the pressure, though he still held me as close as he could. 'Then will you concentrate on getting better and trust me that when this war ends, I will find a way to be free?'

His undamaged hand traced my face, learning every part of it, committing it to memory, every gentle caress a kiss that could not be given.

'I will wait for you, Elin, for as long as you need.' His fingers brushed my lips. 'And if you change your mind...'

'I won't.'

'If you change your mind, I will understand.' His lips touched mine once more. 'I want you to know that I will understand, and I will never blame you.'

* * *

The sun was sinking that evening as the train went round the headland and the familiar curve of Port Helen came into view.

I walked up the path from the village feeling energy flowing through me. The walled garden was neat, all ready for tomorrow. Even with the windows blacked out, Hiram looked welcoming as I made my way to the kitchen door.

Cook was stirring soup over the stove. I stood for a few minutes watching her and the familiar scene. An ache tugged at my heart at the thought of leaving my home, the place that had been my world for as long as I could remember. At the same time, I knew I had no choice. Not if I wanted to live free of regret for the rest of my life.

Mrs Hughes heard my footsteps and turned. 'Miss Elin!' There was something in her face. In the way she didn't rush to welcome me. Something that only meant one thing.

'Hugo.'

'Oh, *cariad*.' There was such a mix of emotion in her face. My stomach contracted.

'Is he…?'

'No *cariad*. He's been injured. The message came not an hour ago.'

I took a deep breath. 'Badly?'

'He was well enough to bring home. So they must believe he will survive. He's been taken to Applebourne. Miss Alice telephoned as soon as he was brought in.' She hesitated. 'She said they would be operating in the morning.'

I sat down in a chair. 'What kind of operation?'

'One of his legs has been badly crushed, Miss Alice said. The surgeon is hopeful they can save it, but even if they can, he may never walk properly again.'

Grief flooded through me. Grief for Hugo, and a terrible, anguished grief for myself. 'I should go to him.'

Cook crouched down by me, taking my hands in hers. 'There is nothing you can do tonight, *cariad*. Miss Alice said he wouldn't know you if you did, he's been so heavily sedated against the pain. He's in the best possible hands now. It's when he comes round from the operation that he'll need you. Whatever happens, he's going to need you more than ever, now, my dear.'

'Yes. Yes, of course.' My whole body was in turmoil, my mind a blank. I felt Hiram's walls close in around me. No longer comforting and familiar, but a prison, crushing the last breath from my lungs.

Part Four

Chapter Thirty-Three

JANUARY 1918

Alice was waiting for me as I pulled the Mercedes onto a grass verge, jumped out and ran between the line of ambulances drawing up at the front door of Applebourne.

She hugged me tight. 'Hugo survived the operation, and it looks as if they've managed to save his leg.'

'Thank Heaven.'

'He's not out of the woods yet.' Alice gazed at me anxiously. 'The doctors are hopeful, but it's still early days.'

'I understand,' I replied. Around us, ambulances were being unloaded. Stretchers were carried up the steps to the waiting nurses, followed by the walking wounded. Behind them, led by a sergeant with two heavily bandaged arms, came a long line of men, their eyes bandaged, shuffling slowly, one after the other.

'You'd better come into my office,' said Alice. 'The doctors will speak to you when they can, but ambulances have been arriving since yesterday afternoon. None of them have left the operating theatres since midnight.' She took me into a little room lined with row upon row of files and sat me in a chair while she fetched a cup of tea.

That day, the ambulances never stopped. It was soon clear that there would be no question of speaking to a surgeon. The operations continued with barely a pause. Every doctor and nurse available had been called in, working in shifts, snatching a few hours rest on any resting place they could find. I could see the greyness in their faces, and the despair as they fought to save lives and limbs beyond saving, and ease the agony of endless lines of exhausted and frightened men waiting their turn. In that great tide of misery, an officer and his wife were simply one amongst thousands, each life a battle in itself.

Thanks to Alice, I was able to see Hugo briefly. He did not move or open his eyes when I spoke to him. He looked so small and pale in the hospital bed, a great cage protecting his mangled leg, that I had no wish to disturb him. There was nothing I could do. Nothing I could feel. Like hundreds, thousands, millions of other women, all I could do was wait. But, like all those waiting, I could not stay idle when there was so much to be done.

As I left Hugo's ward, I joined the nurses and the VADs helping in any way I could, fetching bandages and carrying instruments, delivering food and cups of tea to those recovering, sitting with the waiting, and the dying, and wiping blood from the floor.

'How long has it been like this?' I asked a young VAD, as we made up a new delivery of beds of all shapes and sizes donated by families in the area.

'A few days.' Clara frowned, brushing the hair from her eyes with a hand reddened from washing and cleaning. 'A week, maybe?' She couldn't have been more than nineteen and with her tiny waist and delicate wrists she appeared more like twelve. I guessed from the look of stunned horror on her face that she had not been at Applebourne long. 'They say there's a big battle in a place called Passchendaele, and Heaven knows how long it will last.' Her blue eyes filled with tears. 'A boy died just now. He wasn't much older than my brothers. I was holding his hand and he was so sure I was his mother and I didn't know what to say. I turned away to speak to one of the nurses and he was dead.'

'At least you were with him,' I said gently. 'You allowed him to be with his mother for those last minutes. That was the best anyone could do.'

I held her while she sobbed her heart out. She pulled herself together and wiped her eyes. 'I don't know how the others get used to it.'

'I'm pretty sure they don't. They just learn to put it to one side so they can carry on.'

'I suppose.' We finished the bed and moved onto the next. 'It feels like the end of the world, sometimes. Whenever an appeal goes out from the hospital, people donate beds and sheets and all kinds of things, but it's never enough. This is the last empty room in the whole hospital. Some of the orderlies were talking about putting up tents in the grounds next, and it's freezing cold already and there's still months of winter to come.'

'Let's hope it won't come to that,' I reassured her.

For all my hope, there were soon tents springing up over the lawns at Applebourne, as there were in every hospital on the south coast. Each time I visited in the months that followed, more had appeared, and still the hospital could not keep up with the injured, the dead and the dying.

Hugo's recovery was painfully slow. Twice he was taken back for further operations on his damaged leg. Infection set in, and for a while it seemed it could not be saved, but then slowly it began to heal and Hugo, though weak, was finally able to take notice of his surroundings.

'My dear,' he said, holding my hand as his eyes finally rested on me with recognition. Spring had arrived and the windows were open to a fresh breeze stealing through the wards.

'Hello, Hugo,' I replied. He was gaunt and pale. Deep lines had appeared on his forehead and shadows lay under his eyes. His skin was like parchment, as if it might tear at the slightest touch. Even his eyes were dull and distant. I fought down a sense of fear that I no longer recognised him. 'The nurses tell me you are getting stronger by the day. We'll soon have you back home at Hiram. You'll soon be well again there.'

'Yes,' he murmured, eyes closing, his hand falling away from mine.

'It will take time, Mrs Helstone,' said a nurse gently, seeing my distress. 'Your husband has months of recuperation ahead of him. But he has survived the worst. I'm sure with your care he can be back to his old self in no time.'

I waited for twenty minutes or more, but Hugo did not stir, exhausted by the effort of even that short conversation. It was impossible to stay still with the rush and bustle around me, so I made my way into the nearest tent, which had to be made ready for the next rush of casualties. I worked steadily for several hours, returning every now and again to see if Hugo had woken up, but mostly thankful for the occupation of making up the beds with clean sheets and every blanket that could be found.

I had just reached the last group of beds, crammed so close to the edges they were nearly pushing their way out of the tent walls, when I discovered a pile of clean – if slightly threadbare – blankets being placed on the mattress next to me.

'There you are,' said a familiar voice. 'Every last one I could beg or borrow. I was told you might need these.'

I swung round. 'Owen!' The VAD at the other side of the bed gave me a sideways look. 'Captain Northholme, I mean.' My heart tightened at the nearness of him. I steadied myself and did my best to sound as if I were speaking to an acquaintance. 'I didn't know you were an orderly.'

'I'm not.' He gave a wry smile. 'At least not in general.' His bandages had been removed, apart from a light covering of his left hand. The burns on one side of his face were still red and angry, tightening the skin and distorting the shape of his left eye. 'I've been working with the doctors who do facial reconstructions. It seems that despite my hand I have an aptitude for photography. I record the face before surgery so the reconstructions can be matched as accurately as possible, and also their progress. It helps the men that I've needed skin grafts myself, that and the way I look. I've been helping out here for the past few weeks, training up a few more men. But I'm not needed today, so I thought I might as well make myself useful.'

He cleared his throat. 'I was sorry about your husband, Mrs Helstone. And I am glad to hear he is recovering.'

'Yes,' I said. 'Thank you.' My stomach clenched at the rawness of his scars set against the remains of the handsome face. The VAD was fussing with the blankets, barely bothering to disguise the fact that she was hanging on every word. In the closed, gossipy world of the nurses' dormitory, I could just imagine the whispers that poor Major Helstone's wife might be taking comfort elsewhere and not so eager to see her husband recover as she appeared, and him such a brave man too. I could see the same thought had crossed Owen's mind. He was already beginning to move away.

'Have you heard from your cousin?' I said.

'I had a letter from her a few days ago.' He gave a quick glance towards the VAD. 'Perhaps you would like to join me for a cup of tea in the canteen, if we can still get one, when you've finished here, Mrs Helstone? I know how fond you are of my cousin, I'm sure you would like to hear all her news.'

'Thank you, Captain,' I replied. 'I would like that.'

* * *

Owen was waiting for me as I reached the canteen. We collected mugs of weak tea and found a table in a corner, half hidden behind a pillar.

'I hoped I'd find you here.' His hand touched mine briefly. 'I'm rather afraid I badgered Alice into telling me when you were next visiting.'

'I'm glad.' Just the presence of him, so near and yet as far from my reach as if he had emigrated half a world away, sent a deep ache into my bones. 'I so wanted to see you, and to explain.' I took a deep breath. 'Owen…'

'You don't have to explain, Elin. I promise I didn't come here to ask anything of you. I couldn't bear not to see you again. And I wanted to tell you that I understand. Heaven knows, I wish I didn't. But I do.'

A deep hopelessness overcame me at the finality of his tone. 'I meant all those things I said, the last time I saw you. I meant them with all my heart.'

'You weren't to know what was going to happen.'

'I haven't changed my mind,' I said earnestly. 'Not one bit. But I can't leave Hiram. Not now. Not with this war still dragging on, and so much suffering. Too many people depend on Hiram. And I can't leave Hugo. Not while he's like this.'

We were silent for a few minutes, staring into our tea. 'I really have heard from Mouse,' he said at last.

'Oh?' I kept my voice neutral. 'How is she?'

'Well.' His hand rested next to mine once more. 'I'm going to see her in a few weeks' time.'

My head shot up. 'Did she ask you?'

'No.'

'Owen—'

'It's all right,' he said gently. 'I know. She told me.' A look of utter sadness came over his face. 'She told me everything. I should have known, the day of Edmund's funeral. I would have if I hadn't been so sunk in self-pity. For that I will never forgive myself.'

'Don't be a fool. You can't blame yourself. I saw how much pain you were in and how frightened you were about the future. Mouse wouldn't let me tell *anyone*. You can't blame yourself for that.'

'That doesn't excuse the blindness. Mouse never could keep much from me, even when we were small. Northholme could be a cold and lonely place for children for all its grandeur. We always looked out for each other. But when she needed it most I wasn't there for her. If it hadn't been for you and Jack…' He shuddered.

'But now I can do something, and I think she needs someone more than ever. I'll stay with her for as long as I can. I'll try and see if she will speak to her father. I'm sure she's far too proud to go begging. But I'll try. And there must be something I can do.'

'You'll be the best thing for her, Owen. I was hoping to go and see her this summer, but now it's impossible.'

A faint smile crossed his face. 'And I would like to meet your Aunt Catrin and visit the cottage by the sea, the things that are part of you and I never thought to see.'

'I envy you,' I said wistfully 'I can't help feeling I'll never see them again.'

'Elin—'

'I can't ask you to wait.' The words had built up inside me until they spilled out in a rush.

'I'll wait for you for as long as you wish. You know that.'

I shook my head despairingly. 'No, Owen. I can't ask you to throw your life away for me. You told me that day in the orchard that you'd never known how precious life was until you faced death every day at the front. You set me free to live, even if you were no longer alive to be a part of it. I loved you more than ever for that. Now it's my turn. It may take years for Hugo to be well enough to run Hiram and start a new life for himself.' I swallowed. 'From the way the doctors have been talking, it may never happen.' I took his hands. 'I can't ask you to give up all hope of a family and happiness. I could never live with myself.'

His hands tightened over mine. 'I can't stop loving you, Elin. I've no intention of forgetting you or giving up hope.'

'Please don't make this any harder than it is.'

'Very well.' His eyes met mine. 'I will live my life. I will never expect anything from you, Elin. But if you ever need help of any kind, or simply a friend, I will be there for you. Whatever happens.'

'Thank you,' I murmured. I let my eyes fall. I could not bear to let him see my pain, or the emptiness inside me. I wanted to rush away to lick my wounds in private, but I could not bear to relinquish his touch.

'Good afternoon, Mrs Helstone. You are well, I trust?' I looked up to find Mr Connors standing next to our table, a look of intense enjoyment on his face.

Slowly, I removed my hand from Owen's. 'Good afternoon, Mr Connors. I didn't know that you were visiting Applebourne.'

He smiled. 'Obviously not.'

Owen looked up sharply at his tone. I could see him rising to his feet. I trod on his foot, hard, beneath the table. To my relief, he subsided.

'You'll find the soup is bland, but the tea is hot,' I said. 'Good day, Mr Connors.' I turned back to Owen. 'I'm so very sorry, Captain. I sympathise with your loss. We all need to support each other at such a time,' I added pointedly. I felt, rather than saw, Connors turn on his heel and make his way towards the food counter.

'He should be given notice for speaking to you like that,' growled Owen. 'I've a good mind to report him to the hospital authorities.'

'And cause a scene?' From the corner of my eye I could see Connors watching us closely. 'That's exactly what he'd enjoy, so he can throw his insinuations all over the place.' I lowered my voice. 'Do you know him?'

Owen shrugged. 'I've seen him once or twice. He delivers medical supplies for the hospitals in London. He must do the same for the ones along the coast. He has a reputation for being able to get anything you want on the Black Market, if you pay him enough. There's always someone prepared to exploit others' misery for their own gain,' he added darkly.

Connors' gaze had not abated. He took a table nearby, easily within earshot, his eyes fixed on the two of us. We drank our tea in silence.

At last I stood up. Perhaps it was a mercy Connors had interrupted us. There were to be no lingering farewells, even though we might never see each other again. I took a last glance at Owen. I would not otherwise have been able to let him go. 'Give my regards to your family, Captain,' I said loudly. 'And good luck.'

I walked up to the wards without glancing back. Hugo was still asleep. I moved over to the windows overlooking the driveway. After a while, I saw Owen emerge from one of the tents. He looked up at the house, his gaze lingering as if he could make me out at the window looking down at him. Then he turned, and within minutes was driving out of sight.

Much to my relief, I didn't see Connors when I visited Hugo in the months that followed. Between the shortages and the rationing, it was difficult to make the journey to the hospital. Petrol was almost impossible to come by and food was scarcer than ever, making the work in the walled garden everyone's first priority. I took fresh vegetables and preserved fruits whenever I visited, which at least made the journeys feel less of an indulgence.

As summer arrived, so did Mouse's baby. It was a little boy she named Francis, after the patron saint of peace. Mouse, being Mouse, did not gush in her letters. At least little Frankie was a true Northholme when it came to looks, was all she would say, that and how she didn't know what she'd have done without Owen's visits and Aunt Catrin's help.

I missed them, and longed to see them. But I could not leave when Hugo might any day take a turn for the worse. I had my train ticket ready and promised to visit as soon as Hugo was back home and settled.

Within months, Mouse's letters were full of plans to buy the Caradocs' abandoned farm next to Aunt Catrin's, as a proper home for her and Frankie. Not to mention the large flat meadows that would be ideal for flying.

'I'm going to teach Frankie to fly, the first chance I have,' she wrote, in her flowing scrawl. 'Then he can help me with my flying school. Children have to be useful, you know.'

I smiled with pleasure to see that Mouse could still make her plans and order the world as she wished it to be. Aunt Catrin's letters reassured me, too. She hadn't hidden from me the fact that Mouse had struggled at first even to look at the baby. But as the weeks went by, she spent more and more time sitting by the cradle, watching her son and gradually falling in love with the new life, with its helplessness and its fears and its attempts to make sense of the world. Until, Aunt Catrin wrote, Mouse, although she would never confess as much, was well and truly besotted.

I also heard, from Mouse, that Owen had begun a new life for himself as he had promised. He was working for a charitable organisation set up to help soldiers so badly wounded they could never return to their former lives, and, using the skills he had learnt with his work for the facial reconstructions, he had begun to make a name for himself as a photographer and journalist. Now and again, when I was at Applebourne, I would flick through a newspaper and come across his name next to an article on the shortage of prosthetic limbs for amputees, or a haunting photograph of wounded men, row upon row of them in great vaulted halls. Mouse gave me no further details of his life, where he was living, or if he was married. I wondered if he had asked her not to. But I did not dare write to her with the question, so it remained unanswered.

* * *

As the year drew on, it seemed the war was to end, after all. There had been so much talk of an ending, and it had dragged on for so long, I did not dare believe it. But as we bottled the last fruit from the garden and stored the last of the vegetables, and Hugo was finally declared well enough to come home, it became a certainty.

There were bonfires on the coast and laughter and music rising up from Port Helen on the day victory was finally proclaimed. We kept our own celebrations in Hiram until a few days later, for Hugo's return. Cook roasted the largest joint of beef she could find, while I made Eve's Pudding and used the bottled raspberries to make Hugo's favourite junket, and brought up last year's Elderflower Champagne, along with a dusty bottle of real champagne Hugo had been saving for a special occasion.

As I waited in the fierce wind of that November afternoon, was I the only wife with a mixture of feelings as her husband was returned to her? I was happy to have him safe, that I would never again dread the telephone ringing or the arrival of a telegram. I was relieved I'd no longer have to bear the entire responsibility for Hiram on my own and that I could concentrate on the walled garden and the best use of its produce. Already I was planning for next year, when we could get back to growing more than potatoes and carrots. I could try more exotic crops, like garlic, melons and even pineapples.

As the automobile from Applebourne turned into the driveway and made its way towards me, I could not help a slight clenching in my stomach and a flutter of nerves at the return of a man I had barely spoken to for almost four years. Four long, life-changing years, during which both of us had been through so much we could no longer be the same as before the war.

The automobile drew up next to me. I could see Hugo propped up stiffly in the passenger seat, his face white with pain. The driver jumped out and lifted a wheelchair from the back.

'There you are, sir. We'll have you out and inside in a jiffy.'

I stopped dead in my tracks, my hand on the passenger door. I couldn't believe it. I cursed myself for being so blind. For not asking questions. How he'd managed it, I'd no idea. But there he was, lifting Hugo down into the chair with an air of this not being the first occasion.

'Thank you, Mr Connors,' I said.

My instinct was to get rid of him as quickly as possible, before he could sidle his way in any further. The last thing I wanted was for Connors to point out the lack of a butler or footman, or indeed any male help in the Hall. But I had to preserve at least the appearances of courtesy. 'Can I offer you a cup of tea before you go?'

'Go?' His smile was a smirk.

'Back to Applebourne.' I swallowed my pride and my unease. 'Unless we can offer you a bed for the night?'

'The room at the far end of the corridor will do,' said Hugo. He looked exhausted but his voice was strong.

'Of course,' I began, my mind racing on the practicalities of moving Molly back to her old room in the attics and making up the bed. 'But perhaps one of the large rooms at the back might be more comfortable?'

'It's not comfort but convenience the man needs,' said Hugo, irritably.

'Convenience?'

'You don't think Applebourne Hospital would have sent your husband home without suitable attendance, Mrs Helstone?' put in Connors smoothly. 'Or, Heaven forefend, expect you to act as a nurse.'

'I'm perfectly capable.'

'In loving kindness, I'm sure, but not in practicalities,' he replied.

Hugo stirred in his chair as if he could not be comfortable. 'Mr Connors has agreed to leave his post delivering medical supplies to attend to me until I am back on my feet. We should be grateful, my dear.'

'Just a few weeks,' agreed Connors. 'No time at all.'

He moved behind Hugo to wheel him towards the house. He looked me full in the face, this time without disguise. In my husband's absence, his look silently informed me, I had dared to deny him the position he had once been promised. Now he was going to take it, and more. And there was nothing I could do about it.

Chapter Thirty-Four

WINTER 1918

That day my life changed. It came so suddenly, so completely without warning, that at first I could not believe it had happened.

For weeks, Hugo remained in his rooms. I tried to see him, to talk to him and maybe re-kindle some kind of understanding between us, but Connors was always there. Always listening. Always stepping in with some practical question about the estate or reassurance that Hugo would soon be able to take his natural place at the head of the household once more. I saw how hungrily Hugo listened to him. Where once he had stalked the grounds reassuring himself his world was as it had always been, now he hung on Connors' every word. I had been quite clearly told that Hugo's internal injuries meant that he would never return to full fitness, and that he knew this. But I was powerless in the face of Hugo's need to believe the opposite.

I had too many battles to fight, between the shortages and the appearance of influenza in Port Helen. Time would tell, I told myself. Meanwhile, the routine in the garden continued with the endless production of food. I worked in the kitchen with Cook, laying down stores, creating recipes to make the most of our resources. Nothing had changed, except for the presence upstairs in Hugo's room. I understood how much he hated me to see him so helpless. His pride, always fragile, had become tattered over the years at the front. There was a thinness to his veneer of dignity that frightened me.

I hoped he might confide in his brother, but when Rupert visited a few weeks after Hugo's return home, he emerged from Hugo's room with a look of despair.

'I only hope Hugo comes back to himself soon,' he said as we walked in the gardens that evening. 'He has changed so. It's as if the brother I knew died out there.' He scowled back towards the house. 'That damned Connors fellow is hanging on his every word. That creature certainly knows how to play on a man's weakness. Hugo won't have a word said against him. Why he can't see it, I don't know.' He smiled at me, a gentle, kind smile. 'I'm sure you will be able to make him see sense, dear Elin. You always brought out the best in Hugo.'

'I will try my best,' I murmured. Although, as Hugo would rarely agree to see me, I could not quite fathom how. When I tried to visit my husband, Connors would be often ready with an excuse. Major Helstone was tired. Or asleep. Or his bath had just been drawn.

'There really is no need to trouble yourself, Mrs Helstone,' he said one afternoon, when I ignored his statement that the Major was resting, and stepped past him into the room. Hugo was sitting by the fire, as I had seen him do so often, his eyes fixed on the flames.

He looked up at the sound of my footsteps. 'Elin!' He glanced towards Connors, as if uncertain what to do with my presence.

I picked up the book next to his chair. 'I'll come and read to you, if you would like, Hugo,' I said. 'I don't mind if you are tired and fall asleep. But we could at least sit together. We have been so long apart.'

'I really don't think that will be necessary, Mrs Helstone.' Connors removed the book from my hands, placing it in its previous position. 'The Major needs to rest if he is to regain his strength. Perhaps another day. When he is feeling stronger.'

I looked at my husband. 'Hugo?'

'Not today, my dear.' Hugo's eyes slid from mine. 'Perhaps tomorrow.'

'Then let me just sit with you. I won't be any trouble. Besides, I'm sure Mr Connors might enjoy taking a turn in the garden. It's so airless up here.'

'Not at all,' smiled Connors.

I gritted my teeth and returned his smile. 'But you are so good to my husband, Mr Connors. We should not ask so much of you. I'm sure the fresh air will do you good.'

'I will get enough fresh air when I begin to take Major Helstone out into the grounds,' replied Connors. 'Which will be very soon, eh, Major?'

'Yes, of course,' muttered Hugo.

I glanced from one to the other. Hugo was looking increasingly ill at ease, while Connors was making it quite clear I was unwelcome. I swallowed my humiliation as best I could, and made my way back into the corridor.

As Connors closed the door behind me, I heard Hugo murmur. 'Perhaps it might be as well…'

'No Major, you were quite right,' said Connors. 'This is no place for the gentler sex. They need protecting, don't you agree? It wouldn't do to go upsetting them. Once you have regained your strength and can go downstairs again, then I'm sure Mrs Helstone will be pleased to see you.'

'Yes.' Hugo's voice was part-eager, part-anxious, as if Connors' assurances were all that he needed to return to full health. 'Yes, of course.'

Unable to bear any more, I hurried away out of earshot.

I did not attempt to make my way past Connors again. At most I was permitted to sit with Hugo for a few minutes once a day, in the evenings when the room was darkened, the lamps low. I tried to talk about the garden, tell him of our progress. Consult his opinion. His replies were few, but at least there was something we shared in this isolated world of his.

Gradually men began to come back to Port Helen and the surrounding villages. But so few of them. Charlotte and Bethany returned home and Kitty went back to help her mother in Port Helen. Women all around me were returning to their homes to take up their old lives again. I was no different, I told myself. It would take time to adjust, that was all.

Eventually Hugo began to attempt walking again, although he still remained mainly in his rooms, only rarely venturing downstairs. I would see him sometimes as I worked in the garden or went to fetch ingredients, a shadow in the window looking down. Watching. I should have been glad that he took some interest, but it made me uneasy.

The influenza did not abate with the end of the war. More deaths. More names in the newspapers. Many from Port Helen succumbed. More black armbands. More faces missing. The rest were left pale and weary. It felt as if we had been through so much and could bear no more.

Alice came as often as she could. Hugo refused to see her and after a while she didn't even try, just asking politely after his health. There was still work to be done at the hospital: men were still sick, still struggling like Hugo with the after-effects of the war. I couldn't help but notice that Alice visited less and less as time went on.

A few weeks after Christmas, Jack's mother died. She had never been strong, and over those last months of the war she had succumbed to one chest infection after another. Each time I saw her, she seemed weaker, and it was clear from the closed in look of grief on Jack's face that it was only a matter of time.

The day after Annie Treeve's funeral, I made my way into the walled garden. With the land girls and the school children returned to their previous lives, it was silent and empty. Only one of Mr Wiltshire's carefully trained gardeners had survived the fighting, but he had left almost immediately he was released from the army to live with his sister in Australia. Connors had found it difficult enough to find young William, who had an interest in growing and was prepared to kneel in mud and rain until his back ached and his fingers turned numb, rather than turn to manufacturing or the warmth of a shop floor.

I found Jack in one of the greenhouses. The last of the vines had been neatly pruned, with the cuttings and the leaves swept up. Jack was propped against one of the benches, lost in thought, an envelope in his hand.

'I thought I might find you here,' I said.

'Mrs Helstone.' He pushed the envelope inside his jacket. 'As you can see, all done. A bit late, but at least it's before the sap starts rising again.'

'Yes.' He wasn't quite meeting my eye. I took a deep breath. 'I'll deliver it, if you like.'

'I beg your pardon?'

'The letter. It's for Hugo, isn't it?' He bit his lip. I could see the torn look on his face. I had barely spoken to him since Hugo's return, and he looked tired and worn. 'You've nothing to keep you here now.'

'It's not that.' He hesitated.

'Mouse told me she would write to you.'

The troubled look on his face deepened. 'Yes. Yes, she did. Just after her baby was born.'

I looked at him sadly. I had grown so used to him working in the gardens and we had been through so much together. I was going to miss his friendship and his reassuring presence more than I dared think. 'Then you know that she needs you. Even though she's far too proud to say.' I wondered how much exactly Mouse had told him, or how much he had guessed. 'And maybe also feeling a little shame?' I added tentatively.

'She shouldn't be,' he returned fiercely. 'Never. She has accepted what happened and has made a new way of living for herself. She is far more to be admired than she ever was before.'

I might never have another chance to say it. 'And loved?'

He turned his face away. 'I can't ask anything of her, Elin. I never could, the gap between us is too great. And now she may never want to love, or ever be able to trust a man again.'

'But she needs you,' I said quietly.

He turned back, with the same troubled look. 'I hate to leave you like this. I know Connors. The man always was in love with power and money. I can see how he is using Hugo's weakness to gain control over Hiram and push you aside.'

'It doesn't matter,' I replied. 'I never expected to rule Hiram once Hugo returned. I shall simply be like any other wife in my situation and find another occupation for myself.'

'It's not that.' He frowned at me. 'You are both my friends, you and Hugo. Two of the dearest friends I've known. I don't like to see what Connors is doing to you both, or the way he is driving you apart.' He took out the envelope, turning it between his hands. 'I've tried to talk to Hugo. Oh, not about Connors,' he added. 'Just to speak to him.' His hands stilled. 'I felt I didn't know him. Even more so than after the war in the Transvaal.' He seemed about to add something, but instead placed the envelope back in his pocket.

'Hopefully when he gets stronger he will become himself again.'

'Yes, let's hope so.'

'I can look after myself,' I said. 'I have friends, and people who care for me. I'm really not your responsibility, Jack. You have done enough already. I can't expect you to keep on saving my life.'

He smiled. 'I would never insult you by trying to look after you, Elin.'

'Then also trust me to make my choices in my own way?'

Slowly he nodded. He took out the envelope, handing it to me this time, as if afraid he might destroy it otherwise. 'I've given a week's notice. There are a couple of young men in Port Helen you might try. I've given Hugo their names.'

'Thank you.' I could hear Connors' voice at the front of the house, admonishing Molly about the lack of sheen in the hallway floors. I'd already been through with him once this week that polishing had been the last thing on anyone's mind during the war, and no help for Molly had yet appeared, meaning she was even more rushed off her feet than ever. I was continuing to help as much as I could, but Hugo's shocked face when he caught me filling the coal scuttle in the dining room meant I was limited to the times when he had returned to his rooms, with Connors dancing close attendance. I could feel another battle looming, one that I felt already I barely had the energy to fight.

'Elin.' Jack had heard Connors too. He grasped my hand. 'Always remember what I told you in France. You can't live someone's life for them, and they'll never thank you if you do.' His grip tightened.

'Hugo will never tell me of his demons. How can I help him if he won't share them?'

Jack hesitated. He seemed about to speak, then gave my face such a searching look it startled me. It was as if he saw something about me I didn't yet understand. Before I could demand an explanation, he shook his head and released my hands.

'You'll find a way,' he said. 'You are strong and resourceful and you never give up. You didn't hesitate to pull a man from a burning vehicle or a woman from the sea, and you never showed fear, even when you were terrified. I know that, somehow, you'll find a way.'

'Applebourne will soon be closing,' Alice announced one day, shortly after Jack's departure, as we strolled together on the lawns in front of Hiram Hall, huddled up in our coats, away from listening ears. 'There are barely any men there now. They are arranging for the others to be moved. The family don't want to move back, and I don't blame them. The Fords lost three sons in the war and old Mr Ford died of influenza on his way home. Cicely has chosen to return to America. A cousin is inheriting and eager to get into the house.'

'What will you do?'

'I'm not sure.'

'You know you are always welcome to move back into your old room. Hiram is still your home.'

'Thank you.' She squeezed my arm and avoided my eyes. 'But I have been speaking to one of the nurses. She has been offered a post in her uncle's firm. She offered to put in a good word for me.'

'As a clerk?'

'No. As a manager in a hotel.'

'Alice, that's wonderful!'

She glanced back towards me. 'It's a hotel in London. A big one. The war has changed things, Elin. So many men were killed at the front and there is a need for skilled labour. It's a good post, with an excellent salary, almost as good as a man's. I'd have my evenings to myself. I'd be able to rent rooms. Even a small house. I've enjoyed being able to earn my own living. You have a husband, Elin. They are saying that many women will never marry, with so many men lost.' She gave a faint smile. 'I'm not sure I'd ever wish to give up my independence now, but it means I do need to find an occupation to support myself.'

'Of course.' We were silent for a while. This was a parting of the ways. First Mouse, now Alice. Each of them moving on to new and different lives in which I had no part. I should have pitied them both: Mouse with a fatherless child she'd never wanted, Alice with no hope of a family of her own. Instead, I envied them with an intensity that frightened me. 'When would you start?'

'Not for some months.'

'I see.' I looked back at the house.

Alice followed my gaze. A shadow at Hugo's window walked away. 'You will come and visit me in London?' she said. 'You can't spend your entire time cooped up in Hiram. We could visit the galleries and the theatres.'

'Yes. Yes, of course.'

'I won't let you say no. I'm not going to leave until you agree and we've spoken to Hugo to arrange a time. He can't stop you from visiting your family.' She cursed under her breath. 'What does that man want? Whenever I come to see you, he's always hanging around. Doesn't he ever leave you alone?'

'Mrs Helstone.' Connors ignored my companion. Had he planned for this summons while Alice was with me? 'The Major wishes to speak with you.' I instinctively looked up at the windows. 'Major Helstone is feeling stronger today. You will find him in the study.'

'Surely it can wait a few minutes? I spoke to Major Helstone less than an hour ago. There was nothing pressing then. I will go when my cousin has left.'

'The Major asked to speak to you urgently, Mrs Helstone.'

'It's all right, Elin,' said Alice. 'It's time I set off back to catch the train to Applebourne.' She kissed my cheek. 'Remember what I said, and I'll speak to you soon.' Without acknowledging Connors, Alice strode away through the walled garden towards the cliffs and the path down to Port Helen.

Accompanied, of course, by Connors, I made my way back to the house.

'Ah, there you are, my dear.' Hugo sat behind the desk, two sturdy walking sticks propped up beside him, leafing through the household accounts.

'I'll leave you, sir,' said Connors. He nodded towards a large bell that had come from the school to sit on the mahogany desk. 'Ring if you should need me.'

'Good man,' said Hugo as Connors left.

I gritted my teeth but said nothing. There was no point in alienating Hugo before we began. My stomach tensed. For no good reason, I told myself firmly. Everything was up-to-date. Everything was clear. There had been no great profit, but with the war Hiram was lucky to have survived at all. Old houses all around were succumbing to the effects of the war, to fortunes lost, sons gone and a lack of the staff needed to keep a great house running.

Hugo looked up as I hesitated, unpinning my hat as my eyes adjusted to the lack of sunlight. 'You've done very well, my dear. I told you Treeve was a good man. It's a sad business to lose him, but it can't be helped.'

I blinked. From Connors' summons, I'd feared I was about to be accused of sending the place spiralling towards bankruptcy. 'Thank you,' I murmured. 'Mr Treeve was a valuable help in the gardens, but I taught myself to do the accounting and the running of the Hall.'

'Of course, my dear.' He smiled at me. 'But I really can't expect you to bear such a responsibility now I am home.'

'No, of course not.' My shoulders relaxed a little. I was being oversensitive. It could not be easy for Hugo to return to the place that had been running very well without him. I smiled. 'I was only keeping the records up-to-date until you were well enough to take over again. I'm delighted to see you returned to your rightful place.'

'Good, good.' He turned back to the accounts.

'If there's anything you feel needs explaining…'

'Oh, no. Not at all. It's all perfectly clear.' Silence fell once more. I watched his face as he pored over each page, uncertain whether he wished me to stay. My mind crowded with a hundred different things I needed to do that day. After a while, I could bear the silence and the inactivity no longer.

'I'll ask Cook to make a cup of tea,' I murmured, escaping hastily to the kitchens. When I returned a few minutes later, Hugo had not moved. 'I've spoken to Cook,' I said cheerfully. 'There will be tea and cake in the drawing room. Unless you would prefer it out in the garden, Hugo? It's a lovely sunny day and quite warm out of the wind, and you've been inside for so long.'

He was frowning. 'You should not speak to Cook directly, my dear, let alone run down to the kitchens, for all the world as if you were a maid.'

'I don't mind. We've had to grow used to very few servants,' I replied with a smile. 'It only takes a few minutes, and I've discussed tonight's dinner and all tomorrow's meals with Cook, so there was no time wasted.'

'But it does not suit the dignity of my wife. We cannot carry on as if there were still a war. We should be employing a Housekeeper.'

My heart sank. 'Staff are very hard to come by now, Hugo, and I'm really very happy organising the house. I enjoy the challenge. It gives me something to do.'

'There are much better ways for you to employ your time, my dear, especially when we have guests to stay. We need a smoothly run house. And I should have my wife by my side.'

Now I was alarmed. 'But Hugo, I've grown used to having an occupation. It won't take all my time, I promise. Not now that you are able to take over the running of the estate. I'll still be able to sit with you when you wish. And we'll still meet for meals and for tea. It will give us something to talk about.' I winced at this, but fortunately Hugo did not appear to have heard.

'There's no need to worry, my dear. I have secured the services of Mr Connors' niece. She comes highly recommended and I'm sure will prove an excellent Housekeeper. She starts on Monday. At last we shall have a house that runs smoothly and is fit for guests to be invited to. The war is over: it's high time the place was full once more.'

I felt the air had been sucked from the room. I could no longer stand there and smile, with Hugo still flicking through the accounts while ordering my existence without so much as a by-your-leave.

'You might have at least consulted me, Hugo! I'm the one who is going to have to work with her. Surely the Housekeeper is a wife's responsibility? I can interview candidates if you feel so strongly that that is what is needed.'

'Why put you to so much trouble when there is a perfectly good candidate on our doorstep?'

'That's not the point,' I muttered between gritted teeth. Hugo did not answer. Dignity imbued every line of his body as he returned to flicking through the accounts book. I stood there, seething, too angry to remind him of the tea growing cold in the drawing room, too proud to leave. At last the silence became too uncomfortable to bear. I was about to turn and help Cook, when a sound from the open window made me stop.

From the gravel beneath, I heard a soft crunch. Footsteps. Slow, pausing, then moving as soundlessly as possible until they vanished into the soft grass.

I moved to the window. There was no one in sight. I turned back to Hugo, who was oblivious. The last thing I needed was to play even further into Connor's hands by alienating my husband by seeming a hysteric, suspicious of every noise. I could almost hear the satisfaction in that retreating tread.

'It sounds as if tea is ready, my dear,' I said. 'And Cook has promised us some of her best seed cake. Perhaps it's too cold to venture outside, after all. Shall we go in?'

Chapter Thirty-Five

SPRING 1919

Sissy Connors was not quite what I expected. For one thing, there was enough resemblance in the shape of the eyes and nose to declare her truly a blood relation to Connors. I'd expected a sharp little miss with an eye for the main chance and an ear at every keyhole. Sissy was pleasant, rather shy, and ill at ease in her new position. She was ridiculously young to be a Housekeeper, being little more than twenty at the most. She had clearly been told by her uncle that I was 'difficult'. For the first week or so she watched me like a startled rabbit, but when I showed no signs of raving or making unreasonable demands she relaxed a little. She even smiled once or twice.

Hugo was smitten, as I knew he would be from the moment I saw her softly pretty face framed by a mass of pale yellow curls. While she soon learned that I did not bite, her awe of Hugo never lessened, a daily reminder to my husband that the equally awed girl he had married had somehow vanished over the intervening years and was now nowhere to be seen.

I didn't dislike her. Poor girl, she was in a difficult enough position. She needed my help to ensure she kept the house in some kind of order, but must not betray any kind of liking or gratitude towards me when her uncle might see.

'I do understand,' I said one morning, when she was flushed with embarrassment at the chill she had adopted in her speech after Connors had interrupted our discussion of the day's meals.

'Ma'am?'

'It's never easy, being in the middle. And I'm not sure I'd want to cross your uncle, either.'

'Oh no, Mrs Helstone. Never. He's got a terrible temper on him.' She bit her lip, as if she had said too much. 'That is, I'm not sure what you mean, Madam.'

'Just that perhaps it's best to keep him happy. I'm sure we can relax the formalities a little when we are on our own?'

I watched a slow smile spread over Sissy's face, then she nodded. 'Yes, Mrs Helstone.'

I thought for a while that all might yet be well. Whatever Connors might have had in mind when he suggested his niece didn't appear to be taking effect. She was afraid of him, cowed by him even, but she had no reason to dislike me or to tell tales. Hugo kept his distance, but remained unfailingly courteous. I began to hope that if I was patient and waited for him to recover his strength, we might yet find some means of making some version of a marriage work.

Molly was the first to go. She had removed herself back to the attic good-humouredly enough when Connors appeared. She grumbled a little at the extra work, but was mollified by my attempts to hire a maid to assist her. The fact that no one replied to my advertisement did not dishearten me. Hiram was not alone in struggling to attract servants back to their old positions. Once the factories and the other means of employment were full, there was bound to be at least one young woman eager for a wage. But no one appeared, and it was Molly who left.

I found her one morning, tearing off her apron and cap as she shot down the stairs, two at a time. 'I will not be spoken to like that!'

'Molly?' I took her arm and led her into the kitchen. Her eyes were red with crying and her hair was wild from the dislodged pins. 'Molly, what is it?'

She sniffed loudly. 'I'm sorry, Mrs Helstone, I will not be spoken to like that. I'm not staying in this house a moment longer.' She flung the cap and apron on the kitchen table.

Cook grabbed her arm, preventing her from leaving. 'Good Heaven's girl, what has got into you? You can't just go. You need to give notice. And what will you do for work?'

Molly blew her nose. 'I'm giving notice now. This minute. I'm not expecting any wages. There are plenty of jobs going in that new Woolworths Department Store. I'm sick of cleaning grates and brushing stairs and not having time with my Ralph, even though he nearly got killed. I want a bit of life of my own.' She caught my eye and hiccupped. 'I'm sorry, Mrs Helstone. I truly am. But he's got no right. No right at all. And I won't stay in this house a moment longer.'

'That's all right, Molly.' There was no point in trying to soothe things over. 'I'll arrange for your things to be taken to your mother's house. Don't worry, I'll make sure you get the wages you are owed, and a good reference too.'

'Thank you,' she whispered, bursting into tears again.

I had no say in Molly's replacement. A fact that no longer surprised me. Her room, however, remained empty, as did the others in the servants' quarters beneath the eaves. Mrs Pettersham, a taciturn woman from Port Helen, appeared daily to clean and help Cook with the preparation of meals. Another of Connors' 'suggestions', I had no doubt.

'That Connors'll be rid of all of us, *cariad*, just you see,' Cook said to me in Welsh one evening, as we watched Mrs Pettersham make her way through the walled garden towards the path down to the village. 'All of us who are loyal to you. Question is, who will be next?'

* * *

When Hugo called me into the study a few days later, I dreaded to think what it might be.

'My dear,' he said, motioning me to sit down in the chair as he propped himself against the desk. 'There is a matter we need to discuss.'

'Yes, Hugo?'

'This business with the walled garden. Connors has tried his best to find a replacement for Jack Treeve, but even he is finding it impossible. There is such a shortage of men, they can pick and choose where they work, and it seems to take up so much of your time as it is.'

'I don't mind working in there,' I put in quickly. My heart had begun to race, my breath was shallow in my chest. 'I enjoy weeding and keeping the greenhouses tidy, and William is very good with the heavy work. It really is no trouble, and I enjoy it, and there is still so much that is difficult to buy and I've adapted so many of my mother's dishes to what we can grow here. It's worked so well during the years of the war, it would be a pity to lose it now.' He was frowning at me as if it had occurred to him for the first time that I had not simply sat forlorn and pining but had been fully occupied while he had been away. I swallowed my pride. 'It's a pleasant hobby for me, and far more suitable than helping Cook in the kitchens.'

'It's very good of you, my dear, but the war is ended. Imports are returning, there really is no need for us to go to the trouble of producing so much food, much of which we give away in any case.'

'There are still families suffering from the effects of the war and the influenza, especially those who have lost fathers and husbands or whose men have returned unable to work. The fresh fruit and vegetables we provide them with costs us very little and gives us a great deal of goodwill in the area, Hugo. Your friends' wives all do charitable work, why shouldn't this be mine?'

A slight frown creased his brow once more. I had a suspicion he was reflecting how his bride would never have questioned his decisions in this way, and that the delightful Miss Connors most surely never would. I felt old and haggard. A sharp-tongued shrew. A witch. And the worst of it was that I no longer cared.

'Let other houses take their turn in providing for the poor of Port Helen. Why should it always be us?' He brushed imaginary fluff from the top of his walking stick with the greatest of care.

I took a deep breath. 'Please let me have this, Hugo. I won't trouble you for anything else. But please let me have the walled garden. I'm not the only wife to have gardening as a hobby. It's perfectly respectable.' His eyes remained on the walking stick. Desperation began to take hold of me. 'I need an occupation, Hugo. Please understand I can't live in idleness. Just a few hours now and again. I promise I won't embarrass you by helping Mrs Hughes in the kitchen any more, or working in the house. I won't even try out any more recipes. Surely you wouldn't begrudge me one thing that would give me a sense of purpose?'

He glanced up at that, and I looked into dark haunted eyes. Briefly, they were clear once more, his smile gentle. 'All I want is for your happiness.'

My heart went out to my husband, lost somewhere deep inside this shell, where I could no longer reach him. 'Think of it as beneficial exercise for me, Hugo. You might find you enjoy the garden yourself. You could join me. It's a restful place to be.'

Hugo shook his head. 'No, my dear.'

'Then cannot you not at least share your thoughts with me?' I gazed at him with despair. 'I don't pretend to be able to fully understand what you went though in that terrible war, but I can try. We had our own fears and hardships here. I might understand more than you think.' He did not move, but I could tell by his stillness that he was listening. 'When I took Alice to Applebourne that first time, I saw the soldiers being brought in. I saw their torn bodies and the horror in their eyes. And besides—'

'Connors is right, of course.'

I blinked. Hugo was frowning over my shoulder into the distance as if I was not there. 'It really is a waste of William's time. He could be useful in so many other ways. Connors has an excellent idea of excavating the field next to the stream to create a lake, like the one at Northholme Manor. I do think of you, my dear. I remember how much you said you enjoyed your boating trip on the lake at Northholme.'

'Not just boating…' I bit my lip. Now was not the time to mention my swim, or the languorous effect of the water and the clinging weeds that set my every sense alight and aching with longing. Or the walk to the fountain with Owen, when my heart had been hopelessly, impossibly lost. I pushed that thought hastily away. 'It was very pleasant,' I muttered.

'There, you see. I'll speak to Mr Connors. The work can start tomorrow.'

'But why on earth would Mr Connors suggest a lake, when there is so much else to be done?' I took several deep breaths. 'Hugo, Mr Connors barely knows the Hiram estate. I ran it all those years you were away, and besides, I've known it all my life. It's in my blood. Everyone in Port Helen speaks of you as a good landlord. Times are still hard and there are so many practical things that need to be done. There is still very little income from the investments. Hiram cannot afford to live beyond its means. Are you sure Mr Connors knows what he is talking about? You are so much stronger now.' I laid my hand gently on his arm. 'Surely we might run Hiram just as well between us, without Mr Connors? As man and wife?'

He flinched, as if I had struck him with a hot iron.

I did not remove my hand. 'Please, Hugo. Please tell me if I have offended you. I never meant to. I know I have my faults. But I can learn. Just tell me what I need to do. I cannot bear this distance between us.'

I felt him shrink, as if the mere pressure of my hand on his sleeve had become unbearable. He turned, making his way painfully towards the chair on the opposite side of the desk. My hand dropped to my side. 'I'll speak to William in the morning,' he said.

I ran upstairs to my room, the only place where I could lock the door and break my heart without being disturbed, without being seen. As I reached my door, something metallic fell in one of the rooms further down the corridor. I could hear it rolling along the wooden panels of the floor. My blood was too hot to ignore it. Forgetting tears, I marched straight towards the sound, flinging wide the half-open door.

'Oh!' It was Sissy, crouched over a small ornament on the floor. She blushed furiously and dusted off the little figure of Achilles, replacing him back on the mantelpiece. 'I'm sorry, Mrs Helstone. I don't know why I was so clumsy.'

'No harm done,' I murmured automatically. On one of the beds sheets and blankets were piled high, next to a leaning tower of eiderdowns.

'It's for the guests next week,' said Sissy, following my gaze. 'Major Helstone wants all the beds made up and the rooms ready.'

'Surely this is for Mrs Pettersham to do?'

'Yes, yes of course.' Sissy was scarlet with mortification. 'But there's so much to be done to get ready, with all the cleaning and washing, and with no maid and so many beds to make up…'

'Of course.' I took hold of one of the sheets. 'Come on, I'll give you a hand.'

Sissy hesitated, but her relief was obvious. Between us we soon had the beds made and the room cleaned and ready and were moving on to the room next door. 'We should be hiring a girl from the village to help you,' I said, as we began on the next bed. 'At least when guests are expected. We can put another advertisement in the newspapers tomorrow.'

Sissy paused in changing a pillowcase. From the closed door of the study below came the sound of Hugo and Mr Connors deep in discussion of something or other to do with the estate. 'It's no good, Mrs Helstone,' she whispered. 'They won't come. No one will.'

'There has to be *someone* in need of a post. There are so many households without a breadwinner.'

'Yes. But they won't come here. Mrs Pettersham only came because no one will employ her because they all know she, well, sold things, during the war.'

'You mean she's a thief?'

Sissy shook her head. The murmur of voices had stilled as if the two men were pouring over plans or lists. She waited until the discussion started up again. 'The black market. You won't say anything, will you? You won't say that I told you?'

'No, of course not.' Hugo would probably only see me as a foolish woman who listened to gossip, so it was an easy promise to make. I looked her straight in the eye. 'Was that how your uncle knew her?'

Sissy nodded. 'He could get anything during the war, anything you wanted. If you were prepared to pay. And my gran said he sold other things, too.'

'What other things?'

'Medicines. And pills and things to make you feel better and make your mind forget.' Her voice sank to barely a whisper. 'And secrets. Gran was always certain he'd been spying for the Germans for years, even before the war. He used to boast to her about how he could find out anything, and how valuable he was to certain people, and how he'd get his proper reward one day. He thought she didn't understand what he meant, but she did. Gran said that's how he came by the money to buy Granddad's farm. They couldn't keep it up, you see. Not after Dad was killed and Granddad died of pneumonia. Uncle James offered to buy them out and Gran said she had no choice.' She glanced wistfully through the window. 'It should have been mine. Dad always said it would be mine, after they had all gone. Uncle James hated that. And he's afraid that someone might tell the authorities what he got up to during the war. He could be tried for treason – hanged. He'll do anything to hurt someone he thinks might know something. Even if it's just his imagination, he has to stop them.'

The world had gone very still. I did my best to keep my voice casual. 'That must be very sad for you, Sissy, losing your home like that. You can see the farm from here, then?'

She sighed. 'Yes, up there, up on the hill. The house is on the other side, facing the sea, but you can just make out the barn.'

I followed her gaze to the dark shape on the cliffs above Port Helen. I swallowed hard. 'When did your uncle take over the farm?'

'Years and years ago.' She sighed. 'Right at the very beginning of the war. Dad was killed that first Christmas. It was soon after that.'

'I see.' My stomach clenched hard into a knot. I was back in the field with Mouse, crouched beneath the hedge as the Gotha circled above our heads and the hint of cigarette smoke drifted from the barn.

'The farm was my home,' Sissy was saying. 'I used to play there with my cousins when I was a little girl. But Uncle James wanted it.'

I glanced at her. She looked very young and forlorn. 'Sissy, why don't you just go?'

'Go?'

'Leave Port Helen and start a new life somewhere else.'

'Oh, but I couldn't leave Gran. Uncle James didn't pay all the money, you see. Not yet. He said if I came and worked here he'd pay her the rest, in a little while.'

'But surely if he agreed to buy the farm you can make him pay what he owes without holding you as some kind of hostage? There's a lawyer in Port Helen—'

'No!' Sissy grabbed my arm. 'When Gran found out he'd only paid half and said she'd get the rest later, she tried. But people are afraid of him. When one of our neighbours tried to stand up for Gran, he was arrested the very next day for being part of a spy ring selling the locations of all the airfields to the enemy. He said there was all kinds of evidence against him that could have got him hanged. It took months and months to prove it couldn't possibly be him.'

Below, a door opened. 'It should be an easy matter build a boathouse at the far end,' came Connors' voice. 'It will be the finest boating lake in Cornwall. We shall be able to see from the terrace, Major.' We stood quite still as the clip of Hugo's sticks faded into the distance, accompanied by the brisk importance of Connors' boots.

'You won't tell?' whispered Sissy.

I shook my head. 'I won't say a word. In fact I think it's best if we both forget we ever had this conversation.' I looked at her. 'And I promise I won't blame you, if you ever decide to take your grandmother and just go. Whatever happens, I'll give you a reference.' Sissy nodded tearfully and took a bundle of sheets downstairs to be washed.

In the silence, I stood by the window looking out over Port Helen and the silhouette of the barn in the distance. Voices murmured in the kitchen garden. Pots clattered in the kitchens. In Hiram Cove the sea rumbled gently, pulling at the shore. Over Port

Helen harbour, seagulls arched and shrieked, chasing each other for fish and scraps above fishing boats rocked in their moorings by the tide.

I stood until the returning tap of Hugo's sticks echoed from the walls of the house. Connors' thin voice joined the echo, still drawing up plans for making Hiram Hall the envy of every great house in Cornwall. Grandiose plans, that would be folly to consider and madness to try. I doubted whether Connors himself believed they would ever be fulfilled. They didn't need to be, in the seductive world he had created and to which Hugo clung: the world that had existed before the war. Every now and again there came Hugo's low murmur of agreement.

I waited until they had returned to Hugo's study, then made my way to the kitchens as quietly as I could.

Mrs Hughes looked up from stirring her sauce. 'Why, Miss Elin.' She glanced at my face. 'There's nothing wrong is there?'

I shook my head. A mixing bowl stood on the table, next to a jar containing sultanas and a small plate strewn with the candied peel of oranges and lemons. I began creaming the eggs and sugar for the steamed pudding, the tension in my body easing. I missed being amongst the scents and the textures, scouring my mother's recipe book for new ways to turn potatoes and swedes and a handful of greens into a delicious meal. Mrs Hughes was the last one left whose allegiance was to me rather than to my husband. I began beating the eggs.

'You know I would hate to lose you, Mrs Hughes.'

She did not look up. 'Of course, Miss Elin.'

'But if you have to go, if anything makes you go, Alice will always be glad to find a position for you. She says there are several hotels who are crying out for a cook.'

'I see,' she replied.

Chapter Thirty-Six

SUMMER 1919

Cook did not wait to be dismissed. A few days later she came into the drawing room where Hugo and I were sitting, during one of our rare times alone together.

'I have been offered the post of Cook in an establishment in London, Mrs Helstone,' she announced, without meeting my eyes. 'I am required to give a week's notice, I believe?'

'Yes,' I murmured. 'Can we not dissuade you, Mrs Hughes?'

'No,' came the abrupt reply. 'I shall endeavour to wait for a replacement to be found, but I shall leave at the end of the week. I have no wish to disappoint my new employers.'

Hugo roused himself. 'Mrs Helstone and I would like to wish you all the best, Mrs Hughes.'

Cook sniffed. 'I could have wished to stay. Nearly thirty years I've been at Hiram. I had intended to remain until my retirement.' Her voice sharpened. 'But some people are too easily led by the nose and should be ashamed of themselves.'

Hugo flinched. He looked up. Suspicion flickered in his eyes. He glanced towards me, as if afraid I might be laughing at him. As if afraid the whole world might be laughing at him.

'Hugo,' I said, placing my hand gently on his arm. Something fought in his face, like a swimmer sunk to a deep, dark place, struggling towards the light. His eyes cleared and he gazed at me with a puzzled expression, as if seeing me for the first time after a long journey, uncertain if he remembered me at all. I smiled at him reassuringly. 'It's all right Hugo, I'm here.' His hand sought mine and clutched it tightly. He was about to speak, when through the open window came the voice of Mr Connors shouting to William to keep his muddy boots off the lawn. A frown crossed

Hugo's brow, his face closed in on itself once more and the moment was gone.

Mrs Hughes sniffed even louder this time. 'I'm sorry, Mrs Helstone, but it had to be said. Ashamed of themselves. That's what they should be.'

* * *

After much searching and advertising, Sissy finally managed to find a replacement cook. Mrs Gorwell arrived from Taunton the day after Mrs Hughes' departure. She was not much older than Sissy, but immaculately dressed and severe. She had the kitchen rearranged within days, and made no bones about not welcoming the lady of the house anywhere near her domain. Her cooking was adequate, but lacking in variety, being heavy in suet and beef. She was no countrywoman, looking askance at the carefully bottled fruits and preserves as if she had never seen anything quite so outmoded – or indeed potentially poisonous – in her life. Within weeks I was convinced her previous employers had died of chronic indigestion.

Hugo made no comment, barely seeming to notice the indifferent meals put on the table, where he and I sat in outmoded state, barely speaking to each other.

I would pass Connors in the hall, or on my brief escapes from the house, when I went to collect flowers from the grounds. Each time he would doff his hat in an exaggerated semblance of servility, while his eyes watched me with his silent smile. I ignored him, but I began to dread meeting him. I could feel the effort of appearing indifferent to my isolation, and the loss of any influence at all with my husband, begin to wear my spirit down, extinguishing the fight.

Chapter Thirty-Seven

SUMMER 1919

I was picking raspberries in the walled garden that last day Alice came to Hiram Hall.

'I'm afraid Mrs Helstone is not feeling well today and cannot receive visitors.' I looked up at the sound of Mr Connors' voice in the driveway immediately outside the entrance to the garden.

'Then I'll leave her a message, if you will give it to her.'

'Of course,' he replied. I moved towards the door as silently as I could. Connors was standing with his back to me. Alice was fussing with paper and pens. Over Connors' shoulder I caught her eye.

'You will make sure she gets it, won't you.' Alice bent over the paper, scribbling furiously as if with every confidence he would deliver it. 'Applebourne Hospital is closing and I'm taking up a post. I know my cousin would wish to write to me, maybe to visit me at some time…' While Alice rambled on, taking no notice of Connors' attempts to get rid of her, I shot as fast as I could to the little door onto the cliffs. A few minutes later, Alice appeared around the corner of the garden wall to join me. I hugged her tight.

'Insufferable little man,' she growled. 'I expect he's burning my note already. It's all right,' she added, as I glanced back. 'The first of your guests has just arrived. We've a few minutes before he will start to look for you.'

'How is Mrs Hughes?' I asked, anxiously.

'In her element,' said Alice. 'I don't know what the hotel would do without her. She's a marvel at being able to turn anything into a delicious meal, and she's marshalled the kitchen staff into order in no time. But I know she misses Hiram dreadfully.'

'I miss her too. I don't get to cook at all these days. It feels as if part of myself has gone.'

Alice kissed me. 'You look so pale and tired, Elin, as if the life has been knocked out of you. Every danger and challenge during the war never left you like this. At times you looked exhausted, just as we all did, but you were always resourceful and full of fight. I hate seeing you like this.'

'It's just taking me a little time to adjust,' I replied. 'I knew it wasn't going to be easy to go back to being simply a wife after all that time running the Hall. But there must be women all over the country going through exactly the same. I'm sure it will get easier with time.'

She glanced at me. 'Mr Connors can't help matters.'

I grimaced. 'He's got the post he wanted and he's successfully made sure all the staff who had any loyalty to me have gone. But Hugo listens to him, and there's nothing I can do. I'm just going to have to make the best of it.'

'That's not like you, Elin. Not after everything that's happened. You deserve more than that.'

I smiled faintly. 'I don't think it's a question of deserving, it's a matter of facing the reality.' From the driveway came the sound of more guests arriving. 'I'm sorry, I have to go.'

Alice kissed me. 'I'll come and visit you in a day or two, once your guests have gone. We'll find a way to make Hugo listen.' She hugged me tight and made her way back along the outside of Hiram's walls towards the roadway.

As I heard Alice drive away, I found I could not face my guests. Not yet. I needed to clear my head. I needed to get out of the oppressive air of Hiram Hall for a while. Voices echoed in the driveway, greeting Hugo. I fled, as I had always done since I was a child, down the cliff steps to the solitude of Hiram Cove. The beach shone brightly in the sunlight. Water lapped peacefully, this way and that. We had never replaced the rowing boat. Hugo had accepted my story that it had broken free one night and been lost in a storm. Its shell lay rotting next to the central rock, already too far gone to be worth salvaging.

I paced to and fro on the edges of the surf, the pebbles crunching and sliding beneath my feet. How much simpler my life might have been if I had followed my heart and left for Owen. I closed my eyes, pulling myself together. I was too old for fairy tales. Aunt Catrin was right when she said that every marriage had its problems that must be worked through. If I had run away to Owen, who knows how things might have been? I still loved him with all my heart. The simplest thought of him sent my heart racing. But maybe that was a mere deception of the senses, as Hugo had once been. Maybe all I was doing was making the same mistake again.

I had seen so much death and suffering, how could I believe any more in something so simple and pure as true love? It was reality I had to face now. Cold, hard, everyday reality. Why should I expect a charmed life with no troubles?

Slowly, I began to calm. There had to be a way to make some kind of life for myself. Connors might not stay forever. He had got what he wanted, but surely Hugo must one day realise that he was being preyed upon? He had always been so careful to take care of Hiram. Surely now he was getting stronger and familiarising himself with the running of the estate again, he must see that I'd spoken the truth. Things had changed. There was less money coming into Hiram. He could not avoid that truth forever. Until things settled down again we would need to be careful, like everyone else. It must be only a matter of time before Hugo would see that the boating lake, for all its grandeur, was simply impractical. Besides, with so few able bodied men to employ in its excavation, the scheme must die a natural death. One day Hugo would see through Mr Connors' grand schemes. And I had to hope that I could win his trust once more…slowly, surely, win his affections back to me.

The sun was beginning to fade as I made my way back up the steps. When I lifted the latch into the garden, I found Connors walking rapidly towards me. 'Ah, there you are, Mrs Helstone. The Major couldn't find you. We were getting quite worried. Your guests have arrived.'

'Have they?' I said vaguely. I was no longer going to allow myself to be riled by him. 'I quite forgot about them. The beach is so lovely at this time of year, don't you find, Mr Connors?' I held out a handful of shells. 'I'd quite forgotten how pretty these are.'

'Delightful,' he murmured in the slightly disdainful tones of humouring a child.

I smiled blandly. 'Thank you for your concern, Mr Connors. I was quite safe.' I swept off in the direction of the house. 'Now I really must go and greet my guests.'

* * *

Dinner that evening was a sumptuous one. Heaven knows how Sissy had managed to cajole Mrs Gorwell to such heights, but not even the most demanding of our guests could fault a single course. I watched it all as if from a distance as I kept up an appearance of quiet cheerfulness. Connors had somehow hired enough staff for the evening to wait on the tables. I could almost imagine Papa walking in through the door, unsurprised at how little Hiram had changed over the years.

As I exchanged pleasantries with my neighbours, I looked around at our guests. The men were landowners from the larger estates around Port Helen, or Hugo's colleagues from the army. A chaplain sat at one end, a General at the other. The women were their wives or their fiancées, accompanied by many an unmarried daughter. Most of them I had never seen before. The men talked business, the women of London and fashions and the latest gossip at court.

I felt as if I had stepped back in time. As if the war had never happened, with its shortages, its bone-aching weariness, its horrors and its grief. But of course it had. After a while I could see it in their eyes. In the mourning still worn. In the lack of young men's faces, young men's voices. In the air of bored dissatisfaction in more than one of the daughters, who had most probably spent the war driving a tractor or up to her ears in engine oil. Surely there was a thin air to the chatter and jollity and the attempt to rebuild a world gone forever?

At last the dinner was over and I withdrew with the rest of the women, leaving the men to their brandy and talk of Germany's complete humiliation and how the Hun could never rise again to trouble us. As the tea was poured and the guests resumed their conversations I caught pitying glances towards me. I could already hear in my mind the snatches of whispered conversation that would take place each time I left the room. *Such a shame she hasn't got more to say for herself. Such a shame the Major saddled himself with a wife so lacking in social brilliance. Such a shame she could never give him a child, poor man.*

'If you'll excuse me,' I murmured at last. 'I must just check that all the rooms are in order. Good staff are so difficult to come by nowadays, don't you think?'

In those precious minutes while the men in the dining room gossiped over their brandy with Connors in close attendance, and the women in the drawing gossiped over their tea with an exhausted Sissy anticipating their every need, I walked restlessly through every room in the house. From the maids' quarters tucked in under the eaves, to the large empty room that had been my mother's, still with the rocking horse Hugo had placed there with such pride and high excitement, a lifetime ago, when my pregnancy had been confirmed. There were ghosts in the house that night. I could hear them in the laughter seeping in between the wainscot. In the smell of violets that crept in every now and again. The billows of dust that swayed in the beams from the lamps.

I walked on and on, my skirts sweeping along the floorboards, gathering memories, until I reached my own room. In the dressing table mirror I looked pale and tired. In the sharp relief from the lamp, my face had gained shape and shadows. No longer that of a girl. No longer that of a young woman. I could make out the memory of my mother in the shape of my nose, the arch of my brows. Already I was her shadow.

I took her necklace from its box and placed it round my neck. It had been her favourite. It was mine, too. I did not have her delicacy or her elegance. But it shimmered blue in the lamplight. I placed it among the opulence of Hugo's diamonds. The blue almost extinguished by the brighter light, but still peeping through in a quiet beauty.

Hugo was waiting for me at the bottom of the stairs. There was a slight sway in his step. A glassiness to his eyes. 'There's nothing wrong is there, my dear? Only Connors mentioned you seemed a trifle, well, distracted, this afternoon.'

'No, not at all.'

'I was surprised to hear you had been down to the beach on your own. Anything could have happened. Connors is quite right: we really must find you a lady's maid.'

A terrible weariness overcame me. 'I don't think such things exist anymore, Hugo,' I said.

'Nonsense. Of course they do.' He patted my hand. 'And we shall find you the best there is. Connors has heard of an excellent one, a relation of Mrs Pettersham. He has undertaken to speak to her tomorrow for us.'

Something deep inside snapped. Fury took hold of me. A deep, hard anger that filled every part of my being. I struggled with my last vestige of self-control to keep my voice quiet and reasonable. 'So that I can be always watched? So I can lose the last piece of independent life left to me?'

He stared at me in utter astonishment. 'My dear, I only want the best for you.'

'Oh Hugo, I'm sure you do. But I need my independence and a sense of purpose. I want to live my life, not drag myself through some half-life, with no say in my future. I have never deliberately hurt you or shamed you, and I have never betrayed you. Would it cost you so much to permit me to have some small existence of my own?'

'Ah, there you are, Major.' The door to the dining room opened and the General emerged. I could hear Connors' laughter following him with the spiral of cigar smoke and the smell of brandy. 'We were just wondering what was keeping you.' He bowed with great gallantry, and even more unsteadiness, in my direction. 'Time to join the ladies, don't you think?'

'Yes, yes of course.' There was unmistakable relief in Hugo's voice at this interruption. 'We'll speak of this tomorrow, my dear.' He held out his arm without quite meeting my eyes. The closed look was back on his face, shutting me out. Shutting out anything that might disturb the gossamer surface of his mind. 'Tonight we must look to our guests.'

At that, the fight finally went out of me. Through the cigar smoke came the harsh edge of Connors' cigarettes, catching at the back of my throat. My mind became cold and very still.

What had I been thinking of, believing that bending myself to my husband's every wish would win the love I craved? Connors had rendered me impotent, and Hugo knew me so little he had not even noticed. Or had not cared to notice. Connors had isolated me. Maybe that was enough. Perhaps now he would feel safe that I had no one to listen to any story I might tell about the barn above Port Helen, and the Gotha circling. About Mouse and the accusations against her that had led to so much heartbreak. Suspicions I could never prove, but which I knew, from all that Sissy had told me about his spying, to be true.

And if they were true, Connors had shown no compunction about using his position as a valued informant for the Germans to send Mouse to almost certain death. Was that what he was intending for me, too? This time using his position of trust with my husband to ensure he could do as he pleased without question or suspicion. Or would he simply confine himself to the drip, drip of uncertainty, undermining my peace of mind as he had already undermined my power? And Hugo would neither see what was happening, nor defend me. Reality. Between them, in one way or another, they were killing me.

I deserved better than this.

'I'm sorry,' I muttered. 'You must excuse me. I have the most violent headache. I've tried to ease it all day, but it has come on again. I really must go and lie down.'

'Of course.' Hugo looked around helplessly. 'Perhaps Miss Connors...'

'No, please. There's no need to trouble Miss Connors. All I need is to rest for a while. I'll be quite well in the morning.' I returned up the stairs, clinging to the banisters in earnest, my legs shaking so much I could barely take one step after the other.

I lay on the bed for a while. When footsteps clattering up the stairs shortly afterwards announced the arrival of Sissy to check on me, I pulled the covers over me, pretending to be asleep. When I was certain she had returned downstairs, I sat there, my mind working fast. It might be months until guests came to Hiram Hall again. Months until Hugo was distracted and Connors and Sissy too fully occupied to remember my existence. By that time, there may well be a maid dogging my every step and watching over everything I did.

Moving as quickly and quietly as I could in my stockinged feet, I retrieved a carpetbag from my mother's room, along with the small amount of money I had always kept in the back of a drawer during the war in case of emergencies. I took her necklaces and a ring and crept back again, feeling my way along the corridors in the darkness, every sense alert for footsteps following me, or the creak of a tread on the stairs. In the safety of my room I quickly packed a few necessities, tucked in my mother's recipe book, a little more worn and grease stained, and the notebooks I had kept to record my own experiments. From my dressing table I selected the plainest of the necklaces Hugo had given me, which I could pawn or sell if it came to it. The rest, including my wedding ring, I left behind. Finally, I changed out of my evening dress into a plain skirt and blouse, selecting a dark jacket that I hoped would give me the appearance of a teacher or a woman of business.

Around me the house slowly began to quieten. The streak of headlights into the night and the retreating of engines followed our guests from Port Helen as they returned home. The rest made their way upstairs to bed, their subdued laughter and whispers passed my door, followed by the creak of floorboards in the guest rooms on the floor above.

Towards dawn the house finally fell silent. All I could do was wait, praying that there were no secret assignations that might mean the furtive return of a lover in the first light before dawn, and that Connors had enjoyed the remains of Hugo's cellar along with the guests and his watchfulness was – for a few hours at least – finally blind.

Chapter Thirty-Eight

SUMMER 1919

I left as light crept into the mist-filled dawn.

I walked without hesitation, looking neither around me nor back towards the house. I made it safely into the walled garden, hastening between vegetable beds neglected and overgrown with weeds and the broken supports of beans and peas. The door onto the cliff creaked on its hinges. I glanced back, certain the whole world was now awake. But the garden remained still, the house silent.

Pulling the garden door to as quietly as I could, I made my way down the path towards Port Helen. Mist rolled in from the sea, muffling the crash of water onto pebbles. Through it, eventually, came the first glimpses of a fragile blue, the promise of the day to come.

Port Helen was barely stirring. Smoke had begun its slow curl from chimney pots. Men stamped their feet in the cold as they set off for the fields. A fishing boat was heading out to sea, swallowed into nothing before it reached the harbour wall. I walked briskly, not avoiding greetings but replying cheerfully.

At the station, I paused and looked back. I could never quite get out of my head that vision of Hiram as it might have been, had the battlefields crossed the channel. The rolling green fields, as far as the eye could see, dotted now and again by farmhouses and tiny villages tucked into hollows. The blasted landscape of France and Belgium must once have looked like this. I shivered as my inner eye turned the familiar fields of my childhood to mud and craters, strung with barbed wire and the stench of death. Trees gone, leaving only poisoned stumps rising from a hellish mist.

Heaven knows how those ruined villages, those blasted lives I had seen would ever recover. How Lisette's family – if any had survived – could find a way to live again. To trust in life again. The mud of Flanders had not been repeated here, and yet we were changed. We might sanitise what had happened, glorify it. But nothing would ever be the same again.

There were a few people on the station waiting for the train. None of them were acquaintances, for which I was grateful.

'Up to London then, Mrs Helstone?' said the stationmaster cheerfully. He had known me since I was a child, overseeing all my comings and goings.

'I am,' I replied with a smile.

'Make a nice change for you, being in the big city, seeing the sights,' he answered with a wink.

I laughed, slightly awkwardly. 'I hope so.'

The train arrived a few minutes later. I took my seat, on the seaward side, scouring the platform anxiously for any hasty arrivals, my ears alert for the sound of the Silver Ghost, or shouts to halt our departure. I thought the wait would never end. Perhaps there had been a telephone call from the Hall. Or maybe a fault with the engine, meaning a wait until the next train. But at last the carriage shuddered into life and the station slipped away behind me. There was no one else in my compartment, so I was free to watch Port Helen, with Hiram Hall just emerging from mist high up on the cliff-top, framed by the field where once – a lifetime ago – a bi-plane had come to a shuddering halt, bringing with it the call of a new world. The last I saw as the train eased round the headland was the house swallowed into nothing within the fields and the darkness of Hiram Wood.

The coastline passed in a blur of tears. The tide was in, crashing on the shore. How could I leave? I gazed at the sea wishing I could go back. I would get off at the next station and return in time for breakfast. No one need ever know. I would have a place to live forever. Many women had a worse fate. Was I just weak that I could not bear the destiny I had chosen?

As we turned the next headland, there was a flash in the water. A school of dolphins were skimming through the sea beside us, keeping pace with the train. They leapt in turn, high, joyful leaps, their dorsal fins shimmering in the sunshine. The line straightened once more and we left the dolphins behind. I watched them for as long as I could, powering through the waves, diving upwards into an alien environment before disappearing back within the sea once more.

We would soon arrive at the larger stations. I would not have my solitude for long. I took out my book, ordered my mind for the story I would tell my fellow passengers if conversation should arise, and composed myself for the long journey ahead.

* * *

We arrived at Paddington to the noise and bustle of London. I had never travelled alone before. Never had to rely on my wits to find my way.

I stood under the great dome of the station feeling life swirl by. Passengers were greeted by friends or family, or made their way confidently to the exit. Everyone seemed to know where to go. Everyone had a purpose.

A sense of panic began to rise. I fought it down. I was not alone in the city. I had money. The appearance and speech of a respectable lady. And had I not driven between the bombed out craters of France, and survived an enemy checkpoint with a fugitive under my care? I could survive anything. In London, a cab driver might disapprove, but could hardly refuse my fare. I knew where to find Cousin Iris, and, if I needed it, Alice's hotel was respectable.

I soon found I was less shocking, being a woman on my own,

than I would have been before the war. Looking round, I saw several other women, smart and businesslike, making their way singly or in twos and threes. There were so few men to go around. It was only natural. I took a deep breath. I had work to do and no time for doubts.

Owen was not at the newspaper offices when I telephoned. The reporter I spoke to told me he was not expected back until the end of the week.

'He'll be at St Benedict's,' she announced cheerily, accepting without question that I was a fellow reporter who urgently needed to speak to him about a story.

'With the veterans?' I hazarded.

'That's the one. There's no point in trying to telephone him there, they're always so busy it's impossible to get hold of anyone in a hurry.' Papers rustled. 'I'll give you the address, if you like. It's not far from where you are, you know. It'll be far quicker to jump in a cab.' There was a short pause. 'That's the one. I knew I had it somewhere. Don't let them fob you off. Owen's bound to be there. It's his passion. But then I expect you know that.'

I took down the address. She sounded young and eager. Envy shot through me at her breezy self-confidence. She worked with 'Owen', she spoke as if she knew him well. They might even be lovers. I quashed my jealousy. I could hardly blame him. I had gone back to my husband. I had set him free. I had told him to live his life.

As I stepped outside the station I came across several beggars in the street. One sat on the pavement just outside the station: blind, one leg of his trousers pinned up and empty, another casualty of the war.

'Where were you?' I asked, placing a coin in his hand.

'France. A place called Ypres. A hellhole it was.'

'So I've heard. I'm sorry.'

His sightless face rose, as if gauging my voice. 'You were a nurse?'

'No.' I hesitated. 'Not a nurse, but I passed through the battlefields near Lille. My friend worked with the field hospitals there. She was injured, I went to find her.'

He chuckled. 'So you know.'

'Yes.' I frowned at his sightless eyes. 'Is there really no other way for you? Nowhere to go?'

'I'm well, aren't I?' There was only a trace of bitterness in his voice. 'No need for the hospitals. Not any more. We're forgotten already. They don't like to remind themselves, see. The war was won. The dead have their monuments. Who thinks of the broken?'

'I do,' I said. I flagged down a cab. 'I'm on my way to St Benedict's, you can come with me.' He muttered darkly about nuns. 'I don't think you'll find any nuns there,' I replied. 'Besides, I need you to help me. I'm on a reconnaissance mission there. You can be my camouflage.'

He chuckled at that. The first cab drove off at the sight of us, in search of a more respectable fare, but the second stopped.

'I was too young to be called up, myself, but I lost two brothers at Ypres,' said the driver, as he helped guide Corporal Samuels to a seat.

Within minutes we had arrived, and I was guiding my charge towards the entrance. As we reached the door, it was opened from the inside.

'That's all right, Mrs Helstone. I'll take him from here.'

I started. 'Owen!' His scars had softened a little and he was looking more like his old self, apart from the tightening of the burnt skin on one side of his face that would never heal. I was torn between relief and trepidation. At least he was smiling. I had been afraid he might make it clear I was the last person he wanted to see.

'I heard you arrive from the window. I'd know your voice anywhere.'

'That's the spirit!' The soldier was chuckling. 'I can't tell you if she's young and pretty, or crabbed and ancient as the hills. But whichever it is, my boy, I wouldn't be letting that one go.'

I was scarlet. From what I could see of Owen's face he was no cooler. 'I don't intend to.' He took the corporal by the arm. 'But first of all we need to get you inside.'

'I don't want no praying,' announced Corporal Samuels, suspiciously.

Owen grinned. 'There's no praying. Not unless you particularly ask for it. Just a bed and a hot meal. They'll look at fitting you a new leg and finding you an occupation.'

The soldier grunted. 'What kind of occupation do you suggest for some poor blind old sod like me?'

'You'd be surprised,' replied Owen. 'We have plenty of men here who have lost their sight but who can still make a living for themselves. What were you before the war?'

'Mechanic,' he muttered. 'I bet that foxed you.'

'Not at all. We'll have you working on clocks and farm machinery before you know it.' Still grumbling, but without any further resistance, Corporal Samuels allowed himself to be guided inside.

As he was taken off towards the kitchens in search of a hot meal, Owen picked up my bag. 'Come on, Elin. Let's get out of here. There's a tea house a few minutes' walk away. You look exhausted.'

The tea house was small, nothing as grand as a Lyons' Corner House, but it was clean and quiet.

'I spoke to your office,' I said as we settled down at a table. Now he was sitting there in front of me I didn't know where to start. 'I spoke to a young woman. She said you would be here. She was very helpful.'

'That would be Rebekiah.' His tone was warm. My heart sank, for all that it had no right to. 'You were lucky you got her, some of the others can be proper battleaxes. Not that I blame them. It can't be easy being a woman in a man's world.'

'No.'

He glanced at my bag, tucked carefully between my feet. 'So, have you come to visit Alice for a few days?' I shook my head. I could not trust myself to speak. 'I see,' he said at last.

'I can't go back to him.' I did my best not to betray my anguish, but I could hear it thin and hard in my voice. 'I can't ever go back to him.'

Owen cleared his throat. 'Elin—'

'I'm not asking you for anything,' I said hurriedly. One day I would be able to endure whatever it was he was about to tell me. But not now. Not when my own feelings were so raw. It was selfish, but I couldn't bear to hear of his happiness. 'I meant it when I told you not to wait for me. I don't want to do anything that might change your life. I've no right.' I hesitated. 'But I do need your help. I have to make sure that I can be free of Hugo, before he can find me. I wish it was anyone but you. But I don't know who else to ask.'

He looked at me aghast. 'Oh, Lord. I see what you mean.' He grimaced. 'I have to say that was the last thing on my mind.'

My heart sank. 'It's all right. I'll understand if it would make things awkward for you.'

'Not at all. But are you sure, Elin?'

'I can't go back to him,' I said. 'It would kill me. But if he finds me in London, or with Aunt Catrin, I may have no choice. I've some money, but it won't last for long and I've nowhere else to go. I don't even know how to go about finding work here, so that I can earn my own living. I know Hugo will never let me go willingly. His pride would never allow it. I need to force his hand.' I glanced at him. 'That's how it's done, isn't it? One or other has to be seen to commit adultery. Isn't that how your godmother got her divorce?'

He nodded. 'She asked a husband of a friend. He'd seen her bruises after her husband nearly killed her with one of his beatings, and was only too glad to help. They played chess all night.' He looked at me. 'I don't play chess. But I'll do my best.'

'Thank you.'

'No need to thank me. Perhaps I'll regain some of my reputation where the ladies are concerned,' he replied, smiling. He ran his hand down the tight skin of his burns. 'Possibly my only chance to appear debonair again.'

'You don't need to appear debonair.' I had clearly embarrassed him. He was staring down into his tea as if he wished he were on the other side of the world. Grief shot through me. But I had no time for a broken heart. I had made my choice. I had set Owen free, just as he had once done for me. I had no one to blame but myself. Now I had to learn to live with my decision.

* * *

We booked into a down-at-heel hotel as Mr and Mrs Smith. Hardly original, but that was not the intention. We had already laid a trail of witnesses in a nearby restaurant, and now only needed the obligatory chambermaid to provide the final, damning piece of evidence. Owen had persuaded one of his fellow reporters to photograph our every move, including our guilty exit from the hotel the following morning. If nothing else, Hugo's pride would force him to petition for divorce after such a public betrayal by his wife.

The man behind the desk looked carefully bland. I made no attempt to disguise the cheapest-looking and least fitting ring I could find amongst Mama's jewellery, or my haste to get away from him. We were shown to our room. Comfortable, but hardly opulent.

In the stillness of the room we looked at each other, the double bed looming large between us. I gazed out of the window. The city lights glittered in the darkness, reflected in the puddles of the streets as the rain fell, almost imperceptibly, on umbrellas and cabs. This was the point of no return.

'What will you do?' asked Owen, as I turned back towards the fire.

'Go and stay with Mouse and Aunt Catrin in Anglesey. I posted a letter on the way, so they'll be expecting me. To be honest, I don't think Aunt Catrin will be surprised. Alice has helped me enough, I don't want to involve her in a scandal that might jeopardise her new post.'

'And that will be your life?'

'No. Not forever. But it will give me a place to be safe until the scandal dies down. A place to plan a future.'

'I see.' I jumped as there was a knock at the door. 'It's room service,' he said, colouring slightly. 'I ordered champagne. It seemed the right thing to do.'

Nerves made me giggle like a schoolgirl. 'Do you do this often, then?'

'Never,' he replied, his voice serious. The champagne in its ice arrived, with two glasses. 'Leave it,' he ordered, as the waiter began to uncork. He tipped him. We looked at the bottle, and then at each other as the footsteps made their way back along the passageway.

'A fine pair of adulterers we make,' I said at last, to ease the tension. 'We should be downing that by the caseful.'

Owen laughed. He eased the cork with a demure flourish and poured the champagne. His hand shook slightly, sending silver bubbles over the tray. We drank in silence. Unaccustomed to it, I felt the alcohol flow through me.

'Thank you.' I said. 'For being my friend – for doing this for me. I hope Hugo doesn't cause trouble for you. I hate doing this to him. I wish there was a more civilised way I could ask for my freedom without having to go through this stupid charade. But I couldn't live in that house any longer. Connors didn't have to murder me: I never had much influence with Hugo, all Connors did was take the small freedoms I did have away.'

Owen filled the glasses with care. 'And now you will be free to live as you please.'

'Yes.'

'At *Swn y Môr*.'

'I expect so. At least I'll be near Mouse.'

'I see.' He looked at me wistfully. 'May I visit you one day?'

'Yes, of course. I would like that. If it doesn't make things awkward.'

'Awkward?' He was scowling. 'Is that for you or for me?'

'For you, of course. The way you talked about Rebekiah…'

'Rebekiah?' The dismay in his voice stopped my heart in its tracks. I forgot to breathe. 'Rebekiah is the best reporter I know. And the wildest. She could drink me under the table and has had more lovers than I've had hot dinners. She'd never want half a love and my heart was lost a long time ago.'

'Oh.' I sat down on the bed. 'I thought—'

'For Heaven's sake, Elin. When a woman asks you to spend the night with her *as a friend*, to enable her to be free of an unhappy marriage, it's hardly the time to start telling her that you never stopped desiring her. Have you any idea how impossible this is, being so close to you?' He gave me a sideways look. 'It's quite all right. You made your feelings quite clear when you said I was the last person you would have wished to ask.'

'Of course I didn't want to ask you!' I glared at him. 'I can't just leave my husband and walk straight into the arms of another man, however deeply I might love him. What do you take me for? These last months have worn me out, Owen. I've got nothing left to give anyone. I lost everything when I walked away from Hiram this morning. I need time to find myself again.'

'You might have explained.'

'Of course I was going to,' I replied, cross. 'I was going to write to you, as soon as I was settled at *Sŵn y Môr*.'

He gazed at me with such intensity shivers ran up and down my spine. 'Elin,' he whispered, leaning closer. I could feel his breath warm on my lips, his warmth burning through my blouse. 'I thought I'd lost you.'

'Never.' I leaned in to meet his kiss. He drew me closer and closer until we overbalanced, landing in a heap on the counterpane. The bed creaked suggestively.

'Oh, Lord,' he muttered, releasing me. I stifled a giggle. 'That is unbelievably sordid.' We lay there grinning at each other like naughty schoolchildren. 'It's good to see you laugh.'

'It's good to see you smile,' I replied. He reached out, his hand brushing my cheek, travelling slowly down towards the neckline of my blouse. I caught the hand as it lingered on the hollow in my collarbone. 'Not here, Owen. Not like this. And I couldn't bear to risk having a child that Hugo's pride might possibly make him claim for his own, and truly break my heart.'

He cleared his throat. 'Of course.' He kissed me gently and slid from the bed, pushing the two armchairs together next to the fire.

'What on earth are you doing?'

'A blanket, and I'll be as fine as in a feather bed.'

'Don't be silly. I'm not going to rest in comfort while you break your back.'

'I might not be able to restrain myself.'

I snorted. 'Balderdash. If you love me, you'll see me as a rational woman who knows her own mind, not a silly little miss who needs to be instructed in what she really wants.'

'True.' He didn't take much persuading. He was already sliding back onto the bed next to me, taking care not to rouse that mortifying creak. 'And I can dream,' he added, whispering in my ear, sending every sense in my body into a wild dance.

It was a strange night as we lay there in the dark, huddled under the counterpane for warmth, murmuring to each other as drunks stumbled and shrieked in the streets below and footsteps creaked on the stairs. Somewhere towards dawn we must have fallen asleep. Even the streets outside were silent when I woke. I crept to the window as grief overwhelmed me, silent tears pouring down my face, as I wept for the life I had left behind. For Hiram and for Hugo. For the only life I had ever known.

I scarcely felt the blanket being wrapped gently around me. But it was there, as my tears finally lessened, keeping the warmth in my body.

Owen was a shadow, face turned away from me on the pillow when I slipped back under the covers. I thought he was asleep, but he moved slightly, so I rested against his reassuring solidity, his feet warming the chill of mine.

We did not speak. There was nothing to be said. We simply held each other safe, until the streets outside began to stir into life once more.

Chapter Thirty-Nine

SUMMER 1919

Mouse was waiting for me as the train drew into the station.

'Oh, thank goodness. I thought you would never come.' She ran towards me, hugging me tight. 'I was so afraid you'd change your mind at the last minute and go back and you'd never be able to escape and I'd never see you again.'

'Never,' I replied, kissing her. Mouse looked just the same as she always had, her skin a little browner, her cheeks rosy from fresh air and exercise.

'Come on, I promised I'd take you to Aunt Catrin's as soon as the train came in. They're all dying to see you.'

They must have been listening out for us. The moment the Chevrolet turned into the drive, Lisette was racing behind us, Jojo at her heels.

'My goodness you've grown,' I exclaimed, as I jumped out at the front door and hugged her. Lisette was tall and willowy, with dark curling hair and an olive skin glowing with health.

'Come on, come on.' Lisette grabbed my hand. 'You've got to see him, Auntie Elin. He's been waiting for you.' She pulled me to the front door, to where Aunt Catrin was waiting, a sturdy, fair-haired little boy clutching her hand.

'*Cariad*,' was all she said, as Frankie waddled headlong towards Mouse, who swung him up onto one hip, kissing him soundly.

'That was a brave thing you did,' Aunt Catrin added in Welsh. 'Your mother would be proud of you.' She held me tight for a few minutes.

'So?' demanded Mouse. 'What do you think?'

I smiled at Frankie, who was staring at me with shy curiosity from his mother's arms. 'He looks like you,' I said.

'Frankie's a true Northholme all right,' said Mouse, trying very hard not to dote and failing miserably. 'He'll probably end up looking like Papa, poor mite, but with any luck he'll take more after Edmund. I can't see anyone else in him, and I never will.' A faint smile appeared on her lips. 'I still can't abide babies, but there always has to be some exception to any rule. I've no intention of ending up as an old stick-in-the-mud like most of my relatives, quite unable to change my mind... He's taking interest in the farm already. I expect he'll be a terrible nuisance now he's walking and getting into everything, but Jack doesn't seem to mind. I even think he rather likes having him around.'

'The kettle's boiling,' said Aunt Catrin.

'Good,' said Mouse, rubbing noses with Frankie, who giggled loudly. 'Because *someone* was helping Aunt Catrin with a *bara brith* when I left, and I'm starving.'

Later that afternoon I stepped out into the garden. From the direction of the nearby village, a figure was making his way across the fields, a hessian sack over one shoulder, a sheepdog trotting at his heels. Jack was browner than ever with sun and sea air and a little greyer at the temples, but otherwise he was the same. As he came closer, I could see that, despite the grey, he appeared younger than I remembered. He had the look of a man who had found peace.

'I was under instructions to wait at my lodgings,' he said, smiling in his familiar serious way. 'Mouse was determined to have you all to herself.' His eyes scrutinised my face. 'I'm sorry, Elin. I know what it must have taken for you to take such a step.'

I bent down to fuss Fly's head. 'I tried so hard not to leave him. But in the end I had no choice. I still wish there could have been another way.'

'Hugo's pride would never have allowed it. And as for Connors…' Anger crossed Jack's features. 'He always was a despicable excuse for a man. He possesses an unerring capability for spotting weaknesses in others, and has no conscience in using it for his own ends.'

'I wish there was more I could have done.'

'Nonsense. You stayed in that impossible position longer than anyone could have asked you to do. You made sure Mrs Hughes was safe with Alice. Not every captain has to go down with their ship, thank goodness.' His eyes were troubled. 'Hugo must make his own choices. You would never have been able to wipe away the past, and you could never live his life for him. And don't ever feel that you should.'

'I know.' From the house came excitable barking as Jojo raced to join Fly. Within minutes the two dogs were racing towards the beach. 'Mouse tells me you'll never give up your pacifist campaigning.'

'Never.'

'I'm glad,' I said, as Lisette came towards us. 'I've seen too much of war and its legacy to think otherwise.'

'It's not just that.' He hesitated, then turned away. 'I'd better take the potatoes to Aunt Catrin,' he muttered.

'You are sad, Auntie Elin?' said Lisette, looking at me anxiously, as we followed him back inside the cottage.

I tucked my arm into hers with a smile. 'No, Lisette. Just remembering.'

* * *

For the next year, I thanked Mama each morning from the bottom of my heart for her gift of peace at *Swn y Môr*.

Far away in another world I was a scarlet woman. An adulteress. A wife who had no doubt betrayed her husband with a hundred lovers or more while he was away risking life and limb for his country only to return desperately wounded. Hugo fought me, as I knew he would, even though I had put myself in the wrong and now demanded nothing from him. I didn't flaunt my supposed lover all over the gossip pages – I didn't even write to Owen, nor he to me, in case Hugo (spurred on by Connors, no doubt) hired a private detective to assuage his pride and punish me for my desertion by blackening my name even further.

I had no intention of remaining in seclusion forever. One night in a hotel proved nothing beyond the desire to obtain the evidence necessary to provoke a divorce. My reputation might be tarnished, but it could, with time, be mended. But any suspicion that I had been flaunting a lover – or even a series of lovers – under my husband's nose while he was away at war would be far harder, if not impossible, to be forgiven and forgotten.

If Hugo did hire a detective, it did him no good. Before long, Alice was able to tell me I had vanished from the papers. There was nothing to embellish the story. Owen was a hero, the nephew of the eminently respectable Lord Northholme, and now openly living a quiet and virtuous existence assisting the rehabilitation of wounded soldiers without a woman in sight. The whole thing was, declared Alice, so clearly one of those polite fictions increasingly used to dissolve an unhappy marriage that it soon attracted only sympathy and was left to run its course.

Hugo finally gave up the fight. I wondered if somewhere in his confused mind he suspected that if I was pushed too far I might be driven to reveal how much of a sham our marriage had become. Hugo could never have borne sniggers behind his back or whispered stories from the past rearing their ugly heads to shame him.

Meanwhile, I lived peacefully. I coaxed a small vegetable garden from the salt-swept land behind the cottage surrounded by lavender and rosemary, and pruned the apple trees back into life. I watched the fishermen in their boats, and seals sunning themselves at high tide. Most days I made the short walk to Aunt Catrin's to help her pickle beetroot and cabbage or create great pans of soup made of green peas and ham, or any vegetable that might be in season, to go with the crusty loaves of bread that fuelled the helpers on the farm. Other times I took pickled walnuts and tarts filled with rhubarb or rosehips, or blackberries when they were in season, the further walk to the Caradoc farmhouse, to the big old kitchen where Mouse was making plans for her flying school. I sat with Lisette as she happily kept Frankie occupied, or helped Jack and Mouse as they planted fields and fed the animals. Some nights I stayed with Mouse and the children, others with Aunt Catrin, enjoying the laughter around the evening fire. Other times, I returned to my healing solitude of *Sŵn y Môr* and my recipes.

It was Alice who first asked me, as shortages lingered, to send copies of the recipes I had created or adapted from my mother's book to make the best use of the produce of Hiram's garden. Mrs Hughes was already noted for her ability to conjure miracles from a carrot and a handful of potatoes and, with her repertoire widened, the hotel was soon, so Alice told me delightedly, noted as the place to be. I thought no more of it until a regular guest who worked for one of the new women's magazines, asked for the secret of making rice pudding on a stove with only two temperamental gas rings and no oven, and any method possible of making offal taste like the daintiest cuts. Alice immediately suggested she write to me to find out more.

I was soon contributing recipes and baking tips. With so many men lost in the war, more women were now earning their own incomes and living independent lives, but without much idea of how to cook for themselves without a servant to hand, and eager to learn. When I was asked to come up with more dishes for one that were simple, nutritious, quick to make and from the cheapest ingredients possible, the challenge was irresistible. I was soon devising ways of creating a mock lobster dinner on one ring, while browning a bread and butter pudding on the other, ensuring both courses arrived at the right time.

It gave me a little income to eke out my money from Mama and saved me from selling her necklace, for now, at least. Aunt Catrin and Mouse would never let me go without, but having found my independence I was determined to keep it.

My wish for solitude was soon tested. By the summer, the editor of the magazine was suggesting we meet up in London and talk through some more ideas face to face. The recipes and tips for single women were such a runaway success she was suggesting a regular column. Maybe in the future a book. The world was calling me back already.

* * *

I was sitting in the sun one afternoon working on the intricacies of a rabbit curry followed by pear and treacle pudding (my two ring dinners were by now growing ambitious) when a figure came striding along the well-worn path from Aunt Catrin's farm.

'I hope I'm not interrupting,' he said, hesitating by the garden gate. I dropped my pencil and notebook.

'Of course not.' The scarring had faded a little more, but the disfigurement would always be there, attracting curious glances, marking him out. To me he was beautiful. I sat there, drinking him in.

'I was visiting an old army colleague in Liverpool,' he said, a little awkwardly. 'It was so close, I couldn't quite resist.' He cleared his throat. 'Perhaps I should have written.'

'Don't be silly.' I pulled myself together and rose to meet him. 'I'm a free woman. I am permitted to have visitors, you know.' He smiled and met my kiss. 'Come on, I'll put the kettle on.'

We sat in the sun for a while, drinking tea and smiling, slightly shyly, at each other.

'It feels strange,' he said. 'I've always known you as someone out of my grasp, another man's wife. I can't quite believe I'm sitting here with you now and no one has the right to stop me.'

'Does that make you change your mind?'

He took my hand. 'No.'

'Good,' I replied. He grinned and the shyness eased. We chatted more easily, catching up with each other's lives, until the sun began to sink towards the sea.

At last Owen stood up. 'I'd better be getting back. May I come again tomorrow?'

'Of course.' He was already turning towards the gate. A sense of utter desolation opened up inside me.

'Must you go so soon?'

He turned back, a smile lighting up his face. 'It seems only minutes to me too, but we've been talking for hours. It's a fair walk and it will be dark soon. Besides, Mouse will be expecting me.'

I took a deep breath. 'Will she?'

'Well, yes of course, I…' He came to a halt. 'Elin, I arrived here out of the blue, without warning. I love you with all my heart, but I would never presume anything.'

'I know.' I took his hands in mine. 'Please stay. I couldn't bear to be parted from you again'

His eyes were on my hands, a troubled look on his face. 'I have my demons.'

'So do I.'

'And I have scars.' He swallowed hard. 'Scars that no one but my doctors and nurses have seen. The scars on my face are nothing to the ones that are hidden.'

I kept my eyes on his as I unbuttoned first his jacket, then his shirt. I ran my hand over the poor ruined skin left by the burns down one side of his body and his arm, then bent to kiss them.

'I will never see your scars, Owen. Only you.' He held me tight. His tears dampened my face as he bent to kiss me. I pulled him closer. 'And the night,' I said, 'has its own rules, you know.'

* * *

I woke the next morning with sunlight streaming through the attic bedroom of *Sŵn y Môr*. I stretched, my body luxuriating in a peace and sense of contentment I had never felt before.

Next to me, Owen stirred. He propped himself on one elbow and looked down at me smiling. 'Well, well, Miss Elin. So that was a first, after all.'

'There's no need to look so smug about it,' I retorted, blushing. I slipped through his grasp as he reached for me, pulling the counterpane around me as I gleefully shot down the stairs and out to the beach. I threw the covering away as I reached the shore, splashing through the waves, Owen close behind.

'Lord, it's freezing!' he gasped as we plunged into the next breaker. 'Is this your idea of fun?'

'Stimulating, don't you find?'

'More like you're trying to kill me,' he grumbled, as we struck out for deeper waters.

'Perfect revenge,' I replied, slipping my arms around him with a kiss.

We swam as the sun rose, splashing back, more slowly this time, amongst the waves to wrap ourselves up in blankets. The fire was still smouldering in the grate. With a few sticks it was blazing again, sending out fragile warmth as it gained strength to boil the kettle.

'I can see why you came here,' said Owen, as we huddled together attempting to get our circulation moving.

'A perfect retreat.' I kissed him. 'It always will be. But that doesn't mean I want to live here for the rest of my life. I want to go out into the world and change and grow. I was terrified every moment of that time I spent in France, but at the same time I've never felt so alive. I don't know what the future might bring, but I'd rather face it than stay shut away all my life.'

* * *

Later that day, we walked between green fields to Aunt Catrin's farm. Lisette was entertaining Frankie on the grass in front of the house, while Jack sat a short distance away, watching them with a smile as he mended the handle of a scythe.

Above us in the blue sky a bi-plane swept over the fields and out into a great arch over the sea before turning back towards us. We waved as, with a flourish, the little craft sank slowly, if slightly unsteadily, to the large field at the edge of the farm. A few minutes later we could see Mouse shaking hands with her pupil before striding back towards us.

She kissed Frankie and Lisette before hugging me tight. 'A bonfire on the beach, I think,' she announced to the world in general. 'Lady Madeleine loved every minute of it, and the hotel in Beaumaris lived up to their promises. She's booked to come back in a few months' time and I've three more pupils lined up already. And this is just the start.'

'I might have known you'd find your way into the air again somehow, Mouse,' said Owen, shaking his head. But I could see that he was smiling.

As Jack and Owen busied themselves building the bonfire, I sat with Mouse and a very sleepy Frankie amongst the sand dunes, watching Lisette gather driftwood while Fly and Jojo chased seagulls along the shore, a streak of spray accompanied by hysterical barking.

'I always said I'd start a flying school,' said Mouse, thoughtfully, kissing the top of her son's head. 'Charlotte is one of my next pupils, you know. She said in her letter that she's never forgotten her time as a land girl at Hiram. She has turned down the offer of marriage from an earl and taken up flying instead. She said he was pretty ancient. There are so few young ones left.' Her eyes rested on Jack, who had paused, a bleached branch of a tree in one hand, deep in animated conversation with Owen. 'I don't know why he loves me, but he does.'

'I know exactly why Jack loves you, Mouse. How could he not? I think he loved you, from the day he met you,' I replied with a smile.

Mouse was frowning. 'I thought he wouldn't. Not after – well, you know.' She adjusted Frankie, who was now fast asleep, wrapping him inside her coat. 'I didn't think anyone could possibly love me. Besides, I didn't think I could let anyone near me, let alone love them. Yet somehow I do.'

'I'm glad,' I replied, kissing her. I looked up to find Jack watching us. The troubled look was back on his face. It was not for Mouse, I saw, as I met his eyes across the flickering flames of the bonfire. At the far edges of my mind, something fell into place. I shut my eyes tight, fighting it, every muscle in my body rigid. I forced my eyes open again, and it was gone.

Around the bay, the tide surged up against the rocks, throwing spray high into the air. I could have been back in Hiram Cove, looking up at the dark windows, where Hugo was waiting.

It would always cause me pain, that I had left Hugo, for all his weaknesses; that I had left him and my family home in the care of a man who had no conscience. But Hugo had made his choice. There was nothing I could do, and if I tried, I might risk the new happiness I had by some miracle found. But it was unfinished business, deep in my heart, still causing me grief when I least expected it.

Chapter Forty

SUMMER 1925

After a while, memories of life at Hiram began to fade. The scandal of my divorce was forgotten by most even before Owen and I were quietly married. I never thought I would see Hugo again.

After the children were born, we began to spend more time in

London. Owen continued to work with the veterans and make a name for himself as a journalist, using the skills he had developed as a photographer while helping with the reconstruction of faces damaged beyond repair. My own column was popular and I published two books of recipes and was working on more. In London, we found a small house to rent in a quiet neighbourhood next to Hampstead Heath, but we returned regularly to Anglesey, to Mouse and Jack and Aunt Catrin, and to the peace of *Sŵn y Môr*.

That Sunday afternoon, Owen and I made one of our regular visits to Alice in her elegant flat near the large hotel she now managed. After luncheon, we took our usual walk in Hyde Park. Owen and Alice were either side of little Rhys, holding him steady as he waddled along the path. I was in front, chasing after three-year-old Lucy, who had raced ahead to see the ducks, laughing so much at her squeals of delight I could scarcely catch my breath.

We turned a corner and there he was. An old man pushed along in a wheelchair, his body frail and bent, hair thin and completely white, his gaze fixed on his gaunt hands clutching at the edges of the blanket covering his knees.

'For Heaven's sake!' cried the boy pushing the chair as Lucy ran in front of them. I rushed towards my daughter, but she was swept out of the way by the woman with them.

An acid taste burned my mouth as she turned to scrutinise Lucy, who had frozen at the near collision and was beginning to cry. I reached to snatch my daughter from her grasp, but Sissy stepped forward and placed her into my arms before I could.

'You have a beautiful daughter, Ma'am,' she said. She did not smile, but neither was her voice hostile. Her face was thin and worn, with the pallor of one who scarcely sees the sun. Even in the midst of attempting to soothe Lucy, I could see the cowed look in Miss Connors' eyes.

'Thank you.'

At the sound of my voice, Hugo stirred. Faded, bloodshot eyes rose to meet mine. Slowly his gaze focussed. A frown creased his brow, as if attempting to clutch at the shreds of memory. His gaze clung to my face, then travelled to Lucy, clinging to me, her arms around my neck. He became very still. His skin assumed an even more deathly pallor. He grasped the arms of the wheelchair, as if attempting to rise.

'Take the Major on, will you, Adam,' said Miss Connors quickly, drawing herself up. 'And take more care where you are going in future. You could have hurt that child with your carelessness.' She bent to settle Hugo back in the chair, lowering her voice to Adam as if we should not hear. 'I'll do what I can to make things well with the child's parents, so there will be no need to mention this to my uncle. But if there is any other incident like it, you will leave me with no choice, and you know what will happen then.'

'Yes, miss,' muttered Adam, moving forward with exaggerated care, as Owen arrived at my side, then Alice, holding Rhys tight in her arms.

'I'll make sure he doesn't say anything,' said Miss Connors. A look of desperation came into her eyes. 'I'm sorry, Mrs Helstone – Mrs Northholme, I mean. I should have written to you. I've so often been on the point of writing to you at that magazine you work for, but Uncle James watches me closely all the time even though I haven't done anything to defy him. I know he'd make an excuse at the Post Office and read my letters, if he suspected.' She glanced in the direction of the wheelchair, which was now almost out of sight.

Owen was gently taking Lucy from me. I felt his hand briefly on my arm.

'Is Hugo very ill?' I asked.

'I'm afraid so. It's all those injuries he had inside him from when he was wounded. They were better for a while, like his leg. But they never properly healed and now they've got worse again. We've been to see a specialist in Harley Street.'

'I'm sorry.'

The wheelchair had disappeared. Sissy grasped my hand. 'I wouldn't marry him, Mrs Northholme. That's what Uncle James wanted. So I would inherit Hiram and he could take control of it. But I wouldn't. I couldn't do that to the poor old gentleman. But now I can't stop him.'

'Stop him?'

'Uncle James has persuaded Major Helstone to sign the Hall over to him. He took him to a solicitor this morning, after we'd been to see the specialist. He did it in London so no one would suspect. He wouldn't let me go with them, but I know that's what he was doing.' Tears started to fill her eyes.

'But why should Hugo hand over Hiram to Mr Connors?'

'He thinks he's signing it over to you.'

I stared at her. 'To *me*? But Sissy, why on earth would he do that?'

Sissy turned scarlet. She took a quick glance towards Owen. 'Because Uncle James told him you needed Major Helstone to look after you. I heard him. He said your...' she swallowed, 'your "lover" had used you and abandoned you, and that you were now living in the most terrible poverty, practically on the streets. I'm sorry, Mr Northholme, but that's what he said. And he thinks he has been sending you money, which Uncle James has been pocketing.'

Owen shook his head. 'But surely Hugo knows that, even if I had been such an unconscionable brute, Elin has many friends?'

'But he wants to believe it.' Her voice cracked. 'It so cruel. He listens to Uncle James. Sometimes I think he's afraid of him, but he trusts what he says. In his poor confused mind I'm sure he thinks he is doing this for the best. I heard my uncle tell him that if he signed Hiram over to Elin he should be named as Steward so he could look after you if anything happened to him. I tried to tell the Major that you were married, Mrs Northholme, and that you were happy and had children and were really quite famous with your recipes and your articles. But he wouldn't listen. Uncle James has told him what he wants to believe. I'm sure, in his heart of hearts, he hopes this might bring you back to Hiram.'

'But surely when I don't—' I caught the look on her face.

'I thought so too. I thought Hugo would finally see what Uncle James was like.' A tear escaped down her cheek. 'But now there's no time. He's dying, Mrs Northholme. Uncle James knows he only has to wait for a few months. A year at the most. And if he grows impatient, everyone will assume it was sudden heart failure because of his injuries.'

'I know the man's a vile parasite, but even he wouldn't go that far, surely?' said Owen.

'You don't know him.' Her grip on my hand tightened. 'Please help the Major. I know I've no right to ask, and I know he gets some strange ideas, and he's not at all right in the head, but he doesn't deserve this. I can't bear to think what Uncle James might do now he's got what he wants. And I can't bear to think of the poor old man living his last months in misery. I don't know who else to ask.'

Before I could speak, Miss Connors had turned and was running to catch up with the wheelchair.

'Poor Hugo,' said Alice, trying to soothe Rhys, who was beginning to cry. I took him from her arms, while she led Lucy back to the lake, distracting her with some enthusiastic feeding of the ducks and moorhens.

'I have to speak to Jack,' I said, holding Rhys tight.

'Of course, *cariad*,' said Owen, watching me anxiously. 'We'll telephone them as soon as we get home.'

I shook my head. 'No, I need to see him. It doesn't make sense. None of it makes sense. I know there's something he's not telling me. I have to see him.'

'It may be that Hugo is simply confused,' said Owen, gently. 'He looked very frail just now, and many of the men I work with who have been terribly injured experience problems with their minds, as well as their bodies.'

'I know.' I bit my lip. I couldn't explain the look on Jack's face, that night at *Sŵn y Môr*, or the understanding that had hovered so close, and that I had pushed away. 'But I still have to talk to Jack.'

* * *

We arrived at *Sŵn y Môr* a few days later. Jack was waiting for us. I could see at a glance the troubled look was back on his face. As Mouse and Owen settled the children, we walked the short way to the beach. He knew what I was going to ask. As I told him of our meeting with Hugo and Sissy, I could tell by the way he wouldn't quite meet my eyes. When I had finished he was silent. I could see the sadness in his face.

'I need to understand,' I said. 'Hugo was your friend. I need to understand. I thought Hugo would be so angry with me, at the humiliation I put him through, that the last thing on his mind would be to want to help me, let alone give Hiram back to me.'

'I think in his confused way he is still trying to look after you.' He hesitated. 'That he still loves you.'

'But that's it.' I wanted to shake him. To make him understand. 'Hugo doesn't love me. He never has. He was fond of me, as you might be of a pet, and he tried to be kind. Perhaps when we were first married he loved me. But not after that. Not after I miscarried our child. After that, it was as if he couldn't bear me near him. He couldn't bear to touch me.' Jack looked up sharply. I could feel his eyes on my face. 'I tried to understand. I tried to make it better. But he wouldn't let me. I thought he blamed me. I thought he couldn't bear me because I wasn't the untouched girl he'd married. That he'd fallen in love with a dream and I would never be good enough.'

'I don't think it was that way, Elin,' said Jack. 'You must never blame yourself. I am convinced that Hugo truly loved you, in the best way he knew how.'

'So it *was* my fault.' I looked at him desperately. 'I have to know, Jack, don't you see? If I can lose Hugo's love without knowing why, I'm terrified that one day I might lose Owen's, too. And that would kill me.'

'It wasn't you,' said Jack, gently.

'I know. At least, in my head, I know Owen loves me. But in my heart I have to be sure. I have to understand. And you are the only person I know who can help me.'

There was a moment's silence. Then Jack stirred. 'I will fight against war with my last breath,' he said. My heart sank. He was changing the subject. Avoiding me. He would never answer. 'I hate what it does and the legacy it leaves. It's not just the deaths, Elin.' He kicked the sand with his boot. 'We rescued three men, the day my brother died.'

I stared at him. 'I thought you said only Hugo survived?'

'Yes. And that's true. It seemed easier to put it that way. More dignified. It's what their families were told, too. The truth was that neither of them could bear the memories and the shame. They weren't as strong as Hugo. One was found hanged, the other shot himself.'

'No.' A wave of nausea flooded over me. The understanding that day of the bonfire as I sat with Mouse was back, a shadow at the edge of my mind.

'Whatever the justice of a cause, war really is the world gone mad. It's a place where people like Connors thrive. And there are worse than Connors. Much worse. More sadistic, more depraved. What happened to Mouse, and those women in the French villages, doesn't just happen to women. It happens to children, and to men, too.'

The pieces fell back into place. This time not to be pushed away. Finally, I had to face, square on, what Hugo had been through, all those years ago.

I ran. I fled, stumbling over the sand dunes, falling and retching, then on my feet again, until my legs gave way and I curled up tight in a hollow, where only the sky was visible and I could not hear the sea at all.

It was Mouse who found me. She put her arms around me without a word and held me tight until my shaking ceased.

'I'm sorry,' she said. 'I didn't know. I knew there was something, but Jack never told me.' Her arms tightened. 'But then I suppose he couldn't. Not after what happened to me. Don't be angry with him, Elin.'

I didn't reply. One day I might be able to answer her, but not now. 'I can't abandon Hugo,' I said at last. 'Those last months I was at Hiram Connors was always telling Hugo how he was protecting him, and how there were things I should not hear. That was an iron grip Connors must always have had over him. I thought it was because he didn't care for me. I didn't understand. I can't leave him to Connors. Not now. '

'Of course not.' Mouse kissed my forehead. 'What Hugo needs is a rescue mission. You came through a war to rescue me,' she added, as I began to protest. 'This is just Cornwall. Jack won't leave Hugo to Connors, not now he knows. And I won't, either. I'm sure Sissy will help us.'

'I'm not sure. She's clearly terrified of her uncle.'

'But from what you said, she's fond of Hugo and can't bear to see what Connors is doing to him. You'll see. Between us we'll find a way.'

She sounded so like her old impetuous self, I found myself smiling. 'Mouse, you can't just kidnap someone. And besides, that would just make it easy for Connors to take over Hiram without even waiting for Hugo to die.' I sighed. 'Hiram means so much to Hugo. I'm sure he would be distressed if he were forced to live anywhere else. I couldn't bear to see him unhappy, now he has so little time left. I couldn't live with myself unless I knew he had found some kind of peace.'

'I agree.' Mouse sat up straight, determination on her face. 'So we'll have to get rid of Connors.'

I sighed. 'Hugo will never do that. Connors always knew how to convince him. He never would hear a word against him. And from what Sissy said, nothing has changed.'

'Well, in that case,' said Mouse firmly, 'we'll just have to find a way to prove it. We'll have to find a copy of the will to show to Hugo, then he'll have to see what kind of man Connors is.' She was silent for a moment. 'And maybe Sissy can help us to find other things. Papers. Anything that might prove all those horrible things he did.'

'Mouse.' I looked at her. 'Mouse, you do know what that might mean, if we succeeded?'

She grimaced. 'That the accusations against me of spying – I know it was Connors – and that I was held prisoner by the Germans might become public knowledge. And about Frankie.'

'Yes.'

She sighed. 'I'm quite prepared for that. And anyhow, in Papa's eyes I couldn't sink any lower than marrying Jack, and he can hardly disown me all over again, even if it did come out. I suppose I'll have to tell Frankie the truth one day, when he's old enough to understand. But Jack will always be his father. And no one can ever take that away.' Her face darkened. 'You can't just let Connors get away with this. Didn't you say Sissy has a grandmother in Port Helen.'

'Yes.'

'Well then you can write to her there, so Connors wouldn't know. I'm sure she will help us.'

I looked at her with misgivings. 'Connors is cunning. And greedy. He won't give up a prize like Hiram that easily.'

'Well, we'll make him,' said Mouse. 'You'll see, Elin. Between us, we'll find a way.'

* * *

And so I made my way once more along the cliff path to Hiram Hall, to the door that lay unchanged and the kitchen garden overgrown with neglect and rotting with time. To the place that haunted my dreams. The place I never thought I would see again.

As I reached the archway, the footsteps on the gravel paused.

'You came,' said Sissy, as I emerged into the driveway. She was pale and breathless. There was no vehicle in the driveway or any sign of life, but her voice was no more than a whisper.

'Of course.' I smiled reassuringly at her. Sissy had answered the letters I had sent to her grandmother's house, but I could tell from her short replies how terrified she was of even letters being intercepted. She had waited until she visited Truro to post the last one. 'I couldn't leave the Major like this.'

She nodded. 'We need to be quick. As I told you, Uncle James always goes up to Grandma's farm on a Friday. He's just left. But he's so sharp, I don't know if he suspected anything this morning, however much I tried to make things as normal as possible. I never know when he might be back again.' A gleam of determination appeared. 'I left a bottle of port on the table in the kitchen. Mrs Pettersham steals whatever she can from the cellar, so she'll never be able to resist it. She was snoring when I went down there just now. The Major's in the drawing room. It's the only place he seems to feel at peace.'

I followed as she led the way up the steps to the front door. Briefly, I lifted my face to the reassuring warmth of the sun then followed Sissy back into shadows inside Hiram Hall.

Chapter Forty-One

SUMMER 1925

Hiram enveloped me instantly.

As my eyes adjusted, I gazed up at the great staircase, down which I had run as a child, rushing eagerly into the sunshine. As a young woman I had glided down – or at least done my best to appear poised and graceful – watching Hugo's eyes light up as they rested on me. I had walked down those stairs on the morning of my marriage, my hand resting on Papa's arm, my heart filled with joy, and just a little apprehension. I had watched the coffins of first Mama and then Papa take their solemn way down. It was where my child who had never lived was taken away, and with it my dreams, Hugo's fragile mind, and my fragile happiness.

I shivered. It was like entering a lost world. Dust hung in the blue and crimson beams from the stained-glass window at the top of the stairs: a fantasy scene of dragons and golden-haired princesses that had entranced me as a child, but was now revealed as cracked and badly executed. My memories, and those I had loved, were no longer here: I carried them with me. They were my essence. But Hiram had been left to slip into the shadows. No longer a home.

Footsteps crunched on the gravel, following us inside. Sissy swung round, jumpy as could be. She let out a quick sigh of relief as Jack appeared, followed by Owen.

'You won't find anything,' she said. 'I've looked and looked, as much as I can. I can't find the will, or anything that could incriminate Uncle James and make him leave the Major alone.'

'But we have to try,' I said. 'Even if we can't find anything and we have to leave Hiram to Connors, at least we can get Hugo away from him. And at least we can try.'

She nodded, her eyes following Owen anxiously as he slipped silently towards Hugo's study. I followed Sissy into the drawing room. Hugo was sitting in his wheelchair next to the fire. The curtains were half-drawn, letting in the faintest light as he gazed intently into the flames.

He looked up as we approached. His gaze was gentle as it rested on Sissy. Slowly it moved to my face.

'My dear,' he said, attempting to rise.

I put my hand on his arm. 'Hello, Hugo.' I did my best to sound cheerful. 'I hoped you'd join me for afternoon tea. There's a charming new hotel in Port Helen and it's a beautiful day.'

'I'm not certain...' He glanced towards Sissy as if for reassurance.

'I'll come with you, if I may, Major Helstone,' she said with a smile. 'And look, you have another old friend come to visit.'

Hugo's shoulders straightened as Jack came in quietly behind us. 'Why Treeve, my good fellow, how are you? I haven't seen you in such a while.'

'No, sir,' replied Jack evenly, as if this were a casual meeting in a park.

From the driveway came the roar of Mouse's automobile making its way towards us. I met Jack's eyes. We had to get Hugo away. We had all agreed that was the main thing. Who knew when Connors might decide to return and use his powers of persuasion to make him stay? Once Connors knew what we were attempting, there would never be a second chance. There was no time to lose.

'Captain Treeve is joining us too,' I said, crouching down so I was level with Hugo. 'I thought you might like that.'

'Yes.' Hugo's eyes travelled between the three of us. A faint colour had appeared in his parchment cheeks, a glow of life in his eyes. 'Yes, I would like that.' His voice was stronger. 'I've been cooped up in here too long. This damned leg of mine.' He patted my hand, still resting on the arm of the wheelchair. 'I should like to see the sea again.'

Jack took hold of the wheelchair and began manoeuvring it towards the front door. 'Come along then, Major. We've a vehicle waiting for you. You remember Lady Margaret, don't you? The ladies will join us a little later, you know what the ladies are like.'

Sissy and I followed them to the front door, where Mouse was arriving at speed, her face gleaming with excitement. Jack lifted Hugo into the front seat, hastily perching himself and the wheelchair in the back. Mouse waved, and they were off, speeding down the drive in a whirl of dust.

Relief flooded through me. 'Come on.' I grabbed Sissy's hand as we shot back inside. Owen had forced the door of Hugo's study and the drawer in the desk that held the account books. For a good hour, the three of us searched. We worked quickly and methodically through the shelves and the papers. But there was nothing.

'The will isn't here,' said Owen, at last. 'And Connors is clearly too careful to leave anything else lying around.' He glanced towards the ceiling.

'It's not anywhere else,' said Sissy. 'I've looked in every place I could think. If it is, it's so well hidden no one can find it. I even looked in the kitchens and in the barns. This was the only place Uncle James keeps locked all the time. I thought it must be here, but it's hopeless.'

We stood for a minute in silence. I could feel Sissy growing increasingly anxious at the lengthening of the shadows. I was beginning to jump at the slightest creak of floorboards myself.

'At least we've got Hugo away,' said Owen. 'Whatever happens, he'll be safe now. We've done our best. There's no point in giving Connors the opportunity to accuse us of daylight robbery. Time to get out of here.'

I nodded. My eye fell on the small pile of account books, still lying on the desk. Hiram may have changed over the years, but I knew the estate. And I knew what the accounts should show.

'I still might be able to prove to Hugo what Connors is up to,' I said slowly. There were several years in the pile. I gathered them up, making sure that I included the years of the war when they had been my responsibility and several from the time Hugo had run the estate. As I picked up the last one, I paused.

'We can look over them properly at the hotel.' Owen was growing anxious too.

'There's something in there,' I said. I opened it, and there, tucked inside the cover, was a small sheaf of papers. There was no sign of a will, just lines of Connor's precise handwriting. I frowned at the top one. 'It makes no sense.'

'It's probably in code.' Owen bent over the papers. 'None of us came across anything that looked like a codebook. Still, I'm sure I can find someone willing to take the time to break it.'

Behind us, Sissy gasped sharply. Owen pulled me out of the way.

'It seems we have burglars in the house.' In the doorway stood Connors. 'I shall have to call the police. Get you arrested for trying to rob the poor Major, after all he's been through.'

'Really?' I raised the account books. 'I think we're the ones who will be calling the police.'

Connors raised his hand. He held a pistol, which was pointing straight at Owen. His pale eyes lingered on the papers in my hand with the slow blink of a lizard.

He'd become a demon in my imagination in the years since I'd seen him. Now again, just as when I first met him, he struck me as a small colourless man.

'I might have known,' he said. He flicked a glance at his niece. 'You always were much too soft to get on in life, Sissy. You were a little too eager to see me go this morning. I had a feeling someone had been meddling.' His eyes glanced briefly back towards Owen, then came to rest on my face.

'I suspected that now the Major's dying, you might be back to try and take all that you threw away when you left.'

'That's enough,' growled Owen. His hand slipped towards his jacket pocket.

'I wouldn't do that,' said Connors. A slight tick had begun on his face, high on one cheekbone. He moved his pistol until it pointed straight at my forehead. 'Not if you want to see your wife alive, that is.' He nodded to Sissy. 'Well, go on. Make yourself useful.'

'I'm sorry,' whispered Sissy, taking Owen's pistol. She flung it through the nearest window, smashing the glass.

'What did you do that for?' demanded Connors. There was a jumpiness to him that made the fear in my belly flicker into terror.

'I thought that's want you wanted,' replied Sissy. 'You've won, haven't you? There's nothing they can do. Now you can let them go.'

I exchanged glances with Owen. We both knew that Connors wasn't going to let us go. The papers still in my arms had seen to that. Even after all this time, he wasn't going to risk being tried as a spy. Perhaps hanged. How many lives had he destroyed during the war? Three more would make no difference. I cursed that moment of inattentiveness, when none of us had been listening for footsteps on the hallway floor.

'Jack Treeve, Lady Margaret Northholme, they know we're here.' I saw him flinch at Mouse's name. 'Hugo is with them. If anything happens to us, they'll know who to blame.'

'Nobody could blame me for protecting my house against burglars.'

'Your house?'

He smiled. 'I've earned it. Major Helstone will back me up. He won't let a word be said against me. He knows who he can trust with his secrets.'

I shuddered. He knew what Hugo had suffered. He'd said from the first he had served in the Transvaal. He was a man who could root out secrets. And he had used it to worm his way into Hugo's trust, to convince him that he was his friend, while reminding him, again and again. Wearing him down. And because I hadn't understood, I couldn't stop it. I wanted to be sick.

'I'll put these back on the desk then, shall I?' I said, doing my best to sound calm. Unsuspecting. As if I believed that Connors truly was about to let us go.

'Go on.' He nodded brusquely. He clearly had no intention of blood obscuring his messages and his precious accounts. I moved slowly, closer towards him.

I flung the account books straight at him. Papers flew up in front of his face. Sissy shrieked as Owen threw himself through the papers, knocking Connors to the ground. As the two men struggled, the pistol flew from Connors' hand across the floor. I grabbed it. From the corner of my eye, I could see Connors slam Owen's head hard against the desk.

The pistol was familiar in my hand. Hugo's pistol. The one Jack had taught me to use, all those years ago. I didn't stop to think. My ears rang with the shot, as I stumbled, dazed with the force. Connors slumped to the floor.

Owen had recovered his balance, and was at his side in a moment. Blood was seeping into a pool.

'Is he dead?'

Owen nodded. Sissy burst into hysterical tears. 'It's all right,' he said, leading her away from her uncle.

I looked at Owen. I felt sick. 'I shot an unarmed man,' I said. I sounded horribly calm. 'People will think I came to try and get

Hiram back, and I got you all to help me.' I looked down at the weapon in my hands. 'The police will think I'm a murderer.'

'Nonsense.' Owen took the pistol from my hand. 'They're not going to believe you could shoot that thing straight.'

'Then they'll think it was you. If they find out about Mouse, they'll think it was you.' I thought of Rhys and Lucy, happily spending the day on the beach with their Aunt Alice, and my heart broke. 'They could hang both of us. Then Connors really will have won.'

Owen pulled a fallen paper from where it stuck to the sole of his boot. His eyes focussed. 'Wait a minute.' He bent over Connors, rapidly searching inside his jacket, then his shirt. I could not bear to look. I had killed a man. A living, breathing man, who had looked into my eyes as I pulled the trigger. I'd seen fear there. Horror. Disbelief. I hated Connors for all he had done, but I knew that last flickering of a life would haunt me forever.

Owen pulled out a small leather bound book. 'I thought he wouldn't have memorised the entire code. If I'd got something like this, that I might still find useful, but might have me hung as a spy, I'd have kept it on me at all times, too.' He gathered up the papers. 'That looks like a key to the code all right.' He peered from one to the other. 'Yes, it must be. And from this bit here, it looks as if Connors was still in touch with his contacts in Germany earlier this year.'

Sissy stopped sobbing. 'You mean, he might still have been spying?'

'I'm not sure,' said Owen. He looked at her. 'We should hand these over to the police.'

Slowly Sissy nodded. She dried her eyes. The look of determination was back. She looked me square in the face. 'That means he might have been killed by anyone. A fellow spy. Or someone who wanted revenge for all those horrible things he did.'

'Sissy,' I began, gently. 'Whatever he was, he was your uncle. I can't ask you to lie for me.'

Sissy shook her head. 'If I was out having tea with you and the Major, because his friends wanted to see him, and you wanted to make your peace with him and see him for one last time, then I wouldn't know who had been here.' She looked around the study. 'You can see the place has been ransacked. Suppose my uncle had told me someone might be looking for him, and he'd given me his papers and his little book to look after? Then when I came back and found him, I'd be so scared that even if he'd told me not to, I'd call the police.'

'I can't ask you to do that, Sissy,' I said. I rubbed my eyes. My whole body ached for all this to go away. For my life to be as it had been, with Owen and the children.

'Yes you can, Elin,' muttered Owen. 'What Sissy is saying makes sense. Don't let Connors win. Whether anyone can prove it or not, the man was a monster. I've seen better men than him die for nothing. I'm not going to let you be harmed by him any more than you have been already.'

'And I want to do this.' Sissy bit her lip. 'You were kind to me, when I came here, Mrs Helstone, when you shouldn't have been, not with the way Uncle James was treating you and driving you away. You told me to leave and live my own life. I know you were right. I should never have stayed.' She took a deep breath. 'I'm the only family Uncle James has. He told me he would leave everything to me. So my grandmother's farm will be mine now. And I don't have to be scared of him any more.'

Owen frowned. 'We're forgetting Mrs Pettersham.'

'If she wakes up, she'll find him. It won't make any difference. Either way, she'll be scared stiff. She was part of the black market and all sorts of things during the war. She'll think she could be next. Please, Mrs Helstone. You've got your children to think of. And it would break the poor Major's heart to see you accused of murder.'

I glanced at Owen. 'I won't stand by and let you be accused of murder, either,' he said firmly. 'So if you don't want to see me on trial for my life you'd better accept Sissy's offer.'

'It seems I have no choice.' I kissed Sissy.

She gave a watery smile. 'I won't change my mind. I promise. I'm glad he's dead. He hurt so many people, I knew someone would kill him, one day. I remember when he found that pistol in one of the barns. After what he tried to do to you and the Major, if I'd found it first, I might have used it on him by now.'

'Don't say that,' I shuddered. I didn't dare look at the lifeless figure slumped in the corner. I pulled myself together. 'Hugo will be wondering where we are.'

The three of us walked rapidly down the path along the cliffs. As we cleared Hiram Cove and the sea opened out into the bay, Owen flung Hugo's pistol, and his own, as far as he could into the depths of the sea.

'I hope and pray I never have to use one of those in my life again,' he said, as we hastened on to Port Helen.

Chapter Forty-Two

SUMMER 1925

A few days later, I returned to Hiram Hall for the last time.

The police questioned us briefly, then let us go. Hugo was too weak and confused to be questioned, and Jack and Mouse swore blind that we had joined them within minutes at the hotel. The war was long over. All anybody wanted to do was forget. Sissy was right about Mrs Pettersham, who had emerged from her port-induced stupor in a state of utter terror and hadn't taken much persuading to give them all the information they might need, and more, about Connors' wartime activities, before decamping on the London train without even returning to collect her belongings. But I sensed no real enthusiasm to pursue it further now that the man was dead. They accepted Sissy's story, and with the papers and the little book of code handed over to the Intelligence Service, they quickly lost interest.

Sissy wanted to return to look after Hugo, but not one of us would allow it, not even Rupert when he arrived. We owed her too much already. It was no life for a young woman, and besides she had her grandmother, and the farm on the other side of Port Helen. She promised to visit Hugo whenever she could, but I was glad that her life was no longer lived within the shadows of Hiram Hall.

I found Hugo sitting in his wheelchair in a sunny patch of the kitchen garden near to the pond, talking to his brother, while Jack piled brambles and dead wood onto a bonfire a short distance away. Sadness crept through me, despite their laughter. Rupert and Jack were men in the prime of life, while Hugo, though not much older, was old and frail.

'Elin!' Rupert came to join me as I hesitated, unwilling to disturb them. He clasped my hands warmly. 'Dear Elin.' His eyes searched my face. 'It's good to see you again.'

'And you, too.'

He coloured slightly. 'I'm sorry, I should have spoken to you before, or at least written. I didn't want you to believe I blamed you.' His gaze fell to my hands. 'I asked too much of you. I was afraid you were angry with me.'

I kissed his cheek. 'I was never angry with you, Rupert. I just didn't want to place you in a difficult position when I left. I hope we will always be friends.'

'Of course.' He glanced back to where Jack had abandoned the fire to take the seat next to Hugo. 'I will need to talk to Hugo, of course, get lawyers in to draft a new will. I'm afraid the one he signed is perfectly legal. Sissy was right: it leaves Hiram to Connors.'

'Did Connors lie about Sissy?'

Rupert shook his head. 'Thankfully not. Whatever he might have been planning, he has no other relations.'

'So Hiram will go to Sissy.'

'Yes.'

'Then there's no need to trouble Hugo. Leave things as they are.'

Rupert cleared his throat. 'Miss Connors came to see me yesterday. She's well aware of the implications, and she was very distressed. She said quite clearly she wouldn't feel right inheriting the Hall. Her grandmother's farm is all she wants. She begged me to persuade Hugo to make a new will, leaving Hiram to you, just as he thought he was doing. It's what is right, Elin. It is, after all, your family home.'

I looked round at the garden. My fingers itched to pull away the saplings and the creeping buttercup, to uncover the vegetable patches and mend the panes of the greenhouse. I ached to gather up the fruit on the trees and bushes that had not yet begun to spoil. The pans for making jam and the jars must still be there, somewhere in the kitchen, waiting to be filled with their richness before the first frosts came. I could stay here forever, as I once dreamed. It could always be my home.

'No,' I said quietly. 'I couldn't do it. I can never live here again. That day I left, I knew I could never return.'

'Yes, Jack thought you might say that.' He gave a wry grimace. 'I have no wish to inherit, either. My boys are well provided for as it is. It seems wise to ensure they follow professions that might keep them from the clutches of the army. I've no wish for them to turn to idleness now.' He cleared his throat. 'There is an alternative solution. One Hugo and I discussed years ago, after – well, when the doctors were so adamant you might not survive. Hugo told me that if he lost you, he would never marry again, and he would leave Hiram Hall as a place for wounded soldiers. Those who can never return to the lives they once had and will always need care. The thought seemed to give him some comfort at the time. Perhaps such places are needed more than ever now?'

I smiled. 'These gardens will be perfect for regaining strength and some peace of mind. There is still so much suffering, even after all these years. Yes, I would like that too.'

'Good.' Rupert's face relaxed as we made our way towards the others. 'Look Hugo, look who's come to visit us.'

Hugo turned. A smile lit up the pallor of his face. His eyes were bright and clear, with the vivid blue that I remembered from so long ago. He clasped my hand in his. 'Elin, my dear, Jack's managing wonders with the garden already. We really shouldn't have let it get like this. Do come and join us.'

'Of course,' I replied with a smile.

'And are you happy, my dear?'

I hesitated, unsure if he thought we had travelled back to a time long ago, before that day of raspberries and champagne, and the biplane soaring across the sea from France.

'Yes, Hugo, I am happy,' I replied at last.

He patted my hand. 'Good. Good. I'm glad.' His gaze remained on my fingers, not long and elegant as they should be, but strong and muscular, adorned only by a simple gold wedding ring so different from the ornate jewel he had once placed there. A shadow crossed his face. 'He lied, didn't he? That day I saw you with your children, I knew I should never have listened to him. Sissy was right. You are well and happy. And you are loved.'

'Yes, Hugo,' I said.

His hand tightened. 'I'm not sure that you were always happy when you lived at Hiram. I sometimes think that perhaps I should have taken better care of you, my dear.'

'You did your best to care for me,' I replied. 'I'll never forget that.'

He smiled. 'Such a beautiful little girl. She has your eyes, my dear. And your bright smile. You must bring her to visit me. And the baby, too. That's what Hiram needs, don't you think? The laughter of children.'

My throat filled. Jack and Rupert had turned away slightly, their faces hidden. 'You must rest now,' I murmured. I didn't know what else to do, so I gathered the last of the roses from the trellis at the side of the pond, placing them on the blanket covering his lap. 'Look Hugo, my mother's roses. Their perfume is so lovely at this time of year, don't you think?'

His hand was painfully thin, the skin mottled and almost transparent as the light glowed between the bones. He grasped the largest bloom, raising it to draw in the heady scent of cloudless summers, of men bringing in the hay in distant meadows with the patient clop of horses hooves, and the quiet murmur of harvest in the kitchen garden. The scent of rosehips swelling crimson in the hedgerows and swallows flitting beneath the eaves. The scent of innocence.

Hugo sighed deeply. 'Perfect.' His hand patted mine. 'The evenings are drawing in. You really should have a shawl, my dear. Treeve will send Elsie to fetch it for you. Mrs Pelham will know where it is.'

I swallowed my tears. 'There's no need, Hugo. I'm warm enough.' But Hugo's head was nodding as he drifted into sleep. 'Good man, Treeve,' he murmured as his eyes closed. 'I won't have a word said against him. Not in my house.'

'Jack, are you sure you want to stay?' I said, as Hugo's breathing deepened and we moved out of earshot. 'Rupert said he'll be with Hugo until a good nurse can be found, and Kitty jumped at the chance to escape her dad's shop and come back to take charge of the garden.'

'I'll remain here for a few weeks. I'm not sure Hugo will settle easily to a new routine. At least I'm a familiar face he trusts.'

'Maybe I should stay.'

'No.' He shook his head. 'No, Elin. It will distress you, and it will not help Hugo…stirring up the past. Hugo needs peace and quiet and to remain in his dreams. With men who've been under fire together there is a bond of understanding. That's what Hugo needs now.'

'Like in the ambulance?'

'Like in the ambulance.'

I nodded. 'I understand.'

A sound of voices came from the direction of the cliff door. I turned as a familiar figure limped his way towards us.

'So he came.' Jack smiled. 'I thought he might.' He caught my eye. 'Corporal Smith and his wife have been working for the family at Applebourne since the hospital closed. I'm not sure either of them has settled back into being below stairs. When I spoke to him on the telephone he was ready to jump at the chance. It looks as if his wife might have agreed.'

Corporal Smith reached us. He had a large knapsack slung over one shoulder and appeared just as wiry and cheerful as he had been racing through enemy lines. He shook my hand. There was understanding in his eyes. I could have been straight back in that ambulance again, when every second might be our last: all of us bound together with bonds that never break.

'Good to see you again, Nurse,' he remarked with a grin. 'And you too, Doc,' he added, shaking Jack's hand in turn. He gave a low chuckle. 'I thought you might like to know there's a young man waiting for you, Nurse. Pacing up and down outside on those cliffs out there he is, fit to wear them into the sea.' He winked. 'Pity none of the lads took me up on my bet. I'd have made a small fortune.'

I smiled. 'Poor Owen. I'd better go.'

Corporal Smith was already making his way to Rupert and Hugo. Within minutes he'd pulled a small and extremely battered paraffin stove from his knapsack and set about making tea. Hugo roused a little at the clatter of tin mugs.

'He'll be safe now,' said Jack.

I nodded. 'I know.' I took a deep breath. It had to be said, or it would always remain a shadow between us. 'You nearly told me about Hugo, didn't you? Before you left Hiram.'

Jack turned his face away. 'I should have done,' he muttered gruffly.

'No, I didn't mean that.' I grasped his hands. 'You have always been such a good friend to me, Jack. I owe you my life, many times over. I didn't see it at first, but seeing Hugo just now, I understood. You knew that if you told me, I would never leave. Whatever Connors did, my pity would have always kept me here. It would have kept Hugo safe, but my life would have been over, however long I might have survived. You once said Hugo and I were your dearest friends. I can't imagine the pain it must have cost you to choose between us like that.'

'It wasn't a choice,' he muttered. But I could see the tears in his eyes.

'Thank you,' I said, kissing him firmly on the cheek. 'And for Mouse and for Owen and Hugo. We all owe you our lives, and so much more.' I turned and made my way past the fruit trees and the canes of raspberries, through the little door onto the cliffs.

Owen paused in his pacing as I emerged, sweeping me tightly into his arms. 'If you feel you wish to stay, Elin, I can look after the children. We'll wait for as long as it takes.'

'No.' I shook my head, brushing my tears away. 'Thank you, but no. Jack is right: I'm the last thing Hugo needs. I knew it would kill me to stay, a long time ago, and now I would only disturb Hugo's peace.' I kissed him. 'That day Mouse landed her biplane up here on the cliffs, you and I found each other. None of us can go back from that. I wouldn't wish to.'

His eyes rested on mine. 'Nor I.'

I tucked my arm into his as we began the walk down towards Port Helen. 'So I'll never be free.'

He grinned, his eyes warm on my face. 'Never.'

We walked, holding each other tight, until we reached the beach just outside Port Helen. The sun was beginning to sink on the horizon, sending a soft glow over the incoming tide and the small strip of remaining sand, where Alice was playing cricket with Frankie and Lisette. Laughter rose up to meet us as Alice raced to make her runs, hat discarded, skirts flying in the wind, while Lisette chased the ball with Jojo jumping at her heels and Frankie shouted encouragement at the top of his voice.

Just beyond them, at the golden edge of the sea, Mouse was paddling with Lucy in the ripples of waves, baby Rhys held between them, their figures a silhouette amidst the dance of light.

'Strange how things turn out,' I said. I took one last glance towards Hiram Hall, high on its hill. The warmth of the setting sun had sent a glow into its windows, touching them with gilded light. Once I had thought Hiram was my freedom. My protection. I had been a little afraid of the world outside. But it was only out in the world, with its kindness and its cruelties, its joys and its griefs, that I had found true freedom. I clung to Owen's arm, aware of all we had lost, determined to treasure all we had found.

And together we walked down to the sea, to where our children were waiting.

Elin's Recipes

These are a selection of the recipes Elin uses, along with ones she inherits from her mother. Some are based on old family recipes, while others have been developed from those found in the newspapers and recipe books of the time. The measures and cooking times are as accurate as possible, but several were intended to be cooked in an old fashioned range, so keep an eye on the cooking times and feel free to adjust the amounts to fit your own taste!

HUGO'S RASPBERRY JUNKET

This recipe uses rennet, but I use a vegetarian substitute, which can be obtained from health food stores. Follow the instructions on the bottle for either 1 or 2 pints of milk, depending on the size of your mould, which can be a simple bowl or an intricate jelly mould (found online or in good kitchen shops).

Take one quart (2 pints or 1 litre) of fresh milk. Warm some of it with a tablespoon of sugar, then pour the hot and cold milk together into a deep bowl. Add one good tablespoonful of brandy (optional) and one of rennet. Stir and stand in a warm place to set.

Turn it out onto a plate, and cover the top with clotted cream, and raspberries lightly stewed with a little sugar. Throw over it a tablespoonful of brandy (optional), then grate a little nutmeg on it and dust with icing sugar. Goes well with shortbread biscuits.

એ

MAIDS OF HONOUR

Eight teaspoons of sugar,
One egg
2oz   60g   Ground Almonds
Pinch of Baking Powder
Packet of frozen Puff Pastry
Raspberry Jam

Beat the sugar and the egg together, then stir in the almonds. Put the baking powder last. Have some patty-pans/muffin tins lined with puff-pastry (frozen is fine), lay a teaspoon of raspberry jam at the bottom of each, and cover with a teaspoon of the mixture. (I decorated them with toasted almond flakes, which worked well.)

Bake in a moderate oven – 200°C (180°C if fan assisted), Gas Mark 6 for about 20 minutes.

છ

These are the sort of recipes I imagine Elin's mother having written in her book, that Elin uses through the war:

OATMEAL CAKES

6oz	170g	Oatmeal
5oz	140g	SR flour
3oz	85g	Butter
1oz	30g	Sugar

One Egg
Two tablespoons Milk

Mix the dry ingredients, rub in the butter, mix up with the egg and milk. Roll it out like pastry, cut it with a shaped cutter. Bake these biscuits for about ten minutes. 200°C (180°C fan assisted), Gas Mark 6.

എ

MALT LOAF

½lb	230g	SR Flour	2 tablespoons Malt
½lb	230g	Wholemeal Flour	2 tablespoons Golden Syrup
4ozs	120g	Sugar	2 cups warm Milk
Pinch of Salt		½ teaspoon Bicarbonate of Soda	
4ozs	120g	Sultanas	

Mix dry ingredients. Add malt and golden syrup to warm milk and dissolve. Stir into dry ingredients. Bake in a moderate oven 170°C (150°C fan assisted), Gas Mark 3 for about 1 hour. (Makes 2 cakes.)

എ

TREACLE SCONES

1lb	500g	Flour	1 teaspoon Ground Cinnamon
2ozs	60g	Lard or Butter	1 ½ tablespoons Sugar
½ teaspoon Bi-carbonate of Soda			1 teaspoon Mixed Spice
½ teaspoon Cream of Tartar			Milk to mix
2 tablespoons Black Treacle			

Mix dry ingredients, rub in lard or butter, and add treacle, then mix with enough milk to make a stiff dough. Divide in four. Roll out on a floured board and cut in four, or with a shaped cutter. Bake in a hot oven, 200°C (180°C fan assisted), Gas Mark 6 for 12-15 minutes.

ᘓ

HAND CREAM

This is an original 1910 recipe, that was meant for people whose hands were affected by frost.

Take a ¼ lb Hog's lard, without salt. Wash in water then in Rose Water. Mix it with the yolks of two new laid eggs. Add two large tablespoons of honey. Stir in fine oatmeal or almond paste to make into a paste.

ᘓ

LEMON SYRUP

To a pint of lemon juice add one pound of sugar. Simmer gently, removing the scum. Once the scum has disappeared, boil for half an hour. For the last ten minutes place thin slices of lemon peel into the mixture. Bottle the syrup, placing a few slices of lemon peel into each bottle.

BERFFRO CAKES

A kind of Short Cake or Sugar Cake

1oz	30g	Sugar
3ozs	85g	Flour
2ozs	60g	Butter

Mix well by hand, roll out fairly thin and cut with a shaped pastry cutter. In Angelsey, where Berffro (short for Aberffraw) cakes originated, it is the custom to mark each round with a scallop shell. Bake in a moderate oven for about 15 minutes at 170°C (150°C fan assisted), Gas Mark 3. When cool sprinkle with sugar.

ço

OLD WELSH GINGERBREAD

This was the gingerbread traditionally sold at the old Welsh fairs.

¾lb	350g	Flour
½ teaspoon Bicarbonate of Soda		
1 teaspoon Cream of Tartar		
6ozs	170g	Demerara sugar
¼lb	120g	Butter
2ozs	30g	Chopped Candied Peel
6ozs	170g	Black Treacle (warmed slightly and mixed with 1 gill (¼ pint/120ml) of milk).

The bicarbonate of soda and cream of tartar are added to the flour and well sifted. Rub butter into the flour, add sugar and peel, mix with treacle and milk. Bake in a greased tin for 1 - 1 ½ hours at 170°C (150°C fan assisted), Gas Mark 3.

PWDIN AFAL PWDIN EFA
APPLE PUDDING OR EVE'S PUDDING

2ozs	60g	Plain Flour	2 Eggs
1oz	30g	Sugar	Approx ½ pint 284ml Milk
1½ozs	40g	Butter	1lb 500g Stewed Apple
Vanilla			

Melt butter in a saucepan, stir in the flour and add the milk a little at a time. Bring to the boil to make a smooth sauce. Pour into a bowl and add the sugar, a few drops of vanilla and the egg yolks. Then fold in the stiffly beaten egg whites.

Grease a pie dish, and cover the bottom with a layer of stewed apples. Pour the mixture over them and bake for ¾ of an hour at 170°C (150°C fan assisted), Gas Mark 6

ℰℴ

TATWS PUM MUNUD
FIVE MINUTE POTATOES

This is still a popular dish, as it takes only five minutes to prepare! Fill a casserole with alternate layers of Welsh bacon, sliced onions and thickly sliced potatoes. Add pepper and salt. Cover with a lid and cook slowly for two or three hours at 170oC (150oC fan assisted), Gas Mark 3. Remove lid for the last 20 minutes to brown the top layer of potatoes.

ℰℴ

BARA BRITH
CURRANT OR SPECKLED BREAD

Original version

2lb Flour	6ozs Currants
1oz Yeast	4ozs Candied Peel
8ozs Brown Sugar	1 teaspoon Salt
8ozs Fat	½ teaspoon Pudding Spice
6ozs Sultanas or Raisins	Warm Milk

Adjusted version

1lb	500g	Strong Flour
1oz	30g	Yeast
4oz	120g	Brown Sugar
4oz	120g	Butter
3oz	85g	Sultanas or Raisins
3oz	85g	Currants
2oz	60g	Candied Peel

½ teaspoon salt

1 teaspoon mixed spice

Warm milk or strong tea, as preferred

Mix yeast, a little sugar and warm milk or tea. Rub fat into the flour, add the dry ingredients. Make a well in the centre and add yeast liquid. Knead into a soft dough. Cover and allow to rise to twice its size in a warm place, for 1½ hours. Turn onto a floured board and if using 2lb version split into two equal halves before putting into one or two greased tins as appropriate. Bake in a moderate oven at 200°C (180°C fan assisted), Gas Mark 6, for one hour. Slice thinly and butter.

᙮

SEED CAKE

Original version:
2½lb Flour
2lb Refined Sugar
12ozs Caraway Seeds
2lbs Butter or Margarine
4 teaspoons Orange Flower Water
10 Eggs
½lb Candied Peel

Modern (scaled down!) version
8oz	230g	Butter or Margarine
8oz	230g	Sugar
2ozs	60g	Caraway or Poppy Seeds
8oz	230g	SR Flour
2oz	60g	Candied Peel

Rind and juice of 1 Orange
Rind and juice of 1 Lemon
3 Eggs

Cream butter and sugar, add eggs one at a time with flour alternately, then add juice of one orange, caraway/poppy seeds, candied peel. Spoon into a greased 7inch/18cm tin and bake in oven at 180°C degrees (160°C for fan assisted), Gas Mark 4 for 1 hour, or until a knife comes out clean. When cool cover with butter icing. (Vanilla or lemon both work well.)

ॐ

Newspapers during the war gave advice on how to cook nutritious meals for large numbers of people without using meat. The next two recipes are based on those found in newspapers of the time.

WAR STEW

Original version
½lb Haricot Beans (soaked overnight)
1½lb Onions
2lb Carrots and Turnips
3lb Potatoes

Brown onions, add water, soaked beans and diced carrots. Simmer for two and a half hours. Add turnips and potatoes and boil for a further hour.

Modern version, for 2 – 4 people
One tin of haricot beans, one onion, three carrots, 1lb (500g) potatoes and half a small turnip, (adjust amounts according to taste).

Fry onions, add chopped vegetables, simmer gently for approximately 30 minutes, until vegetables are cooked. Add beans and warm through. Add seasoning. Serve with rice or toast.

ح

A 'MEATLESS MEAL'

Based on a 1918 recipe, but on more manageable lines and with the addition of cheese to improve tastiness. Serves 2 or 4, depending on how hungry you are (but be warned, it is delicious!). Adjust the amounts (especially the cheese) to your own taste.

Chop three leeks. Fry gently in butter until soft. Add a clove of garlic and ten chopped mushrooms (add more if you like mushrooms).

In a saucepan melt two tablespoons of butter, slowly add one tablespoon of flour and stir for one minute. Then add approximately ½ pint (284ml) milk slowly until you reach a consistency of double cream. Add approximately 4oz (113g) grated cheese. Stir in leek and mushroom mix. Pour over 2 – 4 large pieces of toast. Place in a fireproof dish, scatter grated cheese on top and place under a hot grill until golden brown. Serve hot.

℘

CHRISTMAS PLUM PUDDING
(A POPULAR PRE-WAR RECIPE)

¾lb	350g	Flour
2oz	60g	Breadcrumbs
1½lb	700g	Suet (or vegetarian suet)
2lb	900g	Raisins
1lb	500g	Currants
10oz	300g	Sugar
2oz	60g	Almonds
1lb	500g	Mixed Candied Peel

Mixed spice to taste

Six Eggs

Milk

Place the dry ingredients in a bowl, beat the eggs and stir in, add milk to make a good moist mixture. Divide in two. Place in muslin bags and boil for 8 hours.

જી

I've added more recipes to my website:
http://julietgreenwoodauthor.wordpress.co

The recipes for treacle scones, hand cream and malt loaf are based on recipes published in 'The Llandegai Recipe Book' by Lady Janet Douglas Pennant, published by the National Trust in 1968.

Books

Elsie and Mairi Go to War – Dr Diane Atkinson
Singled Out – Virginia Nicholson
The Roses of No Man's Land – Lyn MacDonald
Under Siege: Portraits of civilian life in WW1 – ed. Robert J. Young
Virago Book of Women and the Great War – ed. Joyce Marlow

Acknowledgements

Thank you to everyone at Honno Press for all their enthusiasm, support and guidance during the writing of this book. Particular thanks, once again, to my wonderful editor, Janet Thomas, whose astute comments guided the way, who pushed me to dig deeper than I ever thought was possible, and to whom I owe more than I can ever express.

Thank you to Literature Wales for the three-month Writers' Bursary that enabled me to concentrate fully on completing the final draft, and for all the help and support during that time.

Thank you to all my friends, family and work colleagues for their patience and understanding – and for dragging me out for walks and glasses of wine if I disappeared for too long! Thank you also to the NW Novelistas – the best and most generous group of authors anyone could wish for.

Thank you to Janet Bark-Connell for help in sourcing the recipes, and Salena Walker for help developing the 21st century and vegan versions. A huge thank you, as ever, to Dave and Nerys, Catrin and Delyth for being the best of neighbours. Also to my local dog walking community, and Fran Cox, Sally Hanson, Annette Morris, Beth Bithel, Claire Liversage and Liz Ashworth for listening and helping me through, picking up the pieces every now and again.

And thank you to all those who shared their stories of war, and the pity of war. They will never be forgotten.

ABOUT HONNO

Honno Welsh Women's Press was set up in 1986 by a group of women who felt strongly that women in Wales needed wider opportunities to see their writing in print and to become involved in the publishing process. Our aim is to develop the writing talents of women in Wales, give them new and exciting opportunities to see their work published and often to give them their first 'break' as a writer. Honno is registered as a community co-operative. Any profit that Honno makes is invested in the publishing programme. Women from Wales and around the world have expressed their support for Honno. Each supporter has a vote at the Annual General Meeting. For more information and to buy our publications, please write to Honno at the address below, or visit our website: www.honno.co.uk

Honno, 14 Creative Units, Aberystwyth Arts Centre Aberystwyth, Ceredigion SY23 3GL

Honno Friends

We are very grateful for the support of the Honno Friends: Annette Ecuyene, Audrey Jones, Gwyneth Tyson Roberts, Jenny Sabine, Beryl Thomas.

For more information on how you can become a Honno Friend, see: http://www.honno.co.uk/friends.php